Master

OTHER BOOKS AND AUDIO BOOKS
BY TONI SORENSON:

Behold Your Little Ones

I Can't Go to Church

Heroes of the Book of Mormon

Heroes of the Bible

He Knows Your Heart: Inspiring Thoughts for Women

Redemption Road

Master

a novel

TONI SORENSON

Covenant Communications, Inc.

Cover image *Hold Tight* © 2008 Liz Lemon Swindle.

Cover design copyrighted 2008 by Covenant Communications, Inc.

Published by Covenant Communications, Inc.
American Fork, Utah

Printed in Canada
First Printing: February 2008

13 12 11 10 09 08   10 9 8 7 6 5 4 3 2 1

ISBN 10: 1-59811-522-7
ISBN 13: 978-1-59811-522-2

My name will mean nothing to you, but my story is a retelling of the greatest story ever told and should mean *everything* to *everyone*.

If you interpret my words as fiction and fiction only, you will miss out on truths that are both historical and spiritual. Search the scriptures. There you will find evidence of my existence recorded in ancient sacred writ, overlooked for millennia. My story comes forth now because now is the promised day when satanic doubt spreads like black ink, threatening to blot out His very name, to reduce Him to nothing more than a teacher, to erase the eternal truths He taught and lived.

That cannot happen.

Jesus was who He said He was.

I know because I was there in the shadows of His holy footsteps.

His miracles were real.

I know because *I* am one of those miracles.

—*Almon*

I am the Lord thy God, which brought thee out of the land of Egypt, from the house of bondage. Thou shalt have none other gods before me.

—Deuteronomy 5:6–7

One

The man was still smoldering when we came upon his body.

I smelled him before I saw him.

In the desert every day brings a new discovery, but this was the first time in my nine years of life that I had seen a burning body. Any normal boy would have been terrified to come upon a human face melted away—his nose, his eyes, even his chin virtually gone—but I shuffled my sandaled feet closer. My nostrils flared to take in the baked desert air. The scent was strong, not sickening like you might imagine; it was that of singed goat hair and overcooked flesh.

"An evil omen," my father said, his voice trembling. He held a straight arm out to keep me back. "This is a sight you do not need to witness."

I craned my neck for a clearer view of death.

"I cannot discern his nationality," Father said, stooping to examine the remains. He held a hand over his nose and mouth and looked to be sick. Beneath his dark beard I saw his sun-baked skin pale a shade. He shook his head, and disappointment clouded his eyes. "The man's cloak is ashes and his feet bare. Any wealth he might have had is already plundered."

The man had been robbed. It was an everyday occurrence in the desert; thieves laid wait along the roadsides and lurked behind dunes. Robbers were as common as jackals and just as deadly, and though I understood the reality, I did not feel the fear that showed on my father's face. Even with danger surely close by, my heart beat slow and steady.

"The body was doused in oil and set aflame," Father said, shading his eyes to scan first the roadway leading toward Egypt and then that leading to Palestine. His eyes rested on a lone hawk against the blue sky above a few rouge palm trees; it was most unusual to have no other sign of life in sight. This was a route worn for generations by caravans, camels, donkeys, even horses; it was used by traders and travelers, Jews and Gentiles, Roman soldiers and those loyal to Herod. It brought men all the way from the East to Africa. Father and I would not be alone for long.

My curiosity soared like the bird above us. Was the man Jewish, Roman, Phoenician, Syrian? Simply a misguided traveler? Did it matter now that he was dead?

I looked closer and guessed the man to be a Jew—like us. The tuft of his charred beard was black, and the hair that was not singed from his neck was curly. What was left of his skin was light as my own; if he'd been Egyptian, his skin would have been dark. Beyond that, there was no evidence of his identity; I had nothing more than a feeling that he was Jewish. If I was right, his body was supposed to be washed, wrapped, and buried on the same day he died. I didn't see how washing him was going to be possible.

The look of concern on my father's face made me wonder if he was echoing my thoughts. Father was Jewish, so by birthright, I was from the lineage of King David—yet Father had not trained me in the laws, the history, or the rituals of Judaism. Father was an intelligent and experienced man who had taught me many things, but not all that it meant to be Jewish.

"If there comes a time when being Jewish is important to you, then there are plenty of rabbis who can train you," Father had told me. "Though why you would want to live under so many laws that will crush you, I do not know. You are too intelligent for such nonsense."

Nonsense?

I didn't know then what being a Jew really meant. Along the desert roads, I saw Jewish pilgrims with their dark curls, long mantles, and white robes. I knew they read scriptures and I knew they never looked happy. I heard them argue, mostly with each other.

Father was right. I didn't want to be a Jew, not like that.

The only time the subject came up was when Father had finished off the wineskin. I once overheard him tell a merchant at the oasis that a rabbi in the Holy City had stolen his faith. He slurred his words, talking so openly, so miserably. He said the rabbi and priest at the synagogue in Jerusalem denounced Father, calling him a sinner and announcing to the whole community that he was no longer welcome to worship with them.

The vein that ran down the center of Father's forehead had swelled up through his skin and throbbed. His brows had come together like two colliding caterpillars, black and fuzzy.

I had wanted to ask him then what sin he had committed, but I knew better.

"Rabbis, priests, what do they know but the law? Study what has happened to our people; they are turning on each other like wild beasts. How can they claim to be *chosen*?

"You have traveled this region with me for years; you see that Jews have invaded every corner of the land. Look around. There isn't a city within traveling distance that is not home to a Jewish population. Why, Alexandria is home to more Jews than Jerusalem."

I didn't understand, but then I didn't care to understand.

While Father often ranted about his disgust, there were rituals he instinctively kept. One day a week he rested and talked of things holy—that is, if he wasn't drunk. And whenever someone died, Father held to the law that said the body must be properly cared for, or else the soul of the departed would remain in torment, would stay around and haunt the living.

I looked at the burning corpse and hoped that the man was not Jewish, because I did not want to have to prepare him for burial.

Father sighed. "The evil men who did this might be out of sight, but they aren't far." He waved a hand toward the dead man. "This, too, could be our fate if we neglect caution."

A sound came from the dead man's face, and I looked to see the last of his flesh pop and sizzle, like fat in a pan. The incineration reduced his ears to a sight that made me think of moth wings. Father and I had once come upon a corpse hanging from the branch of a tree; it had been left baking in the sun where it had fed vultures and beetles for a very long time. The bones of the man's feet had been picked and baked to an alabaster color, while his arms and face had been mummified to brown leather.

I remember standing there, staring in awe. That man had been hanged for a crime against the government, and Father told me to feel no pity for his demise.

I tried not to.

Death was a picture the Sinai and Negev deserts regularly displayed. Growing up at the side of my father, never settling in a single place for long, our desert had shown us the close of many lives. Snakes bit, scorpions stung, the unrelenting sun stroked life from the frail. No, death was no stranger, no monster to me. Its greedy hand had reached out on the very day I was born. My mother gave her life in exchange for my own. I knew that every breath I took was one she would not. The guilt of that reality sat at the bottom of my heart like a millstone.

Death's most gruesome picture had come when King Herod's rule had draped death throughout all the land. Two years earlier, his deranged decree had swung a bloody sword against the neck of every babe in the land. Threatened by a prophecy that a child had been born who would rise up and reign as the new king, Herod had commanded his soldiers to slaughter every babe younger than two years of age. The sights, the sounds, the sorrows that had filled the land at that time never ceased to stalk my nightmares. There were nights when even Father woke up crying, "No! No! No!"

More than two years later it was not an uncommon sight to see mothers still draped in black, mourning inconsolably.

No . . . death was no stranger, and as I peered at the smoldering corpse I thought about my own departed mother. Her body had lain beneath the soil for nine years. Had it turned to dust? Was her spirit content, or did she mourn my absence from her life the way I mourned hers from mine?

I studied the dead man's remains and wondered if he was guilty of a crime that merited such a horrific fate.

Father appeared to read my mind. "Perhaps Romans attempted to cremate this man for some crime." He spit in the sand at the mention of Romans. Father hated the soldiers who paraded through the land, their cruelty and unholy practices tarnishing the Jewish way of life he said he cherished.

Father was a Jew, but he had seldom taken me to synagogue. He talked of his ancient fathers—Abraham, Isaac, and Jacob—like they were still alive, and yet he once stole holy parchment scrolls and sold them for the price of a meal.

It was ironic that Father was so adamant about the Torah and its endless laws—considering what he and I did to earn our living.

Our donkey suddenly brayed and clopped backward. His nostrils went wide and I saw fear in his eyes, the same fear that glinted in my father's eyes.

"We are not safe in staying, but no matter who he was, no matter what he did, this man deserves a decent burial," Father said, retrieving a small shovel from the bag draped over our hesitant donkey's back. "Once his body has cooled, we will move it to a lawful disposal spot."

I backed away. While I wasn't afraid, I wasn't anxious to travel with the charred corpse—and I was certain our donkey, Boaz, felt the same way. The nearest lawful disposal spot was at the nearest oasis, and that was at least a half day's journey away.

My body shivered even though the Sinai sand was hot enough to scorch a small red bug that scampered near my toes. He sought refuge in the shadow of my foot and I lifted my sandal to accommodate him, careful not to step wrongly and bring him harm.

While Father doused the corpse with sand, I carefully slid closer until I could reach out and touch the dead man's finger. I lifted it and set it in the center of my palm. It was gray and warm and long, heavier than I had supposed. The base of the nail was still attached. The color was dappled gray and the bone was not yet baked clean. There was no ring on the finger to steal. I wished there was. I found myself wishing the robbers had left behind a ruby ring, one that would allow Father and me to eat for weeks.

"Back away!" Father ordered. "Now!"

I wanted to explain what I was thinking. Instead, I turned to see a more intense fear burning like the sun in my father's eyes.

Then I saw why.

Just over the nearest rise came three robed men who moved toward us as smooth and rapid as cobras over sand.

Two

The men were bandits.

Bandits were dangerous, especially this cloaked breed who kept their identities sweltering behind black, hooded robes. I had seen men like them before, mostly on the stretch from Jericho to Jerusalem, a road thick with thieves. It was familiar territory to us because Father and I were thieves . . . desert robbers . . . but not bandits. Bandits were a class far below us.

Bandits stole lives. We stole only treasure.

Of the three, one was taller, broader, and obviously older than the other two—a father perhaps, and his sons. Whenever we had encountered bandits like them before—men known as Cobras, with their black hoods fanned, ready to strike—Father had told me to keep my head down and move past them with haste. Now I stared openly at them, trying to see eyes beneath the shadows of their hoods. The leader went directly to the corpse and knelt to study it.

"Why have you done such evil to this man?" the leader asked in Greek, his tone raspy with venom. "What did this man do to bring such harsh judgment?"

"My son and I only now came upon the man," Father explained, also in Greek. "He is a stranger to us. We brought no harm to him."

To show fear in the face of an enemy was to show weakness.

Father was not known for his bravery, but his cunning had saved us more times than I could count. His tongue, fluent in a half-dozen desert languages, was sharper than a blade, his words slicker than oil. Part of me was anxious for him to work his wiles on these men, to free us fast, while another part of me dared to face them down.

The leader stood and moved toward Father, who gave me a wide-eyed stare that without words told me to take cover behind Boaz.

In that moment I felt caught between being a child and being a man. A child would hide. A grown son would stand beside his father and offer aid.

Reluctantly, I surrendered to the child in me, and my feet inched backward until I was hidden behind our donkey. Of course I could still be seen, but I felt safer. My hand reached into our supply sling and I felt for the sheath that held my father's small silver saber; I quickly slipped it beneath my robe. If pressed, I would prove my manhood.

I suspected that these bandits were the executors of the dead man; if I searched their pockets I would surely find the loot they had taken at the cost of a life. To kill us and burn our bodies would not weigh on their empty souls. And they *would* . . . kill us . . . if they knew that our pack held two small but valuable figurines made of African ivory. The man we had robbed had begged us not to take his precious idols—*teraphim* he claimed came from Ur, the Babylonian city that was home to Abraham. He had offered us shiny bracelets instead. In the end, we had robbed him of everything, and now I remembered his face, his fear, the shine of his tears on his cheeks. I had heard his pleading, and I was sorry for what we had done. *After* the act, I was always sorry.

The tall man spat in Father's face. "You and your brat are not unfamiliar to me. You are nothing but common dogs. You murdered this man and were attempting to bury him."

The fear that swam in Father's eyes was familiar to me. I had seen that same fear on every face we had ever robbed.

"No. No. You are misinterpreting the situation. My son and I are innocent."

All three bandits laughed.

I tried to swallow, but my tongue had gone dry as the sand beneath my feet. I coughed and the leader spun to look at me. The other two came closer.

"Leave Almon alone!" Father demanded in a voice that was stronger than I knew he felt. "My son has nothing to do with anything."

"*Almon?*" The man looked at me with narrow eyes and malevolent interest. Customarily a man would address only my father, but this man turned to me. "Almon, do you know what your name means in Hebrew?"

I knew. Almon meant *forsaken*. It was a name that had breathed with me every day of my life.

I stood motionless, looking at the man, trying to appear fearless, but my heart was thundering in my chest. I hated the fact that I was afraid.

The man threw his head back to laugh again and his hood came partway down. I saw his face. He looked no different than a thousand other men of the desert.

In that instant the other two men were on each side of me. I looked up into the shadowed eyes of the bandit at my right. His face was light-skinned and smooth. He was young, not much older than Bar Mitzvah age. The other was older, but not by much. He stood so close I could smell his sour breath.

I thought I understood. These sons were their father's accomplices. They were desert criminals just as Father and I were. Only Father never admitted what we did to earn money. We were more than mere robbers, Father told people; we were in the trade business. What we traded was *me*.

Slaves brought a high price, especially a boy as strong and compliant as I was. Father would negotiate with travelers, using the variety of language skills he had mastered when he had worked as a money changer on Temple Mount. That was before I was born.

Selling me was much easier and more lucrative than robbing weary travelers. Selling me was much more profitable than weighing coins for tightfisted worshippers.

Father targeted men from the East, who paid the highest prices; seamen from the Mediterranean were also eager bondsmen. Romans were cautious, as were Jews. I had never been sold to anyone traveling to Africa.

Our plan might sound sinister, but really, it was simple. Father would trade me for coins, pretend to bid me a sad good-bye, and then, like the practiced thief he was, he would shadow me wherever I was taken. Sometime during the night he would creep into the camp where I was and release me. We would sneak to safety and savor our earnings until necessity made us repeat our routine. The risk of being found out was kept to a minimum because Father was very cautious about whom he approached and because he was gifted with disguises.

For a moment I feared Father would attempt to sell me to these bandits. But he did not have the upper hand as he usually did; his smooth tongue had gone dry, like mine. Now as I looked to Father, I saw that his knuckles were white from the tight grip he held on the shovel.

"You have left nothing more to plunder," the leader said, venom in his voice.

"We did not rob or harm this man," Father insisted.

I felt a sudden pressure on the back of my neck and realized that the pale boy had taken hold of me. I squeezed the handle of the saber, but wondered if I had the courage to use it.

"Inspect the pack," the man ordered. "Search their belongings."

I coughed again, and felt fingers tighten around my neck.

"We have nothing of value," Father lied.

"Then you have buried it here in the desert."

"No, we have not."

"Are you Jews?"

Father did not hesitate. "Yes."

"You do not look Jewish."

"And how does a Jew look?" Father asked, a hint of his strength returned.

That made the tall man laugh again.

"How do you earn your living?" he asked.

I held my breath, waiting for Father to tell him that, as thieves, we held much in common, but that was not his reply. "For now . . . we search for work. We are on our way to Temple Mount. I once earned my living there, changing money."

The man adjusted his hood so that his face was impossible to see. "Work is not difficult to locate. Archeleus continues his father's building. The wage is fair."

Knowing how Father felt about Herod's son, I wondered how he could hide his disdain. Father put on a show of confidence I knew he did not feel. He gave me an assuring glance and then turned his back to the man and began to shovel more sand on the still-smoldering body.

I jerked from the boy's grip and when I did, his hood slipped free. I saw his eyes and could not help but stare—they were *yellow*. I did not look away. I had seen cats in Egypt with eyes the same haunting color.

The boy seemed more embarrassed than angry and reached to grab me again. His brother did not touch me, but moved toward Boaz, toward the sling that concealed the ivory teraphim.

Our donkey brayed and kicked his hind feet into the air. He threatened to run off, but only moved a few steps.

I jerked free, but only for a second. Now both boys held me tight, their fingers around my throat. I could barely breathe, and that was when I saw in the distance the coming of a small band—two or three people and a donkey. They weren't much, but at least we were no longer alone in the desert with the bandits.

I aimed my arm to draw attention to the caravan, hoping the men would be alarmed and would disappear as quickly as they had appeared. But my flailing turned the tall man's attention to me, and he came at me.

"No!" Father yelled.

"Where do you claim home?" he asked me.

I said nothing, even though the boy had released his grip on me.

"Almon is mute," Father said. "He *never* speaks."

The man stopped and moved his hand inside of his tunic. I was sure he was reaching for a blade.

Father must have had the same inclination because he lunged to put himself between the man and me.

My own fingers moved swiftly and subtly beneath my robe to unsheathe the saber. I felt the sharpness of the blade and felt my courage sharpen in turn.

"Almon," the man said, addressing me, "where is your home?"

I remained silent.

He stepped closer. "Where did your father hide the treasure he stole from the dead man?"

I flinched with the realization that this man already knew we were not the murderers—he was. Yet, he was toying with us, as a cat before the pounce. He was evil and insane.

The knife blade sliced into the side of my thumb.

The man pushed Father back.

"I told you, my son is *mute*."

"He does not look mute."

Father scoffed. "How does a mute *look*?"

The man stepped toward Father and gave him a hard shove, hard enough to rob Father of his balance. He landed hard on the packed sand. His eyes went wide, and I saw a sudden flash of silver. Was it Father's sword or the killer's?

I made my move and as I did, a hand gripped my wrist. I felt a sharp, burning pain up my arm. My saber fell to the ground. I fought hard to get free, but four hands held me tight. As I struggled I saw the tall man put his foot on Father's neck and spit in his face.

I kicked and jerked and used every ounce of my strength to free myself. The cat-eyed boy looked as frightened as my father, but his grip remained sure.

"Hold him!" the man shouted at the boys.

The fingers around my throat tightened.

Father made a sudden lurch and bounded to his knees. I was proud of him and longed to fight alongside him, but my strength was the strength of a boy.

I hated myself for being so silent, so weak.

Why didn't Father just give over the ivory idols and the shiny bracelets? Why didn't the little band moving toward us hurry faster? Couldn't they see that we were in desperate need of rescue?

Father and the leader cursed at each other.

Then I saw another flash of silver as Father raised the shovel. With a thud and a moan the leader collapsed to the ground beside Father. But he was up again, and lunged at Father. They wrestled and shouted, throwing accusations like they threw sand.

The boys who held me seemed amused at the struggle.

"Your father, he is rich?" the larger boy asked me, his sour breath blowing like a putrid wind in my face.

I shook my head.

"Your silence speaks lies. Where is your treasure?"

My tongue flicked out snakelike, but it formed no words.

Hatred flared in the boy's dark eyes. "We will kill you and set you aflame like we did the stupid merchant."

The yellow-eyed boy hissed. "Be silent, Brother!"

My throat felt dry and helpless at the brutal revelation.

They knew that we had not harmed the burning man—they had. It was their intent to rob us and then leave us just as dead.

Where? Where was that small band of desert travelers? Surely they would chase these bandits away. Surely this was not how Father and I would meet our demise.

I felt dizzy. The pain from my injured arm now filled my head. Through blurry eyes I saw that Father and the tall man were still kicking sand. Father seemed to be taking control.

The tall man rolled toward us and his mouth opened. "Help!"

The larger boy left me and ran to offer assistance. He kicked sand in my father's eyes and then stepped on his chest. I saw him bend down to pick up my father's shovel.

I looked over into the face of the yellow-eyed boy and summoned my last surge of effort. I didn't need it. The boy released me and I ran to help my father.

I opened my mouth in a futile attempt to tell him I was coming, but as my body lunged forward, a fast and blinding pain cracked the back of my skull.

I knew I was falling, but it seemed to take forever for my body to hit the burning sand. I felt only heat, as if I had been immersed in a pool of steaming water. My eyes remained open and as I sank beneath the surface I looked for a final time into the yellow eyes that would haunt me forever.

Then they were gone and all I saw was the endless blue of the desert sky fading . . . fading . . . fading . . . until there was nothing left but the blackest of nights.

Three

My eyes were heavy, as though coins had been placed on the lids to keep them from opening. It was a practice the Romans performed on their dead.

But I was not dead.

"Awake."

The man's voice was not familiar.

I struggled to move and felt my head throb. My whole body shivered in pain. Then there was water at my lips, drizzling down my chin. I opened my mouth and gulped. It was ointment to a burn.

"Good," said the voice, "drink all you can hold."

My right eye was swollen shut; my left eye slowly opened. We were in the desert, a place where no one offered water with such generosity. Through the curtain of my lashes, I saw a man's bearded face. He was not one of our attackers, but a different man. A Jew for certain. A complete stranger. *Friend or foe?*

"Are you able to sit?" he asked in Aramaic.

I tried to sit, but felt as though my spine would explode.

"It is best to be still," the man said. "You are injured."

I swallowed more water and let my body relax for an instant, and then . . . then I remembered and forced myself upright in spite of the pain.

Father!

My heart cried. My mouth opened and closed, but as always, no sound emerged. *Father!*

Through a single eye, I discerned that I had been moved from where we had been. It was no longer daylight, but dusk, and the heat was giving way to the coolness of the desert night. It was hard to focus, to understand what had happened. It was impossible to make myself understood.

"I know you are frightened," the man said, cradling my head. "You were alone in the desert when we came upon you."

I wasn't alone. *Father!*

He must have read my lips . . . or my heart . . . because in tones as soft as a dove's fluttering wings, the man explained to me what I did not know. "We came upon you in the desert. You had been injured and left there. It was clear that a fight had occurred, but when we discovered you, you were alone. I searched the area but found only you and your donkey."

I tried to shake my head, but the pain was too great.

"I am certain you were abandoned."

No.

"Can you speak?"

No.

"Do you wish for more water?"

No. I wished only for my father. *Where was he? Where was I?* All my silent life I had longed for a voice to tell the world my feelings, my thoughts, and now my great fear. *Was Father dead? What had become of the bandits? The burning corpse? How had this man missed so much in his search?*

"We are at the oasis now. You will be cared for here until you are strong again. I fear your arm is broken."

The oasis he spoke of had to be the twin wells oasis, the only one between the desert and Palestine. Father and I had been headed to this very destination. He had to be close by. He *had* to.

I tried to bring my vision into focus; all I could make out were palm trees and the form of a donkey tied to a gate. The scent of the burning corpse still clung to my nostrils and I suddenly felt nauseated.

The man held me while I vomited bile and blood. I had bitten the inside of my mouth and my tongue; my lip was as fat as a pond toad.

The stranger's arms were strong and sure, his words kind. His embrace was comforting, but it only made me that much more concerned for Father.

I glanced down at my arm and saw that someone had made a splint for me; two pieces of soft wood were on either side of my arm, and strips of swaddling cloth held the splint in place. I reached up and touched my head with my uninjured hand. It, too, was bound with strips of cloth. *Who had taken care of me, and how long had I been unconscious?*

Vaguely, I recalled seeing a tiny caravan in the distance while Father and I were under attack. *Had that been the source of my aid?*

I had been two steps into the land of the dead. Now I was alive. My fear for my own life was gone. A different kind of feeling swelled within my heart. I felt grateful, so grateful I had to blink back tears.

"Let your concern go," the man said. "My family and I will stay beside you until you are strong enough to be on your own."

More tears.

Father!

I could not be on my own. Without Father, what would become of me . . . a *mute?* I gritted my teeth and tried unsuccessfully to hold back the flood of tears that burst forth and flowed down my cheeks. Tears were for babies, and I was no baby.

"We will not leave you alone," said another voice, this one even softer than the wings of a dove. This voice was a woman's voice, and I forced myself to look for its source.

Slowly, an image came into focus, one that even now I can still picture with perfect clarity. Kneeling beside the man, there she was . . . a young woman with fair skin and long dark hair. Her veil was thin, and when I saw her smile, my tears stopped. My mind pictured a desert sunrise, a dawn of hope.

"We will not leave you," her sweet voice repeated. "You will heal and be whole again."

How could she know that I had never been whole? I was born incomplete. I tried again to sit upright and find out about my father. I was too weak, and I fell back into the man's arms.

"Rest now," said the woman. "Our family found you, and it is our honor to watch over you."

Her *family?* Her *honor?*

"Yes," said the man. "This is my wife, Mary, and that little boy playing in the sand is our son, Jesus."

Four

I woke before dawn. My very sinews hurt.

At first I did not remember where I was or what had happened, but as soon as my head cleared, I thought of Father. This was the time for him to come and rescue me. Countless times after he had sold me, he had crept into camp to locate me, had untied my wrists or unshackled my ankles, and we had escaped together, laughing and celebrating in the cloak of desert darkness.

I lay still and waited, hoping against hope that he would come for me now.

Nothing came but the sound of the desert sleeping and my empty stomach growling. How long had it been since I had eaten?

A breeze barely blew. Carefully, I pried open my eyes and tried to make out my surroundings. I was alone in some sort of small tent. I could see an orange moon through the gap where the flaps parted. The air was cool and the scent of fresh camel dung strong.

Should I rise and try to run? Where would I go?

Should I stay where I was and hope that the hospitality of the man Joseph and his young family would linger?

Oh, Father. I thought I knew the meaning of my name . . . but now I felt it defined anew. I was truly *forsaken.*

The sound of a distant rooster crowing stirred the oasis, and I soon smelled wood smoke and heard the stirring of people.

"How are you?" Joseph's voice asked.

I saw him peering into the tent and did not expect the sudden wave of relief that rippled through me.

I wished that I had the ability to reply, but all I could manage was a smile.

He smiled in return. "Surely you are hungry."

I nodded.

His smile widened, and he handed me a baked corn cake. I gobbled it greedily and gulped the cup of warm goat's milk that accompanied it.

"How is your arm?"

I touched the splint and nodded again. It did not hurt as much as it had earlier.

Joseph helped me to rise, then held on to me while I stretched and walked. As morning dawned, my eyes searched for Father. Joseph seemed to understand two things about me: I was unable to voice my thoughts and feelings, and I was desperate to find my father.

"Do you have a family?"

I wasn't sure how to reply; Father was my only family.

"Do you make your home close to this oasis?"

I lifted my uninjured arm and gestured in a circle, trying to tell him that the whole region was my home.

We kept walking, past tents and merchants to the twin wells, where women were lined up with empty jars and waterskins, waiting their turn. No one gave us more than a passing glance. I was grateful because I did not want to draw attention to myself. I knew that if I had made it here, the three robbers could also be here, and so could my father. But how could I find him?

The oasis always amazed me. It was a small city in the middle of sand and nothingness. The wells watered the parched earth and life sprang forth: green grass, green trees, green palm leaves. Yellow flowers blossomed at the foot of the trees.

Yellow! I thought of the bandit boy's yellow eyes, and I felt shame that I had not stood up to him, stabbed both him and his brother with the saber. I had been worthless to my father.

Joseph took me to a small shaded area where men relieved themselves and used water from a common tub to clean the desert dirt from their bodies. I had not realized how filthy my hands were, my fingernails ringed black. Joseph was gentle as he wiped caked sweat and blood from my brow.

Again, a sense of gratitude threatened to bring tears. Who was this stranger so thoughtful and generous? He had no obligation to me, and yet he felt bound. I had no words to express how I felt.

We walked in silence through the morning din of the oasis. It was home to a few hundred inhabitants, a cacophony of people from different nations. Mostly, though, the people were like us . . . on their way to somewhere else. I had stopped here to water our donkey and rest several times with Father, but now when I searched faces and dwellings, there was no sign of him.

A group of priests walked toward us, and Joseph stopped to beg their attention. He motioned for me to stay put while he spoke to the men in private. I could tell from the way he moved his arms and motioned in my direction that he was telling them about me. I imagined that he was explaining to the priests how he had come upon a lone boy in the desert. What should he do? Could he rely on their mercy to take over my care?

Oh, Father, rescue me now. A heavy sense of foreboding told me that Father was not at the oasis—that he was not coming to rescue me this time, or any other time.

Battling a new flood of tears, I pulled a dry branch from a nearby tree and stooped to scribble in the sand.

Joseph approached me and touched my shoulder gently. "You are skilled as a scribe?" He seemed astonished.

I shook my head. Father, who had learned the bare basics of reading and writing from his boyhood rabbi, had taught me to write in the language of our ancient fathers. By firelight, he had taught me to read. He was not educated enough to polish my skills, but could see that I had a gift for the written word, while speaking eluded me. He told me that his dream for me was to become an official scribe.

"Are you able to write your name?" Joseph asked.

I used the palm of my hand to smooth out the sand so it could serve as my parchment. Carefully, I made the characters that revealed my name.

"Almon." Joseph said my name and I knew he understood its meaning, but there was something in the way he said it that brought me no shame.

He asked me a series of questions, and I did my best to write my reply to every one. I lacked the skills to make myself as clear as I longed to be, but Joseph had an ability to understand beyond symbols and silence.

He now knew that Father and I had been robbed by three hooded bandits. He understood that I feared for my father's well-being. I told him that no, we claimed no particular place as home. I told him Father was in the trade business, but I did not tell him that I was the commodity traded.

By the time we headed back to meet his wife and son, Joseph knew as much about me as anyone did. Besides Father, no one had ever shown so much interest in my life. Even my numerous owners had never displayed such curiosity about me.

We stopped at the back side of the largest well so that Joseph could tend to the animals. His donkey was younger than Boaz, who now stood bareback. Joseph said that when he found the animal it had no saddle, no bags, no bridle. While Father and I had no wealth, the few items that we carried with us—tools, cooking pots, clothes, and a worn sacred text from which I'd learned to read—were all gone. Had they been buried? Burned? Would I ever have answers to the questions that swirled inside my head?

Part of me wanted to return to the desert so that I could search the area myself, but the more logical part told me that I would not be able to locate the exact spot again. If the burned body was dragged away or buried, if Father and our belongings were gone, what would there be to mark the area except shifting sands?

I petted our donkey's neck and felt another wave of surety that Father was not coming back. Not ever. Grief choked me as surely as a hand around my throat.

I watched Joseph and thought that I had never seen a man so kind with animals. As he adjusted the rope tethering his camel, I noticed for the first time that two of his fingers had been hacked off at the knuckles. I wondered what tragedy had taken them? While Joseph now knew so much about me, I knew practically nothing of him.

The wail of a child stole my attention and I turned to see a small, curly-headed boy across the way. His mother, Mary, waited in line to fill her waterskins at the well.

Jesus had fallen and now ran to his mother for consolation. Tears ran down His dusty cheeks and Mary knelt to comfort Him, using the side of her thumb to wipe away her child's sadness.

I moved closer.

"Jesus," she said in a tone as gentle and pure as a perfect flute. "Jesus."

As surely as her arms, the words Mary spoke to her son lifted Him. The flow of sorrow stopped, and in spite of His wound, the boy returned His mother's smile.

I could not stop myself from staring. I had never witnessed such a scene.

When the boy realized I was staring at Him, He stopped, and through His tears, He smiled right at me—an open-mouthed, bright-eyed smile. There was a power in His smile and His laugh, a power that drew me to Him as sure as the moon lined up the tides.

He was just a little boy, and yet there was something about Him that caught my attention and held it. The rising sun backlit the boy's curly hair and the edges of His tiny tunic. He danced in the light with His arms stretched out like a waiting angel.

I heard laughter and looked to see unbounded delight in His mother's eyes as she watched Him.

I, too, kept staring, feeling drawn to the child. When His sandals danced my way, when He beckoned with the folding and unfolding of His little fingers, saying, "Come," I could not help but follow Jesus.

Five

The next day there still had been no sign of my father or the three cloaked bandits, but I had come to know Joseph, Mary, and Jesus as well as I had ever known anyone . . . except Father. My mind now grasped that I was utterly alone—truly *forsaken*—but when I was in the presence of Joseph and his family, the terror that of that reality was kept at bay.

Then Joseph approached me with pity in his eyes. "We have been dwelling in the land of the pyramids, but we are now directed toward Israel—our homeland," he said. "My family and I are returning to the land of our fathers."

Panic squeezed my heart. I inhaled a shallow breath and knelt to smooth the sand, a routine that had already become familiar to us. Desperately, I sketched the Hebrew symbol for *slave*. If Joseph would take me with him, I would be his slave. I would work night and day, do whatever was required. I would give the rest of my life if he would spare it now.

Joseph shook his head. "I am a simple carpenter, not a wealthy bondsman."

My eyes stung. I rubbed the sand smooth and sketched again. *Home*. I would be a slave in Joseph's home. I would unlatch his shoes and the shoes of everyone who crossed his threshold. I would wash their feet. I would sweep his carpenter's shavings and help to care for Jesus. He was a happy child, easy to laugh and enjoyable to be with. How could I convey so much with so little ability to communicate?

Joseph stooped on one knee and looked into my eyes. "Almon, I have never owned a slave."

Another wave of terror gripped me. Joseph did not understand—I was willing to be the carpenter's slave. I *wanted* to be his slave. I had nothing else to offer but myself.

If Joseph, Mary, and Jesus left me behind at the oasis . . . what would become of me? Father was not returning to rescue me this time. I had lived long enough to know that an unprotected boy my age was prey to a variety of desert predators.

Joseph seemed to understand my fear. "It is true I am not prosperous," he said. "Yet prosperous is the man whose household serves the Lord God."

I will, my heart shouted, *I will serve your god if you will take me with you. I will serve with all my heart and all my soul. Oh, Joseph, take me with you to Israel!*

"Mary, Jesus, and I will be honored to have you accompany us if that is what you desire."

My body gave no warning. My arms, both the one broken and the one not broken, reached out to embrace Joseph's neck. Without shame, I clung to him.

Joseph did not push me away, but allowed me to hold on to him until I felt strong enough to let go.

The next morning before sunrise, we set out across the desert to the land Joseph and Mary called home. Galilee. It was a region I did not know, beyond Judea and Samaria. Father had I had wandered mainly in the desert and as far into Judea as the Holy City. I had heard that Galilee was a land of hills and farms, a land of the great lake. I was anxious to see it, to put this sandy region behind me. I was desperate for a new life.

Joseph walked beside me while Mary and Jesus rode their donkey. Boaz carried both a backpack and an under-the-belly sling. I was glad he was able to make a contribution to this family, and hoped I would, too. The family didn't have much to carry—pots, bedding, some clothes, and an odd-looking wooden toy Joseph had fashioned in Egypt to help Jesus learn to walk. It had a handle and two poles with a rounded wheel. It was awkward, but clearly important to the family.

What would it be like to have a real family?

I had never missed one because I had never known one.

Now it was all I wanted . . . to belong to a family.

The sand-packed road was wide, and we were not the only caravans leaving early to reach the borders of Palestine. Others also drove
camels and donkeys; most walked on foot, and a few of the wealthy
rode by carriage. I searched for a sign of Father in every face we
encountered. It was fruitless and I knew it, but still, I looked.

We kept a steady pace, and I sought out ways to assist Joseph. He
seemed pleased when, even with only one good arm, I helped to load
the bags and tend to the animals. His pleasure turned to surprise that
I was able to coax both donkeys.

"Almon, you are a boy capable of much," he said.

His words made me feel like I could scale the highest pyramid in
Egypt.

The sun rose fast and hot. Jesus began to squirm, and Joseph
paused to lift Him off of the donkey. Then he reached to help Mary
down, and I saw that her second child was due soon.

I looked away, embarrassed.

We all quenched our rising thirst from the waterskins, and then
Jesus raced toward me, took hold of my good hand, and wrapped His
little fingers around mine. I looked to Mary and she smiled her
approval, so Jesus and I walked together as we continued our journey.
In His presence, I nearly forgot that my father was gone, that I had
given myself, without condition, into slavery. To be around that little
boy was to be in the company of joy.

A fat-headed lizard darted in front of us, and Jesus giggled with
delight. A pair of eagles circled above us, and Jesus did a dance with His
arms spread open wide. Boaz let out a sudden bray, and Jesus mimicked
him with such authenticity that even Joseph laughed out loud.

If helping to care for Jesus was my responsibility as his father's
servant, then I hoped that my duty would never end. Though I had
no reason to be, Jesus compelled me to be happy.

Six

I soon learned what Father had meant when he said that Jews were their own bondsmen. Joseph and his family lived by more rules than I could count. In the morning there was prayer. There were separate prayers for the bread and wine. There were midday prayers and prayers to close the day.

I had heard rabbis pray aloud on the streets in Jerusalem. Their voices were raised and their words were more of a chant. When Joseph prayed, his words were set, but there was feeling to them. I especially enjoyed hearing him recite *Shema*.

Hear, O Israel: The Lord our God is one Lord.

I loved how his faith filled me with a sort of peace, but guilt stirred deep within me. If Joseph discovered that I was not some poor innocent boy, but a robber, he might leave me by the wayside. I kept remembering people we had stolen from; why did I suddenly feel guilty *now?*

The journey was long, but there were new sights every day. Jesus kept me happy. Everything to Him was a reason to smile. I was awed at how Joseph taught Him of faith and family by telling stories.

The way Joseph's voice changed and his expression altered, he made King David seem alive. First he was a young shepherd boy, then he became the lion, and then the bear, growling and making Jesus laugh.

My favorite part was when Joseph made himself tall by stepping up on his toes and spreading his robes wide to become Goliath, the giant. I barely knew the stories, but longed for Joseph to tell them over and over.

"One day you will read from the Torah," Joseph told Jesus.

Only he wasn't telling Jesus. He was telling me.

"One day you will be a scholar, Almon."

But I was a slave. Only and always a slave.

They were devout Jews, obedient to every law.

On the eve of *Shabbat* we stopped to rest and observe the holy day. We purified ourselves in streams because the water was moving, which meant it was living. Living water was the only kind used for purification.

Mary prepared bread and stew a day ahead so there would be no work performed on the day appointed for rest.

I had so much to do and so much to learn. Joseph and Mary assumed that I knew more than I did. I let them assume and showed myself eager to learn and to do.

Once we were within the borders of Palestine, Joseph stopped to converse with two Pharisees who were outside the courtyard of a synagogue. I thought of Father and his disdain for these men who had chased him from Judaism. Now that Father was gone, I would never know the whole truth behind his departure from his faith.

Jesus was up on the donkey with His mother's arms circled around His waist. It had been a long day, and His little brow was damp as He leaned against Mary.

We watched with interest as Joseph gleaned information from the Pharisees. One of them, a bushy-browed man, kept looking at me, curiosity etched in the wrinkles of his face. I could not hear what was being said between the men, but I could tell that the conversation was animated.

When Joseph returned to us he said nothing right away, but guided us down a pathway that led to the village well. There, Mary filled our waterskins while I kept Jesus occupied, gathering pebbles that seemed as important to Him as gold coins. He kept studying them, turning them, touching each one.

His little hand went out and He wanted me to look at them, to see them the way He saw them. I looked and almost expected to see the tiny stones glow. To me, though, they were merely dull, gray pebbles.

Later, while we were eating our meager meal of barely cakes and dried fish, Joseph told us that King Herod's domain had been divided between three of his sons.

He looked grim. "Archelaus is the Roman appointee over Judea, Samaria, and Jerusalem. Philip now reigns as tetrarch along the coast."

Mary's dark eyes fell. "What of Galilee?"

"Perea and Galilee have fallen to Antipas."

Mary sighed. "Oh, what are we to do?"

Joseph looked at me and I knew the look; it was one of dismissal. As a slave, even a household servant, I expected to sleep with the animals or outside of the fire's warmth, but Joseph had already constructed the simple tent close by made of tanned hide and wood—the same structure I had slept in every night since they had taken me in.

I crept in and curled up on the softness of sheepskin infused with the scent of wood smoke. I intended to stay awake, to listen for the cry of Jesus in case He needed tending to, but my eyelids were heavy. I closed them and opened them again to find a new day had dawned and with it, Joseph and Mary's plans had changed.

"We are no longer headed toward Judea, but we will go to Galilee," he told me. "How is your arm?"

I tried to raise it to show him that it felt much better, stronger.

I was able to brush the donkeys, to pick their hooves clean of thorns and pebbles. I was able to fold my tent and pack the bags. Jesus was with His mother, eating figs. He ran to offer me one.

Instinctively, He seemed to understand that I communicated without words, so instead of saying anything to me, He held the offering out and bounced His head up and down.

I accepted, and He laughed and ran to get me another.

I wanted to keep Jesus beside me, but this day He walked along with His father. I listened with keen intent as Joseph taught. He spoke of Sadducees, the men who claimed their priesthood lineage through Zadok, the high priest who served King David in his glory times.

"Your mother and I presented you at the temple when you were a baby," Joseph told him, "and soon, there will come a day when we will return to the Holy City. For now, we will not travel through Judea, but soon."

Jesus was even more attentive than I was. Though He was just a few years old, Joseph spoke to Him as if He were much older. Jesus hung on everything His father said. He asked question after question.

I had not been around children, but even I knew that Jesus was no ordinary child. Was I that curious about the world when I was His age? Did my father answer questions as patiently and thoroughly as Joseph replied to Jesus?

How would my life be different if my father had remained loyal to his Jewish faith?

Thoughts and memories of Father came when I least expected them. When Joseph spoke to Jesus of the Pharisees, he did so with reverence and respect. When Father had spoken of them, he had mocked them. I could almost hear his voice hanging in the desert air, ridiculing the Jewish leaders.

The days passed with a routine pleasantness. Joseph taught Jesus of one true God. Mary tended to her family and showed great kindness to me.

Each night we made a fire and camped where we could. Joseph's stories of Jonah and the big fish were told best with the fire flickering in his eyes, the shadows of the dancing flames bouncing around us.

It did not matter whether Joseph was caring for the animals, comforting Mary after a long day of travel, or swinging Jesus around and around—he did everything with care and a level of love as high as Mount Sinai. He did not once treat me as a slave.

The direct route to Galilee would have taken us through Samaria, but Joseph went a longer way through Perea. Even my father had avoided the land he referred to as "half-heathen." For generations, Samaritans had laid claim to Jewish rites and religion; it was on their land near Sychar that Jacob's well was dug and still brought forth water. It was in the land of the Samaritans where Joseph's bones were buried. It was holy ground, and unholy people inhabited it.

They were pagans who burned their own people as sacrifices, who ate the flesh of humans. For all I knew, the desert bandits were Samaritans.

I woke up in the night from terrors, seeing the yellow-eyed boy, feeling my arm break, hearing my father cry for my help.

I bit back the pain by taking my bottom lip between my teeth until I tasted blood.

Because I was in my own small tent, I did not know if my whimpering woke Joseph and his family. They never told me, but acted the next morning like nothing had happened during the night.

We passed farm after farm, vineyards, and finally the skirt of the great Galilean lake. I loved its blue water and heady scent. Fishermen flooded the waters—both those who cast from the banks and those who fished from ships.

Joseph stopped to ask after a kinsman: Zebedee and his wife, Mary. He seemed disappointed to learn that they were on an errand and would not return for weeks.

The great lake, called the Sea of Galilee, fascinated me, and I wanted to stay and camp along the water. So did Jesus; He waded beyond the shore and out into the water, splashing and laughing, but Joseph and Mary were anxious to reach their destination.

The land and the people had suffered greatly under the cruel hand of the Herods. Whole villages had been ransacked. Men accused of disloyalty had been crucified, and the crosses were still up along the roadsides. Mary was expert at diverting Jesus' attention. His young eyes would not fix upon the signs of death.

Death did not attract my interest now.

The city of Sepphoris, only a few hours from Nazareth, had been hit hardest. Every street moved with mourners. Women's hair was gray with ash. Clothes were rent. Men were busy trying to rebuild homes and businesses. Even the synagogue had been burned.

"There will be a rising need for carpentry," Joseph said, looking shocked. "The demand for timber will be at a premium."

Mary held Jesus close to her. She looked tired and so sad that I wished Jesus would sing one of His happy songs or do a dance to bring a smile to His mother's face. I could not stand to see tears in her eyes.

"Joseph," she said, "what of Nazareth?"

"Everyone I have spoken with reports that our village has been spared. Soon, Mary, you will have a real home. We will finally be safe."

"The God of our Fathers willing."

Finally we entered the steep terrain of Nazareth, a village familiar to both Mary and Joseph. First we stopped at the home of Joseph's brother, Joel. The abode was far from poor. It had two levels, which meant the owner was a man of station.

I had never seen a house constructed of such fine, lengthy timbers. The entrance door was double and hand-carved with the sacred star of David. The courtyard was lush with green leaves and white flowers.

I stayed on the street, holding the donkey tethers. Joel and his wife, a woman named Naomi, seemed overjoyed to see Joseph and Mary. Naomi hugged and kissed Jesus until He wiggled His way free and ran to me. The women kept talking as they made their way inside the home.

"Who is the boy?" Joel asked Joseph, nodding toward me. As Joel turned to expose his profile, I saw an older version of Joseph mirrored in his brother's features. They shared the same prominent noses, camel-colored beards, and lanky statures.

"The boy is called Almon," Joseph answered. He then dropped his tone and turned away; I was certain he was explaining to his brother how he came to be the owner of an unfamiliar boy, now bonded to him.

I stood as still as a pillar, wanting to be accepted by Joseph's entire family.

Joel listened and then motioned toward me. "Come, slave."

Fast as a snake strike, Joseph reached for his brother's arm, stopping him. Joel looked shocked.

"Almon is *not* a slave," Joseph said, loud enough for the neighbors at the end of the cobblestoned street to hear.

Joel frowned. "The boy is now your property; that makes him a slave."

Joseph shook his head. "I do not think of Almon as a slave."

I kept my head bowed, fearful that Joel would convince Joseph to be rid of me, to perhaps sell me. *No! Please, no!* I was happy to be Joseph's slave.

I could not hear all that the brothers said to each other, but I did hear the tone, and after a few moments it mellowed. Then I heard laughter and saw Joseph's arm go around Joel's shoulder.

Later, when Joseph came to help me with the donkeys, he said softly, "There is a great difference between a slave and a servant."

I could not think of a single difference.

"You may serve my household, Almon, but you will never be my slave."

Seven

The household of Joel became a little larger that day, as Joseph's family joined his brother's.

Immediately, a gray-bearded servant named Dan approached us to take the donkeys. He spoke to me, and when I did not reply he went about his business. I did not know what to do . . . *should I follow and try to help? Should I stay where I was?* Joseph was engaged in conversation with Joel. Mary and Naomi were busy, and His mother held Jesus by the hand.

"Come," Naomi said, ushering me toward the house.

I had never entered a home so luxurious. The courtyard was constructed of hand-chiseled stone; even the ground was cobbled by the finest masons. I thought of the temple, of how only the whitest stone was allowed.

I laid my hand to the heavy wooden door and felt the depth and precision of its carving. The wood was sanded finely and stained dark, but the outline of the star left lighter so it gave the illusion of shining. I was mesmerized by it while Jesus was taken by the garden blooms, so soft and bright. He touched them carefully, as His mother had taught him. He smelled them and wanted me to smell them, too.

Naomi seemed anxious to escort us inside. "Welcome. Welcome."

Mary kissed the tips of her fingers and touched a metal case, a *mezuzah*, attached to the doorpost. Joseph would later teach me that the case contained a sacred parchment, or *klaf*, an excerpt of God's words from the Torah.

The main room was large, with a stone oven and enough pots to supply a merchant's shop. The table was made of thick, smooth slats of lumber with chairs to seat six people. Couches and embroidered pillows were there for reclining. Above us were more beams of perfectly shaped and sanded wood, these stained dark with berry juice.

Mary and Naomi immediately went to the cooking pot and lowered their voices to whispers.

I could not help but stand and stare, trying to take in such a place. It wasn't just the furniture and the stone floor; it was a feeling of *belonging*. And the aroma that filled the air was rich and wonderful, that of baking bread and simmering spices.

This was a place I never wanted to leave.

Joseph took the seat of honor at the head of the table while a boy not much older than I rushed to fill a water bowl and snap a towel. He was a household servant eager to wash my master's feet clean. I felt an unexpected sense of jealousy flood over me—Joseph was *my* master.

I stood by the door, unsure of what to do. I had not been given a task, and as much as I ached to belong, I was not a member of this family. I was an outsider—a simple servant at best, a slave in truth.

Jesus looked over at me and smiled. Then He rushed to the window and pointed excitedly at a hummingbird in the garden. I knelt next to Him and watched the bird float from bloom to bloom. One instant the wings were blue, the next they turned to green.

"Come to me," Naomi bid Jesus, her voice quiet so she would not disturb the men who were speaking. Even I knew that it was not permitted for women to disrupt men who were engaged in conversation. "Let me feel those precious curls on your head."

Jesus did not want to leave the hummingbird, but did as He was asked.

Mary saw my predicament and whispered, "Almon, are you hungry?"

Embarrassed, I shook my head no.

"Does the boy not speak?" Naomi asked, keeping her voice low. She was stirring a black pot, adding herbs to it. The smell was pungent and made my stomach growl.

"No," said Mary, "Almon does not have a working tongue, but we are learning to understand each other."

Her smile gave me confidence and her nod gave me direction. I took off my own sandals and moved across the cool stone floor to help wash Joseph's feet. Both he and Joel were engaged in fast-paced conversation. They spoke of Egypt, the land of the pyramids. They spoke of Herod and the dark days of his murderous decrees. They looked to Jesus, who had crawled onto His mother's lap for comfort. His Aunt Naomi could not keep her hands from touching the boy's curls, and Jesus, though heavy with exhaustion, managed to smile at her.

Joel also spoke of lumber and business. It didn't take long to understand that the brothers somehow worked together. Joseph was the carpenter while Joel traded in the timber business.

The servant boy seemed kind and whispered that his name was Asher.

I had no way to tell him that I could not speak.

He guided me in the proper order of washing feet. It was a custom that I knew, but no one had ever washed my feet and I had never washed another's feet.

Joel spoke with excitement. "Our family will make a fine caravan when we travel to the Holy City for the festival."

The upcoming festival was Passover. Jews traveled from every corner of the land to descend on the Holy City. It had always been a favorite time for Father and me to rob unsuspecting pilgrims.

"I have missed the temple," Joseph said.

"Yes, I am certain that you have, though you have returned home at the perfect time. We will celebrate the festivities as we celebrate your safe passage home."

For a moment I thought Joseph was going to weep. I glanced at Asher, who was drying one foot while I washed the other. This was not the disdainful task it might have been because the feet belonged to Joseph; I had walked alongside him. I knew how he had acquired such caked-on dirt. Washing Joseph's feet made me happy.

He smiled down at me and then said to his brother, "I am not in a position to offer the sacrifice I had hoped. When Mary and I presented Jesus at the temple for purification, all we could offer was a pair of turtledoves."

Eight

It was true that I knew little of God, especially the God of the Jews. He was the God who meant everything to Joseph—and Joseph had quickly come to mean everything to *me*.

I wanted to learn of Joseph's God, to keep His endless laws.

What would my father think of me, knowing my heart had changed so completely? It did not matter. Father was gone and Joseph was before me, showing me only kindness and opportunity. If I were his son, he would never have sold me for profit.

While I did not understand my own emotions, I could not stop them from overtaking me without warning. All I had to do was *think* of Father and I was overwhelmed with sadness, anger, or a combination of both. Now that I had seen Joseph with Jesus, I knew that a genuine father would never allow his son to suffer the treatments I had—not even for all of the coins in Arabia.

I wanted to learn quickly of faith and family. I wanted to know everything. I feared making a mistake that would take away Joseph's favor.

Asher led me through the courtyard, around an abundant vegetable garden to a back dwelling. The servants' quarters consisted of a simple room with stone walls and a packed dirt floor. Yellow light came through the cracks in the flat shafts. When I breathed I smelled earth and cinnamon.

Asher paused to wipe the foot bowl clean and dry. His eyes took me in and I could not tell if he approved or not. "You are unpracticed," he said. "Are you recently sold?"

I sighed. Most of my life Father had protected me from strangers. Now it seemed I had to explain over and over that I was not a boy of words. I pointed to my open mouth and shook my head.

Asher's brow wrinkled. "You don't talk?"

My head shook again.

"Not ever?"

No, I tried to say with my eyes.

"Then I will talk," Asher said. "I heard the man, Joseph, call you Almon."

I nodded.

"This outbuilding is for our dwelling. Your family will stay in the big house of Joel until your master builds a new home."

My heart jumped a little to hear Asher refer to Joseph, Mary, and Jesus as my family. I listened with great interest to what Asher taught.

"Joseph and Joel are brothers. I knew Joseph before he left for Egypt, before he and Mary were wed. Before all of the talk about . . . " Asher's tongue flicked out to lick the corner of his mouth. He had something to say, a secret to share perhaps, but decided instead to say, "Your master, Joseph, is a skilled carpenter and very popular down on Carpenters' Street."

Asher showed me to a corner with a mat, my new sleeping quarters. He showed me a small oven where we cooked our own meals. There were pots, tools, and a beautifully woven reed basket; I had seen such baskets in my travels with Father. Baskets like these were woven by Egyptian artisans, the reeds plucked from the black banks of the great Nile. They were expensive to purchase. It was a basket that did not belong in slaves' or servants' quarters.

"A gift from my master," Asher said. "My master, Joel, is a very kind and giving man. He presented it to me when I completed my studies in the House of Prayer." His chin went high and I saw the pride reflected in his eyes.

Asher was educated? Would I have the same opportunities? Oh, my heart wanted to dream of the possibility, but it was enough just to be here safe with people as good as Joseph's family. I told myself to be content. I was fortunate just to serve. What right did I have to wish for so much more?

We walked outside to where the animals were kept in a large stable. It had a tall beamed lean-to, built to shade a full-grown camel. Our donkeys were there, along with a single-humped camel, two more sturdy donkeys, and a variety of sheep and goats. I was not used to seeing sheep and goats penned. Sheep were usually in pastures and on hillsides with shepherds. And the goats I knew roamed free in the hills of Judea.

A brown-faced billy with a ragged beard charged toward me. I reached out to grab his horns, but he was stronger than I expected. Before I realized it, I was sitting on the ground and Asher was laughing.

I smiled, and the goat soon lost interest.

"Is your arm all right?" Asher asked, pointing to my sling.

I nodded. There were times I forgot that it was still broken. There were times I forgot that just days ago I was living a completely different life, a life that now brought me so much shame.

Asher introduced me to the man I had seen earlier. "This is Dan. He serves outside. I aid him when it is necessary, but my duties are those of a household servant. It is much better than one who shovels dung and milks goats morning and night."

Dan looked at me without smiling. His face was creased and pitiful. His shoulders were stooped and his skin had a yellow cast. His robe was soiled and his beard as faded as noonday sand. He looked as ancient as Noah.

"Tell me of Jesus," Dan said, pleading like a starving man begging bread.

I could not.

"The gods have taken Almon's tongue," Asher said. "The child does not speak."

I resented being called a *child*. If Asher only knew the things I had seen and done, the things that had been done *to* me, he would realize I had never really been a child.

Dan seemed direly disappointed. He came to me and looked deeply into my eyes. "Jesus, the child, He is the Son of David."

I did not understand. Jesus was the son of Joseph. *Jesus bar Joseph.*

Dan sucked his bottom lip; the way his eyes darted between me and Asher made me anxious. The old man seemed possessed—tormented even. "Listen if you cannot speak. Jesus is a wonder." He leaned toward me and his breath was hot on my face. His cloak reeked of camel. "I must know . . . does the child own powers?"

I had no way of understanding his question.

"The angel . . . the angel came to Mary in this very village. She was in the garden by the *mikvah* when it happened."

"Dan, swallow your words!" Asher's tone showed no respect for his elder. If I had ever spoken to Father with such dishonor, he would have broken my teeth with his fist.

"Do not say so much so early."

"He is a mighty prophet, your Jesus."

Angels? Prophets? What did Jesus have to do with them? He was just a boy, kind and curious.

Dan's voice trembled. "You care for the holy child. You must know that He is no ordinary son." His fingers, thin as reeds, grasped my shoulders. I was surprised at his strength. "You must know who your Jesus is."

Asher looked at me and rolled his eyes. "Dan is old. Forgive him."

But Dan's fingers pressed harder into my shoulders. "Heaven was rent at his birth. I heard Joseph retell it all . . . I heard the words come from Joseph's mouth. He told of Bethlehem. He told of angels and their music. He told of shepherds and their worship. Men of the East came following the star . . . " Drool dripped down Dan's chin, and his milky eyes filled with tears. "The treasure they brought still sits hidden in my master's house. All for the child Jesus."

Dan spoke the name with such reverence that Jesus almost seemed holy.

"Leave it be!" Asher said, again in a tone of disrespect. "There is much work to do and Almon is weary."

Dan came closer to me. "Profess your silence, Almon, but my eyes will be on Jesus. He will not escape my watch."

The old man's words did not make sense to me, but they did make me uneasy.

"Joseph will be well rewarded by God for honoring Mary . . . for raising her son as his own."

"Close your mouth, old man!" Asher ordered. "Your words will bring the wrath of God against the house of Joel!"

Dan dropped his head. He let go of me and stepped away. With the back of his hand—a trembling hand gnarled and lined with veins, blue and bulging—he wiped away his drool. "I have spoken out of order. Forgive a foolish old man."

At that moment Joseph's shadow darkened the doorway. Both Dan and Asher stepped away, as if caught stealing.

Joseph only smiled. "Almon, I came to see if your new quarters suit you."

I nodded and, at his invitation, went with him back to the house.

"We will reside here for a time with my brother and his family," he explained as we walked. "You will help me build a home of our own."

I opened my mouth. My lips formed the word for gratitude, but of course, no sound emerged.

Joel spoke as we approached. "Be comforted, my brother. There is great demand for your skills in Sepphoris, even here in Nazareth. You will find more work than you can do. Soon you will provide your household with prosperity. Soon you will be able to afford an unblemished lamb."

"That is my wish."

I turned back to Mary and saw that Jesus was fast asleep on her lap. Naomi was still touching His curls as though they were made of pure gold.

"Your son is no ordinary child," Naomi whispered.

Mary only smiled and bent to kiss His forehead.

Naomi poured some steaming liquid into clay bowls and approached the men. The aroma reminded me that my stomach was empty. I did not know when or how it would be filled, but I knew Joseph and Mary. They would not neglect me.

Asher, who had been washing Joel's feet, finished with the towel and handed it to me, urging me with his eyes to complete the task so Joseph could dine with his brother.

I wiped my master's foot dry and cleaned up the dirt and water from the stone floor.

Joseph looked at me with gratitude while the look Joel gave me was one of superiority. His eyes told me my only value was in what I could do . . . wash feet, feed donkeys. But I would prove him wrong. In time, I would prove to him, to me, and especially to Joseph that I had value untapped. In time, I hoped to prove that acquiring me was not a burden, but a blessing.

Nine

And so the days passed and Asher proved as good as his word. He showed me by example how to care for every detail and every responsibility in Joel's house. There were many details to attend to, because Joel kept a house of order.

In addition to Joel and Naomi, there were two children. Malik, their son, was a brute of a boy, older than me by years, and stronger. He had a head of bushy black hair and a habit of pushing me from behind when no one was looking.

They also had a daughter who was not much older than Jesus. She was named Deborah, after the honored judge and prophetess. I thought it odd that she wore a thick veil. Most girls did not put on a veil until they reached the age of twelve.

"She wears the veil to hide her ugliness," Asher told me, and he laughed quietly.

She did not seem ugly to me. She was kind, and the rope of red hair that fell down her back caught and held the sunlight. I liked Deborah very much, but did not have occasion to see her because she was shy and kept mostly to the house or clung to the folds of her mother's skirts.

Dan did not speak to me often, but I saw how he watched Jesus at play. It made me uneasy, and I began taking Jesus away from the house, up into the back hills where the shepherds ran sheep. Jesus loved the lambs and bounded after them, mimicking their leaps and bleats.

At night Asher recited his synagogue lessons, learning one law after another. He seemed fearful of making a mistake, and more than once I saw tears on his cheeks. I did not understand what went on each morning while he was off at school, but at night when he took to his studies, he was very serious.

I had been raised by a renegade father—a rogue, a lawless man. But Asher's life was layer upon layer of laws. Asher taught me that in addition to the 613 commandments, there were also 365 prohibitions and countless other injunctions.

"Why do you not know the laws?" Asher asked, though he knew I was unable to answer. "Have you not been brought up as a Jew?"

I shrugged, trying not to give away too much of the truth.

"Learn them well now. Our masters are strict in keeping all of the laws. Disobedience can cost a Jew his status—even his life if the offense is great."

I felt as though an invisible hand held my throat. What was I to do to learn so many laws? It seemed impossible, even for someone as good and kind and devout as Joseph. Yet, Joseph never complained, just went about his day with utter devotion. I found myself shadowing him just to hear him recite the ritual prayers. His voice rose and fell in perfect rhythm and brought balm to my wounded soul.

Jesus, too, loved to hear His father pray. But Jesus also knew the prayers and was able to say them aloud.

I felt the weight of a millstone crushing against my back. Even if I did memorize the commandments and the prayers, I would never be able to recite them aloud, prompting Joseph to look upon me with the joy he cast upon Jesus.

If it weren't for the way I felt about Joseph and his family, I would have run off into the night, going back to take my chances in the desert.

"Snakes," Asher whispered to me one night while we lay on our mats, "are more predictable than the shifting commandments of the Pharisees."

I sat up and tried to see him through the darkness. He had returned from his schooling at the synagogue upset, his eyes red and swollen.

"I was scolded today because I quoted Rabbi Asa's words."

I had no way of knowing who Rabbi Asa or what his words said.

"They hate each other, the Pharisees. They interpret the laws so differently. How am I to know that Rabbi Zeev never accepts the interpretation of Rabbi Asa?"

I lay still, but felt sympathetic.

"If I am cast out of synagogue school, I may well be cast out by Joel. I will bring him dishonor and shame."

Maybe I did not want to attend school, not if making a mistake would cost so much. It wasn't something to concern me anyway. Joseph seemed perfectly content to keep me occupied tending Jesus, helping with tasks in his brother's house.

Whenever a guest entered, his shoes were unlatched, his feet washed and dried. The fireplace had to be cleaned, the fire stoked, the woodbox filled. Weeds that choked the colorful flowers in the garden had to be pulled before they were allowed to take deep root. The vegetable garden required hoeing once each day.

Naomi and Mary enjoyed sitting in the shade of the garden while Jesus played. With each day that passed Mary's stomach grew larger, and I wondered how life would change once a new baby came into the family. I had never been exposed to a tiny baby and I hoped no one would ask me to tend it.

Each morning after chores, Asher and Malik walked off to the synagogue to attend school. Asher followed the proper seven steps behind, like an obedient servant. Malik had him carry all the books and both writing tablets.

One day each week Naomi walked Deborah to the synagogue for her lessons. It was unusual for a girl to receive a proper education, but in Nazareth, daughters who belonged to families of station were permitted to learn the basics of reading and writing. They were also taught the holy laws.

I found myself searching out Asher's thin study book. I was especially taken by the wax writing tablet he kept on the workbench. He did not have the patience for making exact letters. I did. And whenever he would permit, I would pour the wax evenly and watch it set. Then I would take the sharpened writing instrument and form the shapes that became words.

"You have a gift," Asher told me once. "Not even the priest has such a steady hand."

Asher and I fell into a daily pattern. While we were doing afternoon chores together, he would tell me all that he had learned at school, then later I would help him form his letters.

I learned quickly to love the Torah, though I did not understand most of its messages. To me, the god described was a god of war and vengeance, a god who waited for a human to make a mistake just so he could be punished.

That did not seem to me the God that Joseph worshipped.

Malik soon came to me for help with his writing, too. I felt honored, but I was fearful of making a mistake that would bring on Malik's rage. The boy had a fiery temper; I had seen him take it out on the goats and the small dog that came begging for scraps.

I did not dare pose the many questions that my mind formed, but I listened intently to Malik, hoping to glean any learning he shared.

I was especially honored when Joseph provided me with an oil lamp and a set of tattered scrolls. "I do not know how a desert boy knows so much of Greek and Hebrew, but I have seen you help both Malik and Asher. I am grateful," he told me.

I was the one filled with gratitude. Whenever a spare minute arose, I studied. At night I kept the lamp burning until the oil was gone. When the day came for me to accompany Joseph to his work-shop on Carpenters' Street, I found myself using my finger to write in the sawdust.

My passion for writing grew like corn in the fields.

Joseph praised me now and then, and his words only made me try harder. Asher seemed to appreciate my help and took on extra chores so I could have more study time. But Malik treated me like a slave, ordering me around, giving me piles of pages to write out. He did not know I considered his burdens a blessing.

Scrolls became my silent friends, every mark on them holy. Greek, Hebrew, even Latin—every word became like a friend I wanted to know and understand. Translation for me was not a challenge; it was a pleasure.

Jesus had His own passion for the Torah and its teachings. I was amazed at His understanding and ability to memorize the lessons— gifts that eluded even Malik.

One day while I was writing letters in the sand, Deborah came by to watch. Jesus ran to her and begged her to join us. I was surprised at how much she knew of the letters and symbols of the sacred text.

"Father says you have intelligence," she said.

I lifted my eyebrows in surprise. Joel hardly spoke to me, only to give me added tasks. I was glad that Joseph's brother found some value in me.

The afternoon sun was low and when I looked closely, I could see Deborah's face through her veil. Something was wrong with one side. Her cheek was covered in lumps, her chin malformed; her right eye was impaired by a terrain that made me think of the great desert mud flaps. Her face looked to be covered in dried balls of manna.

I felt pity for her, but she was not pitiful. She smiled and laughed, secure behind her veil.

Deborah took Jesus by the hand. "Come with me. I will take you on a walk through the village."

Jesus bounded to her like a forest antelope.

It was my duty to watch Jesus. I could not allow Him to wander off, so I followed behind. Deborah led us up and down the steep streets of Nazareth, past humble homes with no courtyards and past palatial homes with courtyards that dwarfed even Joel's.

People knew Deborah and called out to greet her. Jesus lifted His right hand and waved, a sign of peace.

God had granted Deborah the patience to answer the unending string of questions Jesus posed. He wanted to know how birds flew, why some flowers were yellow while others bloomed red. In the common courtyard with the village women looking on, He leaned over the well and made His voice echo, then asked who was down there shouting at Him.

When we returned home I feared Joseph would reprimand me. Instead, he scooped Jesus into his arms and swung the boy around until He squealed with delight. He thanked Deborah for taking Jesus through the village, and he thanked me for following to be certain Jesus was kept safe.

"Almon, never leave my son. Promise me that you will watch over Jesus when His mother and I cannot."

I nodded and a great warmth swelled inside of me. I did not vow aloud, but nevertheless, I vowed to Joseph that I would do as he asked. Jesus would be my charge and I would be His protector.

After that first walk through the village, Jesus wanted to wander every day. Some days Deborah went, others she did not. I learned to follow Jesus, careful to stay in His shadow so I would not disturb His adventures and learning experiences. I just wanted to be near the boy. His enthusiasm was contagious. I never thought of the sky as anything but blue or gray. Jesus saw it in countless shades. He prophesied the weather by the changing colors of heaven's canvas. He was most accurate.

He watched with interest the farmers as they planted, tended, and harvested their crops. He showed particular compassion to the beggars, plentiful on the streets of Nazareth. I thought it strange that in a land populated by Jews who were supposed to be the most holy of all people, there were so many who went without food, money, or care. It seemed to me that there were more needy people in the villages of Galilee than I had seen anywhere else.

The local language also took some adjustment on my part. Because Father spoke so fluently in many tongues, I had learned to understand more than just Greek and Hebrew, but Aramaic was different and I had to listen carefully to understand. I knew enough to grasp the fact that the Jews, as a people, were terrified by Roman rule. They feared that their freedom and their faith was being taken from them, and they feared that they had not the power to battle—not at that time, anyway, but soon . . . soon a Messiah would come who would deliver them and wreak havoc on the Romans.

It was impossible to go anywhere among the Jews and not hear talk of the coming Messiah, the day of insurrection and vindication.

I wondered at this Messiah . . . Father had never mentioned him at all.

Once while we were walking through an olive orchard, a waterwitch came up the furrow toward us, crying that for a coin she would tell us where precious water could be found. She carried a double-pronged stick and wore robes as dark as the robbers who had taken my father. The woman gave me chills, even though the day was scorching.

Deborah did her best to pull Jesus free, to steer Him away from the beckoning witch, but Jesus ran across the path to the woman, unafraid. She seemed perplexed at the child's presence more than she seemed amused at His words. His little arm pointed to the common courtyard. He was trying to tell her that if she was looking for water, she would find it at the bottom of the local well.

That made me laugh, and Jesus turned to smile at me. Even though I did my best to stay apart, to keep hidden in the shadows, Jesus was forever aware of my presence.

On the mornings when Jesus stayed with His mother, I loved accompanying Joseph to his workshop. Carpenters' Street was lined with shops, crowded with craftsmen. The air was thick with the sounds of saws ripping wood and hammers hitting nails. The delightful scent of fresh-cut cedar perfumed the air and made me want to stand still and breathe deeply. I enjoyed helping Joseph set up his tools, arrange his lumber, and sweep his shavings. One of my favorite tasks was to help Joseph match the grains in the wood.

I liked it best when Jesus came along and used His imagination to assist. He saw images that I had to search for. His little finger pointed to a swirl in the wood's grain, and He told me it was the sea swallowing Jonah and the big fish. In another piece of wood Jesus saw the sacred Jewish star; in still another, He pointed out the snout of a pig, an animal the Jews despised.

My feelings seemed strange. I was a Jew by birth; I was circumcised. Yet I felt apart from the Jews around me. I did not belong to them.

I watched Joseph work with awe. He treated wood the way he treated his animals: with care and respect. He did not craft a bowl without caressing the wood, running his hands over it, smoothing it until the olive wood felt like marble.

I also took note how his hand, the one missing two fingers, did not always work the way he wanted it to. There were times he tried to grasp a tool only to have it fall to the ground—or times he tried to saw with accuracy but found the blade veering.

Joseph never complained.

He gave God thanks over and over for His every creation. For the trees that provided the wood, for the sun that fed the trees, for the very earth that nourished us all. He had a special prayer for the rain that fell.

One day when just the two of us were in the shop, Joseph looked over at me and offered the saw to me. I took the tool, careful and unsure. Joseph then took a scrap piece of wood and helped position my body and my hands so that I could saw it. I lacked the strength to pull the blade back and push it forward like the task required. Joseph put his arms around me, held my hands, and offered his own strength to make up for my weakness.

When the board was cut he praised my effort. After that Joseph taught me to use a plane, to sand the grit from a board, to nail properly, and even to finish a small shelf we took home for Mary.

She embraced me when Joseph told her I was the craftsman. I never tired of her touch or the sound of her voice. It made me forget all my worries, all my doubts.

On an evening when we were about to close shop, I looked at Joseph and thought of my own father. I had not remembered him in days, and guilt overtook me.

"Almon?" Joseph said.

I felt my cheeks blush. I had been caught staring at his scarred hand.

Joseph did not seem irritated. "You are curious," he said, holding out his hand with the two missing fingers.

I bit my bottom lip.

"You wonder how I lost these fingers." He picked up his saw and showed me how the blade had taken both fingers with one hack. "I was a boy about your age when the accident occurred. Time has taught me to be more careful."

I felt sick. I felt sorry. I felt that I would give my own fingers to replace his.

"Do not feel pity for me," Joseph said. "I am able to work. Prosperous is the household whose God is Jehovah."

I did not understand then what his words meant, but I knew they made me feel better, and for a time that was enough.

Ten

Joseph and Mary needed a home of their own. I heard them talking at night in the courtyard when most of the household was sleeping. I had taken to climbing the ladder to the rooftop. It was cool up there and the view of the stars unmatched. It also provided perfect acoustics to hear what was being whispered below.

"Two women under the same roof is an invitation for contention," Mary said, always in her soft voice.

Joseph laughed. "It won't be long until we have a home of our own."

"That is my fondest wish."

"My wish is that the home will be ready for dedication before the new baby arrives," Joseph sighed.

Mary chuckled. "That will require haste on your part."

There was a lull and I felt guilty for hearing what they said; words between husband and wife should stay between husband and wife. I rolled over on my mat and put my hands over my ears, but I could still hear their voices.

"It is not that I do not appreciate the hospitality of Naomi. She is so kind and generous. I just long to have four walls to enclose my own family," Mary said.

"I understand," said Joseph. "You shall have more than four walls, Mary. Because your father was so generous with the dowry, the land is ours. You have seen it. I have already raised a home you can be proud of."

"And I *am* proud, Joseph. My heart is filled with gratitude. The Lord be praised."

"Yes. The Lord be praised. I know you are anxious to have a home for the new baby. I promise you that when Joel returns with the timbers, we will set the beams for the roof. Soon, Mary, soon."

Mary sighed. "Oh, Joseph, you are a good man. I am grateful to have you for my husband."

"And I am grateful for God's hand in bringing you into my life, Mary. His favor has shone down on all of us because of your worthiness and willingness."

There was a long silence when all I could hear was the sound of the animals shuffling in their corral. Somewhere in the distance a night bird cawed.

"Joseph?"

"Yes, Mary."

Far away I heard the closing of a door.

"There are moments . . . moments when the weight of what has fallen to us seems so . . . so heavy."

"Jesus."

"Yes, Jesus."

I wondered if I had heard right. Raising Jesus carried hardly any weight. He woke happy and went to sleep happy. He was ever obedient.

"You are an ideal mother, Mary. God knew what He was doing when He chose you to be the mother of His Son."

Now I knew my ears were deceiving me. *Jesus, the Son of God? What was this crazy talk between Mary and Joseph?* It made no sense.

"My father could not have chosen a better husband for me. And *you* will be the father of this child, this child that I am about to bear. I know you will love this baby as much as you have come to love Jesus."

"I do love Him, Mary, as though He were my own."

Through the darkness and the confusion of my brain I heard Mary softly crying. Maybe even Joseph, too. I dared not to breathe. I had imposed on a conversation so private I deserved to be banished for listening in.

After awhile I heard footsteps on stone. A door moved on its hinges, and then all was quiet. Mary and Joseph had gone inside and left me to wonder.

Eleven

I was alone in the workshop when the man came in. Joseph had left to fetch supplies. No one was due and I had no way to communicate.

The man was short and stout and wore a dark brown tunic. He greeted me with respect, but all I could do was stare.

"Is this the shop of Joseph?" he asked.

I nodded.

"I am Nathan, a physician from the city of Sepphoris. I have come to hire Joseph to build shelves for my office. Is he here?"

I shook my head.

He squinted and approached me with confidence. "Is something wrong with you, son?"

I pointed to my mouth and shook my head.

He looked concerned. "You are mute?"

My head bobbed again.

"Clearly, you are not deaf . . . a most unusual situation."

I backed up until I was pressed against Joseph's workbench. I could not tell if this man was simply curious or if he intended to harm me.

"Open your mouth," he said.

I pressed my lips together.

"Open. I will not hurt you. I am a physician."

At that moment Joseph entered through the door, ducking because he was tall even in his own shop. He and the physician exchanged greetings and I could tell that Joseph was pleased a man of station had chosen to enter his shop among the many that were along Carpenters' Street.

"I have come to hire your services," Nathan said, "but first . . . tell me about your slave boy."

"Almon is my servant. He is *not* a slave."

Nathan clearly did not discern between slaves and servants.

"He is mute. Why?" Nathan asked.

"It is a condition he had when we came upon him in the desert."

"Tell me the circumstances," the man said, pulling up a stool.

Joseph looked at me with assurance in his eyes. "Almon has proven his value. He has become part of our household."

"That is not what I asked. I am a trained physician. Tell me the circumstances of acquiring him and I might be able to help the boy."

Light danced in Joseph's eyes. His words retold the story of their coming upon me in the desert, finding me alone, with obvious signs of a fight, but no sign of my father or anyone else.

I had not fully realized how thoroughly Joseph had searched for any other victims.

A stabbing pain shot through my arm; it was as though his words took me back to that day and that drama.

"Terror can cause someone to go silent," the physician said. "Tell the lad to open his mouth so that I may inspect it."

Joseph nodded at me and I opened my mouth, allowing Nathan's fingers to touch my teeth, lift my tongue, and push it down again until I gagged.

"He is not tongue-tied," Nathan said. "That would have been a rather simple procedure. I see nothing physically amiss at all."

"Almon is able to communicate. He is actually very intelligent."

"In carpentry?"

"In Hebrew, Greek, and Aramaic."

"How can he be fluent in three languages if he cannot speak?"

"He reads and writes."

The physician looked astounded. He whirled to face me. "How . . . where . . . did you learn to read and write?"

I wrote the symbol for *father* in a fine layer of sawdust.

"Have you sent this boy to school?" Nathan asked.

"No."

"Can you afford to pay for his education?"

"No."

"Would you be opposed to my paying for his education?"

Joseph looked dubious. I could hardly keep up with speed of the conversation.

"If I paid the cost, would you allow the boy to attend the local synagogue school?"

Joseph stood with a mallet in his hands. He seemed uncertain—not of the offer, but of the man's motives. I wondered, too, why a stranger would make such an offer.

"Rabbi Asa heads the school," Joseph said. "Perhaps you are familiar with him."

Nathan frowned. "No. I do not know the man, though your Rabbi Zeev carries much authority. He is renowned."

Joseph's lips went tight, and I wondered about this Rabbi Zeev. What kind of man could bring such uneasiness to Joseph?

The awkward moment passed, and then Joseph smiled again. "When you become acquainted with Rabbi Asa, you will discover that he is good and kind. He knows the Torah as well as a shepherd knows his flock."

"I have seen your synagogue with its small but fine school."

"My father donated the lumber for the structure," Joseph proclaimed. Then his face suddenly went red and he pursed his lips into a tight, straight line. "Forgive me, sir; my father has been dead several years. It is unlawful of me to mention him."

Nathan looked sympathetic. "It is difficult to keep every law every day."

"It falls to me to put forth my best effort. I fail from time to time."

Nathan chuckled. "We all fail, my carpenter friend. We all fail."

I had never seen Joseph look so uneasy. He coughed and sputtered. "Well . . . back to the synagogue school. My nephew attends school there. Almon helps him with his lessons." Joseph gave me a quick smile.

Nathan jerked his head toward me and looked at me like I was a two-headed donkey.

"Rabbi Asa reports that Malik is doing very well."

My heart thundered.

"Your offer is very generous, but I cannot accept."

My heart stopped.

"Why is that?"

"I am not a man who enjoys being obligated."

"There would be no obligation."

Joseph looked at me, but I kept my eyes downcast. I did not want to appear as eager as I felt, nor did I want to seem unappreciative.

Nathan put his hand on my shoulder. The way he peered so intently at me made me squirm.

"How old is the boy?" he asked Joseph.

"Almon has ten years, if his accounting is accurate."

Nathan turned to me. "You have never attended a formal school?"

I shook my head.

"His father was a man of skill. He taught Almon to read and to write."

To steal and to lie, I thought, but pushed the memories to the back of my mind, shoved them as hard as Malik shoved me when I failed to meet his approval.

"I fear that the boy has not been trained in the way of the prophets. The only training Almon has received of that kind is what he has acquired living with us."

"That is a beginning."

"I feel sorrow that it could not have been more."

Nathan grinned. "He is young. As you know, Jewish boys do not study the law until they are ten. Almon . . . " he looked at me and his grin widened, "can be trained properly at synagogue."

"I lack the funds to provide such an education." Joseph said, turning a piece of olive wood in his hand.

"If cost is the concern, I assure you I am capable of providing such an opportunity."

"Almon, though . . . he is my servant."

My heart stopped once more.

Nathan scratched his chin. "Yes, it is most unusual to educate a slave—rather, a servant."

"I would ask to see a demonstration of his skills," Nathan said, looking at me but addressing Joseph.

A bright square of light came through the window and shined on Joseph's face. His eyes sparkled. His hand moved to set the mallet down and he cleared a space on the workbench. Then Joseph scooped a giant handful of sawdust, spread it evenly, and told me to write. But he failed to tell me *what* to write.

I tried my best to keep my hand steady as I scribed the words of the holy *Shema*, my favorite prayer because it was so simple and so true: *Hear O Israel, the Lord is our God, the Lord is one.*

Nathan watched, peering closer and closer. His tongue kept clicking.

I took plenty of time to be certain my symbols and letters were precise. I ran out of room before I finished.

"The boy has skill," Nathan pronounced. "I am willing to provide him a chance to prove himself."

The wrinkles in Joseph's brow smoothed. "I would be indebted to you, lord."

"No. There will be no obligation. My own son died before he was old enough to study the law. That was many years ago, and I have dedicated my life to helping other young boys who possess potential, but lack funds."

Joseph bowed his head, and I wondered if he could hear the hammering of my heart. "Allow me to contemplate the possibility," he said. Then, lifting his eyes, he changed the subject with firm resolve. "Tell me, Nathan, for what purpose do you require my carpentry skills?"

Twelve

I did not know the date of my birth. When did I achieve ten years of age?

It did not matter.

In the next weeks everything in my life changed. Time became a blur.

Joseph and Mary moved into their new home, a two-room square, washed white as lambs' wool. In the back was a small shed for me and our animals. The roof was flat, like Joel's, and seeded for grass so it made a perfect sleeping place.

The land had been deeded to Joseph when he married Mary. It was a large parcel that had been in the family for generations. Asher told me that Mary and Joseph were kinsmen, so it was close to Joel's house, but also central to Joseph's workshop. There was still much work to do to make it as complete as Joseph envisioned, but it was clean and new and the day I moved there it became the first home I had ever known.

Jesus preferred to be outside with me rather than stay in the house. It fell to me to help landscape the courtyard. Mary chose the plants and flowers, mostly gifts from Joel and other relatives who lived in Nazareth. Every day I became acquainted with more kinsmen and neighbors. It was impossible to keep track of them all.

Jesus showed love to everyone. He remembered names when I could not. He found joy in the rain and the sunshine. He learned to imitate the sounds of birdsong. His whistle fooled even the birds.

At night, when the heat was oppressive, Jesus joined me on the flat roof where we slept beneath the stars. He talked of heaven like he had just come from there. He counted the stars and spoke of the one true God who was author of all that was great and all that was small.

He made me believe.

I lay there listening to Him and wondered again and again . . . *Why had Mary and Joseph referred to Jesus as the Son of God? Was Joseph, the carpenter, not this boy's earthly father? Was there some secret, some shame, about his place in the family?*

It mattered not. Jesus had become so dear to me that the very sight of His flying feet headed my way made me forget any of my burdens. His curiosity and passion for life infused me with strength and hope. I treasured our moments together and was grateful that it was my assignment to shadow Him.

Jesus understood me even though I could not speak. He shared with me truths from the Torah and the prophets. Like His father, Jesus had a gift for making every story live. When he recited the story of Cain and Abel, I could feel the purpose of sacrifice. God deserved our best, our first, our finest.

Jesus made *me* come alive. When I was with Him, my bravest dreams seemed somehow within my grasp, especially my aspiration to become educated, to have a family, to find purpose in my life, to find value in myself.

Nathan proved to be a man of honor. He and Joseph met with Rabbi Asa. After much discussion and much persuasion, I was permitted to become a pupil at the synagogue.

Malik was not pleased, but Asher congratulated me.

Rabbi Zeev, a man just older than Joseph but with the thick black hair of a bear on his arms and toes, peered at me with the same curiosity that the servant Dan showed to Jesus. He had a fast tongue, and I had to listen carefully to understand him. Fortunately, he did not spend a lot of time in Nazareth. Later, I learned that his ambitions rested mainly in the Holy City.

Rabbi Asa was not as old as he appeared. His hair and beard were white and short for a rabbi. His stature, too, was short. I was almost as tall as he was, but his belly bulged and his chest was broad as an ox. He had lived most of his life in Nazareth, but trained in Jerusalem at the temple and in the ancient synagogue there.

His smile was generous.

I liked him right away.

"So much of Jewish history is oral," he explained during my first day's lesson. "For generations, our people had no written word, so they told and retold our history, our laws, our traditions.

"Almon, since you cannot tell me, I would like you to write down your history. Be complete."

He handed me a tablet laid with fresh wax. I was given my own writing instrument, a sharpened reed.

It should have been a proud moment; I had the ability to fill the tablet. But what words could ever tell the story of my simple life? For the longest moment, I sat at the cross-legged desk on a cross-legged stool. Malik, Asher, and the other boys fixed their eyes on me.

The double doors leading out to the courtyard were open and Rabbi Asa spoke to another teacher, leaving me to my first—and what would prove my most difficult—task.

No breeze stirred, and the air inside was stale and warm. I felt the back of my neck go damp. My head started to hurt.

In the end, I did what came easiest. I lied.

I wrote that I had been raised by my father. I wrote that my mother had died when I was a baby. I did not know my grandparents or any other kinsmen. I did not write that Father had learned much as a money changer on Temple Mount. Money changers were not well thought of by Jews. I twisted the truth to make Rabbi Asa believe my own father had gained his education at the temple. In a way, it was true; in another way, it was not true.

I wrote of life in the desert. As the son of a successful trader, I had traveled much and met many people.

I wrote of Joseph's heroic rescue of me. I wrote of the burning body, the bandits, and my father's certain demise.

I gave my life color and texture with my lies. I also told enough truth to warrant Rabbi Asa's sympathy.

"A single-generation history is a sad history," Rabbi Asa said upon reading my tablet. "I am glad the hand of God has guided you here. Here you will learn what you have not yet learned. We are a covenant people. God has chosen us . . . "

I listened carefully, vowing to understand, to accept, and to serve. I wanted to make Joseph proud of me. I would come to know the

God of the Jews and I would serve Him to the last day of my life. These were promises I not only made to Joseph; I made them within the chambers of my own heart.

The lies of my past were past. I would bury them deep and keep them buried.

From that first day at synagogue school, I told myself I was a new person. The Hebrew word for convert was *gerut;* I would convert completely. No one would ever have to know the real truth of my past.

Though Mary was due to deliver any day, she worked hard to construct the proper clothing for me to attend school. She was gifted at the loom and skilled at designing clothing out of the simplest cloth.

Her eyes looked tired, but her face smiled when she called me into the house to present me with my new robes for school. As she helped me try them on for proper fit, her hand reached up and the side of her thumb brushed against my cheek. It took me back to that first day when I had seen Mary wipe tears from Jesus' dusty cheeks.

"You are weeping," she said.

I had not realized my own cheeks were damp.

"Are you sorrowful, Almon?"

No. No. Not sorrowful at all. I now knew what a mother's touch felt like.

Standing before Mary, draped in new robes she had sewn just for me, living with a family who treated me so well, I knew a level of happiness I had never experienced.

"We are pleased that you are able to attend school at the synagogue," she said. "Joseph says one day you will make a fine scribe."

My heart was overjoyed. My own father had wanted me to become a scribe, and now Joseph believed it was possible.

God was indeed great.

Every day that followed seemed no different from the one before. The sun rose over Palestine and set every night behind the great lake. Fishermen fished. Farmers farmed. Carpenters turned wood into walls and walls into homes.

To me, no day was taken for granted. Every sunrise was a gift as surely as fresh manna to a starving boy, a boy no longer *forsaken.*

Thirteen

Rabbi Asa assigned my learning to a younger teacher, another rabbi who had only recently finished his training. Rabbi Micha was a thin, nervous man who sneezed at every unfolding flower. He seemed young to me, with his sparse beard only slightly dappling his smooth skin. Malik told me a man had to reach thirty years to attain the status of rabbi. Thirty years seemed ancient to me, and Rabbi Micha did not seem ancient.

Not long after we settled into the new house, the entire village of Nazareth celebrated Rabbi Micha's marriage to the coppersmith's daughter. The festivities lasted two days. I stayed at home with Jesus and Mary, who was cautious about her public appearance since she was expecting a child so soon. From the rooftop we watched people dressed in their finest clothes wind their way to the common courtyard. We heard the music and laughter and smelled the roasting meat.

Jesus called to the people, and they looked up and called back their greetings, grinning at such open friendliness. I did not think there was any person Jesus did not like. His little heart held enough love to shower the world with good will.

Watching the festivities, I began to contemplate my own future and the possibility of marriage. If I intended to follow my deepest dreams and become a scribe, the law required that I take a wife, but who would marry me? I was a servant. All I could offer were poverty and silence.

Rabbi Micha took his task of training me and the other boys my age very seriously. He proved neither kind nor patient, but ready to reprimand us for any sign of disrespect or ignorance. To him, the law was everything.

He had taken his example from the Pharisee Ovadya. Ovadya resided in Sepphoris, but extended his authority over our Nazarene synagogue. Both Rabbi Asa and Rabbi Micha seemed eager to bow before the man—as much out of fear, I thought, as respect. I deemed Ovadya's eyes too close-set, his voice as high as a woman's, and his hair oily, like unbrushed camel. More than that, his interpretation of the Torah was not steady. On one visit he would interpret the law a certain way, then on his next visit he would contradict his own teachings.

No one dared point this out to Ovadya, because he held the authority to expel any student he wished from the synagogue. The appearance of his colorful tunic with its elaborate *tzitzit*—fringes that resembled a fox tail— was enough to wipe the smiles off every face in the synagogue.

Whenever Ovadya visited, my thoughts brought my father back to me. I remembered all he despised about Pharisees—and looking at Ovadya, I began to understand. Ovadya carried a long pointing stick that he used to strike any student who did not supply the answer he wanted. I even saw him bring it down on Rabbi Micha's hand once when he failed to find a passage quickly enough. I did not favor the man, but never let my feelings be known because his office demanded respect, even if he did not.

I grew fond of Rabbi Asa and felt pity when I realized he had long ago lost the respect of his students. Late one morning while Rabbi Micha was away, he sat on a stone bench in the center court-yard. The heat had driven us out into the open air; even the birds had sought refuge in the shade. Sweat dripped down the back of my neck and I reached up and felt my damp hair beneath the rim of my *yarmulke*.

Everything around me was the same shade . . . that of fresh goat's cream—the stone of the synagogue, the stone beneath our feet, the stone bench. All of us boys wore the same light-colored cloaks. I stared at my colorless surroundings and tried not to yawn.

Jude, the pupil next to me, wore a smile. "The old man is drooling in his whiskers," he whispered to me, nudging me with his elbow.

I managed to keep a straight face, but it was true. Rabbi Asa's mouth was open, and saliva dripped from his beard.

A fat black fly landed on the drool of his lip, and the rabbi's head jerked up. "Ah . . . in Greek, *synagogue* translates to *place of meeting*. It is here in this very courtyard you pupils will hear the wisest men expound God's holy word. It is here you will meet truth."

And with those words, his chin dipped, his eyes closed, and he was asleep again.

I heard someone behind me laugh out loud, and I turned around to see Malik. In his hand was a long thin willow. He slid closer and closer until he was able to reach out and tickle the rabbi's exposed foot.

Of course, the old man jerked. Everyone tried not to chuckle.

Malik held an audience and he obviously savored the attention, so he reached out and tickled the old man's foot again. He got the same response, only this time the chuckles were not so subdued.

"Get closer," Jude urged.

Malik could not help himself. He slid even closer, and this time he raised the willow to tickle the rabbi's beard. The tip of the willow touched it, but Rabbi Asa only snored on. Again, Malik's stupid bravery urged him closer. He pushed the willow harder until it actually touched the rabbi's cheek.

As fast as a viper, Rabbi Asa grabbed the willow, rose to his feet, and held Malik by the ear.

I did not know a holy man could say the words he uttered. He let Malik know that he was an absolute disappointment, a pitiful student, and a boy who could await the wrath of both Rabbi Micha and the feared Pharisee, Ovadya.

With a shove, Malik landed back down on the stone. We all watched as his face grew red and moisture dripped from both his nose and his eyes.

Jude laughed, but when Malik turned, his eyes fixed on me—and I knew I was the one headed for trouble.

Fourteen

The walk home after synagogue was fast-paced, up and down the steep streets. The potter sat out in front of his shop and called out his greetings.

I lifted my chin, but Malik huffed along, ignoring the man. He could hardly keep up with me even though I carried the supplies for both of us.

I slowed, looked back at him, and offered all I could—a thin smirk.

Malik spit, and his fig-like cheeks went red. "The physician Nathan has taken pity on you, Almon. Pity."

His words stung, but did not injure me. What was it to me if Malik had no faith in me? Joseph did. Nathan did. I did.

I tried to gesture to Malik to make him understand. I wasn't rushing because I wanted to show him up; I was hurrying because I had double duty to do for Joseph, with chores to do at both the house and the shop. Only after I had given my best to Joseph's household did I feel I could settle down in the glow of an oil-burning lamp and study. It was my reward to myself.

Malik's huffing sounded like an angry ox, but I did not slow my feet. I walked faster.

"Slow down," he said.

I looked back and shook my head.

"I order you to slow down, Almon!"

My feet flew faster.

"Slow down, slave! All you will ever be is a slave!"

I didn't slow down—I stopped. My eyes narrowed and my fist clenched. My arm was long out of the sling and strong enough to put a chokehold around Malik's fat, red neck.

He looked as surprised as I felt. Malik was twice my size. He was my superior, and yet his eyes bulged with fear.

What had I done? My anger put everything in jeopardy. If I hurt Malik—if he even *claimed* I hurt him—his father would surely demand justice from Joseph.

Slowly, reluctantly, I released my grip.

Malik stumbled backward and narrowed his eyes until they became dark points of malice.

I did not belong to Malik.

He scoffed and spat again, his spittle hitting my toes. "You *are* a slave. You belong to everyone."

A sense of powerful fear grew rapidly inside of me. I turned away from Malik and broke into a full run, afraid of my own temper.

I heard the sound of women before I turned the corner toward home. At first I thought there had been some tragedy, the way their voices wailed. Instead, I soon learned, Mary had given birth to a son.

Naomi was there and she approached me with haste, the skirts of her robe flying. "Where is Malik?"

I jabbed a thumb in the air, indicating that he was behind me.

"There is much work to do. Go in haste, Almon, and see to the chores. Asher is here to assist you."

The house was packed with people: friends, relatives I could not name, neighbors who barely knew Mary and Joseph. Rabbi Micha's wife carried a big platter of sweet dates.

A baby had been born. More than that, a *son* had been born, and there was great cause to celebrate in the household of Joseph!

I saw Joseph first up on the rooftop where I went to sprinkle the plants and grass with water. He was in the far corner, kneeling beside a young palm tree. He was on his knees in silent prayer. I did not dare to move. I stood silently looking at him, and I saw the tears of gratitude and joy flow from his eyes.

I said a silent prayer of my own. I thanked God for Joseph's happiness. The child was named James.

I quickly learned that an infant—tiny as a man's sandal and swaddled in strips of linen so tight he looked like a cocoon—could rule a household. Every time the baby cried, Mary reached for him. Naomi rushed around cleaning up after every mess.

Joseph presented James with a hand-crafted cradle he had made at the workshop. It moved from side to side with a simple touch.

"You would think our child is royal," Mary said, inspecting the fine work of her husband.

"All of our children are royal," Joseph said, staring at James but not moving to lift him.

Jesus was fascinated by the baby and begged to hold him. Mary allowed it, only if she had her arms around both of her sons. When I peeked in and saw her cradling Jesus and James, a part of my own heart hurt. My own mother's arms had never held me, and they never would.

That pain eased when I thought about my new studies. Already Rabbi Micha said that I was the keenest student he had ever taught. I took no stock in that because he was a new, inexperienced rabbi. And though Malik made no trouble over our encounter, I knew he was able to strike at me when I least expected it. Any praise I received at school seemed to be an insult to him.

I did my best to avoid Malik, though each day that Asher did not attend school, I was summoned to carry Malik's supplies.

I did so with a false sense of submission.

I was a servant, but inside I did not always *feel* like a servant. A voice as silent, but true as my own told me repeatedly that I was meant for something greater than servitude.

I tried to still the voice, but it would not be silenced.

It spoke loudest when others spoke for it. Like the time I heard Rabbi Asa tell Joseph that he attributed my ability to memorize to the fact that I listened while most of the other students talked.

"God's ways are not man's ways, and the mute boy has been favored by a high hand," the rabbi suggested.

"He is gifted in many ways," Joseph said.

"I look for great accomplishments to come from the boy," the rabbi said.

When the dark voices like Malik's started stalking, I went back to the words of Joseph and the rabbi. I played them over and over in my head until I felt stronger and more sure of myself.

During the days following James' birth, I was forced to miss some precious mornings of schooling. I must have washed a hundred feet.

It fell to me to clean up after people feasted. If they brought gifts, I presented them to Naomi, who in turn presented them to Mary and Joseph.

Joseph assigned Asher and me to take the donkeys and ride into Sepphoris, the largest city in Galilee, to post letters. One was addressed to Mary's parents in a town by Mount Carmel; the other was addressed to Joseph's eldest brother, a scribe who lived in Bethany, just outside of Jerusalem.

Jesus came running out of the house as we were preparing to leave. He begged to go with us. Joseph, usually so overprotective, gave his permission.

"Let him ride in front with you," Joseph told me. "Almon, hold tightly to the boy. You know how Jesus can squirm."

I did not know my way to Sepphoris, but Joseph pointed to the hill country north and assured me it was not far.

"Go in peace and safety," he said.

I nodded and kicked the beast swiftly to launch our journey. Asher and his donkey were already disappearing in a cloud of dust.

Fifteen

I now knew how Malik had felt when I had raced ahead of him. I was sorry for not being more considerate. Now I was the one desperate to keep up.

Whether it was the added weight of Jesus or something else, Boaz was stubborn. No matter what I did to urge him along, he was in no hurry. Since I could not raise my voice to plead with Asher to slow his pace, after several turns around a few corners, he disappeared from sight.

My silent shouts did nothing to urge Boaz forward.

Desperation crept up like a white desert spider, there before I realized it. I jumped down, took the reins in my hand, motioned for Jesus to hold tight. Then I tried to lead the donkey as I ran alongside. But Boaz would not be led.

Jesus thought the sight of me fruitlessly tugging and pulling, pushing and prodding, was hilarious. He threw back his head and giggled. A woman with a bundle high on her head looked at us from across the street and joined in the laughter.

"You need a switching stick," she called. "Switch him and he'll pick up those lazy feet of his."

My father would have whipped the donkey into obedience, but I had seen Joseph with the animals. He used kindness to get them to obey. I had neither kindness nor a switch. All I could do was pull from the front and push from the back.

Asher was nowhere in sight.

I could feel my face go red. Sweat beaded on my forehead and the backs of my hands. I could still turn around now and go home, defeated. What would I tell Joseph? Never before had I longed for my voice like I longed for it now. I wanted it to shout at the donkey, to curse him with words. I wanted it to be able to ask for directions to Sepphoris. I wanted it to assure Jesus that we were all right, although He was happy and seemed to share none of my worry or frustration.

I smiled at His laughter and soon found myself seeing what He saw. The image of me pushing and pulling *was* funny. Soon I found myself joining Jesus, and when I started to silently laugh, old Boaz started to move.

Finally, after what seemed an eternity, we reached the top of the main road out of Nazareth, and all I could see of Asher was a tiny gray dot in the distance. At least I knew we were headed in the right direction. And what could he do without me? The letters to be posted were in *my* donkey's bag.

Jesus enjoyed Himself even as my frustration turned to fear. He found delight in every face we passed. No one could look upon the child without smiling.

The further we went, the more displaced I felt. I chose to keep to the main road, but it was not a straight path. Instead it veered and forked, and I kept choosing my way with growing uncertainty.

Jesus seemed oblivious to any trouble. He was fascinated by every new tree, every bird, every human face.

Galilee was a densely populated region, one village connected to another. An hour did not vanish before we passed through two smaller villages. They were not situated on a steep hillside like Nazareth, for as we descended, the terrain flattened out and gave way to great fields of grain, verdant orchards, and the largest vineyard I had ever seen.

We could not help but stop.

The press in the vineyard was made of stone. It was huge and gray, stained by the darkness of the grapes. It seemed to me the entire village was there, working to turn grapes into wine.

Jesus was mesmerized by the press and all the associated activity. True slaves, so thin I could count their ribs and with skin as dark as old bananas, stomped the fruit of the vine. They were in chains; I thought back to a time, years earlier, when I had seen men this dark and slender carried by a caravan across the desert. Father told me they were men of Africa.

They had fascinated me then. They fascinated me now.

Jesus, too, could not take his eyes from the assembly.

More slaves carried overflowing baskets, clusters of dark grapes hanging over the edges. Farmers barked orders and women scurried about.

I had seen winepresses before, but nothing so efficient. I held tightly to Jesus' hand while we watched. Finally a man noticed us and tossed a cluster of fat, juicy grapes at my feet.

"Consider yourselves blessed," he said, turning back to the hum of his work.

Jesus cried out our gratitude.

The man whirled back and looked at him and nodded.

I recognized the kindness and generosity of his gesture, its *unusualness*. I wanted to ask the man where Sepphoris was, if we were headed in the right direction, but I couldn't even figure out a way to have Jesus ask for us.

A growing tightness in my chest made it difficult to breathe. Fear squeezed me just as the winepress squeezed the grapes.

More and more I realized how often my father had spoken for me so I would not have to try to communicate. Now that I had to, I couldn't. Why would God do this to me? He had taken my mother on the same day he took my voice. It was not fair, not if God was the loving, just God that Joseph worshipped.

Jesus popped one grape into His mouth and rolled His eyes with delight as he savored its sweetness. I had never known anyone to experience life as deeply and fully as Jesus did. The most mundane aspects of every day came alive through Jesus.

In spite of myself, I had to smile at Him.

I handed Him the water-skin and He took a drink, then handed it back to me. I shook my head. I was too worried to drink. The road at the end of the vineyard forked, and I had no sense of which way to go.

I was about to plead for help, to write down my query in the dirt and hope that someone would be able to read, when Jesus tugged at my sleeve.

I did my best to assure Him there was no need to worry, though I had never been so worried. How would Joseph react if I was truly lost, if I could not be trusted with Jesus' safekeeping? What if harm came to Jesus? Oh, where was Asher and why had he not stopped to wait for us?

Jesus sensed my worry, offered a wide smile, and told me not to fear. Then He led me to a quiet spot away from the business of the press. When we were off a distance and sheltered between rows of vines, He bowed His head and prayed for direction. I had never heard such a prayer. It wasn't prescribed; it wasn't memorized. Jesus spoke to heaven like He was actually talking to God.

He gave thanks for our safe journey. He gave thanks for the vineyard and the man who had offered us grapes at no cost. He gave thanks for Israel and for prophets of old. He gave thanks for His family and His new baby brother. He gave thanks for *me*. His words stirred something as deep as the ocean floor within my heart.

His gratitude seemed unbounded. Jesus then explained our situation, acknowledged *my* worry, and pleaded for personal direction. His plea was *personal,* as if God cared about two boys lost somewhere between Nazareth and Sepphoris—one a child of faith, the other a frightened mute, a mere servant.

I felt warmth on my shoulders, sure as sunshine, and closed my eyes. The world around us went quiet, though I knew we were a mere stone's throw away from the chaos of the massive winepress. It was as if we had been lifted to a higher, more serene plane. I did not want to open my eyes. I did not want Jesus to close His prayer. I longed to stay right on the spot where I was, hanging on His every word.

How long we were there I don't know, but when Jesus ended the prayer His little arm lifted and His finger pointed—not in the direction I had determined to go, but in the opposite direction. His faith was our compass.

By the time Asher's tired donkey reached Sepphoris, Jesus, Boaz, and I were waiting in front of the post.

Sixteen

Sepphoris was the largest city in Galilee; we had passed through it on our way to Nazareth months earlier. I recalled little of it, though I knew this was the home of Nathan, my benefactor, and of Ovadya, the Pharisee.

In the latest rebel uprising, the whole of the city had been destroyed by Herod's army *and* by Roman soldiers. Now it was under construction, being made new by the very people who had burned and broken it. On every street walls were being lifted, lumber being sawed, new replacing old.

It was very different from Nazareth; the streets were wider and straight. The houses looked very much alike, and there were people everywhere—not simple farmers and carpenters, but men and women dressed in fine clothing, looking like they were headed to the synagogue.

After we posted the letters, we rode to the outskirts of town and sat beneath the shade of the synagogue wall to eat our midday meal. While we ate olives, bread, and figs, Jesus talked of the City of Enoch and told us how it had been lifted to heaven because the people were so righteous.

"He knows more than the rabbis," Asher said, only half-joking. Then the easy expression on his face turned hard. "Look to the end of the street. Do you see that mob?"

I did.

"They look angry," Asher said.

He was right. The group of men, a dozen or more, had red faces and clenched fists, and they were shouting at someone in the center of their circle, someone blocked from view.

I pulled Jesus to me and raised my eyebrows to ask Asher what the matter was.

"A stoning," he said, flatly.

I stood up, and that's when I realized that another group was approaching from the opposite direction. I recognized some of their robes . . . they were holy men, priests and rabbis. We were caught in the center of their fury.

I could not allow Jesus to witness such horror. Once, when I was about His age, Father and I had seen a man stoned. The entire town came to cast their judgment at him. I did not recall his crime, but I could not forget his terror, the blood that ran down his forehead and into his eyes, the way he stumbled and tried to protect his head with his hands. I could still hear the shouts of his accusers, and they sounded just like the mob that had gathered in front of us.

I could still hear the *thwack* as each stone met its mark.

I would not allow Jesus to hear such hatred.

I had to get Him away. Behind us rose the rock wall; in front of us the mob was circling. To the left, people were running. To the right, there were even more.

I lifted Jesus into my arms and tried to get Him to bury His face in my shoulder. I pressed my hands against His ears and tried to muffle the accusations of the holy men. The crowd crushed in, and people everywhere were shouting.

I gave Asher a desperate look.

"I want to watch," he said, still on the ground. "I want to see the woman stoned."

His words were cold, but described the scene accurately. There was a woman at the core of the rage—a woman who looked very much like Mary, young and with long dark hair. I saw her eyes, and in them I saw fear flaming as sure as fire. Her hands were up near her ears; she was trying to protect her face, her head. The head was the first thing the mob tried to hit.

"She is probably an adulteress," Asher said flatly, "or a harlot."

My eyes searched both ends of the street for help . . . I knew how Rome hated the practice of stoning, but there were no haughty Roman soldiers on their high-stepping horses to put a stop to what was about to happen. There were only Jews—holy people with rocks clenched in their fists and murder etched on their faces.

My whole body trembled. Death had never frightened or sickened me, but I wasn't thinking of myself.

I placed Jesus on Boaz and climbed on in back of Him. I would get Him through the swelling crowd at any cost. Pure, perfect Jesus, a boy who knew only how to love and laugh, could not be witness to death—not like this. Pray, I thought; pray now, Child. Pray as You prayed in the vineyard that we might be delivered.

I reined Boaz with all of my strength and he turned, bumping into a man who held yellow stones in both fists. His eyes shot daggers at me, but then he was gone, off to push his way ahead of the others, to position himself at the front line for the kill.

I shook my head violently. I was trying to get Jesus away as fast as I could.

Asher stood up and snorted. "Fine. I will come with you, but you are going to make me miss the show."

I didn't care about anything except getting Jesus through the crowd, away from the cheers and wailing, away from the sound of stone meeting flesh.

It was too late.

Jesus whirled around at the sound of the woman's first scream—so shrill, so desperate. I looked, only for a moment, and saw a small stream of blood running down her cheek. Her veil was torn and hung away from her face. Her hand moved to reposition it, and a stone hit the back of her hand. More blood. More cries for help.

Pray for her, Jesus. Pray hard.

In a small, shaky voice He asked me why she was crying. Why? He kept asking, Why? Why . . . why?

I had no answer for Him. I only kicked the donkey's sides over and over and over. The beast proved brave. He no longer balked, but plodded past the people who pushed and shoved and burned with contempt. Men, women, and even a few children clenched rocks in their fists as they rushed to take aim.

The woman screamed again. And again. And again.

How could I erase this horror from Jesus' mind? I should have sheltered Him better. I should have seen the mob coming sooner. I should have done more. How would this affect Him?

It was only after we were out of Sepphoris, only after the shouts and screams could no longer be heard, that I allowed old Boaz to slow his pace. That's when I saw it—something I had never seen before— utter sorrow in the tender eyes of Jesus.

Seventeen

We did not speak of the stoning. Not a word.

Even Asher said nothing.

Neither my heart nor my head could make sense of such an act. I knew the law. I knew that women were stoned for adultery. It wasn't an everyday occurrence, but it did happen. I was just so sorry that Jesus had to be there, because after that, even though we did not speak of it, there was a shadow over Him that had not existed before.

I felt obligated to tell Joseph what had happened. I wrote it carefully on my wax tablet so that my words could be melted, never to be read again.

Joseph laid a hand on my shoulder and looked stern. I feared he was angry with me, but he simply pressed his lips together, bowed his head in thought, and looked up.

"Never speak of it again," he said.

And that was the end of it, though I woke up from time to time, damp from the woman's screams still echoing in my memory. Did Jesus, I wondered, suffer the same night terrors?

Because it was the law, and because Mary and Joseph lived the Mosaic rule fully, James was circumcised and officially named when he was eight days old. Later, when he was crying, Mary allowed me to hold him and to comfort him. Swaddled like he was so that his limbs would grow straight and strong and true to God's commands, James could only open and close his tiny fists, curl and uncurl his little toes. I remember thinking to myself that I must have gone through the same agony. Had Father taken me to a priest, or had he taken the blade to

me himself? There was no one around to ask, and I realized how little I
knew about my own upbringing.

At least I knew that because of my bloodline, I was a Jew. King
David's blood ran through my veins. I *wanted* to be a Jew, though I
did not fully understand or even agree with practices like stoning.
Never would I dare let my doubts be known any more than I would
let my sins be known. If Mary and Joseph knew the black acts I had
done, they would surely cast me out. I had to go on letting them
believe I was a simple victim who they had rescued. I was an innocent
boy made to suffer. Part of that was true, but only part of it; the rest
of the truth I kept buried inside.

Somehow I would make up for my past. I would make it right
with God. I wanted to know and understand the ancient fathers, their
traditions, their commandments. I wanted very much to be a son of
the covenant, and in fewer than three years my bar mitzvah would be
cause for celebration in the household of Joseph.

I would make Joseph proud. The day would come when I would
be counted as neither slave nor servant, but as a man of worth. If the
whispers of my heart were true, the good whispers that told me I had
value in spite of my sins, then one day Joseph would look to me and
see a man of value.

More kinsmen arrived to celebrate the birth of James, filling not
only Joseph's house, but Joel's house as well. Mary's parents, Anna and
Joachim, arrived to a royal welcome of shouts, embraces, and more
kisses than I could count. They had traveled from a region near
Mount Carmel, and came bearing several pouches of spices and fine
linen for Mary.

Anna was a thin woman with fast-moving hands and feet. Never
did I see her idle. If she wasn't in the courtyard plucking blooms or
telling me to firm up this plant or that, she was in the house, moving
the few items that were Mary's.

"The cradle is too close to the door. The poor babe will feel the
chill first."

Mary smiled and allowed her mother to slide the cradle to the far
corner of the room. That smile never left her face as her mother
moved her dishes from the top shelf to the bottom and as she moved
the reclining cushions from one wall to the next.

"I am so relieved you have come, Mother. I have missed you," Mary said, taking her mother into her arms. I backed out the door slowly so I would not intrude on such a personal moment.

Anna was busy, but never unkind. She followed me out to the courtyard *mikvah* to be certain the water was kept flowing. Joseph had bartered his carpentry services with a mason in Tiberias who had crafted a beautiful two-tier *mikvah*. If the water level was kept at a certain height, the water poured from one basin into the next and returned again. It was like magic, and Jesus and I would sit in the sunlight and watch it work for hours.

Anna asked, "You are certain that the water you fill the *mikvah* with comes only from the freshest cisterns?"

I nodded. Joseph had taught me to carefully catch the rainwater that fell so sparsely in this region. Every drop was precious.

Anna smiled and I saw that Mary was surely her mother's daughter. They shared the same dark eyes and deep dimpled cheeks.

"I am told that you are of great service to my daughter's household," Anna said, picking a leaf from the surface of the water. "Mary is fond of you, Almon."

I bowed in appreciation and respect, and kept my head bowed so Anna would not see the wave of emotion that her words had caused.

Joachim, a stout patriarch whose hair had not yet gone gray, was a quiet man who shadowed Joseph to the synagogue and to the workshop. He was an educated man who carried a small book of scripture in the pocket of his tunic. He read whenever and wherever he found time. The wineskin he brought for Joseph was crafted by artisans from Africa. It was sewn with thick black gut, and held more than any wineskin I had ever seen. Joseph seemed most appreciative of the remembrance.

Jesus was not well acquainted with His grandparents, but immediately took a liking to Joachim. He latched on to the old man's hand and listened as His grandfather read from the Torah. He told Jesus stories of the prophets, of Adam and the garden, of Daniel and the den, of David and the giant.

I found myself eavesdropping. While the man did not possess Joseph's ability to portray the characters, he did provide myriad of details. His words painted a perfect picture of the garden first planted by God's own hand. Joachim told of a lion so real I could see its razor-sharp teeth, yellow at the base and long as daggers. I could smell Goliath's sweat as the fearless shepherd boy David came at him.

Jesus begged for more stories.

"Tell me, Jesus, what you know of the law and the prophets," Joachim invited his grandson.

We were all there in the shade of the courtyard, taken in by the stories, and now we waited to hear what Jesus had to say. Those of us who lived with Him day to day knew of His spiritual skills, His uncanny ability to memorize entire passages of scripture. I watched the grandparents' expressions when they discovered how gifted their grandson was.

As Jesus recited commandments and teachings word for word, Joachim's mouth dropped open. His eyes went wet. Anna's chin quivered. They looked at Mary, and Joachim uttered, "Surely, this is *the One.*"

I watched to take in Mary's reaction, but there was nothing in her expression other than calmness, steadiness, and love.

Eighteen

Over the days more kinsmen arrived; with them came an aged woman named Elisabeth and a child, her son, John, a boy just older than Jesus. They were kinsmen of Mary, and the two women embraced so long I doubted if they would ever release each other.

Jesus, always excited at the prospect of a new friend, ran to John. Though the older boy was shy, Jesus took him by the hand and led him to the back of the house where a new batch of chicks had just hatched.

Anna looked up from the loom where she had been working in the shade of the courtyard. She seemed as delighted to see Elisabeth as Mary was.

"Look how John has grown," Anna said, catching the boy by the arm before he rounded the corner with Jesus. She stooped to embrace the shaggy-haired boy with dark, serious eyes. "It has only been since Festival that I saw you last, yet you have grown so much, John."

John looked to his mother, pleading for release.

"Go, son. Follow your cousin and enjoy the day."

Jesus whooped with delight and waved for John to follow Him.

I stood at the gate waiting for instructions.

I suppose the women forgot that I was there. They were too caught up in passing baby James around and in talking of family. These were the moments I savored so much, and yet I felt like the outsider I was.

They talked of purification, of the rumored riots in the Holy City, of the temple and their upcoming trip there. They would travel as a family caravan. It was the first I had heard that the household of Joseph was planning a trip to Jerusalem.

I wondered if I would be going.

I waited in silence, held fast by the love these women shared, by the bond that distance could neither bend nor break. Finally, Mary looked over and saw me.

"Almon, this is my cousin, Elisabeth. Her boy, John, is around back with Jesus. Watch them closely, please. Jesus will want to take him up into the hills to chase lambs. Please keep a close watch over them."

I turned to take my leave and as I did, I heard Mary whisper, "Almon is mute."

"Mute?" Elisabeth gasped, excited, as if Mary had announced I was of royal blood.

I quickened my pace, not understanding. Not understanding at all.

The days that followed brought more people and more plans.

I learned that I would go with the household of Joseph to Jerusalem. We would take both donkeys. Joel and his household and their animals would travel with us, as would the household of Joachim and the animals he had brought to Nazareth. In addition to a riding donkey and a pack donkey, he had a horse, a strong chestnut with three white socks. In his fine robes with red bands woven into the cloth, Joachim appeared almost regal as he rode, his back straight, his head high.

The horse, their fine clothes, and the educated manner in which Mary's parents spoke and presented themselves let me know that the household of Joachim was well-to-do. I feared just a little for Joachim—the empire's army was known for its fine horses, and Jews rarely rode anything other than donkeys. Riding into Jerusalem, Joachim might draw unwanted attention, and such a simple act might give the impression of rebellion.

So long ago that it seemed another lifetime, I had seen a common man pulled from his horse and stabbed repeatedly by the greedy dagger of one of Rome's own. Father was quick to drag the dying man's body to the side of the street. As soon as no one was looking, he had urged me forward and had told me to pull the man's money pouch from his pocket. My hand had come away bloody.

The memory turned over in my head, and as it did, my stomach also turned over. Joseph would have nothing to do with me if he knew that I was not an innocent child abandoned in the desert—if he knew that I had been a filthy thief, the son of a thief.

No matter how many times I told myself that I was no longer that Almon, that I was born anew, and though my hand had been scrubbed a thousand times since, it was still not free of blood.

Joseph and Mary might not see the stains, but I did.

The days before our journey passed quickly. In the mornings I attended synagogue. Sometimes Jesus attended with me, always at the invitation of Rabbi Asa. Jesus was not quite yet five years old, the age when most boys started training, but because He was special, the teacher asked that I bring Him for certain lessons.

My afternoons were filled with chores at the shop and around the house. I was quick to finish so that I could study. The day that Nathan, my benefactor, stopped by to check on my progress, I had just swept the floor of shavings.

Joseph greeted the physician with respect. "We are honored at your presence."

Nathan smiled. "Yesterday I spoke with Ovadya. He has high regard for Almon's dedication to learning the law."

I did not know that the priest even knew I existed. I had seen him when he visited the synagogue, but he always seemed to look through me, like I was invisible.

Joseph wiped sawdust on his apron. Without thinking, he did something I saw him do many times: he rubbed the stubs where his fingers used to be, like they ached. "I am most happy to hear that. Almon loves to study, and his writing skills improve with each lesson. Rabbi Asa believes that if Almon is dedicated, he will develop the skills to be a fine scribe one day."

Nathan did not appear surprised, but my own heart pounded. There was no way anyone could know that becoming a scribe was a dream kept alive in the farthest corner of my heart. How I hoped he had come to tell Joseph he would continue to provide for my schooling! If not, what would I do? I could never go back to a life without scrolls, books, and writing. I hungered for learning the way James hungered for milk. I would die without it.

The kind physician walked across the shop and stopped before the pile of sawdust I had swept. He lifted a large handful and spread it out on the workbench. Joseph slid a stool over to him, and the physician sat down. He looked at me with great intensity.

"Almon, today I am your teacher. I have come with a list of questions, and I expect you to answer me from your Torah studies. Do you understand?"

My heart still pounded. I nodded and shuffled toward him.

He posed question after question, each one growing more difficult. Joseph gave up any effort to work; instead, he folded his arms across his chest and directed his attention at Nathan and me.

"Name the sons of Father Israel."

In the depth of the dust, I wrote my answer slowly, making sure my letters were precise. *Reuben, Simeon, Levi, Judah, Issachar, Zebulun, Dan, Naphtali, Gad, Asher, Joseph, Benjamin.*

I could not read Nathan's reaction.

"And the name of his only daughter?"

Dinah.

He asked me about the priesthoods and how they were responsible for different upkeeps in the temple. I felt nervous, though I knew of Aaron, Levi, and the sons of Zadok. I understood their roles and how each was important.

He questioned me of prayers, especially the meaning of *Shema.*

Hear, O Israel: The Lord our God is one Lord.

As I wrote my declaration that there existed only one true God, a burning rose up inside of me, sure as a fever. I thought of all the idols I had seen, all the gods that people in different lands worshipped. At that moment, I knew I truly believed in one God and one God only.

His questions continued, becoming increasingly more difficult, but not impossible.

Finally, he turned to Joseph. "Is your household making the pilgrimage to the Holy City for Festival?"

"Yes. We are making preparations even now."

"Good. Almon needs exposure to the temple. Some day he will train there to become a scribe. Perhaps I will encounter you during the festivities."

"That would bring me much pleasure."

Before he left, Nathan told Joseph that as long as I was making such progress, he would continue to fund my education at the synagogue. He did not bid me good-bye or even tell me directly that he was pleased. Still, I felt relieved and grateful to know that my education would continue.

Nineteen

At the close of one particularly stifling day, when the heat refused to leave and the air was uncomfortably hot to breathe, Joseph told me to take Jesus and John to the rooftop to sleep beneath the stars. The grass we had planted had already taken root, and the flowers gave off a soft perfume. It was my favorite place for slumber.

We climbed the outside ladder, laid our mats flat, and listened to Jesus tell stories. John seemed enthralled with his cousin's ability to weave a tale, and listened with hardly a blink as Jesus spoke of Noah rounding up the animals, of Solomon and the imposter mother, of Enoch and his holy city.

I don't know who fell asleep first, but I woke when I heard the sound of the door to the house creak open. The boys lay on either side of me deep in slumber.

"Oh, Elisabeth," I heard Mary whisper, "Joseph and I . . . we did not know the details . . . the only word we received while we were in Egypt was that Zacharias was dead. We did not know until you arrived of the horror, the senseless brutality of his death."

Soft sobs rose on the air and went straight to my heart. John's father was dead. I felt a stab of pain for the young boy sleeping beside me. I felt a stab of understanding. At least he had his mother, though she was old. Her devotion to him was clear. John was only half an orphan, and that was so much better than to have no parents at all.

The thick sorrow of the women rose as powerfully as smoke to burn my eyes. I looked at John sleeping so peacefully and my heart ached, knowing he would grow up without the shelter of his father's arm to guide and protect him.

I knew Joseph was not my father, and yet when I was with him, I did not feel fatherless. But who would be father to John?

In a raspy whisper Mary continued. "We prayed that you were all safe in Judea. We heard of the horror . . . the unspeakable horror."

Elisabeth wept. "When Herod decreed . . . Oh, Mary . . . how could such evil exist in one man? He murdered his own sons, his wife. He killed the prophets. He slaughtered our people like we were animals." She sucked in a ragged breath. "He killed so many of our children—our innocent babes."

"He didn't kill them all. Jesus is safe, as is John. We must give God praise."

"God be praised indeed. How . . . how did you know to leave for Egypt when you did?"

Mary paused. "An angel appeared to Joseph in a dream, warning him to take us and flee. We left in the night under the cloak of darkness."

"Did the angel tell Joseph what was to happen?"

There was a small ledge formed by the tallest grass on the roof; I scooted over to it and peered down, careful to conceal myself. In a blue shaft of moonglow I saw the two cousins embracing. I heard the quiet sobs they were trying to quell.

To me, they might as well have been speaking a foreign tongue. Angels? *Angels?* My mind whirled.

"Joseph was warned, but he did not understand everything. We left with haste and had no time or way to warn others." Mary looked at her cousin. "It must have been unthinkable, what that madman did."

Elisabeth's crooked back straightened and her voice grew strong. "Herod was out of his mind with fear and jealousy. We knew he had soldiers, our fellow Jews, in his employ, but we never suspected the power and number of his army. Murderous men were everywhere; no home, no child was safe. My own Zacharias gave his life to protect John and me."

"Tell me, if you can, what happened."

"I only know what the temple priests reported. They said that my good husband was brave and true to the end. He would not give up our location, not even for his life."

"If the priests were there, why did they not stop Zacharias' death?"

"I have never stopped asking myself that question. Mary, there is only one answer . . ."

Mary's question was met by thick silence. I knew it was wrong to be eavesdropping, but I had to hear more.

Elisabeth finally spoke. "Tell me of your journey into Egypt. I have only heard bits and pieces. What was it like?"

Mary sighed. "It was long and wearisome; each step we took felt like a hundred. The land is so different from Palestine. The pyramids are just as you have heard. Great as mountains. And the women . . . they do not veil themselves, and they wear paint on their faces and bracelets climbing up their arms. The temples there are built to worship gods that I do not wish to know.

"Joseph had great faith that no harm would come to us, but still . . . we found it hard to trust anyone. I do not think I garnered a good night's sleep in all the time we were there."

Elisabeth said, "I cannot sleep even now without waking time and time again, remembering and wondering what lies ahead for John . . . for Jesus."

I held my breath and waited for someone to continue. I strained to hear what I was not meant to hear, but a more curious part of me hungered to understand the mystery of Jesus and His birth. All I had were bits and pieces of information, a puzzle that did not yet make sense. My mind spun, turning around the information I had learned . . . Joseph was not the father of Jesus. Mary and Elisabeth believed angels communed with them.

"Perhaps the angel that warned Joseph," Elisabeth said in a quivering voice, "was the same angel that appeared to my Zacharias by the altar of the temple that sacred, glorious day. I well remember that day. Zacharias had been such a faithful temple servant, and to think the lot finally fell to him, that he would have the honor of burning the incense. And then the angel appeared and told him that his prayers had been heard."

"Not just *his* prayers, my cousin; your prayers were also honored with the news that John would be born to you."

"It was one of God's miracles, I tell you."

"I can imagine your wonder," Mary said.

"Yes, cousin, I suppose you, and *only* you, can understand how I felt. I was so shocked and so joyous to know that the very hand of God Almighty had reached down to touch an aged couple like us."

"And John—he is a wonderful boy. So serious. So bright."

Elisabeth coughed. It seemed her voice was fading. "No razor has touched his head, nor will it. No fruit of the vine has passed his lips, nor will it. I believe John understands that he is not his own, but consecrated to God."

"I believe Jesus, too, has a growing understanding of who He *really* is."

My ears strained to hear. What did Mary mean?

Elisabeth spoke. "I am only sorrowful that Zacharias did not live to see John grow, that he is not here now to rejoice with our family—to become acquainted with Jesus, and to see the boys together."

"I wish I could believe that with Herod's death our people will know peace, but Archelaus rules Judea now. His mind is as dark as his father's. He is just as cruel, if not more cruel."

"Jesus will bring peace to our people," said Mary.

"Peace."

Mary seemed to speak more to herself than to Elisabeth. "I look at Jesus and wonder . . . how can one child . . . even when He reaches manhood . . . be given the strength to carry so many on His shoulders?"

"He is the Son of God, and with God all things are possible," Elisabeth whispered. "Look at us, Mary. John and I have survived under His watchful eye. If my son is to serve as the Elias, then your son will be raised for whatever duties God requires."

"The Lord God is great."

"Yes, He is."

Mary slid her hands beneath her veil and bowed her face into her cupped hands. "Jesus, our Messiah. Lowly me, his mother. Oh, Elisabeth." Her voice broke off and I saw that her face was now turned skyward. I heard her moan.

I wanted to scurry down the ladder and tell her that whatever all of this meant—angels, John as Elias, Jesus as Messiah, whatever it meant . . . Mary should not cry. Mary was the kindest woman imaginable. Seeing her tears made my own eyes sting.

Elisabeth waited and then asked, "Are you burdened by the holy call that has come upon you?"

Mary turned to face Elisabeth, rapidly drawing in her breath as though she was surprised. "No. There are moments when I still wonder at all that it means. But the angel did appear to me right here in Nazareth. Joseph has had angels commune with him. Jesus' mission is real, and no human hand can stop His destiny. But even though I am sure of all that, the fear never leaves me that someone, in some way will bring Him harm."

"There are still stories from Bethlehem. They talk of the miracles in Jerusalem, even among the Essenes."

"It seems like a dream at times, but it was no dream. It happened just as they say . . . the angels . . . so many angels and shepherds who saw the very heart of heaven split. They heard angels sing, and the wise men, whose decision to avoid Herod led to your Zacharias' death. Oh, when I think about it all . . . how one event connects another . . . my mind does not quit spinning."

"It is all so great, but what of Joseph? Does he tell you his feelings?"

"Joseph is a choice husband and father. There are times I catch him looking at Jesus, and I see pure joy in his eyes. I have never known a more attentive or worrisome father. Once Jesus slipped from the donkey and bumped his head. I was concerned, but my emotions were nothing compared to Joseph's—he cradled the child all night long."

"You are fortunate to have such a man for a husband."

"Oh, Elisabeth, I'm sorry if I was insensitive to your feelings."

"I am a strong woman, blessed to have had Zacharias for so many happy years. Now it is different. A widow is looked on with pity, and I am no ordinary woman. Even in Judea, even among the Essenes, there are rumors. I see the way people look at me, like I should be the grandmother of John. They, too, carry stories. They whisper that he is destined for a great work. Already the child draws people to him; I'm certain you've noted, his manner is bold, his speech direct."

"I've thought him to be shy."

"No. No, my son is not shy. He is bold, but eager to learn, eager to follow God's will."

"He is a fine son, Elisabeth. We must trust the God of our fathers."

"And what of Jesus? Does your son suspect . . . or know . . . who He *really* is?"

My breath seemed to be knocked out of me. The question held me like a trap, and I could not move while I waited for the answer.

"His Father will unfold the truth to Him as Jesus is ready. I have to trust the only One trustworthy. Now that James has been born, now that Joseph has a son, I look at the two boys and know that God divides a mother's heart equally. That gives me comfort, but there is so much to frighten me. I hear the men talking. I know that there is turmoil in the streets of Jerusalem."

"Yes," Elisabeth said, "at the last festival, Jews were attacked, stabbed, and left to die in the streets with their loved ones there wailing . . . and why? Because our people are tired of being beaten down and made to pay homage to anyone but Jehovah, praised be His name."

What did her words mean? I could make no clear sense of them.

"Joseph is set on our pilgrimage to the Holy City."

"God's hand will shelter us as it has."

Mary seemed worn out; she sat down wearily on the stone bench and patted the empty seat beside her. "While I do not consider my calling a burden, it does carry weight. When we were in Egypt, no one knew of us. But here, here I cannot go to market without women pointing at me and whispering to each other. They have not forgotten the circumstances surrounding my wedding."

Elisabeth scoffed, and she lowered herself to sit beside Mary. "Allow women to wag their tongues like mongrels wag their tails. God knows that He has chosen you to bear and rear our Savior."

The shock slammed forcefully into me, and I thought I might tumble from the roof. *Jesus as Savior?*

"Cousin, I will never forget your visit to me and what it felt to have John recognize your Holy Child. I can still feel the life that moved within me."

"Your kindness meant so much to me then."

"As does your kindness to me now, Mary. Do you recall my words to you when you took refuge in my home?"

Mary bowed her head. "I recall."

"I said then the same thing I say now: Blessed art thou among women, and blessed is the fruit of thy womb. You are truly the mother of my Lord, and I am honored to have lived to see my Savior in the flesh."

I could not trust what I had heard. Surely, Elisabeth was not speaking of Jesus.

Their veils shimmering in the moonlight, the two women leaned on each other but said no more. I watched them, wondering at all they had divulged, as my uninvited ears listened.

Finally, I crept back to my mat and looked at John, whose chest rose and fell steady as the call of night crickets. *Who was this boy, and what was his divine destiny?*

Then I turned to look at the child who had become the brother I would never have. Jesus lay there with His eyes wide open.

I touched my ear to ask Jesus if He had heard the women talking.

He nodded that yes, He had heard; He had heard *every* word.

Twenty

There were ordinary days and holy days. Festivals and feasts. I learned to fast and to give thanks for both the mundane and the majestic.

I was changing from the inside out.

Every seventh day was Sabbath, or *Shabbat,* my favorite day. It was set aside as the first, the prime day of the week . . . reserved as an offering to the Lord, just as were the first fruits or the firstling of the flock. Only the first and unblemished were worthy sacrifices to the Lord. I was learning so much, and not just by study. Though I cherished every new bit of knowledge that found its way into my head at the synagogue, I learned even more by observing the manner in which Mary and Joseph lived. Every commandment was kept, every law observed.

I thought back to the days of living with my father, how he had cursed the Jewish laws and had said they were burdensome and unbearable. He had denounced them and defiled them, but there were truths that beat to the rhythm of my father's life as certain as his heart beat. You could not run away from being a Jew.

An ugly thought haunted me: if Father had been killed in the desert by those three bandits, what had become of his body? Had it been burned? Was it buried beneath the sand? Was it left in the desert to be devoured by wild dogs and insects? If his body was not properly washed, wrapped, and buried, was Father's spirit still lingering in torment?

I could not endure such thoughts and instead forced myself to ponder on better things—good things that made me happy.

I loved everything about the Sabbath, perhaps because it was a day of study and learning. It was a day Mary's skill with spices led to her most delicious meals. They were eaten slowly and with great savor, as fasting was forbidden. People wore their finest clothes, put on smiling faces, and went to the synagogue to worship. Any disharmony they might have felt toward one another had to be reconciled. There was no room for malcontent and no voice for complaint on the Sabbath.

On the Sabbath, all in the entire village left their homes and went to the synagogue. People spilled from their courtyards dressed in their best robes, their hair oiled, their fingers heavy with rings.

I felt privileged to attend synagogue with the household of Joseph. I was not old enough to sit with the men of Israel, so I took my place with the women and children. Malik looked down from his station and sneered at me.

I was sorry for the way I had treated him, for the thoughts I'd held against him. I said a silent prayer in my heart that I could forgive him, and that God could forgive me. Malik was a bully because his mind struggled to hold on to any thought. He resented me because once my mind got hold of a thought, it gripped the thought tightly.

My favorite of all *Shabbats* was the one when I sat between Jesus and John. Mary smiled at me, and I knew my happiest moment. Elisabeth, too, gave me a gentle smile.

We listened to the law read—first in Hebrew, then translated verse by verse into Aramaic. It was easy for me to make the translations in my head, faster and usually more accurately than the one appointed to translate.

No one could know what I was doing in my head. But seated there among family, for those fleeting moments, I felt like I belonged.

As that favored day drew to a close and the sun sank into a scarlet sky, I sat out in the courtyard. My back rested against a young palm tree, and I held my scroll in my hand.

The door opened and Elisabeth stepped out. "Such a lovely holy day," she said. "I see you are reading from the Torah. Mary tells me that the teacher has deemed you worthy of your own scrolls."

I didn't know how to respond, so I tried to keep my mouth straight, my eyes devoid of any emotion. Elisabeth had always been kind, but now she spoke to me like I was *not* a household servant.

"Today is a day to rejoice in the goodness of the Lord."

I nodded my agreement.

Elisabeth sat on the same bench she and Mary had sat on the night I overheard them from the rooftop. The shadows were long in the afternoon sun, and the wrinkles on her hands looked deep. I could see her eyes through her veil, but only glanced at them once.

"I am glad you have come to live here," she said.

My smile widened.

"You are very patient with children, though you are really just a child yourself, Almon."

The way she spoke my name brought to mind the first time Mary had said *Almon*. The same warmth I had felt then washed over me now. I wanted to tell her that I was not a child—that I had never been a child, not happy and carefree like Jesus. Even John, serious and sober, was the child I never was.

"John has grown very fond of you."

I cupped my hand over my heart to demonstrate that I felt the same about him. I would have written my response to Elisabeth, but I did not know if she could read. It was a rare thing for a woman to be educated, though I knew that Mary was able to read and write.

Elisabeth shifted a strand of gray hair over her shoulder. "I am a widow, as you probably know. What you don't know is that my husband, Zacharias, was also mute—not deaf, only mute, as you are."

My fingers almost let the sacred scroll slip. I had encountered the deaf and dumb, but never someone simply mute. What had this fact to do with me? I raised my eyebrows and waited for understanding.

"Yes, for a time Zacharias was mute. I learned to communicate with him through written words and gestures. I have seen you do the same with Mary and Joseph. I can only imagine your life before you came to live in this household."

I wondered if she was trying to glean information from me, but it did not seem so. It seemed rather that Elisabeth wanted to tell me something important, but was having a difficult time. Besides, she had no way of imagining my life before Joseph found me. How could a woman as pure as Elisabeth fathom the sins that had been committed against me as a boy who was sold into slavery again and again?

I squeezed my eyes shut and willed the dark demons to leave my head. I screamed silently that the Almon from my past was as dead and gone as was my father.

Elisabeth leaned forward and I heard her aged knees creak. "Almon, you can see that I am an old woman. I have made arrangements for members of my distant family to care for John in the event that I do not live to see him to manhood. I have faith that he will grow to be as kind as you are."

Her unexpected words tugged at my heart. I felt guilty for overhearing the secrets I had overheard. I felt guilty for hiding my sinful past. I felt a burden on my back as sure and heavy as a pack of large stones.

The sky was cloudy, but the air was warm, and life grew all around us, green and lush in Mary's garden. Elisabeth turned to watch a bee, fat and busy, burrow itself inside a red flower. She watched until it emerged and flew to the next blossom. "Almon, today is the Sabbath. I am not allowed to mourn, though there is not a day when I do not feel the loss of my husband. I would like to tell you the story of his muteness."

I felt honored and moved closer to her until I was situated at her feet. It was very much the same position in which I sat to learn at the feet of Rabbi Micha and Rabbi Asa in the courtyards of the synagogue.

"Oh, where to begin," Elisabeth said with a sigh. "I suppose I will tell you that our home is outside of Jerusalem in the hill country. Do you know it?"

My head bobbed.

"Good. Then you can picture the distance Zacharias had to travel to the holy temple. He did that faithfully twice a year to officiate for six days and two Sabbaths, once during the time of the blossoms and again during the time of the falling leaves.

"My husband was an honorable priest. Even when he was old and it was no longer easy for him, Zacharias made the journey with joy. In the Hall of Polished Stones the priests gathered to offer their prayers. Then, as our ancient fathers did, they cast lots to see who would receive the honor of burning the incense. That day it became God's will that the duty fell to my gentle husband. Oh, what joy he felt. God be praised."

I closed my eyes for just a moment and imagined what I thought it might look like—the ancient man, Zacharias, overjoyed to burn incense at the holy altar. I pictured him surrounded by his fellow priests, some happy for him, others envious. I did not understand why Elisabeth was telling me this or what it had to do with my muteness, but I was grateful to hear her words, grateful for the interest she showed in me.

"It was there and then that an angel from God's presence appeared to my Zacharias."

An *angel?*

Angels appeared to holy people.

It seemed impossible, yet being so close to Elisabeth, so close that I could see through her veil into her eyes, I believed her words.

"Gabriel was his name. Standing on the right side of the altar of incense, he made the miraculous announcement: 'Fear not, Zacharias: for thy prayer is heard; and thy wife Elisabeth shall bear thee a son, and thou shalt call his name John. And thou shalt have joy and gladness; and many shall rejoice at his birth. For he shall be great in the sight of the Lord . . . and he shall be filled with the Holy Ghost, even from his mother's womb.'"

She laid her hand on her stomach.

My ears felt hot, and I reached to lift my prayer shawl.

Elisabeth showed no embarrassment, but her face seemed to glow warm and golden. "I have memorized the angel's words, Almon. I repeat them in my dreams. Gabriel said that my son would go before the Messiah to prepare a people for the coming of the Lord. John is to be an Elias."

There was that word again: *Elias.* I furrowed my brow and narrowed my eyes to ask for a definition.

Elizabeth understood. "An Elias is one appointed to go before, to prepare the way for something or someone greater."

John was an Elias to Jesus.

Could what I had heard be true . . . Jesus was the promised Messiah, the Savior who would save us from the oppression of Herod, of Caesar, of evil itself? I had read the scriptures; the promised Messiah would *not* be a Jewish boy from Nazareth, but a mighty man, a great warrior, capable of freeing our people from oppression, of changing our way of life, of giving us true and lasting freedom. He would be royal and victorious in His reign.

Jesus was no king. While He was a gifted, joyful child, He was just a boy, not a force of power. The only power Jesus had was in His compassion. I felt a wave of guilt for doubting Elisabeth, for doubting the revelations I'd overheard, but Elisabeth's story seemed far-fetched. How could I believe it?

"Zacharias did what any man might do who was married to a woman of my age. My body had long ago passed the time for child bearing. Together, we had mourned the fact that I was barren, and yet Zacharias had not divorced me or taken another wife. He had stayed beside me, and together we had given up hope. Long after the time had passed for possibility, only *then* did the angel come from the presence of God to announce the impossible. We were to be parents to a son that we were to name John.

"It was no wonder Zacharias laughed. He laughed in the face of heaven."

My mind pictured an old man, stooped and white-haired, laughing into the face of an angel—a being radiant and white. Yes, Elisabeth's words painted a strange portrait.

Elisabeth continued her story. "Did he get by with such dishonor? No. He was struck mute. Like you, Almon, my husband could not utter a single word."

I held up my hands and narrowed my eyes to ask: *How did Zacharias communicate this miraculous experience if he could not speak?*

"Zacharias wrote what he had to convey on a tablet. I believed him, though some of his fellow priests and others expressed doubt. They mocked him and said my husband had gone mad."

I held my gaze steady into the veiled eyes of this woman. *How much—if any—of her story was true?*

"With God, all things are possible. Just as the angel said, a son was born to us in our aged years. It was a celebration for all who had known us and stood beside us in our barren years."

I shifted on the stone-laid ground, more curious about Zacharias's muteness than the miracle of John's birth.

"Only after the trial of his faith, only after John was born, only after Zacharias repented of his sin, did God restore his tongue."

I felt crestfallen. Was Elisabeth telling me that I was mute because I had sinned? That could not be . . . I had always been mute. I was mute before I ever sinned.

Perhaps I was mute because my father sinned—my mother too, for all I knew.

Was Elisabeth calling me to repentance? In a way she was right; my birth had brought on the death of my mother. And what had I done after that? I had followed my father through the desert, breaking one commandment after another.

I was not worthy of all the kindness I'd received since coming into the house of Joseph. I knew it, and I was certain Elisabeth knew it as well.

She proved my thoughts wrong.

Her voice turned sharp and her hand reached out to touch mine. "Almon, my cousin is very fond of you. She thinks of you more as a son than a servant. I have watched you these last days. I have offered prayers on your behalf. I tell you this so that you might know that God has a purpose and a time for all things. If it is His mighty will, if there comes a day when God requires your voice, you will speak."

If.

She heaved herself up, adjusted her veil, and concluded, "Be as patient with yourself as you are with the children. Observe the commandments. The day will come when you will see the hand of the Lord touch your life. One day you will testify of this moment and all the glorious moments to come."

Her voice rose full and powerful as a gathering wind. It fell over me and chased away the doubts that swirled in my head.

"Praise be to God, who is our king. Praise be to God, who is our deliverer. Praise be His, and His alone."

She went back inside the house, closed the door, and left me alone in the courtyard. I wanted to call after her, to thank her for what she had said, to declare my faith in her words, but I did not open my mouth. For, in spite of her prophecies, I was still a boy unable to speak, a boy with no voice.

Twenty-one

Forty days of purification were coming to a close.

The caravan of Joseph's household was large and loud. The men talked, the women sang. Animals grunted under their burdens as their feet clopped over the stone streets and dirt roads.

We passed through Nazareth and through more villages beyond Sepphoris. As the terrain descended, farms spread before us in rippling waves of green and gold. Vineyards were laid out in straight rows. Olive trees grew tall and wide.

I had never felt such excitement. We were dressed in the finest clothes we owned. We were going to Jerusalem, the Holy City, so James could be presented at the temple.

The household of Joel was part of our assembly. I wondered how Malik would manage to walk the long distance—his stomach bulged like a full waterskin, and every time I saw him he was stuffing food into his mouth. He barked orders at Asher whenever Joel turned his head.

I did not resent Malik as much as I felt pity for him—for Asher, too. Asher was a kind boy—not really a boy, but a youth on the verge of manhood. He was a servant as I was, but he seemed content with that designation. I longed to rise above my level.

Deborah danced around, excited to be going on such a trek. She wore a robe embroidered with green leaves and pink flowers, a masterpiece crafted from her mother's skill. The veil that covered her deformed face was heavy, but when she turned into the light, I could see her smile. Her laugh made the corners of my own mouth lift. Deborah's spirit was almost as joyous as Jesus'. It was her habit to make up little songs, and I found myself listening to them, playing their pleasant melodies in my head.

Once, I caught Deborah staring at me, and when I looked at her, I felt my face redden.

The servant Dan was assigned to stay behind, to watch over the houses we left empty, and to watch over Joel's lumber business and Joseph's carpentry shop. I was glad Dan did not accompany us, because he still whispered rumors of Jesus to me. The way he fixed his eye on Jesus still made me uneasy.

Every detail of our preparation had been considered, and we were on a sacred journey. But I felt uneasy; until now, all my experiences with the Holy City had been anything but holy. I told myself to pretend that this was the first time I had visited Jerusalem. I was new, and everything I experienced there would be new.

Jesus was excited, and moved from His mother's side to His father's shoulders. For stretches He walked alongside me, thrilled over the simplest things—black birds with red-tipped wings, a white butterfly that left dust on His outstretched palm. When we paused to rest, Joseph allowed Jesus to climb an olive tree. John followed right behind, both boys urging themselves so high I feared for their safety.

Not Joseph. He laughed and was there to help them scurry down the bark of the massive trunk.

We passed through village after village. We ambled past the same vineyard where Jesus and I had stopped, where Jesus had prayed. It was quiet now, the gray stone press stained dark from the grapes.

An ancient woman, toothless and withered, sat on the steps begging.

Jesus tugged at my sleeve. He wanted to be certain I saw her.

Joseph called to Jesus, pressed a coin in His hand, and told Him to give it to the woman. She smiled through a rent veil and reached out to take the coin. As she did, her hand went out like a claw, taking sudden hold of Jesus' wrist and pulling Him close.

Fear and surprise shot from Jesus' eyes.

The woman's head bent back and she laughed, a shrill and crazy laugh. It scared me, but before I could get to Jesus, Joseph had pulled Him away.

The woman kept laughing. Jesus was safe in Joseph's arms now, but His face was turned to the woman, and I saw worry in the boy's expression. He asked Joseph what was wrong with the woman—why she laughed so.

"I don't know, Jesus. She could be vexed."

"She *is* vexed," said Malik, stepping close to me.

Jesus wanted to know what *vexed* meant.

"It's when a devil gets inside of you," Malik said—not to Jesus, but to me. He whispered in my ear. "Devils enter people when they sin. We learned it at synagogue. Sometimes they make you crazy like that woman, and sometimes they make you mute. Isn't that correct, Almon?"

I did not stop. I did not look at Malik. My feet kept moving me forward, but his cruelty pulled at me. When we stopped by a stream to take our midday meal, I could not swallow. My throat seemed swollen shut.

I saw Elisabeth look at me through her veil. I remembered how her husband had lost his voice because he had sinned against heaven by laughing. I had done much, much worse. I had lied, stolen, and deceived.

Maybe . . . just maybe . . . Malik was right. Maybe I *was* vexed. Maybe a demon lived within me still, stopping my voice from all it wanted to say. When I got back to Nazareth, when I returned to the synagogue and had a moment alone with Rabbi Asa, I would ask him how I could repent. If I confessed my sins to him, if I told him what Father and I had done, would he be obligated to tell Joseph? And what would Joseph do?

It was a risk, a risk that could cost me all that mattered.

Twenty-two

Our journey did not continue peacefully. We passed two villages that had been almost completely burned by bandits. Even a small synagogue had been broken into and plundered. Smoke hung in the air like low clouds. The streets were lined with debris, and lost, confused people wandered aimlessly, looking at us, trying to determine if we were friend or foe.

As far as I could decipher, both Jews and Gentiles had been attacked. It seemed to me that no one had been left unharmed.

Immediately, I turned to protect Jesus, but He rode on the donkey seated in front of Anna, His grandmother, and she held a hand lightly over His face, pressing Him into the shelter of her robe. Still, I could see His eyes darting, taking in the terror of a battlefield where a village should have thrived.

Women wailed in the streets; children walked with their eyes downcast, their fingers laced through their mothers' fingers for protection.

Our chatter and singing ceased. Instead silent prayers went up, like the smoke all around us. Our men asked other men what had caused such destruction.

"If it is not Romans, it is our own people under the rule of Archelaus. If it is not Archelaus, it is slaves risen up in rebellion. They ride in on horses with swords and daggers drawn. They steal what little we have. They spill our blood just to watch it run red. How long? How long must we live under such oppression?"

Joseph spoke quietly to those in our group. A shadow darkened his face as surely as the sun gone behind a cloud. "God be praised. Nazareth has been left in peace."

"So far," Joel said solemnly.

I pictured what Nazareth would look like if it fell to the horrors around us. All of Carpenters' Street would burn like a torch. Every house would be plundered, *mikvahs* overturned, the synagogue destroyed.

"Perhaps we should turn back," Joel said. "Rumors abound that Jerusalem is not safe—not safe, and it is home to our people."

"You turn back if you must, but my household is going on to Temple Mount. We will present James there just as we did Jesus. God's Almighty eye is upon us, brother."

Joachim no longer rode high on his fine horse. He stepped down and redistributed the other loads, tying bedrolls to his saddle. He led the horse and walked along with the rest of us. Elisabeth, Mary, and Anna rode donkeys. Naomi walked with her daughter, Deborah.

We paused by the synagogue and Joachim called out to see if anyone was still around. An old, stooped rabbi emerged, his shawl uneven, his step uncertain.

Joachim approached him first and was soon joined by the other men. I stayed back with the women and children.

Malik pushed his way toward the rabbi and returned to us a moment later. "He says that a priest was killed here yesterday, or maybe the day before."

The women pulled the children tighter to them. Mary's arms cradled James, and Jesus leaned into the embrace of His grandmother.

Elisabeth called to John, who stood beside me.

"Who would kill a priest?" Mary whispered.

Malik said, "I heard the rabbi say it was men in black hoods."

My blood turned cold. John's sensitive brown eyes read my fear. I tried to offer a smile of assurance, but the muscles in my face were frozen.

Joel came near us and reported, "Rebels. Rebels who claim they want to free us from the house of Herod, but look what they have done. This synagogue will have to be cleansed and rebuilt. A priest fought back with his only weapons—stones—and was stabbed to death right here on these steps." He waved his hands, and we could see the dark stains of blood that had spilled down the steps.

"The old rabbi said he was the only one unafraid to move the body. He said while he was washing the body for burial, a band of young men, hooded and dark, ripped it from his hands. They dragged the body to the street, poured oil on it, and set the priest aflame."

The women gasped as one. Anna's hands muffed Jesus' ears. Joachim spat in the street.

My mouth opened, but no sound came forth. I had a story to tell, but what would my words matter even if my voice was strong and clear? What happened in the desert had happened here. It would happen again, and there was nothing I could do to stop the men who rode possessed and empowered by evil.

Joseph stepped back and I could see the rabbi, old and defeated, his hands still trembling. On his cheek was a deep wound, dark with dried blood. His eyes looked like gray storm clouds.

"His spirit lingers here," the holy man said—not in Hebrew like I was accustomed to, but in Greek, the favored tongue of my father. His quaking arms lifted upward and he looked right at me, right into my eyes. "*You* feel it. Boy, you feel the priest's restless presence."

I did feel it. We all felt it.

Joseph, Joel, and Joachim accompanied the rabbi into the sanctuary. The rest of us waited outside, no one saying much.

Malik stood close to his mother. "Where is the dead man's body now?" he asked.

His mother hushed his question.

"What does it look like?" Malik persisted. "I want to see what a burned body looks like."

I *knew*. I knew because I had seen a man burned. It was a sight that did not frighten me, but neither did it leave me, not in my brightest waking moments or in my darkest dreams.

After a long, uneasy silence, the men returned.

"The rabbi is settled."

I was not sure what that meant, but I knew Joseph would never leave someone if they still needed him. When we continued our journey, then, all I felt was relief.

Our pace was faster now, our caravan gone quiet.

At night we camped in the open meadows, away from the pillaged villages. We kept our fires low and tried not to attract attention. I noticed how John rarely took his eyes off Jesus. He watched Jesus closely, and I wondered what he was watching for.

I could not sleep because when I closed my eyes, they were back. The three bandits. I kept seeing the one with the yellow eyes, and every time I did, he grew younger instead of older. His eyes grew browner. He seemed to shift from the appearance of a distinct killer into a face so ordinary it could have been anyone.

Jesus, too, woke in the night with dreams that left Him crying and shaking. His mother held Him. Then His father held Him.

No one held me.

"You are afraid of the dark."

I knew the voice. It was Asher, and he had misinterpreted my fear.

I shook my head, trying to see by the glowing embers of the fire.

"There is no need for shame, Almon. Every soul is tormented by demons."

I propped myself up on my elbow. There was no accusation in Asher's words, and yet I felt shame.

"I fear vipers," he whispered. "The warmth of the fire draws them out from their holes. I once saw a black snake, no larger than Rabbi Micha's pointer. It slithered out of the wood we were burning. Before we saw any movement, the snake had attached itself to my master's hand."

I looked over to Joel's tent.

"No. Joel was not my first master. My first master died from that snake bite. I was sold again and again." His eyes dropped. "You cannot imagine what it was like for me, no more than a boy, to be sold from one trader to another."

I didn't have to imagine. I knew.

"God be praised. Joel came to the great sea to purchase lumber and found me there at auction."

One morning as we were rolling our beds, a band of refugees came by. They were hungry, and Joseph offered them the same meal we had eaten: dried dates and jerky. They had recently passed through Jerusalem, and they reported that the city was strong, the temple undefiled. Roman soldiers were more tolerant than Herod's army, which roamed the streets, harassing, spitting on, and provoking fellow Jews. But for now the army had not dared to set fire to or pull down the houses, businesses, and holy buildings.

One man bowed his head and prayed the deliverance prayer. I had never heard anything so pitiful in my life. It wasn't the words; it was the pain and suffering that came out of him like the blade of a jagged knife.

"Annas, the high priest in the Holy City—why does he not help his own? We have no voice to speak for us."

No one said a word.

The man's mournful prayer rang out. "How long, Lord, how long must we suffer in the wilderness?"

When he was finished he looked to Joachim, the patriarch of our clan. "How long, Father, how long until the Messiah comes to deliver us from this oppression?"

Jesus was beside me, and I found myself reaching out for Him, trying to protect Him. He was just a child, but two women I knew to be faithful and true—Mary and Elisabeth—had said He was the One, the *One* all of Israel waited for.

I looked down at Him. He made a fist around my thumb and squeezed. His eyes were filled with compassion for the desperate man, for those with him.

He was just a child, innocent and unblemished. I had never known a child more obedient. All that I had heard, all that I felt, whispered the truth about Him. It made no sense, yet a fire flickered within me and I knew at that moment—as the boy looked up into my eyes, smiled, and gave my thumb another squeeze—that the smallest, darkest part of my heart had been lit. Somehow, some way, I believed the unbelievable.

Twenty-three

Oh, Jerusalem!

What a city. We arrived in the afternoon, and before we ever set foot on holy ground, the white stone streets and buildings glowed in the sunlight. If I did not know that so much of Jerusalem was constructed of limestone, I would have sworn it was gold glinting off gold.

Joseph paused at the crest of a hill so we could all take it in.

Joachim offered a prayer of thanksgiving for our safe arrival.

Before, when I had been in Jerusalem with Father, it had been a perfect place to rob people. On any given day, almost thirty thousand people lived within the city borders. During festivals, the pilgrims who flocked to the city were particularly easy prey as they wandered in the dark tunnels that ran through the city. Jewish pilgrims here for Festival always carried a surplus of coins. They thought they could outsmart us by sewing secret pockets on the insides of their tunics, but Father had worked in the marketplace long enough to know every trick.

While the household of Joseph stood pondering the beauty before us, my mind raced back to the three different times I had been sold from the auction plank just outside the city. Father had fetched premium prices all three times, twice from bands headed for Egypt and once to a land owner from the farms in the lowlands.

It had been no trick to escape from the traveling traders, but the farmer had been harder to deceive. Father had rescued me just outside the city gates, where he had cut the rope from my ankles. We had hidden in a ditch while the farmer had practically stepped directly over us, searching for me. It was the only escape I ever made during daylight; all the others had been accomplished after dark.

Mary came up beside me, James tucked securely in the sling she wore close to her heart. As always, her tone was soft as down. "Almon, we are grateful for your presence. This journey has been difficult, but it would have been more difficult if you had not attended to Jesus and John with such diligence."

Her sweet gratitude chased away all my bitter memories.

Temple Mount was grand, breathtaking, perfect—so large, and unlike any other place on earth. The walls were high and exactly straight, stone upon white stone. Those walls seemed to stretch forever. I had seen the temple before, but now it was as if I was viewing it for the first time. When it rose before me this time, I saw it as God's house. It was holy beyond holy.

The city was white, but the temple was whiter. It was what made Jerusalem the Holy City.

"Herod's temple is flawless," Joseph finally uttered.

"It is one thing to his credit," Joel said, reluctant to give the great builder any credit at all. But in truth, Herod the Great was the only reason we had our temple at all. He had convinced Rome to allow him to have it rebuilt as a tribute to the God of the Jews. No expense had been spared. Rabbi Micha said that thousands of lives had been sacrificed in its making. He did not mean that Jews sacrificed humans, as did pagans; he meant that slaves and common laborers had worked night and day for years and years to build a temple and surrounding grounds that deserved Herod's approval.

To me, the mount was a city unto itself. The temple sat in a center court with high stone walls that enclosed everything, separating the secular from the sacred. It was atop those sturdy walls that marksmen could take aim—and had taken aim—at both unsuspecting rebels and worshipping Jews.

Today was a peaceful day, and I, too, gave God silent thanks.

From our hillside, we faced the double gates of the Outer Court. At the opposite end, the Fortress Antonia rose even higher than the wall.

"It is a disgrace to Jehovah to have a heathen dwell so close to our temple," Joachim grumbled, his voice low. "Herod may have rebuilt our temple, but he did it on the backs of slaves and Jews."

I understood his bitterness, but couldn't he see that before us stood the grandest sight man had ever created to honor God?

Joseph hoisted Jesus up to straddle his shoulders, giving the boy the best view of any of us. His eyes reflected the glow from the city; His mouth stood open in awe.

Malik did his best to lift John, but it was Asher who held the stout boy high so John could see what Jesus saw. It wasn't only the sight we all took in, it was the feeling that penetrated our hearts.

"Zion." Joachim uttered the word with reverence. The Holy City was often called *Zion,* which meant a "fortress" or a "citadel." Joachim explained that just as our history had been built layer upon layer, our temple was also constructed layer upon layer. The first temple of Solomon had been destroyed by the Babylonians; later it had been rebuilt on the same foundation, only to be destroyed again by Roman infidels, then rebuilt by Herod the Great.

"It is still under construction," Joseph whispered. "As grand as it is now, Temple Mount is still being rebuilt, as is much of the city."

It looked finished to me.

Joel frowned, and when he did he looked older than Joachim. "Herod the Great lives on even after he is gone."

"Yes," said Joseph quietly. "His dream was to rebuild the entire city with Temple Mount as the pinnacle."

"As it should be," Joel said, tears glistening in his eyes. "The Lord is great."

"Yes, great."

Elisabeth gasped. "Holiness to the Lord God!" She slid sideways and nearly fell from her donkey. The other women rushed to aid her.

"What is the matter?" Naomi asked. "Tell us quickly that we might aid you, cousin."

Even the men drew in around her. Her fist pounded at her heart.

"Is it your heart?" Mary whispered.

Elisabeth's old eyes opened wide. "Yes, my heart. My heart is full this day. All of it . . . all of this holiness . . . all of it is His." Her eyes locked on Jesus, who still sat astride His father's shoulders. "He is Master. He is Lord. He has come to save us."

No one dared to move.

"Jesus is the Chosen One." Her voice grew strong. "Jesus is the Chosen One!"

The women closed in around her, offering comfort and caring, though no one—not even little Deborah—seemed perplexed by Elisabeth's outrageous declaration.

"He for whom we wait is already among us." Her voice stayed strong, and though I could not see her for the crush of women, I could hear her.

Already among us.

I looked at Joseph and saw a man who was not even startled.

The revelation Elisabeth declared to these people was no revelation at all.

Twenty-four

Guilt rose in me like bile, bitter and hot. Every step I took toward the temple battered me with memories from my tarnished past. I wanted to be exactly where I was—yet I was not sure I had the right to be here. Would God strike me down when I set foot on holy ground?

Malik, who was normally eager to whisper about my sins, said nothing. He did not even look at me, but walked silently beside his father, falling in slow and steady step.

"Be still and do not provoke anyone," Joachim told us as we entered the city. "Avoid looking into eyes." He gave a firm glance at Elisabeth. "We must not draw unwanted attention, sister."

"I understand," she said, lowering her head. Her claims of Jesus' high holiness had ceased as quickly as they had begun.

The streets of Jerusalem were packed; people from all over the empire called this holy place home. All around us rose the sounds of Greek, Aramaic, Hebrew, and languages I had not heard spoken since living in the desert. I thought of Rabbi Micha's lessons on Babel and the great tower, how so many languages had been spoken that people could no longer understand each other.

My heart pounded; my limbs grew heavy. John still walked beside me, though he would not let me clutch his hand. Joseph held tightly to Jesus, whose eyes were wide with wonder.

We left our animals with caretakers at the outer city gates. Our beasts would eat and rest while we were at the temple. The excitement in Mary's eyes was bright, and when she and Joseph looked at each other I felt safe and secure, even though there were soldiers, just as we had been warned.

We made our way through crooked streets and narrow, winding alleys. In the blackness of the tunnel, I felt so guilty I could barely lift my feet. It was here that Father and I had carried out one of our most successful schemes. Father would choose the richest party—almost always pilgrims unfamiliar with the layout of the city—as they would make their way beneath the archway and into the tunnel. When they would reach the area that was dark and crowded, he would push me in front of the men. Their feet would trample me and I would cry out, pretending to be more injured than I was. Often I did not have to pretend, because I was really hurt; once my ankle was cracked as the boot of a Syrian came down on it.

Father would then feign anger. *How dare you be so careless as to crush an innocent child? And how am I, a poverty-stricken father with no wife, to pay for his care?*

The men would always express sorrow and would hand over money to pay for my injuries.

"Are you ill, Almon?" Mary's soft voice turned my head around and brought me back from yet another unsavory memory. "You look ill."

My eyes and smile told her that I was fine—that she had no need for concern.

Close by I could hear the bleating of sheep interspersed with the barking of courtyard vendors who were selling sacrificial animals. We were so near I could smell their scent in the air. It was all familiar to me, yet all new at the same time.

I smiled at Mary. I was fine. At least, I would be.

This was not the old me passing beneath the archway into the tunnel. This was not the old me headed to the temple. This was Almon, born anew.

Before the courtyard expanded and we were allowed to scale the huge stone stairs leading to the Temple Mount, our party was divided. The men went one way, and the women went the other.

Though we were not bound by law to do so, Joseph had us go to the baths to wash the grime from our bodies.

No unclean thing.

The cold water could wash away the dust and sand and sweat, but it could not cleanse me from within.

No unclean thing.

I clenched my jaw and tried to force from my mind the flood of memories with their associated guilt. They did gradually vanish—slowly, like cool mist dissipating in the heat.

Though we were never fully undressed, I felt uncomfortable bathing with other men. There were not just those in our party, but strangers as well, washing their bodies in water so cold it made bumps rise on my skin, like chicken flesh.

The man next to me appeared as nervous as I felt. He wrapped himself in a clean robe. We all dressed in the fresh clothes we had brought with us.

The man cleared his throat and asked of me, "Is that man your father?"

His chin pointed to Joseph.

My face flushed. I was not only unworthy to be present at the temple, I was especially unworthy to be thought of as Joseph's son.

Before I could shake my head, Joel pushed past Asher and Malik to give a quick reply. "No, the boy is not his son; he is the *servant* of my brother."

The man nodded, seeming to understand.

Joseph then moved to my side and addressed the man. "The boy is called Almon, and though he is my servant, he is very much a son to me."

New bumps rose on my skin. My heart swelled so big it pressed against my ribs. I knew then that even if I was struck by heaven's heavy hand, even if I died minutes from that moment, I had tasted heaven's sweetness.

Twenty-five

As we entered the courtyard, it was a stark contrast to our clean bodies and fresh clothing. Money changers called to every passerby. Sheep bleated incessantly. Droppings from doves and pigeons lay in thick layers.

Joseph's lips pressed tightly together as they tended to do when he was upset. He said nothing, but it was clear that he thought it wrong to have such filth so close to such sacredness. When I had been there with Father, I hadn't even noticed how vile and irreverent the temple courtyard was.

John held tight to my hand. I could tell he was bothered, but he appeared more angry than sad. He was still a child, but his face and manners were those of a mature man. The fact that his hair was long and unruly and that his robes were made of tanned hides and goat hair gave him a wild look that I really liked.

Jesus walked between Joseph and Joachim, His head bowed as if He were offering a long, silent prayer.

The hawkers and vendors were not bothered by our solemn demeanor; they screamed at us to buy their lambs, their doves, their pigeons. Hundreds of lambs were penned in such tight quarters that they did not have room to lie down. Reed cages filled with birds were stacked higher than Joseph's head.

Joel spoke loudly to all of us. "If we were here during Festival, the chaos would be ten times as great. There would be no room to move."

I could not imagine such a scene.

A man in a filthy robe splattered with muck and dung stepped out in front of John and me. His toothless mouth was sunken, reminding me of a piece of fruit left too long in the sun.

His greedy eyes focused on me. "A sin offering! The Lord requires an offering for the sins you have committed against heaven."

I stood still as stone. The man was a stranger; was there any way he could know the sins I had committed against heaven?

John tugged at me. "Pay him no mind, Almon. Come."

What if a sin offering could wipe away some of the guilt that fell on me like afternoon rain, heavy and damp?

"Come, Almon!" John again urged me forward.

Joseph visited many vendors before purchasing two white turtle-doves, the most perfect he could find. I heard him say it was the same lowly offering he had made when he had presented the infant Jesus at the temple.

As the mother of the child, it was Mary's responsibility to make the offering. Knowing that, I wondered if anyone had presented me. Of course they hadn't. I did not wish to think about it, but being there made me question and remember.

The money changers called out in so many languages it was hard to discern just one. Father had been young when he had worked on Temple Mount, before he had married my mother. It dawned on me that I did not know how he had acquired his skills. Of course, his father had taught him—my own grandfather, a man I never knew and never would know. Father never really spoke of his childhood or his education. There had been only a few words here and there, and now I would never know more.

A group of men dressed in white passed us, and I thought how clean they appeared—how orderly. They stepped together in rhythm, like they were soldiers, though I knew they were holy men.

I had no way to ask about them, but Joseph noticed me watching them. He moved to my side, leaned down, and whispered, "Almon, those men are temple scribes. One day you can be employed here. You can write and translate and record the history of our people."

How I wanted to believe his words!

Then without my hearing the clop of its hooves, a horse appeared from no particular direction. On it sat a soldier employed by Herod. He was tanned and dark, and his arms were so muscular they made me recall a black slave I had once seen—a fighter from Egypt who was paid to wrestle other men.

"What is your purpose here?" he demanded of Joseph.

"We are come to present my infant son at the holy temple."

Joseph's voice did not tremble, though I felt John squeeze my fingers. Our women clustered together, their heads down, their faces veiled. Deborah hid herself completely in the folds of her mother's robes.

I knew what everyone was thinking and feeling. The images of burned villages, of blood in the streets, were still fresh in our minds. We knew that Herod's soldiers were capable of utter and unprovoked destruction.

I squeezed John's hand to assure him, though I had no reason to assure him of anything. For all I knew, the man could unsheathe his sword and smite Joseph's head right off. I hated the image that flashed through my mind. I hated the fact that the horror was real.

Joseph stood firm and his answer appeased the man.

"Be about your business, Jews."

Once inside, only Joseph, Mary, and baby James were allowed to approach the high priest to present the infant. I stood back with the kinsmen and grandparents. Malik came to my side.

"Are you weary?"

I shook my head.

"I am. I am tired and I am hungry."

We had come fasting to the temple, and we would not break our fast until the sacrifice had been made.

"Father is going to buy a real meal for all of us," Malik whispered. "There is a feasting place outside the city on the way to Bethany. They have big spits with roasting lamb. We have eaten there before."

Asher stood behind Malik. He rolled his eyes and mocked the boy who loved food so.

Malik leaned toward me and whispered, "Asher is our servant, but eats with the rest of us. It is my father's way. He will offer the same generous treatment to you. When we get there and you find your stomach full, give me of your meat and bread. The sweets baked there are filled with honey and nuts. Give me your portion."

It was not a request.

John looked up at me and I knew he felt sorry for me.

"You don't have to do it," Asher said. "Malik is always after scraps, like a hungry mongrel."

Malik gave Asher a hard shove.

Joel was there in a blink. He wrapped his fingers around the back of Malik's neck and squeezed until his son squirmed in pain. "This is the Lord's holy house. You will *not* be disrespectful."

All Joel had to do to bring Asher into obedience was shoot him a piercing look.

My stomach growled as we waited. Just the mention of food made me realize how hungry I was, but if an offering of meat and bread and sweets would change Malik from my foe to my friend, then it was a sacrifice I was more than willing to make.

I did make that sacrifice. I ate some of the roasted meat and fried bread, but I gave the rest to Malik, who held his hand out to me when no one could see. And when the sweets were divided, Malik was right next to me with his pocket open. I slipped my sweets into his pocket, and Malik moved toward his younger sister.

Deborah rushed away from him to the shelter of her mother's skirts.

After that, I learned that I could buy Malik's favor with anything delicious. Fortunately for me, Mary was a wonderful cook and generous with her serving spoon.

Twenty-six

After we finished our feast it was time to bid farewell to Mary's parents and to John and Elisabeth. This was their land; Judea was their home.

Jesus did not shed tears, but His eyes welled up as He said good-bye to His cousin and playmate.

John stood next to his mother, strong and somber.

"I can see the fear in your face, Mary," Anna said. "Do not allow your fears to torment you. Your father and I will be fine, and we will see that Elisabeth and John get safely to the hill country."

The women passed James around again, each bathing him in their kisses. They kissed Jesus, too. When Mary took Elisabeth into her arms, I knew the thought that plagued their minds. Elisabeth was old; this might well be the last time the two women would be able to embrace and to draw comfort from each other.

Joachim pulled down his lion's head walking stick. "We will be going now."

After the final good-byes, we stood there in the street, watching until the figures of Joachim, Anna, Elisabeth, and John grew too small to distinguish in the distance.

He was gone, and I knew it, but I still felt the squeeze of John's hand in mine.

Our excursion to Jerusalem had been memorable, but our journey back to Nazareth was uneventful. Here there were the familiar routines that brought me such happiness and peace. Joseph worked harder than ever, adding another room onto the house. He hired a mason from Tiberias to lay a stone floor, one that reminded me of the temple courtyard.

I stood beside Joseph as we inspected the work. "One day we will make a guest chamber above this room," he told me, "a chamber for dining and celebrating the Festivals. One day the household of Joseph will boast a large family and a home to bring Mary comfort and pride."

I looked up at him and in that instant realized that Joseph, the greatest man I knew, held unfulfilled dreams of his own.

I was more determined than ever to make my own dreams come true. There were three favorite places where those dreams were best entertained: the synagogue, where all things were in order; the rooftop at home, where the canopy of stars was my ceiling; and Joseph's workshop, where stacks of lumber were turned into the finest furniture in all of Nazareth. I loved the smell of fresh-cut wood. I loved listening to Joseph teach stories from our ancient fathers. And I loved being with Jesus.

With John gone, Jesus seemed lonely and restless. He followed me around more than usual, asking questions and pleading with me to search the scrolls for answers I did not hold in my head. He especially loved to hear passages from Isaiah read aloud, over and over, until His eager mind committed them to perfect memory.

Deborah still came by to take Him for long walks around the village. I always went along, tagging behind, watching over the boy who made me marvel.

Finally, Joseph grew weary of Jesus' nonstop questions and gave Him a task in the workshop. He asked Jesus to gather the wood splinters and form wooden nails from them. Each one had to be cut and carved and shaped just so.

It was a job I thought both too difficult and too dangerous for a boy so small. I was years older than Jesus, and Joseph hadn't even given me such a task. But he was patient and loving, and in time Jesus was skilled at taking castaway wood and creating usable wooden nails.

Jesus no longer danced and laughed as He had just months before . . . before the stoning at Sepphoris, before the horrors we had witnessed on our trip to Jerusalem, before the tension and fear grew in Nazareth as sure as sprouting green vines.

Jesus still asked questions. He was still happy. He still smiled and sang, but He did not dance like a carefree child. Those days were gone, and as I watched Him chisel perfectly shaped nails from scrap wood, as I watched Him line them up in equal rows, as I watched Him change, I wondered . . . would Jesus ever dance again?

Twenty-seven

Precious rain had fallen on Palestine; every drop was counted, and cisterns flowed full. Now the clouds were clearing, but the air was still damp and a mist rose from the ground outside. Inside, I worked between Joseph and Jesus in the workshop.

Jesus was busy lining up His nails, making certain every one was uniform and each tip was sharp. While He worked He recited passages of scripture, more to Himself than for our ears.

Joseph was fashioning great pillars from cedar logs brought all the way from Lebanon. I loved the smell that clung to everything when he planed the cedar wood.

Someone rapped on the door, and before I could answer, the physician Nathan opened the door and let himself into the shop. The hem of his green flowing robes picked up the shavings and sawdust as he walked.

Nathan rapped his walking stick sharply on the plank floor.

"Welcome," said Joseph, rising from where he was stooped to do his work.

"I have come again to inquire about my pupil."

I felt my ears go red like they always did when I felt uneasy.

"Have you spoken with the rabbis at synagogue?" Joseph asked.

"Not recently. I stopped by to see the Pharisee Ovadya, but he has taken leave to the Holy City. How was your pilgrimage to Jerusalem?"

"Our journey was fruitful. We did encounter some discord along the way, but Jerusalem was fine."

"And your new son?"

"It is kind of you to ask. James is fine."

Nathan tapped his walking stick again. "And Almon—did he get to walk the grounds and see Temple Mount for himself?"

He spoke of me like I was not present, and I listened with pleasure as Joseph reported my progress. "I have clear expectations that Almon will one day become a gifted scribe. His talent lies with the written word."

At first Nathan's interest was keen. He listened to Joseph and looked at me, nodding from time to time, but then Jesus caught his attention—Jesus, who was in the corner lining up His wooden nails on the bench; Jesus, who was muttering passages from Isaiah.

"O Lord, have we waited for thee; the desire of our soul is to thy name, and to the remembrance of thee. With my soul have I desired thee in the night; yea, with my spirit within me will I seek thee early: for when thy judgments are in the earth, the inhabitants of the world will learn righteousness."

Nathan's jaw dropped, and he looked completely dumbfounded. "This child is your son?"

"Yes, He is my son."

"I have never seen such a miracle in all of Palestine!" He waved a hand in my direction. "Almon is a smart boy, for a mute—but *this* boy, this child you call Jesus, He is so young, and yet He quotes the ancient prophet with assurance and accuracy. Surely, He is no ordinary child."

I stepped back into the shadows, obscured.

Joseph's look held both joy and caution. He went to Jesus and lifted Him to the high stool.

"It would be my honor to pay for this child's education as well as Almon's."

"No," Joseph said quickly. "I very much appreciate what you have done for Almon—for what you continue to do for him. Jesus is my son and my responsibility. Business is steady, and I am able to provide for my own. God be praised."

Nathan seemed disappointed. "Yes, God be praised. You will continue to allow me to fund Almon's education?"

"Of course. We are all very grateful for your generosity." Joseph attempted to divert Nathan's attention. "The teacher is particularly pleased with Almon's writing abilities. His hand is steady and his patience endless." Joseph moved from Jesus to me, pulling me out of the shadows and placing me in front of Nathan. Joseph laid his hand on my shoulder; instinctively, I reached up and touched it. I felt for the first time the place where the saw had taken off his fingers. Again, I wished I could have given him my own to replace those he'd lost.

Jesus was restless. His legs dangled and He seemed almost bored.

"You know the writings of Isaiah?" Nathan asked him.

Jesus lifted His shoulders.

"Recite another passage, please."

Jesus looked to Joseph, whose expression granted permission.

"Behold, the Lord God will come with strong hand, and his arm shall rule for him: behold, his reward is with him, and his work before him."

Something happened during the speaking of those words. We stood still and silent as Lot's wife. It was as if the whole village went silent; saws stopped, hammers stopped, the whole earth listened to Jesus quote Isaiah.

Nathan tapped his stick again, as if he were Moses. "Jesus will be a rabbi of great standing one day, a Pharisee perhaps at the holy temple."

"I am most humbled by your observations, Nathan," Joseph said. "One day Jesus *will* be great. For now He is just a boy, a boy devoted to the prophets and the law, a boy particularly fond of Isaiah."

Twenty-eight

The more familiar I became with the community of Nazareth, the more I heard the rumors—in the marketplaces, at the village well, in the streets outside the synagogue where the household of Joseph worshipped. Rumors about Mary and Jesus. Dan, the slave, wasn't the only one whispering. Even Rabbi Zeev was often heard passing gossip, and I was glad that he appeared only to take the lectern on *Shabbat* or to correct the other teachers.

The fact was, Jesus *was* no ordinary child.

It was evident to everyone who knew Him that He was extraordinary. But everyone did not treat Him with the awe and kindness that Nathan showed.

Most people talked when they thought the family was out of earshot. Few people referred to Jesus as the son of Joseph; instead, they called him "son of Mary," which was slanderous—it meant the child had been born in shame.

Those words angered me, but they also brought to mind the conversation I had overheard between Mary and Elisabeth. In truth, the rumors were not unfounded.

I wanted to protect those I had come to think of as my own family, to stand as a shield between them and the rumors. My fists clenched and my stomach burned when I heard the way people slung words around as sharp as stones. If *I* heard what they were whispering, then I knew that Mary, Joseph, and Jesus heard, too. I also knew that Malik's loose tongue fueled the rumors like dry wood on flames. More than once I heard him whispering to the boys at the synagogue about angels and wise men. Something had happened in Bethlehem; I didn't understand it, but even after all this time people still talked.

"Jesus means *anointed*," Malik told Thomas, one of our fellow pupils. "My name means *king*. Yet in our family Jesus is favored. My Uncle Joseph watches over Him like He is royal. Mary hardly lets Him out of her sight. My own mother speaks of Jesus like He is better than me, as if He is something more than a mere boy. I tell you that's all Jesus is—an odd boy who laughs too much and never stops asking questions."

We were in the synagogue courtyard, under the shade of an ancient tree. It was our appointed time to socialize. As always, I was off by myself with my tablet and a scroll. Still, I was close enough to hear the vicious words Malik spread. I thought of all the food I had sneaked to him, just to buy his decency.

"Jesus is as ordinary as dirt," he said, laughing at his own cruelty.

I looked at Malik, at his big round head and the greasy black curls plastered against it. He had the eyes of a cobra, black and beady. I didn't plan to, but before I knew it I lunged at him and shoved him to the stone courtyard floor. He landed with a grunt.

Malik seemed stunned, and he stared at me like he was seeing a mirage. I balled my fist and struck him in the nose. My fingers came away smeared with red—the same red that stained his tunic, the same red that dripped onto the white stone beneath our feet.

Malik was screaming. My own mouth was open, pouring rage, but no sound came out. I burned with white-hot anger.

I wasn't finished. I lunged again. The boys shouted. Thomas cheered. Malik cried and cursed me. He hit me in the face, in the neck, and in the stomach. I felt the pain, but it only urged me on.

I hit him back. Again and again.

"Stop!" he cried.

I did not stop.

His skullcap came off, and he screamed with rage. "You are a worthless slave boy! You smell like sheep. You are a mute and have no right to be here! You are a slave! A mute! A slave! Never will you be anything more!" His nose spouted blood like a babbling spring. He lumbered to his feet and glared at me.

One punch from his fat-fingered fist and I went down hard. My whole face burned. It hurt to breathe. I felt my nose, and I knew it was broken.

A nose for a nose. The thought made me smile. I wasn't afraid, and I was no longer angry. Still, I lunged again, this time with the purpose of a wounded leopard: simply to do harm.

It took the strength of both rabbis and a visiting scribe to pull us apart. I had started the fight, but Rabbi Asa scolded Malik, and he did it in front of everyone. He accused Malik of being jealous of me because I was superior in my scholarship.

"Almon is more than a servant," Rabbi Asa said. "With his intelligence and devotion to Israel, someday he will be a valuable scribe. With your temper and a tendency for laziness, what will you be, Malik?"

Rabbi Micha touched his prayer shawl and set his jaw straight.

With the power of a gathering storm, a darkness spread across Malik's face. Hatred flickered in his black eyes. He bowed his bloody head and apologized.

I did the same.

When we looked up our eyes locked.

I knew then that the day would come when we would fight again. Perhaps not soon, but one day Malik would take revenge for my small victory.

Twenty-nine

The days, weeks, and months wore on.

I made a sacred vow to myself that I would not squander all that I had been given. I would reign in my temper, my fear, and my secrets. Someday, I knew in my heart, it would all come undone; my life would turn to rot like hoarded manna. The Torah warned, "He shall pay for the loss of his time," and I did not want my time to be lost. Not a single minute.

I spent my time searching for God. The daily prayers, the weekly *Shabbat* service, the festivals all gave life a rhythm that I cherished. I found peace in studying the Torah and in observing the laws.

But I did not find God.

Joseph worked much of his time in Sepphoris, where his skills were in high demand. He returned at nightfall, tired and hungry. He brought with him talk of rebellion spreading region by region, missing no corner or crook of Palestine. Archelaus, a ruler with a hand heavier even than that of his father, had to be ousted from power in Judea.

Antipas was appointed to rule Galilee. Joseph said there was not much difference between the two brothers. Philip was the only one who did not invite rebellion.

Joseph, who never showed anything but charity, loathed both Archelaus and Antipas. He did not mask his feelings and spent many nights discussing politics with Joel and other Nazarenes.

While I washed the feet of guests, I heard their talk.

"Archelaus' exile will surely bring an uprising."

"Nazareth will not be spared this time."

"How long must we wait for deliverance?"

Mary sent letters of concern to Judea to her parents, Joachim and Anna, and sent word to Elisabeth, hoping it would reach her and John in the hills of the Essenes.

Carpenters' Street was a favored gathering spot for those eager to share news. Men there told of a violent uprising in Jerusalem. They talked of terror on Temple Mount. The empire was armed with horses, swords, and daggers. Jews threw stones and curses.

I tried to picture the scenes they described.

"Anyone suspected of rebellion is executed. Crosses dot every hill."

One evening Joel came over, and he and Joseph met in the courtyard to talk of their concerns. Unlike so many other times, I made noise to let them know that I was on the rooftop, able to hear their conversation.

"Rest well," was all Joseph said to me, and he continued talking in low tones to his brother. His concern was what could be done to protect our own people, our faith, and our very way of life.

I remembered well the destroyed village we had encountered on our trek to Jerusalem. Though I had tried, it was impossible to erase that old rabbi's wounded face from my memory. If rebels invaded Nazareth, what would become of our hillside village?

Joel's voice rose and I heard every word he said. "No one is safe in Judea. We must summon our family to Nazareth; it is one of the few safe places in all of Palestine."

"People do not want to leave their homes, no matter the danger."

"If Archelaus was not such a vicious beast . . . "

Joseph sounded tired. "But he is."

"It is ironic that idol worshippers show more respect for our faith than do those of the house of Herod, supposedly our own."

I had heard it all before, but this night I heard fear in Joseph's voice. It made him sound like he was being choked. It made my own throat ache.

The brothers talked on into the night until Joseph finally said, "Prosperous is the man whose Lord God is Jehovah. Come what may, we will be strong and believe."

The conversation went silent.

Long after the men were gone, my mind was still awake, rehearsing one memory after another. I had seen war in the desert, tribes fighting tribes. I had seen torture and death.

My heart wanted to protect Jesus. Already, He had seen more than I ever wanted Him to see. He was too pure, too innocent. It was my responsibility to protect Him. But how? I couldn't even protect Him from the rumors that raged throughout Nazareth—rumors of His birth and His destiny.

How then, was I supposed to protect Jesus from the power and force of the mighty Roman Empire?

My fears were realized. Every day the horrors of war crept closer to Nazareth. Men were crucified for any hint of insurrection, and crosses dotted the hills as close as Sepphoris. Others were slaughtered by the sword or were hung from trees in front of their own families and fellow villagers. Women wailed and mourned in the streets and would not be silenced.

The clatter of Roman horse hooves sent Nazarenes scurrying into the outlying caves and vineyards. Our neighbors dug a tunnel beneath their home leading up to a hillside orchard. It was their way of ready escape if the Romans or Herod's hired henchmen came without warning. And they weren't the only ones.

Joseph refused to hide. He told both Jesus and me to show no fear, no matter what happened, no matter what we felt. "The Lord be our shield," he firmly admonished.

Always obedient, Jesus presented only a happy, confident face. His prayers took on an even deeper sentiment. I could listen to Jesus pray for hours, but what was the purpose? To me, prayers were just words. Where was God when His innocent people were being stabbed, crucified, and killed just to please the evil men who roamed the land?

Malik and Joel visited often, showing both fear and seething anger. To me, Malik was a mimic of his father. Since our fight at the synagogue, Malik had steered away from me, not even asking for my bread or sweets from Mary's kitchen.

One day Joel and Malik seemed particularly disturbed. A business associate of Joel's was crucified when someone reported to Herod's men that he was selling lumber to the rebels. One of Naomi's cousins was stabbed in front of his family because he did not have the money the tax collectors demanded. Others were cast into prison without trials and without justice.

Joel stood tall and firm when he made his declaration. "Until the days of uprising have ended, I am taking my family into the hills to hide in the cave country. Join us, Joseph."

"No," said Joseph. "I am grateful, brother, but I will stay in Nazareth. I will stay and show my faith. The Lord be our shield. His guidance and protective arm will not forsake us now."

"Tell that to the faithful who are in need of proper burial. Bodies are being found burned along the roadsides—burned by the same bandits who burned the priest in that village on the way to Jerusalem. Remember?"

"Yes. I remember."

Joseph could not change Joel's mind, and Joel took his family into hiding.

Sabbath worship at the synagogue switched from talk of the Torah to talk of torture. The rabbis, priests, scribes, Pharisees, and Sadducees all had their own interpretations and predictions. Their feuding made for a different kind of war, but a war nevertheless.

Publicans increased their vigilance, making certain that Caesar received his unfair share of workers' money. We were used to the collectors coming by the shop, but now they were also stopping by homes, harassing women.

Word reached us that in Sepphoris, the townspeople stoned a tax collector. In revenge, the Romans burned so many buildings and houses that from the hillside of Nazareth we could see the orange flames leaping and licking the night sky. We could smell the smoke. We could hear the distant cries of death and the unending wails of mourners.

Death crept closer and closer toward us.

There was no way now to shelter the tender ears and eyes, the untouched heart of Jesus.

Thirty

The Pharisee Ovadya brought two men from the north country to show our school how papyrus was made. He wanted us to understand so that we would never waste it. Long ago I had seen papyrus growing in the Nile Delta like a grass-like sedge, but now that it was spread before us, it was much taller than even Joseph fully stretched. I was amazed.

The workers soaked the stems so the fibers could be separated for weaving. The stems were then cut into thin strips and joined together to make baskets, robes, sandals, and the precious paper I so loved.

My refuge was in words—in the way ink dyed the parchment, the way it bled into its veins and valleys, the way it touched what was blank and left it blank no more. I loved the feel, the smell, the lines, and the swirls and dots. I loved making words.

To commemorate my upcoming Bar Mitzvah, the physician Nathan brought a small but elaborately designed inkpot made from faience, a glassy material. It was colored blue and had been crafted by an artist in the Holy City. It was truly beautiful, and I kissed the physician's hands in appreciation.

His gift meant a great deal to me, and yet Joseph's humble present— a bundle of handcrafted writing instruments—meant more; he styled for me a variety of hardwood pens, providing a small knife with which I could sharpen them. I had been using sharpened reeds and ink made from the carbon of our burned lamps. The new pens were more precise and stronger in my fingers; they made my lines thinner, my curves and swirls and tails more the envy of my fellow students.

Jesus, the budding woodcarver, also crafted a pen for me. It was rough and crooked, and I treasured it.

Jesus was now old enough to attend synagogue with me every morning. Of course, the rabbis marveled at His understanding of the Torah, which made the students mock Him. Even little boys as young as Jesus took their lead from the older students who shunned Him. They did not bother to whisper behind His back, but belittled Jesus to His face. He did not understand the names they called Him. He knew He was a target of cruelty—He felt it—but He did not understand what He had done to merit it.

More than once, I saw Jesus use the back of His hand to wipe tears from His cheeks. I did not think Him weak for His tears, because my own pillow was often damp in the morning after a night of dreaming that I had lost the life that had become so precious to me.

It broke my heart to see Jesus suffer so. He was being punished for doing right. What justice was there in that?

I yearned for a voice, for the ability to assure Him that He did not deserve such cruelty. The words of the students were as unwarranted and deadly as the weapons Herod's men used to torture and undermine innocent Jews. The dark side of me wanted to stone the boys who belittled Jesus, who caused tears to run down His cheeks.

But Jesus was different. He forgave them before His tears were dry. It was His way.

James, no longer a babe in arms but a strong, fast-growing boy, was pulling himself up and taking a few unsteady steps across the room. Jesus loved to play with him, to make James laugh out loud.

He tickled the baby's bare fingers and face with soft, green stems. He told James stories from our ancestors, making all of the animal sounds for the tale of Noah and the ark.

No one told me, but I could see by looking at Mary that there would soon be another baby in the house. In spite of the unrest going on all around us, all was well within the household of Joseph.

Because it was not safe for women and children to travel through Palestine with such volatile unrest, Joseph summoned Joel from the hills above Nazareth where he had taken his family into hiding. He and Joel, along with the servant Dan, traveled to the Holy City for Passover. They represented our clan at the temple. I say *our* clan, because that is how I had come to think of myself: as a member of the household. Though I knew I was not worthy of such an honor—and never would be—still I moved forward as though I was part of a whole, and not just an individual.

"Watch over Jesus while I am gone," Joseph said. "Keep Him safe."

I nodded. How many times had Joseph made the same request of me? It was not a chore, but an honor to shadow the boy I thought of as my own. I would protect Him.

Malik, Deborah, and Naomi stayed with us while Joel was away. Weeks earlier, Asher had been sent to Galilee to work in the lumber business with one of Joel's partners. Joseph said the boy would be back, but I doubted it.

Deborah loved to play with James and spend time with Mary at the loom. Once she showed me a scarf she had woven, and I nodded, thinking it beautiful. That night when I went to bed, I found it folded neatly by my mat, tied with a single strand of string.

For days after that neither one of us dared let our eyes meet. I kept the scarf hidden beneath the box that housed all of my writing supplies. Sometimes I would get it out just to touch the softness, to know that Deborah's fingers had made it—for *me*.

When the spring blossoms bloomed red, I chose the biggest, brightest flower. I tied its stem with the same strand of string Deborah had used to tie the scarf, and while she and Jesus were walking down by the fields of new wheat, I presented it to her.

Jesus giggled, but I gave Him a look that sent Him scurrying after a white butterfly.

Deborah seemed uncertain, and in that moment my heart fell.

"No," she said, reaching to take the stem. "I want it."

That was it. She took the flower, and I was glad.

Deborah had proven she was my friend. I didn't care how deformed her face was behind her veil; to me, she was beautiful.

Malik would not have approved. He had said little to me for months, but there were times I caught him cornering Jesus, pressing Him for information.

"What does an angel look like, cousin? How are you going to save our people from Caesar? What is so special about you, Jesus?"

One evening I came around the corner by the animal shed and found Jesus backed against the crib, Malik's elbow pressed to the terrified child's throat.

"Tell me where the gold is!" Malik growled the demand.

Jesus said nothing, but His hands trembled and blood dripped from His nose.

"Wise men brought you gold. Where is it hidden?"

I plowed into Malik like an ox gone mad. I threw him to the ground, pushed his face into the muck, and pummeled him with my fists, over and over. The air went out of him and his filthy face burned red. His arms and legs flailed. He opened his mouth to scream, but my fists took the air from him before he could make any sound at all.

He had wounded Jesus. He had hurt His spirit—and because Jesus was a little boy who was incapable of harming another, because His father was not present, and because I had come to think of myself as His elder brother, I exacted the uttermost farthing on Jesus' behalf.

When I was finished with Malik, when his face was bloody and bruised, when I made him swear to never injure Jesus again, I had my vengeance. But it did not empower me.

Malik crawled away, crying like a baby. As he did, Jesus ran to him, threw His arms around Malik, and helped his cousin stand.

I marveled. Jesus was filled with compassion for the one who had hurt Him. I stood there staring, feeling sudden sorrow for what I had just done. I feared that Jesus would reject me, that He would see me for the brute I really was.

I also feared what Naomi would do, what Mary would do, and what Joseph would do when he returned home. I had jeopardized everything.

But Jesus spoke to Malik in hushed tones, in words so tender I could not hear, yet I could feel their power. I saw the expression on Malik's battered face go from dusk to dawn.

Jesus looked at me, and I was afraid to meet His gaze. When I did, I saw the same thing I always saw in His eyes . . . love and forgiveness.

It was as if a wave washed through me, cleansing me of so much darkness and dirt, as if I was born again—a different boy. As fast as I had lunged at Malik in anger, I rushed to him in sorrow. I begged his forgiveness.

Malik too, had been changed.

"I forgive you," he said, smiling through his tears.

If Naomi, Deborah, and Mary knew the truth of how Malik's face got cut and bruised, of how my knuckles got scraped to the bones, they never let on. They simply offered us words of sympathy and the cooling ointment of aloe.

Compassion, I learned, was more healing, more powerful even than vengeance.

Thirty-one

In return for all that I had been given, I wanted to do something for Mary and Joseph and their household. I started with a simple piece of parchment Rabbi Micha had given me. I wanted to replace the sacred *klaf* set inside the *mezuzah* located on the family doorpost. Mary was faithful in kissing her fingers and then touching the *mezuzah,* a sign to all that Mary was aware of and obedient to God.

The *mezuzah* was in fine condition, but the *klaf* inside was faded and almost impossible to read.

Careful to make every letter uniform and styled without flaw, I took my time. I worked by lamplight late into the night in the outbuilding where I stayed. I had a little corner with a mat and a blanket. I also had my clothes and the few items I had acquired since Joseph had taken me in. To me, it was the place I felt most safe.

Among the words I wrote on the *klaf* were these: *Hear, O Israel: The Lord our God is one Lord: And thou shalt love the Lord thy God with all thine heart, and with all thy soul, and with all thy might.* I was especially attentive when I formed the three Hebrew letters that symbolized the name of God.

Though our everyday language was Aramaic, I knew that Joseph was most fond of Hebrew, so that was the language I used to fill the parchment. I also used the pens he had crafted for me. I used ink made from the oil Mary had burned in the household lamps. The ripped edges were decorated with the stars of King David, six on each edge to represent the tribes of Jacob.

As I worked I thought of how my life had changed since the day Joseph, Mary, and Jesus had come upon me.

I thought of my father. In my heart I knew that he had been killed. There were moments when I missed him, when I loved him desperately; in other moments I loathed him for the suffering he had allowed into my life.

I thought of God and tried to get an image in my mind. He was all-powerful, all-knowing, all-present; He was quick to anger, and His jealousy was unmatched. He had more rules than a simple human could follow. His punishments were swift and often barbaric.

I knew *of* God, but I didn't really know Him at all.

I could not think of God without thinking of Jesus. Elisabeth believed He was God's own Son. I didn't know what I believed; I only knew I loved Him.

My tears dripped on the page and slightly smeared one of the stars, but I left it as it was, a symbol of my broken heart . . . a new heart given to me by this family I had grown to love.

I waited to present my offering until a peaceful Sabbath afternoon. I handed the simple gift to Joseph, who leaned back on his pillow on the floor. He said nothing as he read it, but then handed it to Mary, who looked at it with tears in her eyes. She passed it to Jesus, who took it, scooted a chair to the doorpost, and replaced the old parchment with the new.

As we celebrated the *havadalah* ceremony, which literally means to be separated from the queen Shabbat, my heart was full. The wine was tasted, the spices smelled, and the prayers sung. Holding her hand near the flame, Mary observed the reflection flicker in her fingernails.

Each action was symbolic of the beauty of the Sabbath and our bittersweet sadness that it was coming to a close. I took heart in believing that the next week would find me in the same home, surrounded by the same family, observing the same rituals.

I might not know God like I wanted to, but I knew it was His hand that had placed me in the household of Joseph, and I knew that same holy hand could remove me from the household just as quickly.

Jewish holy writ consisted of the Law, the Prophets, and the writings. I loved them all, but fancied myself as a writer. After finishing the *klaf,* I began a special scroll, a record of all that happened in our lives. I wrote of Jesus and His enthusiasm for life and His unending quest for knowledge. There were days His questions baffled even the teachers. When Rabbi Asa did not have a ready answer, he tugged on his prayer shawl and his lips formed a circle beneath the wispy beard he brushed soft and white. I was often the one he sent to the ark to search the scrolls for answers.

More and more I noted that Jesus was not exactly learning as the rest of us did. Though He did study lesson by lesson, it was as if He already knew the course—knew the prophets, knew the law, and knew its interpretation.

Of Jesus, I wrote that He was no longer a boy of countless questions, but a boy possessing more and more answers. I watched Him. I waited. I quit wondering who He was and began to wonder about the man He would one day become.

I wrote of Joseph and how people from as far away as the Gentile regions of Tyre and Sidon were coming to him to have their furniture built. The demand for his skills in Sepphoris was steady.

I wrote of James, who was determined to do things on his own—to feed himself and dress himself and walk without assistance, no matter how many times he landed on his backside. I wrote of the newest babies, twins named Jude and Joses. They still slept most of the time, snug in matching reed baskets crafted by one of Mary's kinsmen.

I wrote of Mary and her goodness to all who came within the circle of her arms. I wrote of her loom—how with wool, dye, and skill, she made beautiful tapestries. I wrote of the Torah mantle she had embroidered for the synagogue. I tried to write the beauty of her lullabies, how they filled the courtyard with music brighter than birdsong. My words failed me.

It seemed for the time that the politics of Palestine were becoming calm. Women went to the marketplace with baskets on their arms and music on their lips. Men laughed and talked of the growing crops—of how Nazareth was budding like a young vine, spreading up, house by house, over one rise and then another.

In the evening when my work was done, I sat on the rooftop and looked up and down at the other houses, the other rooftops. In the lowlands, I saw farms laid out in even parcels, packages wrapped in the colors of earth—green in the spring and gold in the gathering season. I could see the orchards and trees lined up like so many soldiers, row after row.

Women liked to sit on the rooftops with their sewing and mending. Men sat on the rooftops too with their eyes closed and their heads back, savoring the last warm rays of sunshine on their weary faces. I wrote of how serene and solitary life on the roof was, how so much of Nazareth could be calculated from where I sat with my parchment and pens.

Joachim and Anna had come back from Judea for the birth of the twins, and they had remained. It was a double blessing to have two sons, and the grandparents were thrilled.

Anna seemed the same to me, but Joachim's memory seemed to be weakened. He kept asking me to tell him my name. When I did not respond because I could not respond, Joachim grew agitated. Jesus showed endless patience with His grandfather and continually spoke on my behalf.

Joseph showed great love and concern for his in-laws and set about adding yet another room onto the house, this one a private area specifically designed for Anna and Joachim. It was on the shady side of the house with an outside door leading to the garden.

Jesus and I did most of the plastering, making it match the rest of the house and the outbuildings. The hue was plain gray, the shade of a newborn donkey, but appeared white when the noon sun shone down on Nazareth.

With the birth of the twin boys, I was introduced to more kins-folk than ever. Brothers, sisters, aunts, uncles, and cousins came to celebrate such a grand blessing to the household of Joseph.

With the threat of political upheaval dimmed at least for the time, Joel and his family returned to their home. Malik had entered manhood, made obvious by the sprout of chin whiskers. But that was not all that had changed about him: he was kinder, especially to Jesus. Instead of being a tormenter to Jesus, Malik became His protector, and he usually walked with us to the shop or home following syna-gogue studies.

I could not fathom a family woven tighter, more concerned about one another. I wrote of their love in my scrolls, and though my heart ached to sit with them as they crowded on the floor, strewn like so many pillows pressed together in one colorful design, laughing as they retold family stories, I knew my station.

Whenever anyone crossed the threshold, I rushed for my towel and bowl. I unloosed shoes and washed the dust from weary feet. I kept the courtyard clean and the cisterns free of leaves and dirt. I scrubbed the stones in preparation for Sabbath worship. I cleaned the benches and trimmed the vines. It fell to me to tend to the animals every evening now that Joseph's workload at the shop had become heavier. The extra responsibility felt welcome; Joseph knew he could count on me.

"Your most important task is always, always to watch over Jesus," he reminded me.

I smiled. It was also my favorite task.

As I filled scroll after scroll with accounts of our days, I realized just how blessed my life had become. I wrote of Malik, who had once been my enemy but who was now my friend. I wrote of Deborah and how her simple, shy acts of kindness never failed to make my heart beat twice as quickly. I wrote of synagogue and Sabbath. I wrote only of the good things. The bad things were engraved forever in my memory and on the back of my heart. Those, I did not record.

I gave my first scroll to Mary.

Her eyes danced with joy as she opened it and realized all that it contained.

"Oh, Joseph," she said, sitting by the window light where it was easier to read. "Husband, will you make me a special ark where I can keep this record, a safe place to protect the history of our family?"

"I will. I will make it from the finest olive wood in all of Palestine."

Mary finished reading and came across the room toward me. I thought she would stop, but she didn't. She opened her arms to me and pressed her lips to my forehead in gratitude.

All the hours, all the effort, all of it was surely paid with interest.

Thirty-two

Thirteen.

Rabbi Asa and Rabbi Micha determined that I was now a Jewish boy of age. It did not matter that I did not know the date of my birth, or even the place where I had been born.

My body changed. Mary and Anna sewed new robes for me, and Joseph helped me make new sandals, large enough to fit my growing feet.

I was now an adult male in Jewish society. Like it or not, childhood was behind me, and I assumed all the legal and religious responsibilities of a man. I felt caught between two worlds. Part of me longed for the days just behind; I wanted to run and play in the rocky hills, to chase the black-socked sheep with James and the twins. I wanted to race Jesus all the way to synagogue, to arrive out of breath and laughing.

Not that I was one prone to do so, but now I could not blame my mistakes and misfortunes on others. I had reached the age of majority; I was responsible for my own thoughts and deeds. *Mitzvoth* was no longer optional—it was my duty.

Bar Mitzvah meant a separation of father and son. Malik bar Joel had separated from his father more than a year earlier. Jesus bar Joseph would make the break in the coming years.

My father's name had been Samuel, making me Almon bar Samuel.

I had been separated from him for so long I could no longer recall the sound of his voice or the look of his face. It was as if desert sands had blown over my memory, layer upon layer, until all that was left was the smooth surface of the sand.

I knew the scriptural passages I was required to know. I could not speak the recitations with my mute tongue, so I wrote them out, word for perfect word.

Rabbi Asa, Rabbi Micha, two priests, and the local scribe came to the house one evening while Joseph rested on the rooftop. A gentle breeze blew the scent of wood smoke upward.

I greeted the men as they entered the courtyard gate, and right away I knew they had come about me. But why? After all these years, had they discovered that I was not the innocent child I had passed myself off to be? Had I academically damaged a scroll in the aedicula?

Joseph heard their voices and climbed down the ladder into the courtyard. Jesus was right behind him.

The men did not enter the house, but stayed in the courtyard. One of the Pharisees, a short man with a red beard, pointed his finger at me and ordered me to get him a drink of water.

I went for the jug inside, but he stopped me. "Water from the village spring," he said. "Go in haste; I must have living water."

Joseph's special cistern flowed with living water, but he looked at me and nodded in the direction of the spring. I left with the jug in my hand and my heart pounding in my chest.

I was halfway up the street when I heard the sound of familiar footsteps.

Jesus had followed me. His face seemed aglow in the dusky light, the sky painted the color of a ripe fig. He didn't say much, just kept pace with me so I wouldn't be alone.

Most of Nazareth was populated by Jews, but the old Arab Alim sat out in front of his house. His tunic was white and his call to us friendly.

We waved and hurried on our way. Half of me wanted to return in a hurry to discover the purpose of the men's visit. Half of me was afraid to find out.

I could have filled the jug from the well in the common courtyard; that would have been easiest, and they never would have known. But I did as I was told. At the top of Market Street, hidden from sight in a thicket of ancient trees tall and gnarled as the eldest rabbis in Nazareth, a small spring gurgled. A large stone basin had been carved to help the water flow, but over generations of use its spout had been worn and never re-carved, so it was difficult to fill the narrow neck of the jug. Ice-cold water ran over my hands until my fingers were hardly able to grip the handle.

Jesus laughed and drank water from His cupped hands.

I drank and thought the water did taste better, sweeter.

Jesus asked me what I thought the men wanted. He was fearful that they had come because of something *He* had done. Jesus had advanced from reciting Isaiah to expounding the holy prophets.

I shrugged and pointed a finger at my chest. *They are not there about* you; *their visit has to do with* me.

It was never difficult for Jesus to understand. It was as if He could read my thoughts. He did not inquire further, but I could see concern in His eyes.

And I was right.

The men were gathered tightly in the courtyard, seated on the benches I had just scrubbed clean that very night. Already, Joseph had lit the night torches to give a flickering glow to all of their faces, faces that turned to look at me.

The chief Pharisee reached for the jug. I saw that Joseph had brought out a wineskin, and the other men were occupied with it.

"I fear to divulge dark news," Joseph told me without getting up.

My feet went to stone. Jesus stood next to me, just as still.

"The physician Nathan has died. He is buried with his fathers in Capernaum."

I knew immediately what that meant. There would be no more funds for my education at the synagogue. Joseph's business was steady, but he had a growing family to provide for. Mary was again with child.

I held my breath, afraid that if I exhaled I would crumble to the ground or dart away in fear. I was thirteen; it was time to prove my manhood.

Joseph understood my anxiety and said quickly, "Nathan left word that he wanted to continue to care for you, Almon, upon the event of his death. These good men believe as he did—that you have a gift with words."

I bowed my head to show gratitude. I exhaled and drew in a deep and welcome breath of cool night air.

"Nathan has bequeathed the means for your continued education. His vision was to see you become a scribe."

My throat closed with emotion: relief, gratitude, shock. Even if I had been able to speak, words would have been inadequate.

Rabbi Asa spoke softly. "Your master, Joseph, has agreed on one condition."

I raised my eyebrows and waited.

"As you know, you are his property. Joseph owns you."

I nodded. It was a fact that someone like me could *never* forget.

"Becoming a scribe is no easy undertaking. It requires an immense amount of time. Joseph has consented to release you to devote yourself to your studies."

I hoped that they could read the confusion I felt.

Joseph stepped forward, and his expression was so intense I hardly recognized him. When he spoke, his voice quaked. "Almon, you have come to mean much to me, to my family. I often go back in my mind to that day in the desert when we came upon you, a mere boy, half-dead."

He paused to gain control of his emotions. Jesus went to Joseph's side and I realized that he, too, was a growing young man.

"Almon, you have served this household well. Your faith is the faith of our fathers. I have watched in awe as you have taken to wood with the same precision you use in your writing. You apply perfection to every task you undertake. I see you when you do not know I am watching. I see how you are with my sons."

Jesus stepped between us. He touched Joseph's elbow to offer unspoken support.

I love your sons as my own brothers, I said silently, hoping he would somehow hear my heart. *I love you as my father.*

Joseph took a deep breath. He placed both hands on my shoulders. "After consulting with these honorable elders, I have decided to grant you something you will need if you are to go on to become a great scribe in the house of the Lord."

What more could Joseph give me than he had already given me? I expected him to tell me he would grant me more time to study—that he would lighten my task list.

"I grant you your freedom, Almon. You are no longer a slave or a servant. You are a free man."

I did not move. I could not move. I was *free?* How was that possible?

"As you know, Almon, in Torah the fiftieth year was the year of Jubilee. It was a time when debts were forgiven, land returned to original owners, and slaves freed. This is your jubilee."

I thought Joseph would spill tears. Instead, he laughed, and all of the others laughed, too. Soon my back was being slapped and I was being congratulated.

What was I to do?

Jesus moved around me, tugging at my arms, telling me it was a good thing that had happened to me.

Joseph read my worries and said, "From now on you are free to live here, free to work for me at the shop for a wage, free to study at the synagogue. You are free to choose for yourself."

Jesus' eyes were filled with utter joy.

I wanted to feel that elation also. Instead, I feared my freedom would lead to a separation from the life I loved so much.

The elders passed around the wine-skin and drank and laughed and celebrated my freedom. I felt like an intruder at my own party. When Jesus left the celebration and climbed back up to the rooftop, I followed Him.

We lay up there listening to the men, watching the stars dance against a sky that had gone black.

No one took note of my absence.

Thirty-three

The servant Dan was gifted at plaiting reeds. Though his fingers were thick and bent with age, they were nimble. He made fine whips and belts and even bird cages. After Joseph granted me freedom, Dan went to Joel and requested that his years of service be counted for more. He did not ask to be released from servitude, but requested that he be allowed to raise pigeons.

Joel seemed amused by his slave's plea and granted immediate permission.

Jesus loved to go by His uncle's house to see the birds that were kept in rows and stacks of cages out back with the animal stalls. He especially loved the nests and the young fledglings. I hated the smell, the filth, and the sight of caged winged creatures. It made me sad.

I will never forget the day I watched Dan open the cage door to release a set of young birds. All but one flew out. One terrified young pigeon clung to the reeds, unwilling to face freedom. Dan lifted the cage high into the air and shook it. The bird toppled from side to side, desperate for a grip. Feathers came loose, but the pigeon refused to fly.

Dan looked at me with malice. "This stupid bird is you, Almon."

I did not feign misunderstanding.

"You could spread your wings and fly. You could soar to the heavens. Instead, you cling to the cage that you know. You stay with the familiar. You are stupid."

Jesus reached into the cage and held out a straight finger. The tiny bird's chest pounded; Jesus stroked the bird's head and cooed to it.

In time, the pigeon finally perched itself on the offered finger.

Slowly, Jesus pulled it from the bars and brought it out into the open. At long last, the bird lifted its tiny head, opened its wings, and gave one determined pump. The pigeon flew into the air and soon disappeared into the sky.

Dan threw his head back and laughed. His spit sprayed the air.

I hated the sound of Dan's laugh. But more than that, I hated the fact that Dan was right: I had my freedom, and yet I was terrified to live free.

Once I was granted my freedom, the household of Joseph treated me no differently, except I now earned a steady wage. Mary and Joseph had never neglected me, but had slipped a coin into my hand from time to time. They had provided shelter, food, clothing, and generosity. In exchange, I had offered my service and obedience.

It felt strange to me, almost sinful, knowing that if I wanted to take a walk in the hills above Nazareth, I did not have to seek permission. I was free to come and go, to spend my wage at any of the shops.

I did not have to wait to study until all of my tasks were finished. If I wanted to study, I was free to take my scrolls and pens and set to work. Instead, I tended to the same routine. I accomplished the same chores. I felt the same fears I had always felt.

In the workshop, I posed my question to Joseph on parchment: *What would you have me do?*

He pressed his lips together like he always did when he fell into deep thought. Finally, he asked, "What does *your* heart desire?"

How could I tell Joseph that all I really wanted was to make him proud of me? I wanted to please him. More than anything, I wanted to be like *him*. Instead, I wrote, *I long to be a faithful Jew.*

Joseph smiled at my answer.

"Keep the law," he said, and turned back to the wood he was staining with the juice of crushed pomegranate seeds.

The laws of a faithful Jew were more confining than Dan's reed cages. No matter how diligent I was, it seemed I always fell short of the highest expectations. It wasn't just the great number of laws and rules to live by, but it was the endless interpretations of those laws. It was so easy to earn the scorn and disapproval of the priests.

There was also the invisible millstone I carried around my neck: the years of sinning that I had never acknowledged. Now that I was a man in Jewish society, I should have acted like a man. I should have gone to Rabbi Asa and admitted my past. I didn't because I could not risk the disappointment that would surely wash across Joseph's face. Even if he forgave me of everything I had done, there would be pain in his eyes—pain that I would have caused.

As Nazareth expanded, so did our contact with the surrounding world. *Shabbats* often brought visiting rabbis from faraway places. They carried news of politics and pagan religions. They also brought fresh interpretations of the law and new ways to tell ancient stories.

One damp and misty *Shabbat* morning we filed into the synagogue, family by family, the men through the main entrance, the women and children through the side door. Rabbi Micha stood ready to greet us. As always, the men were seated at the right, the women were seated at the left, and the children were spread out on the floor everywhere—though the youngest were supposed to stay at the left with their mothers.

Jesus sat surrounded by His younger brothers. The twins had been warned to sit still, but already they were crawling over Him like eager pups. James held a finger to his lips to warn them to sit still and show respect.

Mary looked alarmed and whispered for them to come and sit with her. Joses toddled to his mother's lap, but Jude crawled next to Jesus and gave James a look of sheer triumph.

Joseph smiled at his sons and then offered that same smile to me.

We prayed. We sang. The benches continued to fill as latecomers poured into the synagogue.

Rabbi Micha announced the presence of a traveling rabbi, a teacher of great renown in the Holy City. A man who had lived in Egypt and Syria, his name was Gur, which meant "young lion."

I straightened my back and opened my ears, but my eyelids felt heavy, and I kept yawning during Rabbi Micha's introduction. But as soon as Rabbi Gur opened his mouth, my fatigue fled.

He had the voice of a shofar horn.

Instead of reading and interpreting, this teacher posed questions and stirred up a fast debate as warm as the air around us.

"There is a division among our people," he said.

Even the children leaned forward to hear Rabbi Gur of the Essenes, those who lived in the desert hills of Judea—the hills where

John had been reared. He spoke of the loathed Samaritans and how they had defiled their true identity and soiled their bloodline by intermarrying with pagans.

He spoke of experiences with the idols he had encountered, the gods and goddesses people worshipped because they did not know the one true God.

"We are Jews!" Rabbi Gur shouted. "Our blood is pure!"

An energy shot through the synagogue.

"We are the Lord's own people! He has covenanted with us and no other people!"

The men around me were practically on their feet with excitement.

Then the rabbi's voice became so quiet that we all had to strain to hear him.

"What does it mean to be Jewish?"

The entire synagogue went silent.

He touched the blue thread running through his robe. "Does it mean we are superior?"

Now the synagogue exploded. Some said yes, others no.

"It means we are chosen," Joseph said, his voice clear above the others.

"Chosen for *what?*" Rabbi Gur asked.

"To teach the world of the one and only God."

"Are you saying we have a responsibility to the rest of the world?"

Joseph did not hesitate. "Yes. We have a responsibility to God."

The rabbi lowered his chin and stroked his beard as he attempted to make eye contact with everyone he could. He then asked, "Why are we here?"

"We are here because we are commanded to be here," a man in the far corner replied.

Rabbi Gur shook his head. "If we are supposed to be teaching the world of God, why are we not out in the rain running up and down the streets looking for someone to teach?"

Rabbi Asa shrugged his shoulders. "Everyone in Nazareth is dry within these walls."

That sent a ripple of laughter throughout the building, which brought frowns from many of the elders. Laughter was discouraged on the Sabbath.

Rabbi Gur turned to look at Rabbi Asa. "At the west side of your village, is there not a group of Syrian families who moved here to raise grapes?"

Rabbi Asa nodded. "That is true."

"Is Nazareth not home to an old Arab named Alim?"

People muttered that yes, that, too, was true.

Rabbi Gur raised the holy scroll. "Why are we not teaching the old Arab and the Syrian families of our one true God?"

"We are waiting," Rabbi Micha shouted.

"For what?"

Rabbi Micha stood from his bench and raised both arms in triumph. "For the holy Messiah to come. He will set us free . . . He will lead our people."

The congregation rose and fell in unison. That was the catchall answer. The Messiah would come and our people would reign in power. Until then . . . there was only waiting.

"When will that day arrive?" Rabbi Gur asked. It seemed everyone in the synagogue had a different answer.

I was disappointed and confused. The debate went on and on, so heated at times that a big vein in Rabbi Asa's forehead pulsed like a trapped worm. Fists shook. Sharp words shot through the air as deadly as arrows. Both Jude and Joses rushed to the arms of their mother.

James crawled beneath the bench by Mary. Jesus had moved toward the open door, where it was easier to breathe.

This was the house of prayer. Yet within there was no spirit of peace, no spirit of love. It was dark and frightening to be in the synagogue when women and children were afraid, when grown men— friends, neighbors, even brothers—argued about what it meant to be a Jew. How could such a basic question evoke such violence and wrath within the walls of the holy house of prayer?

My heart felt sick.

I nudged Joseph and motioned that I needed to go outside for air. He stood up to allow me to pass.

Outside the air was damp but warm. I leaned against the trunk of an old olive tree and wondered how long it had stood growing in that same spot. Had the rabbi who planted it been waiting for the Messiah to arrive and set the Jews free? Was that a hundred years ago? Two hundred? A thousand?

I told myself I was free. I could walk away from this contention and never look back. I could return to the lawless life that I had lived as a child in the desert.

I was free to leave, and yet I stayed.

The shouts and fighting grew louder, and I covered my ears like a tormented child. My knees bent and my back slid down against the tree until I was curled into a ball on the ground.

I stayed there for a time, long enough to let the damp of the earth soak the bottom of my robe. My feet were cold. My head ached. Then I sensed I was not alone. I opened my eyes and saw that Jesus had come out of the synagogue, too.

He seated himself on the ground close by me, His legs crossed, His elbows propped on His knees. Like me, He had outgrown such childish poses, yet we were both on the ground, curled up like little boys.

There were no tears in His eyes, yet there was pain.

I could feel it.

Pain and confusion.

In that moment I realized that Jesus and I desired the same thing: to be good Jews. But how could we do that when those in authority couldn't even agree on what it meant to *be* a Jew?

Thirty-four

Joel made the offer in front of Joseph.

"It is an opportunity for you to make your own way." He folded his arms in front of him and his toe rhythmically tapped the hard earth. I had always been intimidated by Joel, but since I had been granted my freedom—and since Deborah had come of age—his favor toward me had grown.

"The lumber will come across the great lake from the forest side. We will harness the oxen and haul the logs to Sepphoris. Your responsibility will be to work alongside my son."

The offer was tempting. Malik and I were no longer foes, and I thought of the promised money. It was more than I could make in months laboring alongside Joseph. It would also permit me to travel. As I grew older, my desire to travel swelled. I longed to see the great desert pyramids again, to smell the black water of the Nile. The days of roaming the land with Father were so distant I sometimes wondered if they had happened at all.

Joseph sighed. There was sawdust in his beard mixed in with crumbs of bread from his midday meal. "Almon, the decision is yours. You are free to choose."

I wanted to go, but more than that, I did not want to leave Joseph if he needed my help.

Joel lowered his arms and gave a grunt. "Don't look so concerned. Joseph and Jesus are coming also."

That made my decision simple, and after a few days of preparation, we were on the road to the Sea of Galilee. It was a pleasant trip, hurried and focused, but I enjoyed being included in a group of men as fine as those who surrounded me.

We passed through the regular villages and saw that the unrest continued. There were still crosses on hills and soldiers on horses who needed no provocation to draw their swords.

"Give no cause for alarm," Joel warned. "Do not look the soldiers in the eyes. If they speak to you, keep your eyes downcast."

But the soldiers were occupied with others, and left us to the business of hauling lumber. I loved everything about the work—mostly the water. The great lake was called the Sea of Galilee because it was so enormous, but it was really a giant lake with water that had the magical ability to change from green to blue.

Villages dotted its scalloped edges. Sand, rocks, and forest decorated its shores. I loved the sights, the smells, the feel of the land. It was easy to draw a deep breath here, to forget the scowls of the rabbis, to bake my skin under the smile of the sun. The birds swooped and dived and called, and I watched Jesus watch them.

He loved anything that was alive. He also loved watching the weather—the gathering clouds, the hues of the sky, the direction of the wind.

We pitched our tents on the rise above the water, beneath the light of a waxing moon, and we roasted fish over a fire. Malik ate until he was full, which was something I had never seen. Joseph told stories, his shadow from the firelight casting itself as big as Goliath.

When the first pink rays of sun sparkled over the water, a band of traders known as "jacks," came by and offered Joel a shipment of massive logs. Joel was expert at bargaining with them, and as I listened to him, I remembered how my father used to bargain in the same manner.

I missed my father. But only for a moment.

Once Joel agreed to a price, we went to the water's edge and waited for the barge to arrive. Jesus seemed as enthralled as I was with the boats of all sizes and shapes that bobbed on the water. Men fished both from the shallow waters of the shore and from the depths of the sea.

Joseph struck up a conversation with a kinsman of his, a fisherman named Zebedee. His skin was weathered, his neck almost black from exposure to the sun. He was kind and outgoing, offering us dippers of stew made from fish, vegetables, and cream. It was so delicious I begged for a second portion.

Malik smiled at me.

Jesus walked the shores with two of Zebedee's sons, John and James, hunting for shells and other sea treasures.

"Look after Him, please." Joseph was at my side. "I will wait here with Joel; you boys go enjoy the water."

How many times had Joseph asked me to look out for Jesus? My eye was already on Him.

Malik stayed behind with his father and Joseph, but I tagged Jesus and His two new friends, also His kinsmen. They were gifted fishermen and showed off their netting skills by casting from a large gray boulder. With the first cast they netted enough fish to feed our family for a week.

The fish went flopping into a tub, and the boys went into the water. James and John dived headfirst; Jesus was a little more tentative. Once He was in the water He seemed overjoyed, shouting and splashing and having more fun than He'd had in years. I found myself wet and laughing, but I held back a little, fearful that Jesus might head into deep water or step into a hole and find Himself in over His head.

I had not been swimming in years and doubted that Jesus even knew how to swim. I didn't need to worry. Malik ran up the shoreline just then to tell us to hurry back because the barge was arriving.

The barge was so laden that water sloshed up the sides, soaking the wood and making it heavier that it already was. The logs were immense, and I doubted that we could ever drag them as far as Sepphoris.

"Show us your strength," Joel said, slapping me on the back.

Malik slapped me good-naturedly as well. "Yes, Almon, show us your strength. You've been building muscle all these years lifting your heavy pens."

He laughed. Inside, I laughed, too.

The plan was to pull, roll, and chain the logs to our wagon. Joel had rented a team of sturdy bulls to tote the load, but I could not guess how they would do it.

It took all of us, even Zebedee and his sons, to shift the first log into place. The second was no easier. Just as we turned to lift the third log, a loud cracking sound made us all whirl around.

"Run!" Joel screamed, and he instinctively yanked Malik out of harm's way.

The log had broken free from the chain and rolled toward us . . . toward Jesus. It came like a massive arrow, newly launched.

I dived to shove Jesus out of the way. So did Joseph.

Zebedee rushed to collar the spooked oxen, his boys on his heels.

"Get out of the way!" Joseph shouted.

Jesus ducked, but not quickly enough. The log hit Him in the shoulder and He fell to the ground with a cracking thud. I threw myself on top of Him and felt my fist hit something hard.

In the same instant, the weight of the wet wood rolled over my back. I felt a sharp pain, a burning in my neck, and then nothing.

I heard Joseph's voice in my ear, but could not understand his words.

When I finally managed to open my eyes, I was laying on my back. The blue sky spread cloudless above me. The light made my head throb.

Where was Jesus?

"Jesus is fine," Malik said, his head eclipsing the sun as he looked down at me. "You're the one who met with death." His laugh was gentle. But why was he laughing?

I sat up. I ached but felt no pain like that of a broken bone. Malik put a strong arm around me and helped me to my feet.

When my vision came into focus I realized I was only a few feet from where I had been when the log had rolled over me. The load was all set, the logs securely chained. Joseph and Joel were ready for the return journey.

They smiled at me as if they held an amusing secret.

Malik offered me the water-skin and I drank, feeling confused and foolish.

Joseph was the one who shattered my moment of pity. He looked at me and broke into a full laugh. "Almon, you moved like a streak of lightning."

Joel grinned. "He meant well."

"Wait until I tell Deborah what a hero her hero is," Malik said.

My face went hot, my ears red. He was teasing me about Deborah, which meant he knew how I felt about his sister and he did not entirely disapprove. And Joel, Deborah's father, was there, which meant . . .

Jesus turned around to thank me for trying to save Him.

My mouth formed a perfect circle.

In trying to save Him, I had caused more damage than the renegade log. Jesus' shoulder was bruised, but it was nothing compared to where my fist had made contact with his eye, now black and blue and swollen to the size of a hen's egg.

Thirty-five

It was to be the grandest pilgrimage the household of Joseph ever made. Jesus was approaching the age of majority. Mary had been blessed with a new baby daughter with healthy lungs and cheeks like rosy apples. The season of Passover was upon us.

Family gathered at the house of Joseph, pouring in like rainwater, filling it to overflowing. The garden was seldom without the laughter of children. James loved to tease the twins, and their squeals could be heard as far away as the village courtyard.

The new baby, named Mary after her mother, slept most of the time. When she wasn't in Mary's arms, Deborah was nearby to rock the baby and to sing psalms.

Anna and Joachim had become permanent residents, Joachim's memory fading faster than anyone wanted to admit. He and Rabbi Asa had become close friends and Joachim spent much of his time at the synagogue, reading the same scrolls over and over.

Joel's lumber business had never known such prosperity. Since our trek to the shores of Galilee, it had grown as fast as summer corn. Malik traveled with his father to purchase the finest, rarest types of woods. They were gone for long stretches of time, leaving Naomi and Deborah free to visit the household of Joseph.

Legally, both Deborah and I had arrived at marriageable age. But neither of us was of marriageable character. I was a free man, but without a home or a skill to offer a bride. And I was mute. What wife would want a husband who could not speak her name aloud?

Deborah was never seen without her veil, and as far as I could discover, she had no suitors. What horrible deformity could cause a girl with a spirit as bright as hers to hide beneath a sheath of perpetual darkness?

The man who won her heart would win a great prize. Only in the private scrolls I kept hidden beneath the floor of my sleeping chambers did I dare to dream that I might be that man.

Joel had taken a liking to me and was generous in the work he sent my way and in the wage he paid. To think that he would ever accept me as a son-in-law was a dream too fragile to share, so I kept it as hidden as Deborah kept her face.

When Malik realized that I had a tender heart for his sister, he whispered to me, "The priest told my parents to put Deborah out on the night she was born."

"Putting out" meant leaving a newborn infant out in the cold night air, out where wolves and jackals roamed. It was what was done to newborns with harelips or who were otherwise misshapen, because most people believed God frowned on the imperfect. Most believed that such infants were cursed because of sin.

I shuddered to think that someone as loving and gifted as Deborah was ever considered for such a terrible fate.

Because Mary and Joseph were so generous with me, providing my shelter, food, and clothing, I was able to save much of the wage I earned. What I didn't spend on writing supplies, I put into a small leather bag I kept stored with my private scrolls. Each month the bag grew heavier and my heart grew lighter, daring to believe that I might have something to offer for the hand of Deborah.

It would take years.

I had years to wait.

I loved to help Joseph whenever I could, and I still did the same chores around the house and yard, but the coins came most quickly when I worked for Joel. The wage he paid me was more than double the amount Joseph could afford. Because I had a head for figures, Joel not only had me lift and tote the lumber, he had me keep inventory and make an accurate record of his business dealings.

Joseph was a dedicated, skilled carpenter, but he did not have the desire for money that his brother did. Joseph found great pleasure in his *work,* not in his *wage.* Mostly, Joseph was a dedicated, skilled father. Now that James and the twins were able to come to the shop with him, it was a busier hub than ever. And it was my duty to watch over not only Jesus, but his younger brothers as well.

As the household of Joseph prepared to leave Nazareth for about a month—the time it would take to make the pilgrimage to the Holy City—there was never a quiet or calm moment.

Cousins I had seen only a few times arrived with their pack animals and families. The sound of children playing and babies crying was constant.

It gave me a happy sense of belonging. I never forgot that I was not a member of Joseph and Mary's family—but I was a member of their household, and that was enough.

Joseph estimated the journey would take ten days, traveling in such a large caravan. Boaz was too old and crippled to make the journey, so he was left behind in the care of Dan, who was also old and crippled.

Our caravan included several other donkeys, two camels, and Joachim's horse, still a grand, high-stepping animal. There were brothers and sisters, aunts, uncles, cousins, friends, and servants. We made a great show, and those who were not also making the pilgrimage came to bid us farewell, promising to keep things safe while we were gone.

Joseph offered a mighty prayer for our safe journey and then made a familiar request of me. "Watch Jesus, Almon. He has grown so in these past months. My son is no longer a child."

And not yet a man, I thought. I knew that span, that limbo, and how difficult it was to find a proper place. I was always happy to keep watch over Jesus.

The women sang to help break up the monotony of the trip; some of the men even joined in. Joachim sat atop his saddle, his head tipped back, his mouth open, singing louder than anyone—and completely out of tune.

Jesus charmed everyone, especially the children, with His larger-than-life tales of the prophets—Elijah and the priests of Baal, Joseph and his dreams, the three friends of Daniel in the fiery furnace. It was obvious that He had learned Joseph's elaborate style of storytelling.

Anna looked at Jesus with pride and a love so powerful it made my heart swell. Mary looked at her mother with a different kind of love, but just as powerful.

As we approached Samaria, Jesus moved to the front of the caravan. He asked why we could not pass through the land.

Malik snorted. "Cousin, you know it is inhabited by infidels."

"That is correct, son," Joseph agreed. "The people of Samaria are despised because of their idol worship. Their blood has been tainted."

Jesus was clearly disappointed.

"Samaria is the land where Jacob's well burps living water," Deborah said, walking in the same group as I was. She took care not to walk too close to me because it would not be proper—and Deborah was always proper. "I would like to drink from it someday."

Malik nodded his head and put his long walking stick forward. "Someday when our people take Samaria away from the unfaithful, then you can taste of Jacob's water."

We were not the only pilgrims headed to Jerusalem. The villages were emptying themselves of inhabitants. The roads were so crowded we were forced to move in single file. Dung and dust littered our way, left by the caravans in front of us.

Jesus did not seem bothered. He was focused on the green grass, the budding trees, the flowers of spring. The top of every tree was home to some kind of bird.

Joseph was right. Jesus was no longer a child. His head already reached His father's shoulders, and His arms bulged with muscles hard-earned by helping both His father and His uncle. His face was still the face of a boy—His skin soft, His eyes intense.

He was very protective of His younger brothers and almost always had one by the hand or atop His shoulders. He loved His little sister, too, and could make her smile when no one else could.

Jesus loved solitude, and I learned how to shadow Him without imposing on His privacy. He sought opportunity to walk alone, to wander among the vines and trees, to pace the shores, and to sit by the river's edge.

Those moments seemed somehow sacred to me. I kept my distance and was glad I could offer only silence.

The first night we camped early in the evening, giving the men time to pitch tents and the women time to prepare food. I worked alongside Jesus and Malik as they set the stakes and hoisted the giant canopy under which the group would gather to eat and tell stories late into the night.

It was tiresome work, and the sun was still hot. When we were finished I sat on the patchy grass and closed my eyes, exhausted. I am not certain whether I fell completely asleep, but when I opened my eyes, Jesus was gone.

Deborah and her cousins were playing a stick-toss game with the children. Malik was by the fire trying to sneak the first bread off the coals. Joseph and Joel and the other men were still putting up the smaller tents.

Jesus was nowhere to be seen.

I went first to the stream at the bottom of the knoll. Other pilgrims were there gathering water but there was no sign of Jesus. Next I wandered through camp, making sure He wasn't hidden behind a canvas. I checked near the animals.

Panic rose in me as sure as fever.

We were camped on a large span of meadow that dipped and rose like small hills. The wild grass was thick and green. The sky was still blue, though the sun would soon set for the night. Other caravans were setting up camps all around us.

I squinted and tried to imagine where Jesus could be. His brothers were all accounted for. So were His parents. I saw no other person missing from our group.

My heart pounded and I felt sweat bead at the back of my neck.

It wasn't the first time Jesus had disappeared. He was always wandering off, which is exactly why Joseph counted on me to keep Him safe.

Should I tell Joseph now, or should I keep looking for Jesus?

Naomi sounded a small gong, alerting everyone that the meal was ready. I had gone to the water again, frantically looking for Jesus. On the way to the river, I had woven through camp. Jesus was not among us.

My mind was overcome with dark thoughts. There were slave traders along this route, men who would have snatched a lone young boy and taken off, never to be seen again. There were grass snakes that could kill with a sudden strike. I didn't think the stream was deep enough to drown in, but I had not actually crossed it.

I felt so guilty, so worried, that I had no other choice but to tell Joseph so the entire camp could begin a proper search. If I let the darkness of night fall before asking for help, there was no telling what might happen.

Everyone was gathered at the main canopy for prayer. I looked across and saw Joseph smile, broad and bright. "There you are," he said.

I thought he spoke to me, but when I turned around, I saw Jesus walking up behind me.

My whole body went limp with relief.

I gazed at the land behind Him; it was flat and grassy. Jesus appeared to have come out of nowhere.

I looked at Him and my eyes asked, *Where have you been?*

He smiled at Joseph and then at me. Joses and Jude broke lose from the other children and came at Jesus like two starved sheepdogs. He grabbed a brother with each arm and swung them high and low, high and low, their cries of delight rising above the clinking of pots.

All I could do was give silent thanks that Jesus was safe and vow to myself that I would never let Him out of my sight again.

It was a vow I failed to keep.

Thirty-six

By the time we entered the Holy City, our caravan had tripled in size. Along the way, we added neighbors from Nazareth, more relatives, and even business acquaintances of Joel and Joseph. They all had animals and children, and soon we were a village unto ourselves.

The narrow streets were packed and sullied, forcing us to travel in one long, winding rope. It was impossible to see the front of our assembly from the back—even more impossible to communicate, because even the deepest voices were drowned in the uproar of so many people and animals.

I remembered Jerusalem as the city of white gold. But now there were too many pilgrims and too much filth. It was impossible to see, to hear, or to appreciate the true beauty that lay beneath it all. The Holy City had been built and rebuilt, layer upon layer. The top layer was now one of dirt and refuse.

The faces of Jesus and Joseph mirrored the same disgust and disappointment I felt. There was little holy about a place so crowded, so loud, and so dirty.

As always, there were soldiers; more of them were Herod's men than were the empire's soldiers. I had heard our men talking of how Rome desired to honor the Jews and their traditions, and they vowed to stay out of the way. In contrast, the brothers Herod felt it their blood right to interfere, to intimidate, to impose their presence. And they did, harassing pilgrims with questions and accusations, knocking people to the ground, shouting, laughing, making a mockery of something as sacred as the high season.

"We are here to honor our Lord," Joseph told us when we paused to leave our animals just outside the gates. "Do not be distracted from that purpose."

And so we pushed and shoved our way toward the Temple Mount. Twice, Jesus stopped to help someone who had fallen. Joseph halted more than that to push a coin into the outstretched palm of a beggar.

When we reached the baths, we separated, the women apart from the men.

The water was cold and the bath crowded. Jesus held on to His grandfather, fearful the old man would stumble and find himself trampled. I did not take my eyes from Jesus. If He wandered off in this crowd, there would be no getting Him back.

We exchanged our dusty traveling robes for the clean ones we had brought. Clean and dressed in fresh robes, we emerged into utter chaos.

The noise alone made me press my hands over my ears. The smell was ripe and sour at the same time.

I had seen hawkers before, eager and edgy, but this was different.

This was the season of Passover, and more than two hundred thousand lambs were being sold for sacrifice. Sellers swore that every lamb was unblemished and unbroken; every hawker had the best and the finest. The prices they demanded were exorbitant.

Though Joel could afford their prices, he growled and grumbled. He seemed agitated, almost angry.

Jesus seemed sad.

Joseph bought a lamb, white and terrified. Its legs were bent beneath it and bound so it would not break away. Joseph carried it securely in the crook of his arm, turning back to Jesus, Malik, and me.

"We are here to honor our Lord. Do not be distracted," he said again, offering us a giant, reassuring smile.

I was glad for Joseph. Before, he could only afford doves. Today he offered the finest lamb he could purchase. Joel also bought a lamb, though he did not smile about it.

I was a little surprised when Malik bought a pair of pigeons for a sin offering. I had no right to question why, but I did think back to how he once taunted me, telling me that I was mute because I was a sinner.

I had money in my pouch. I could make the same purchase as Malik, but I did not believe such a sacrifice would wash away my sins any more than it would loose my tongue. I would always be a mute; I would always be a sinner. I was resigned to those facts, and determined that the sins of my childhood would never be known to anyone in the household of Joseph. Never.

We proceeded to the altar and found that parts of the temple were still under construction. Amid all the chaos, masons were still laying stone, carpenters were still working on the gates and doors. Slaves, practically naked and baked to the color of the rich Nile silt, ignored the crush of pilgrims and kept working, no doubt because there was always an overseer with a ready whip in hand.

Jesus asked about His cousin John. Would he be joining us?

Joseph shrugged his shoulders. "Your cousin is kept safe in the hill country—*preparing*. He will appear in good time, but not here and not now."

Jesus touched the bleating lamb in Joseph's arms. He rubbed one of its floppy pink ears, and the animal calmed itself immediately. Jesus walked next to Joseph as they often did, talking only to each other. I stayed back, careful to keep a respectful distance, but also careful to not become separated in the crush.

I had not thought of John or Elisabeth in so long. John would be taller and broader than Jesus by now. Elisabeth would be . . . I did not want to think of her fate. She had been so old then. She would be far advanced in years now, if . . . .

Before us, lined up as steady as were the sacrificial animals, we saw the beggars, the lame, the blind, the diseased. This was the season of almsgiving, and Joseph was generous with his hard-earned coins.

We passed the money changers and I thought of Father. I could no longer remember his face or the sound of his name.

Blood that had not been caught in basins at the holy altar ran down the hill to the streets below the temple, draining into the gutters and staining the white stones of Temple Mount. Slaves were assigned to clean up the gore, but the blood was too much for a thousand slaves, even ten thousand slaves, to make vanish. My own hems and sandals were splattered with the dark splotches of death, and I realized that the beat of my heart despised everything around me. In that moment, a new wave of guilt washed over me. This was a time of celebration, of family, of sacrifice. This was a time of great gathering, a coming together of our people in one place to honor the one true God.

What was wrong with me?

This was Passover, the season when the holy men put on their finest clothing, brushed and trimmed their beards, and calculated their greatest earnings. For every sacrifice a priest made, he was granted his share.

This was the season when scribes recorded the happenings, writing on behalf of those unlettered and unable to pay the usual fees. I tried to imagine myself among the holy writers. Though the idea of being surrounded by the sacred scrolls, by all of the finest papers and writing instruments the world had to offer, was enticing, I could not picture myself *belonging*.

Word came to us men that Mary had fallen ill and had been taken to Bethany by Naomi and Anna. Joseph was alarmed at first, but assured us that Mary had just been overcome by the crowd. We would meet her and the others later at the house Joachim had rented, the place where we would roast our sacrificial lambs and embark on our seder feast.

I did not feel well myself. The sights, the sounds, the smells—all of it made my head ache and my stomach burn. Standing beneath the blistering sun, we had to wait for hours holding the bound and bleating animals in our arms, waiting for our turn at the altar. By then the aprons of the priests dripped with blood, and the scent that rose thick in the air was a scent no amount of incense could erase.

I could taste the smell on my tongue, feel it on the backs of my hands.

Jesus was drawn to the courtyard of the temple where the noblest teachers sat expounding the Torah and other holy writ. I followed Him carefully and watched as He listened to their lessons. It was almost impossible to hear because people were talking, some shouting; animals were dying; and below, the hawkers were still selling their goods and the money changers were still weighing their profits.

By the time our sacrifices had been made, by the time we managed to wend our way out of the Holy City, the sight of Bethany was most welcome. It was a quaint village not far from Jerusalem, but was humble and peaceful in comparison.

Joseph went to Mary, concerned for her health.

"It was all just too much," she said. "I feel well enough now."

The chamber was already prepared, the grill hot to roast the Paschal Lamb. The great tables were set, the bitter herbs and unleavened bread ready. I had celebrated Passover with Mary and Joseph before, but this was different. It was grander and much more elaborate.

Our songs and recitations used the same words, but to me, they carried more power. Joachim was given the place of honor as the eldest patriarch. Joseph read from the Haggadah. The prayers had never seemed so potent.

I felt the devotion of Moses, Aaron, and Miriam.

I felt the stubbornness of Pharaoh and understood how he doomed his own people.

I felt the power of God's hand over the Jews—those who would obey Him.

More than ever, I wanted to obey Him, and I silently vowed my allegiance anew. I would honor God. I would become whatever He wanted me to be. If that was a scribe, then that would be a dream realized. If it was something lesser, I was willing.

I felt chilled and lay down outside by the fire, wrapped in a blanket Mary had given me years earlier. My head ached, and I closed my eyes.

"Almon?"

I opened my eyes to see the silhouette of Mary. Stars danced behind her head against the blackest sky.

I tried to sit up but felt a pain in my stomach.

"You are shivering; I fear you have fallen ill."

No, I thought, *you were the one who felt ill. I am fine.* But I wasn't fine. She held a cup out to me.

"Drink this. I have boiled mustard leaves. It will ease your discomfort."

I drank the bitter liquid, but it did not stay down. I spent most of the night in the bushes, so sick I didn't even know when the sun rose or when we broke camp to make the return journey to Nazareth.

Joseph lifted me up on one of the pack donkeys and allowed me to ride. It was something I hadn't done since I was a little boy, too young to walk across the desert with my father.

I thought of old Boaz, and then I thought of nothing else.

My fever finally broke and I was able to walk beside the donkey. Only then did I realize that Deborah was walking beside me. Malik was just behind her.

"I am glad to see you have returned from the land of the dead," Malik laughed, poking his sister with the tip of his walking stick.

She turned toward him and frowned.

"You still look like a corpse," Malik said, "but you smell better." He laughed again.

I was horrified. Deborah had seen me sick . . . had smelled me.

My ears felt like they were on fire . . . my embarrassment was that hot.

Deborah kept her head bowed, but said to me, "I am glad your strength has returned."

I wiped my mouth and tried to smile my appreciation.

"Would you care for a piece of fruit or a cup of broth?"

I shook my head.

I didn't know how long I had been ill or how long we had been traveling. I only knew that my legs felt broken and my mouth tasted like curdled milk. I paused to grab a handful of mint growing along a stream. I chewed it and spit, then chewed some more and spit again. I drank from the stream, washed my hands and face, and let the cool water shock me into the present.

Deborah paused when I paused. She kept her distance, but stayed near me. I was glad for her closeness and longed for the trek to take ten years instead of ten days.

Then I heard the voice of Joseph, and I knew immediately something was wrong. I couldn't see him, but I could hear him. Finally, he broke through the people and the animals and ran toward me.

"Almon! Almon!"

My eyes went wide. *What is wrong?*

He took me by the shoulders. His hands shook and his eyes reflected absolute terror. Sweat dampened his hair.

What? What is so wrong?

Joseph drew a shallow, ragged breath and then asked the question that took the air from my own lungs. "Where is Jesus?"

Thirty-seven

No one seemed to know the time or place where Jesus disappeared. He was there for the feast, they were certain of that. But following the feast . . . well, they couldn't be sure.

I was certain of one thing: Jesus' disappearance was my fault. I had fallen ill and had neglected Him completely. Even when I recovered, I looked to Deborah instead of Jesus.

Joseph borrowed Joachim's horse and rode to the front of the caravan, stopping it to inquire and search. No one could provide the answers he sought.

An intense search party was formed. Everyone took part, buzzing like angry bees, searching everywhere, asking passing pilgrims, doing whatever they could to locate the lost boy.

Malik's jaw was set. "Jesus has *enemies*."

"What do you mean?" Deborah asked her brother. "No one is kinder than Jesus."

Malik's small, dark eyes shot me a look that said more than words. "Jesus knows too much. He says things that offend people."

Deborah stood between us, so close her arm brushed mine. "What kind of things? You're frightening me, Malik."

"He believes He knows enough to correct the priests. You've heard Him, Almon. Jesus knows things no boy His age should know."

"I still don't understand. What are you talking about?" Deborah's lip quivered.

Voices around us called out the name of Jesus, making it sound like an echo that would not be silenced. How I wished I could have lifted my voice to call His name, but there was no sound on my tongue. There was no reply from Jesus.

Malik took his sister's elbow. "Jesus reads the scriptures and interprets more than they say. I heard Him tell the Pharisee Ovadya that Judaism is perverted."

Deborah pulled away. "No, He didn't!"

Malik shook his head. "Forget I said a word about it. But don't be surprised if Jesus has been taken by someone in authority, someone He has angered."

Cold fingers of fear clutched the back of my neck. Deborah didn't understand. How could she? But I had been there when Jesus had angered the priests, the rabbis—yes, even the Pharisees. I knew He hadn't set out for that purpose. It was His understanding of the laws and the prophets. He knew more than the authorities, and that incensed them.

The Holy City and all the streets had swarmed with those in authority. If one of them had taken Jesus, what might they have done? I remembered seeing Him at the temple courtyard. Perhaps He had spoken out of turn or challenged their thinking the way He was prone to do.

Why hadn't I paid closer attention to Jesus?

Mary made her way through the swarms of people. Her face was gray with worry and grief. "Oh Almon, you will find my son." It wasn't a question, but it wasn't confident enough to be a statement. "I know He speaks like a man, but He is still very much a boy."

Joseph rode up rapidly and reigned the horse hard. "We must turn back," he said.

"Yes, husband. We must do so with haste."

Deborah was there to take the baby girl from Mary's arms. "Do not worry, aunt. I will watch over your baby until you return with Jesus." She smiled and my heart swelled with a warm feeling for Deborah. She had great faith and compassion. She reminded me of Mary.

Mary kissed the baby and then kissed the cheeks of Deborah. She hiked her robes and turned back toward the Holy City. "Come," she said, pointing at me. "We *will* find Jesus."

But we didn't find Jesus. We searched the road, stopped other pilgrims, asked everyone who passed. We searched the hills and the streams. I thought back to our journey here—of how He had disappeared and then suddenly reappeared.

I hoped that He had already rejoined the caravan. If that happened, Malik promised to locate us quickly. He had kept Joachim's horse, because if Joseph rode into Jerusalem on a horse, it could be interpreted as a sign of insurrection.

Not having the horse was actually better for us, Joseph claimed. He believed we could conduct a more thorough search on foot.

By the time we reached the city gates it was night, and our only vision was illuminated by the flame of torchlight. The inns were shuttered and barred. Homes were closed tight against the threat of robbers.

"State your business." It was a soldier, a Roman on horseback, blocking our way. In the flicker of the burning light I could see the hair on his arm, thick and black as that of a ram.

"We have come in search of our lost son, Jesus."

The statement stabbed my heart, sure as a dagger.

"You are Jews?"

"We are."

"Your son is young?"

"He has twelve years. Please, sir, allow us passage. I believe Jesus to be somewhere within the city." Joseph seemed to shrink; his shoulders sagged, and his head bowed in desperation.

The man laughed. "How can you be certain your son has not run away from the cruelty he faces at home?"

I went to Mary. Joseph held her to him, but I could see her tremble beneath her shawl.

We waited in taut silence. My own heart pounded in my throat.

The man spit at Joseph's feet. "Go on. Be about your business," he said, backing his horse away so we could enter.

Joseph stopped within a few yards and led us to the shadows of the first archway. There was no torch there—only blackness—and I could not see the expression on Joseph's face as he spoke. "Almon, search the stockyards. Search the alleys. Be careful for your own safety, but find Jesus."

I raised and lowered my chin, telling him I would. I would, no matter the cost. I turned to leave, but Joseph's voice called me back.

"When He is located, bring Jesus back here and wait. Mary and I will check this spot regularly."

I did not slow, but kept my feet flying as I began my search. The stockyards were all but empty; the lambs that had not been purchased for Passover would be taken back to the fields. Some would be held here for other sacrificial rites. The filth of two hundred thousand Paschal Lambs was thick and ugly.

I passed by cleaning crews, slaves with brooms and buckets. I could not ask them questions and I could not explain myself. I simply ran through the yards, up and down the stone streets. I slipped a few times, and I could feel the skin peel from my knees.

I thought back to the day I first met Jesus. He had been just a toddler. He had fallen and scraped His knees and gone to His mother's arms for balm. If He was hurt now, bleeding or afraid, who would comfort Him?

I searched the whole of the night. At dawn I went to our meeting place to tell Mary and Joseph that I had failed. How I longed to see them there with Jesus! But before I reached them, I could see that they had been no more fortunate than I.

"We went to Temple Mount," Joseph said. "I was certain that's where we would find Him."

Mary said nothing, but I had the impression that she had been crying.

I knew that Joel and his family—and others, too—would have joined us if they had suspected we would not find Jesus quickly.

I bowed my head with Mary and Joseph in supplication, but that did not give my heart hope.

As the sun rose, the city came alive. I went searching one way; Mary and Joseph went in the opposite direction.

A few times I thought I saw Jesus, but it always turned out to be a stranger. Whenever I returned to the archway, there was no sign of Mary and Joseph. That could only mean they were also unsuccessful.

I shared Joseph's suspicion. Jesus would be drawn to the temple, but He was not there. There was no indication that He had been there since the day of Passover, which now seemed so long ago.

A Pharisee I approached mistook me to be a beggar, and turned away with a scowl. A rabbi offered me a coin that I refused.

A man with fingernails so long they curled like a ram's horn called out to me. I paused before him and saw that his eyes were milked over.

"I am a prophet," he said. "I can answer your question. Ask anything."

My silence perplexed him.

"Ask anything and I will provide you a truthful answer . . . for the price of a coin."

What I wouldn't have given for the vision of a true prophet, someone who could point the way to Jesus.

By the second unfruitful night I was more weary than I had ever felt. My back ached. My feet were blistered and bloody. When I went to the archway I found only Joseph.

"I have taken Mary to Bethany. She waits there, regaining her strength and praying."

He offered me a slice of melon. I ate it, feeling unworthy. I drank from his water-skin and followed him outside the city where we camped by a ditch dug deep for irrigation. There was a familiarity about the place. Then I remembered I had hidden here once with Father, escaping from one of my would-be masters.

"Almon," Joseph's voice cut through the darkness. "I cannot rest. I must find my son."

We walked to Bethany, stopping as Joseph asked every stranger we encountered if they had seen a boy matching the description of Jesus.

Mary waited at the front door, ready to continue the search. She looked as old as Anna, and I hated myself for what I had brought upon her.

"Joel came by while you were gone," she told Joseph. "No one in our caravan has seen Jesus since we left the Holy City. There is simply no sign of him."

"Where is my brother now?" Joseph asked, the exhaustion etched on his face.

"He has returned to the caravan, hoping to bring more searchers."

"He is a good brother."

We left the house and walked back toward the Holy City. Mary and Joseph did not blame me, and yet I knew I was to blame.

It was a chilly night. I wrapped myself in a blanket I kept in my pack. I wondered what wrap was keeping Jesus warm.

Please God, He is Your Son. Keep watch over Jesus.

Just outside the city gate Mary collapsed. Her legs would no longer hold her frailty.

"Have you fasted this entire time?" Joseph asked her, dripping water on her cheeks from the tips of his fingers. Her head was in his lap; his lips were pressed to her forehead.

"I will fast until Jesus is found."

"As will I," said Joseph.

The lingering taste of melon was sour in my mouth. I had eaten. I had drunk. I was still concerned more for myself than for Jesus.

We waited there until Mary was strong enough to stand. Then we made our way, passing more traders than pilgrims now that Passover was finished.

The day arrived with an eager sun. It was scorching by the time the first bread was baked. Mary appeared withered and worn. I didn't know how she would face another full day.

Joseph looked at me with pleading in his eyes. "Almon, you go around the gates. Leave no corner unsearched. We must find Jesus today."

I did as he told me. I searched the outskirts of the temple. It was a path I had already taken. I walked slowly, being certain that my eyes did not miss anything. I was looking for a boy wearing the same camel-colored robes that Jesus had worn. But what if He had been taken? His robes might have changed. His hair might be cut. He might be naked and chained, halfway to Egypt by now.

I felt sick and vomited, though there was nothing but bile to heave.

Next, I searched the shops of the city. I made my way up and down the rows of money changers. I passed hawker after hawker.

Life in the city continued as it always did. Yet my life without Jesus was wrong, incomplete, miserable.

I heard a voice I thought I knew, and I turned toward it. For a fraction of a second, I saw a man familiar. It was Father! My wobbly legs rushed to him and I held out my arms for his embrace, but when the man turned, he was not my father.

He was Joseph.

I fell back, embarrassed and shocked.

"I will not leave," he told me. "I will not leave Jerusalem until Jesus is found."

I looked around him, but Mary was not in sight.

"I left Mary at the common well. There she inquires of the other mothers if there has been a sign of Jesus."

I nodded and indicated that I wished to make another round. I had to leave the company of Joseph. My heart could not stand the sight of his sorrow.

It was not yet night, but I was unable to keep my eyes open. I went to the archway and waited. A soldier came by and prodded me with his sheath.

"Leave, beggar."

I could not explain myself and turned to leave.

"Almon."

It was Mary, and I knew instantly from the relief on her face that Jesus has been found. At that moment I saw Him, coming up behind her with Joseph's arm around His shoulder.

"He was teaching at the temple," Joseph said. "He has been there the three days' time, but we did not locate Him until now."

Jesus said nothing. His face was impossible to read, and I asked no questions. I just fell in step and walked behind them.

We stayed at the house in Bethany where Joseph and Mary were always welcome. There was much rejoicing over the return of Jesus. A feast was laid and I ate, but only a few bites. I was simply too exhausted.

As I fell asleep, Joseph came to me. "Almon, I must beg your forgiveness. It was not fair or right of me to expect you to watch over Jesus. He is my son."

I sat up. *No! I failed you. I wanted to watch over Jesus, and I swore by all that is holy that I would never leave Him alone again.*

"Mary and I have spoken. We have decided it is time for you to begin a life of your own. You are free, but our desire for you is to receive the education of a true scribe. Soon, if you are willing, you will return to the Holy City to begin the years of study that will lead you to realize your fondest dream."

Thirty-eight

My dream shifted like the desert sand.

It buried me, and soon I was bound like a lamb to the altar.

Even now as I retell my story, the years of my temple training drift together and the very memory becomes a blurry sandstorm.

No one in the household of Joseph blamed me for those three days of torture when Jesus was lost, but I blamed myself. I believed that had I not forsaken Jesus, I would be made welcome to stay with the family in Nazareth—indefinitely.

That was not to be.

There was still money left from Nathan's generous gift on my behalf, enough money to give the temple priests and scribes for my care and training.

"We will miss you," Mary said, offering a bundle filled with her best sweet cakes and breads. "There will always be a place for you in our hearts."

"And in our home," Joseph said. He stood outside the courtyard gate, his arms folded across his chest. His eyes were dry, but filled with sadness. "Almon, you are as a son to me, and I am very proud of all that you have learned—of all that you will yet learn."

Jesus came to me and embraced me with the arms of a brother. "Fear not," He whispered.

The younger boys shed tears. Baby Mary slept through my farewell.

Joel had lumber business to conduct just beyond Jerusalem, so he was chosen to take me back to the Holy City, to pay my fees, and to present me at the temple.

The days leading up to my departure were not wasted. I spent them shadowing Jesus. He was more studious, more serious than ever. I spent as much time around Deborah as I could.

"I will study more diligently," she promised, "I will learn my letters well. You and I will be able to communicate with little effort."

I presented her with a tiny scroll on which I'd written the desires of my heart. It was for her eyes only, and I prayed that no one would discover it and mock me for my sentiment.

I did not take Deborah in my arms, not even when we found ourselves alone in the courtyard or the vineyard. I wanted to embrace her, to hold her and never release her. I wanted to put my mouth on hers and kiss her.

I didn't, but how I longed to.

Instead, I presented her with the scroll, smiled, and turned away.

I did not know if I would ever lay eyes on her beauty and kindness again.

A skilled scribe would never be without funds. His talents were always in demand, and perhaps one day I would return to Nazareth to claim Deborah's hand.

No, I told myself, that was a dream that was not to be. It was as hopeless as the dream of my boyhood: that Father would rise from the desert sand and return a changed man.

Dreams came to nothing. And yet it was a dream of mine to become a scribe, and here I was about to embark on that very journey.

I was going away for years.

Deborah was already fourteen and would surely be married with a child or two by the time I made it back to the little hillside village I thought of as my home.

The last words I heard her speak were the exact words Joseph spoke to me: "Go in peace."

I went.

And peace did come to me.

As I traveled with Joel—not Malik, who had stayed behind to build a home of his own for a girl who had become his betrothed—I learned something of myself and a great deal about Deborah.

"You are fond of my daughter," Joel said.

I kept my eyes focused on the sand.

"I have seen it in the way you look at her, but you would not look upon her with such fondness if you could see through her veil. The left side of her face is soft. It falls in. No man would want her for a wife. No man would want her for the mother of his children."

I wanted her! It mattered not to me what Deborah looked like beneath her veil. To me she was beautiful. How could I make Joel understand that?

"The priest wanted me to put her out."

I nodded, indicating that I already knew.

"I thank God every day that His power stayed my hand. Deborah has become a great joy to me and a great comfort to her mother."

For days after speaking of Deborah, Joel said nothing more of her. We walked at a steady pace, mostly in silence. One day, without any warning, he turned to me and said, "Almon, if you wish to marry Deborah, make your intentions known."

I bobbed my head like a fool.

A look of relief washed over Joel and he smiled. "Thank you."

That was it.

He did not bring up his daughter's name again. He just seemed happy, and he offered me the wine-skin.

Life within the temple walls was not a lot different from life inside the synagogue. But the temple was more elaborate, more beautiful than anything I had ever seen. The tapestries were intricate and colorful. The delicate embroidery made me think of Mary with her sewing needle. The walls were lined with polished cedar that made me think of Joseph every time I saw their grain or smelled their perfume.

I missed my family.

I missed my home.

And yet here I was surrounded by more words than I could ever read. The scrolls were endless, and I spent every minute I could in the library.

The priests were kind to me—most of them were, anyway—and patient with my muteness. They seemed impressed that I knew as much as I did of ancient scripture and writing.

One Pharisee, a man named Bart, took me on as his cause. He reminded me very much of Nathan, and I was grateful for his attention.

"It pains my heart that you cannot aspire to be a rabbi," he said.

I looked at him with uncertainty.

The old man touched his white beard. "It is forbidden that one with an impairment . . . a missing limb . . . in your case, a missing voice . . . can become a rabbi. I am sorry, but that is the law."

I did not feel sorry. I wanted to become a scribe, and I was grateful that my impairment did not hinder that goal.

And so I wrote.

I wrote on parchment and carved on slate.

I learned something new every day, mostly about laws that were impossible to keep. I loved my work. I loved learning. But I did not love the life.

I hated the fact that I lived in fear. Would today be the day I made a mistake and got expelled? Why were the leaders so quick to judge and punish? They seemed holy, but they did not seem godlike.

To me, God should be loving and kind, merciful. Most of the men who taught me possessed none of those characteristics. They were arrogant. Arguments rose up like smoke, choking out any sense of peace. They were tightfisted; so much of their lives revolved around money. They were jealous, seeking cause to take offense when it was clear to me that no offense was intended.

My time was spent with lessons, studies, and practice.

I learned to observe all the holy days and rituals of a devout Jew. I missed Joseph and how we lived the Jewish way without making such an effort and such a show. With him, I'd been taught to pray in secret. Here, we were taught to pray where we could be heard.

Whenever one of the Pharisees made a donation to the poor, he came to me to have it recorded. When Joseph gave alms, he never spoke a word of his own goodness.

I missed Mary's cooking. I missed her voice.

I missed the children. At night I woke wondering where Jesus was—if He was all right. It was no longer my place to look after Him, and it was impossible to do so, but I still felt a cord binding me to Him. I wondered what all this time had done to change Him.

After I had been training nearly a year, the household of Joseph returned to the Holy City for Passover. I was summoned to join them at the home in Bethany.

I ran all the way there.

The family greeted me with loud shouts and already prepared food. I was thrilled to see that Mary had a new baby, a boy named Simeon. His cheeks were fat and his legs even fatter. He laughed when I touched his toes.

The twins hardly remembered me and backed away in shyness.

Baby Mary didn't know me at all, and she toddled toward a chirping cricket.

James was tall and strong. He shook my hand, and the power in his grip surprised me.

Jesus was the one who surprised me most. He was nearly as tall as Joseph, and His face had changed. His nose was wider, His eyes deeper. His shoulders were broad, and I could tell that He had been working hard, lifting much.

He greeted me with the same embrace He'd left me with—the hold of a brother.

It was then that I realized how much I had missed everyone. My heart was torn; I rejoiced in their presence but sorrowed because our reunion was only temporary.

Joseph seemed unchanged. He held me and kissed both of my cheeks. "I am told you are doing so well that the temple is making money from your skills."

I could not help but smile. It was true. The Pharisees were hiring out my skills to those who wanted to record an event or an experience. I wrote logs and letters and kept journal entries for those who did not have writing skills but who did have money.

My mind swam with questions for the family, and I wrote them down on the same old wax tablet I had used for years. Where was Joel and his family? Joachim and Anna? Joseph had come in a very small caravan. Why?

"Deborah has fallen ill, as has much of Nazareth," Joseph told me. "They were not well enough to make the trip."

My heart stopped beating at the thought of Deborah stricken. Years ago, a rage of river fever had gone through Nazareth. Many people had died. Jesus had even succumbed to its clutches and we had all feared because the illness had left Him so weak for so long.

I felt worry creep up my spine.

"Do not fret," Joseph said, reading my mind as he was so apt to do. "Your Deborah will be fine."

My Deborah.

"She sends her best to you."

By the time the household of Joseph returned to Nazareth, I felt stronger and happier than I had. They left me with a determination to be the best scribe in Jerusalem, and the faintest hope that one day I would return to Nazareth to set up the household of Almon.

Thirty-nine

Time grew as sure as the vine. It twisted and stretched, yielded and went dormant, only to shoot forth tender new leaves. There were spans in the temple when I was never alone, and yet I had never felt so alone. There were other times when I was so full of gratitude that I forgot to count the days . . . the months . . . and, finally, the years.

My body changed. My mind changed. My life changed.

I became an official scribe, learned in the letters of the Jews and the Egyptians. I learned a level of Latin that impressed even the great Pharisees. With little effort, I was able to translate Aramaic into Hebrew, Hebrew into Greek, and Greek into Aramaic.

The law and the prophets and the writings were engraved upon my heart.

My coin purse was full.

Finally, I had earned my dream.

A Jewish man of my stature was obligated to marry by the time he was thirty. I was ready to marry Deborah, a woman now considered by age to be a permanent maid. I knew better. She had proven faithful, and over the years we had exchanged letters—six, to be exact. I had every word memorized.

Though we had not engaged in a formal betrothal ceremony, in my heart we belonged to each other.

I had an obligation to serve in the temple and decided that I would go to Nazareth, pay a dowry to Joel, and take Deborah for my wife. For the first season of our marriage, we would make our home in Jerusalem.

I had solid, attainable plans. My life was on the verge of becoming everything I had ever wanted it to be.

And then came word that ripped my dreams apart.

Joseph had been in an accident and lay dying. He had gone with Joel on a lumber expedition. The load of logs had come loose, crushing him in one horrific instant.

The ten-day journey to Nazareth took only seven days because I seldom stopped to sleep. All I could think about was losing the man who I had worked so hard to return to. I wanted Joseph to see me as a man of honor and education—as the man he had inspired me to be.

Whenever I pictured my life with Deborah, I pictured Joseph standing in for my father at our wedding. I pictured Joseph teaching my own sons how to carve. I heard him telling my children stories the way only Joseph could.

I thought of Mary and Jesus and all the children who depended on Joseph for everything. Surely they were suffering.

And they were.

Already, the family was so changed I barely knew them.

The house was a house of mourning. It took me by surprise that I had to duck when I entered the doorway. When had I grown so tall?

Mary had grown old. The main table had been moved to make room for a simple pallet where Joseph lay bandaged and motionless. Mary sat next to him and barely lifted her eyes at my entrance.

James and Joses sat on a bench in the corner. They nodded at me but said nothing. Joses' cheeks were streaked with tears.

The air was still and smelled of despair.

I kissed my fingers and touched the *mezuzah*. A flash of memory came to me of the time I had rewritten the *plaf*. Mary had kissed me.

My heart shattered at the scene before me.

Joseph was badly bruised and scraped. His head was wrapped in linen. His face was so swollen it would have been impossible to recognize him. His hand lay limp at his side, and I saw that the stubs of his fingers had gone black.

Kneeling beside him, I took his hand and touched the places where fingers should have been. That hand had taught me so much. It had grasped my shoulders and had given me strength and direction.

I sobbed silently. I wanted to comfort Mary, to return health to Joseph.

Mary kissed Joseph's forehead, then held a cup of steaming broth to his lips. "Joseph," she said softly, "Almon has arrived from Jerusalem. He is here beside you."

Joseph made no sign of understanding. He simply laid there without moving.

I sat on the floor and waited. The only sound in the room was Joseph's ragged breathing. I prayed that the sound would never stop.

Joel came to the door and motioned for me to come out into the courtyard.

"Thank you for making the trek. My brother hovers between this life and the next."

Joel's red and puffy eyes swam with worry. His shoulders sagged. I felt a wave of sheer pity for him. He and Joseph were as close as any brothers could be.

"Joseph's death is on my head."

I cocked my head to imply my confusion.

"I asked Joseph and his sons to bring in the shipment of logs. I should have gone to help."

"Jesus should have helped!" I turned to see James standing behind me. His face was twisted by anger.

"It is true," he affirmed. "Jesus could have helped Father, and He chose not to."

I tried to imagine logs coming undone and Jesus doing nothing to protect Joseph. It was not fathomable.

I was there once at the great lake when the chain had failed to hold the logs. Jesus was the one in harm's way then. It was not possible for Him to withhold his help; it was His very nature to help.

Where was Jesus?

"He hides," James said. "He hides even now when His power is needed most."

His power?

Joel went to James and wrapped a long arm around the young man's shoulders. "This is not the time or the place for such rage."

James jerked away and marched through the courtyard and out into the street. Joses stood in the doorway, his brother's anger also etched across his young face.

Joel released a long breath. "As I hold myself responsible, His brothers hold Jesus responsible."

Why?

Joel sat on the stone bench near the *mitvah*. The trees had grown so large in my absence. So much had changed, and yet I could not believe that Jesus would not help when His help was so desperately needed.

"I see you are perplexed," Joel said. "Jesus was not with His father and brothers when the logs came loose. He was at the workshop. When they carried Joseph to the house, Jesus was summoned and He came running."

Joel cradled his head in his hands and pressed against it, trying to push away the pain.

I could imagine the scene. I saw nothing in Jesus' conduct to merit the anger that James held.

"We all begged Him," Joel said, "beseeched Jesus to pray for Joseph, to touch him and make him whole again."

My eyes went wide. This was the power that James spoke of. How dare they expect Jesus, a mere human, to perform what only God could do?

I had been away for years. I did not know all that had happened in the household of Joseph during that time. But I knew Jesus.

The sun sank lower in the sky and a deep, golden cast spread over the courtyard.

Where is Jesus?

"He has gone where He often goes . . . into the hills to pray. Jesus is not a man of predictability. He speaks with a tongue we do not always understand. Though He is a skilled carpenter, He shows no passion for wood."

I heard an echo from the past, something I had heard so many times from so many mouths: Jesus is no ordinary child. Now . . . Jesus is no ordinary man.

I pictured Him, kneeling among the grasses and boulders, not far from the hillside sheep. I imagined Him imploring God on Joseph's behalf.

If I lay dying, I would want Jesus' faith extended to heaven on my behalf.

A woman came to the gate holding a plate of dates and a jug. "Surely, you hunger," she said.

I looked up, thinking the voice was one I knew.

"Deborah," Joel said, standing.

I stood also, only to have my knees refuse to hold me. I nearly toppled.

Deborah!

She turned toward me, her face still veiled. I imagined her smile was as wide as mine. I longed to rush to her, to take her in my arms, to find consolation.

I stood still as stone.

"My mother watches over Mary's children at our house," she said. "I have come to offer you sustenance."

I took of the dates, cut and pitted, and tasted their sweetness. I drank the wine she brought. It was medicine to my broken heart.

Joel did not leave, but ate and drank with me. After an awkward silence between us, Deborah excused herself and went into the house to offer her aunt dates and drink.

"I see you still favor my daughter."

Yes.

"We will speak of your betrothal when my brother—" His voice simply stopped. He could not speak the words he feared. After a few moments of pacing the courtyard, Joel walked through the gate and out into the street.

Confusion and sorrow tore at me. I went to the animal sheds, to the corner that had once been my sleeping quarters. It was used for storage now, for tools and baskets.

I heard the sound of sandals on stone and turned to see Jesus enter from the garden side of the house. I had seen Him periodically as the family came to Jerusalem for festivals, but I did not remember seeing Him so fully grown. Now I saw that He was a man laden with a burden beyond measure.

He greeted me with the proper embrace, then entered the house to be with His mother.

I washed my hands and face in water taken from the cistern. I prayed. I waited.

Deborah came to the door in a rush. Her hands waved violently. "He stirs. My uncle stirs! Go and collect the children from my father's house. Collect everyone. Tell them Joseph stirs!"

My feet ran like they were aflame. I lacked the words, but made my message clear. Joel and Naomi gathered the children and followed right behind me. I noted that neighbors and other kinsmen joined us, and I was grateful for the support.

Joseph was rallying!

We all crowed into the house, filling it so full one body pressed against another. The air was rank and hot. Jesus, James, and Mary knelt beside Joseph. James no longer looked angry. The edges of Mary's lips were turned up in hope, and Jesus kept His eyes closed. I was certain He was in deep prayer.

I bowed my head in gratitude and looked over and saw that Naomi was smiling at me. I couldn't stop myself from smiling in return.

Deborah managed to edge her way to my side. In her arms wiggled Salome, the newest baby of Mary and Joseph. The little girl sprouted a head full of black curls; her eyes were the same jeweled blue as Jesus'.

Deborah leaned toward me and whispered, "Jesus touched him."

I did not understand.

"He has power, Almon. I've heard my parents whisper. I know who Jesus is. You know, also."

There was no way I could deny what she said. I did not understand . . . I did not know everything, but I knew that Jesus was in no way ordinary.

Joseph's eyes suddenly fluttered and everyone leaned in, waiting with hope and faith.

"Oh, husband," Mary said, caressing his wounded hand.

We waited.

Mary sobbed quietly. I could almost feel her heart breaking.

James pressed toward Jesus. "Do something! Heal our father."

Every person in the room looked to Jesus. He said nothing. What could He say? What could He do?

"Almon?"

It was Joseph who spoke. His voice was thin and brittle. I fell to my knees at his bedside. I took the hand that Mary did not hold. It felt hot and bloated.

"Almon is here," Mary said. "He is beside you."

Joseph struggled to open his eyes and I could see how bloodshot they were, red as seasoned wine. I ached for the voice to tell him how I felt—that he was the best, most loving, strongest man I would ever know.

"Almon is beside you," Mary said again.

With pained effort, Joseph turned his head toward me. I had to put my face to his mouth to hear what he wanted so desperately to say to me. "You are as my son. You are free."

I squeezed softly to let him know I understood.

"I have no right to ask yet another favor, but I must."

Anything. Ask anything.

"Jesus." Joseph coughed, and blood dribbled from the corner of his mouth.

Mary was quick to wipe it with a piece of white linen. It came away stained the color of both birth and death. Red.

"Watch over Him. Watch over Jesus. Keep Him safe, Almon."

I squeezed again. Only Mary and I were close enough to hear Joseph's plea. Jesus was a man by every weight and measure, and yet Joseph was asking me to vow that I would continue to watch over Him, to tend Him as a shepherd over a lamb.

I made the vow.

"The time is soon at hand," Joseph said, coughing again.

Mary wiped the blood and I backed away so that others who loved him could have their time with Joseph.

Malik had made his way into the room. His eyes were full and the look he gave me wiped away any feeling but devotion. In that moment I realized that Malik, too, was my brother.

He was a married man with two children. The port of his youth had been worked into muscle.

We had all changed.

And we all waited, hoping that Joseph would rally and rise from his bed.

We hoped.

We prayed.

Jesus touched Joseph. He held his hands and kissed his battered head. He prayed with might and meaning. His brothers and sisters did the same. Even little Salome bathed her father with kisses.

James and Jude and Joses looked to Jesus and then to their father.

"Heal him," Jude begged, falling at the feet of Jesus. "Please, brother, show mercy, show forth your power and heal our father."

Mary, too, looked to Jesus. Her mouth opened like she wanted to make the same plea, but Mary said nothing.

While all eyes turned once again to Jesus, Joseph's chest rose and fell, rose and fell, and did not rise again.

Forty

All of Nazareth mourned the passing of Joseph, the carpenter. The air rang with wailing, and sobs ripped from the very souls of those who loved him.

I loved him and could not bring myself to believe that a man so sturdy and true could be gone from this life—from *my* life.

Women wailed. Some brought food. Rabbi Asa brought the precious ashes of the red heifer, burned at the altar in Jerusalem. Rabbi Zeev provided the aloes and myrrh, purchased in the Holy City. Rabbi Micha and his wife announced that they were soon leaving Nazareth for another village synagogue, but that they intended to name their next son in honor of Joseph.

Mary seemed grateful, but not completely aware of all that was going on around her. How I wanted to take her pain away.

A stooped, withered woman came out of the shadows, her arms heavy with linen to wrap the body. Only when the light struck her did I see that it was Anna.

I looked behind her, expecting to see Joachim, but then I recalled having received word that he had died . . . last year, or was it the year before?

Jude ran from the house to take refuge in his father's workshop. I wanted to follow him, to be certain his sorrow did not overcome him. I couldn't. Already, the promise I had made to Joseph bound me and I waited near Jesus.

It was not a charge he had made of me—only a request, and one that made no sense. Jesus was a full-grown man who had lived without my shadow for years. He did not need me watching over Him, and yet that is exactly what I felt bound to do.

So I stayed nearby, close to the family that had so suddenly come apart.

Mary's skin took on the gray color of the ashes sprinkled in her hair.

The sackcloth we put on was made of the darkest goat hair. It was so rough it tore at our skin, reminding us that we were in bitter mourning.

"Where are the children?" Mary asked, gazing around at so many people racked with despair.

"My Deborah has taken them to my house," Naomi said. "There she will care for them and give them comfort."

"I am grateful," Mary said, sobbing on the shoulder of her sister-in-law.

James excused himself and went with Joses to the workshop. They went to care for Jude, to share his grief. They passed Jesus without speaking to Him.

Mary turned to Jesus, who stayed with Joseph's body. "Son, do not forsake him now."

I wanted to stand and shout, *He did not forsake Joseph!* He could not forsake Joseph any more than He could do what they now asked of Him. What did they know of Jesus that I did not?

Then it came back to me . . . angels . . . rent heavens . . . wise men . . . babies brutally murdered because He threatened the great Herod. The Son of God. The Messiah.

I knew the writings. When the Messiah came He would deliver His people.

But Jesus was just Jesus. He lacked the power to stay the hand of death.

And yet an old feeling stirred within me, telling me that He was more.

I watched Him take His mother's grief unto Himself. He held her in His arms. Their tears dripped onto the same wood planks that Joseph had laid so many years earlier.

The pipers came and the music started. The mourners sang their songs of sorrow. The whole world darkened as Joseph's body was wrapped and anointed. Even the servant Dan and the Arab Alim came to pay their respects.

He was buried in the family tomb, and I feared that Joel would collapse under the weight of his grief. Malik walked beside him, saying nothing. No words could ease the pain of such a loss.

Yet the next morning the sun rose round and yellow. The birds sang and the animals needed tending. Little Salome cried for her mother, and I was grateful that Mary's arms were full.

The anger His brothers felt toward Jesus did not dissipate with the dawn.

James had not slept since the accident; he had been the one who had brought his wounded father back home. "Jesus could have done something more," he said. His hand clenched into a fist.

"He chose not to," Jude spat.

Jude then looked at me like I was not only mute, but simple. "Jesus has magic," he said. "We all know it. But He refused to use it to help our father."

Magic?

Power?

Call it what they would, it made no difference now . . . Joseph was gone.

James and the boys were with me in the workshop. I did not want to sweep the shavings, because they had been made by Joseph's labor. I did not want to disturb the tools from the places where his hand had set them. I did not want to lose the sound of his voice or the sight of his face. Time had long ago robbed me of my own father's memory. How could I stop the same thing from happening to my memories of Joseph?

Forty-one

As the eldest son, Jesus became responsible for His father's duties. He made the transformation with both strength and humility. It was evident to all who knew Him that His heart was not in woodworking. Still, He was a gifted carpenter and made certain His mother and siblings were cared for, that Joseph's memory was revered.

He was extraordinarily kind to me, providing the rooftop chamber for my sleeping quarters. I appreciated the gesture, but I could not help but feel that I had taken a step backward on my journey of life, when I should have stepped forward.

I was a man of skill; I wore the belt of a temple scribe. I had a full purse and I was ready to give my all for the hand of Deborah.

Yet, my vow would hold; I would honor Joseph's last request of me.

In watching Jesus I saw how He returned unkindness with kindness. During the high holy days of Yom Kippur they taunted Him, saying He had no need to repent because He was the only one who never sinned.

Jesus said nothing, which aggravated them further. They wanted to fight, but Jesus lived in peace. Their condemnation was reciprocated with forgiveness.

I saw Jesus as a master teacher, instructing His brothers and sisters in the teachings of the Torah. He knew more than any teacher I had known at the temple.

Rabbi Zeev, the man who had always been so curious about Jesus, often invited Him to read during synagogue services. Rabbi Zeev reminded me of the traveling Rabbi Gur, who came posing more questions than answers.

I found myself shadowing Jesus just so I could learn from Him.

Gradually, I accepted the fact that Joseph—the patriarch, the voice of faith—was really gone. He was gone, and yet he lived again whenever Jesus opened His purse to a beggar's outstretched hand. Joseph lived again as James pressed his lips together when he was deep in thought. He lived again in the way Jude measured and then measured again each piece of wood before taking a saw to it. He lived again in the way Simeon told stories from the prophets.

He lived on when the girls scrubbed the tables, the chairs, the benches their father had crafted with his hands. Even after years of use they did not wobble, but stood strong beneath their load.

He lived on in the heart of Mary. She spoke his name often, always with reverence and devotion. As long as she lived, Joseph would never die.

As the years passed, little changed in Nazareth. The spring still gurgled fresh, cold water. The synagogue was still crowded every Sabbath morning. Sheep still roamed the hills. Farmers still grew fields of golden grain.

The workshop stayed busy because Joseph's reputation lived on in the craftsmanship of his sons. As eldest son, Jesus saw to His mother's welfare and to the safekeeping and care of His siblings.

Slowly as a long-overdue spring, life without Joseph became life again.

One morning while I was cleaning the animal stalls, I heard a sound that lifted my heart. Mary's lullaby made the sun burn brighter.

Long after the season of mourning had passed, Joel came to ask me the question that helped to stitch my wounded heart.

"Do you still desire Deborah as your wife?"

I nodded with such vigor that my head nearly fell from my shoulders.

"Walk with me, Almon." He turned out of the gate and onto the street. I fell in eager step beside him.

"I have given this moment years of contemplation. Since you do not own property, it is my obligation to provide a lot for your house so that my land is kept within the family."

I had enough money to purchase a parcel of land on my own, but keeping the household of Joel intact made sense. It would allow me to furnish the house, to provide more than just necessities for Deborah.

"You are a skilled carpenter, Almon. You will build the house."

I nodded again. Thoughts were swirling in my head like a desert storm.

"Malik and I will help you. Joseph's sons, also. With such assistance, the house can be completed in haste."

Joel turned toward his own house. I knew that Deborah was helping Mary with the children, so I did not hope to see her. Joel's house looked smaller than I recalled; it was overgrown with a vine, green and thick.

The door that had been so impressive was still impressive, and I could see that Joel kept the wood well oiled. It shone in the sunshine.

Instead of stopping at the gate he continued to walk up the hill behind his house. "This lot will be yours. I hope it is not too close, but Deborah and her mother must not be separated. They share all things." He laughed, and I realized I had not heard the sound of laughter since I'd returned to Nazareth.

The lot was larger than my purse could have ever purchased. It was not flat, but slanted, and vines and fruit trees grew in rows. I immediately imagined where our house would stand. I saw it in my mind, flat with a grass rooftop. We would start with two simple rooms, but with plans to add more as our family grew.

How long had I waited for this moment? My happiness soared.

I wanted to break away from Joel and rush to find Deborah, to walk the land with her, to share our dreams.

My feet stayed put and I listened as Joel shared dreams of his own.

"When Deborah was born I was certain she would live the life of a maid, that no man could love her with a face so deformed. But you proved me wrong. You love her, and she feels the same devotion. I give you my blessing, son."

Son.

The only thing I could do was to kiss Joel's ring to honor him. I did so with a joy I had never known.

The betrothal ceremony was simple, since our family had so recently suffered the death of Joseph. His sons built the canopy; Mary made my new robes and the dress that Deborah wore. Her mother embroidered the veil.

What face would greet me when I lifted that shield?

It mattered not to me, for Deborah had given me her heart, and that made me the wealthiest man in all of Galilee.

Forty-two

I was atop the roof of our new home, straddling the beams that Joel had provided, when Dan came up as slow as a sloth. "I seek Jesus."

My hand pointed left, to the workshop. Jesus had been helping me, but had an order to deliver—chairs that He and James had crafted together. I took that as a sign that James' heart was softening toward Jesus. Joses and Jude were working with Malik, traveling to Sepphoris at least once each week.

A semblance of order brought a level of comfort to the household that would always belong to Joseph.

Now that Deborah and I were officially betrothed, it was just a matter of finishing the house before the second ceremony of our marriage could transpire. Then I would take her for my wife and surely have every desire of my heart fulfilled.

"What do you want with Jesus?" Little Mary was in the shade of a tree, playing a game of sticks and rocks.

Dan laughed. "I have come to fetch your brother on behalf of Rabbi Asa. He has news for Jesus' ears."

Now Dan held my attention. While I did not keep Jesus in sight at all times, I did keep myself available to Him should He need me. I motioned to Dan, trying to make him understand that I would go after Jesus. I would relay the message.

But Jesus returned just as I reached the ground. He called a kind greeting to Dan and scooped little Mary into His arms.

She kissed his cheek and He turned His other cheek for an additional kiss, which made Mary giggle.

Dan lifted his walking stick. "Rabi Asa seeks your presence, Jesus. He has news of a new prophet."

I smiled. During my years on Temple Mount a new prophet appeared almost daily. They came in all stations—the rich dressed in their woolen tunics with embroidered blue trim, carting scrolls written by the finest scribes. Others preached in rags, claiming they had been called of God. After a while, I learned that none of them was worthy of news.

Jesus agreed to go to the synagogue. He looked at me and motioned with His head that I was welcome to join Him. We all went, walking slowly so Dan could keep the pace.

Rabbi Asa and Rabbi Zeev were in the courtyard, surrounded by what appeared to be a Sabbath-sized crowd. When Rabbi Asa saw that Jesus had come he hurried to greet Him.

"A prophet like no other has risen."

Jesus did not even raise an eyebrow.

"I tell you, I tell you all . . . " Rabbi Asa stood on the rise. His voice sounded as full and clear as I remembered it years before. "I have recently returned from the Judean wilderness. I have seen John for myself."

John?

I looked to Jesus, but He still did not look surprised. His eye was on little Mary, who played by the fountain.

"He is as Moses returned. An Elias . . . sent to prepare the way."

Now Jesus lent His ear to the message. His head cocked and His eyes narrowed.

Someone near the open door shouted, "What is the message of this so-called prophet?"

"John calls us to repentance. He baptizes by immersion." It made sense to me, but the crowd rumbled.

"I heard he is Elijah, returned," someone else called.

"He is not," Rabbi Asa said, and he lifted his arm and pointed toward Jesus. "He is John bar Zacharias, the goodly priest from Judea. John is kinsman of our own Jesus bar Joseph."

John? Elisabeth's son. My mind went back to the weeks he had spent here in Nazareth. I remembered a serious boy, odd enough with his rough clothes and his uncut hair. My memory went back to the night we had all slept on the roof together, the night my ears had listened to words not spoken to me, the night Mary and Elisabeth had whispered of angels and children destined for greatness beyond human imagination.

I had not heard mention of John in so long. Had he not gone to live among the Essenes, the community at Qumran in the barrenness of the hills? Elisabeth was surely gone by now. How, I wondered, did John become a mighty prophet?

Jesus spoke softly, but with surety, affirming His kinship to John.

Rabbi Asa lifted both hands. "People are flocking to hear his message. He foretells imminent divine judgment. Never have I heard a voice so driven, a message so clear. He cries baptism and repentance."

Harsh voices rose from the far corner. "What right does he have to call *us* to repentance?"

Rabbi Zeev appeared to scoff.

Rabbi Asa lowered his voice and his chin. He looked at Rabbi Zeev with a piercing stare. Usually he seemed intimidated in the presence of the other rabbi, but not now. "Is not that the duty of a prophet?"

That stilled the crowd.

"John says our people have lost their way from the true and straight path."

Rabbi Zeev kept his fist clenched, but did not raise it again, though his eyes bulged. "We are the chosen people. God's own. We have His holy word. We keep His holy *mitvah*. We are not lost."

People murmured. Some agreed, others did not.

"I returned to Nazareth anxious to testify to you, my fellow elders. John is unlike any other."

Two young rabbis I did not know stepped up to flank Rabbi Asa.

The youngest teacher added his testimony. "This John—I, too, have heard him preach in the Jordan Valley. He teaches a new way, that forgiveness comes by holy immersion."

"What of our law? What of sacrifice? That is how sins are forgiven."

Emotions heightened. I felt my own face begin to burn. Jesus stood listening, but He did not seem anything but interested.

I walked away from the crowd to join little Mary at the fountain. It was almost bone dry. The season of the sun had drawn the moisture from the ground, even from the leaves, and had left everything dry and hard.

Rabbi Asa thundered, "John has come to prepare us for the Messiah!"
Now the assembly roared.

Any mention of the Messiah turned my eyes to Jesus. I saw Him step back until He was pressed against the wall, His attention divided between the teacher and His sister.

A feeling I recognized, but could not name, crept through me, warm and as powerful as a bolt of lightning. I did not understand; all the words I had at my disposal could not explain it, but I knew that Jesus was more than any rabbi or priest there. Whatever John had become, Jesus was greater.

"The time is at hand," Rabbi Asa announced, stirring the crowd to frenzy. "Soon we will be set free from the oppression of the Romans, from the house of Herod, from the unrest and uncertainty that has held us captive for generations!" His voice continued to rise until it filled the courtyard, bouncing from the stone walls of the synagogue and scattering the pigeons from the trees.

The assembly exploded.

Jesus came to join little Mary and me.

I bowed my head when our eyes met, something I'd never done. Whatever feeling stirred within me led me to believe I was in the presence of royalty.

Jesus lifted Mary to His shoulders as we walked away from the crowd, away from the village, into the thicket by the village spring.

The spring did not rush the way I remembered, but the trickle was cool and sweet, and we took turns soothing our parched throats.

I could not take my eyes from Jesus.

He knew *I* knew.

Little Mary clung to my hand while Jesus walked ahead of us, looking suddenly like He had taken on the weight of Mount Hermon.

He asked me how committed I was to honoring Joseph's request.

I did not realize Jesus was even aware that Joseph had uttered the deathbed request.

He assured me I was free to break that oath, that He would not hold me to it.

I thought of Deborah. I thought of my life at the temple and my aspirations to become a truly great scribe. But I gave no indication.

Then Jesus told me that He had put all His affairs in order and that at dawn's first light He was leaving Nazareth. He was going to see His cousin John, the new prophet who baptized at the river.

If I was going to shadow Jesus, I would have to shadow Him to the barren hills above Judea. I would have to leave behind my betrothed, my unfinished home, my dreams.

I knelt and wrote in the sand with my finger, just as I had done hundreds of times to communicate with Joseph. Only this time my answer was a single word that said everything I felt: *Master!*

Forty-three

Rabbi Asa spoke the truth.

John had grown into a mighty prophet.

When I saw him standing there—atop a sand hill in the desert, the sun behind him, the wind blowing around him—I thought of ancient fathers like Abraham, Jacob, and Moses, who possessed more than human power. It was clear that no razor had touched John's head, and his skin had been baked by the sun. He looked wild in his camel-hair robes. His eyes were dark, but shone like polished stones.

Jesus brought all the bits and pieces of information I knew of John into one single picture. He told me how His cousin had spent his life away from the corruption that threatened to crumble all of Judaism. Even the practices at the temple were impure. I knew He spoke the truth.

Jesus made me understand how the laws, the prophets, and the writings had been twisted and turned into burdens unbearable . . . how evil hands and dark hearts had perverted those things that God intended to free men into chains that instead bound the spirits of men and women. The time had arrived to break those chains with a better way and a new law.

I was not the only one to follow Jesus into the hill country. Word of His teachings was whispered throughout the land, and disciples begged to tag along. In the years that we had been separated, Jesus had forged friendships along the shores of the Sea of Galilee and in many of the villages. He made all welcome, but Jesus made me feel as though my servant's station was a place of honor.

My heart was eager to serve, but more often than not, Jesus served me. He set the morning fire and cooked the fish. When I left to fetch water, I returned to discover my bed rolls already packed. When my sandals broke, it was His needle that stitched them sturdy again.

He made no show of His service, and I learned much. All of His life, Jesus—who did not *need* to serve—had served others, even me. He did so with ease and merriment.

We arrived in the desert in a crowd, a steady stream of the curious who had come to hear John preach. I had never seen a man more revered.

"Prepare ye the way of the Lord, make his paths straight."

I listened as I had never listened before. It was as if my heart heard his message, so simple it could not be misunderstood: repent and be baptized, turn from sin, turn again to the sacred covenants between God and our fathers.

Jesus made no show of His presence, but John sensed it. He stopped midsermon, made his way from the mound, and came among the people. Hands reached to touch him, grabbing and pulling at him. Many begged him to heal them. Many cried out for deliverance. There were men old and decrepit, men strong and as young as Simeon, women and children. All had come to hear the mighty prophet John cry repentance.

Then John's arms went wide, his eyes grew moist. "Jesus."

The name I'd heard ten thousand times, I now heard for the first time. *Jesus.*

Who was this man I shadowed, this man who commanded a prophet as powerful as John to bow in reverence? I looked to my Master. There was nothing about Him that would beg attention, and yet, like the moon, His pull was undeniable.

The cousins embraced and the throng around them moved away, parting to allow Jesus and John a private moment. These two men spoke scrolls without uttering a single word.

A woman next to me cried out, "Is this the Christ?"

Did she mean John?

Or Jesus?

And so commenced a work that changed my life as nothing had before. The days that followed opened to me a realm higher and brighter—and an understanding of John, Jesus, and even myself.

Though I had been acquainted with Jesus most of His life, even loving Him as a brother, I realized I had never really known Him.

Now each day thinned the veil between humanity and divinity. With every dawn my eyes were opened to all that I had not seen before.

I watched Him serve, listened to Him teach. The crowds grew thicker and I felt honored to fetch water, to gather food, to tend to the chores that needed tending. Thoughts of Deborah and our unconstructed home, memories of Joel's confusion at my decision—so many causes for concern were set aside. My life was in God's hands, and for the time being, I knew the work I was doing was the work I was meant to do.

Slowly but steadily, beneath the unrelenting glare of the desert sun, I came to know that I held a place of honor, as holy as the ground around the burning bush, to stand in the shadow of my Master.

The people came without ceasing, seeking out the Baptist. The humble came to repent and be baptized. This baptism was different from the ritual washings I had experienced since joining the house of Joseph—the *mitvah* washings for *Shabbat*, the sprinklings to cleanse from death, the washings before entering the synagogue. This was *different*. This was complete.

John admonished people to return to their homes committed to living improved lives, making a higher level of contribution to society. Most left, but there were those who stayed, vowing to become John's faithful disciples.

The numbers grew and grew and grew.

Then came the soldiers of Herod, sent from the palace, seeking John on behalf of the king.

"There is but one king," John said boldly, "and it is not Herod."

The soldiers left, but a dark foreboding told me they would be back.

The Pharisees, who could quote the law and how it related to the cruelty of Antipas and the idolatry of the Romans, sought occasion to challenge John. They came with their tongues aflame, prophesying John's downfall. It did not take a wise man to see they were envious and threatened by John's growing discipleship.

I feared for the day when they realized John was merely a forerunner to my Master. I still did not know what the future held for Jesus, but I sensed its grandeur with every setting sun.

The Sadducees, too, came with clenched fists and red faces. Dressed in their soft, flowing robes and linen girdles, they were in stark contrast to John, who wore a battered leather girdle.

John raised his voice to them, crying, "O generation of vipers, who hath warned you to flee from the wrath to come?"

I understood what he meant. In the desert poisonous snakes hid in the shade and took refuge in holes. They lurked to destroy life, just as the self-righteous Pharisees and Sadducees sought to destroy the simple, sacred truths of Jewish faith.

The faith I had come to know under the tutelage of Joseph—the rituals, the repetition—made for a meaningful and peaceful life. In the household of Joseph, the law was lived out of love for God. But there was no love to be found in the anger, hatred, and competition of the fighting rabbis, priests, Pharisees, and Sadducees.

More and more I understood that God's way was always simple and straight. Man's way was complex and crooked.

The truth John taught was straight and simple.

I was frightened by how angry the religious leaders grew at John's preaching. They shouted at him, called him an imposter. They made threats, even vowing to see him dead in order to silence him. I did not doubt that they were serious, and yet they could not stop the people from coming to the Baptist.

They came in droves.

We moved east to the banks of the Yored-Dan, the river located on the land claimed so long ago by the tribe of Dan. John knew the river like an old friend. The water ran from Mount Hermon down to meet with the water springing up from the ground as our tiny spring in Nazareth. The river was wide and deep, sometimes green and sometimes blue. It smelled of life, damp and growing. John called the site *Yardenit*, with its overhang of trees and the water running deep and calm. John led us to a babbling brook that added to the flow, one of his favorite places for preaching.

The lines of people stretched and stretched; it seemed to me they would never end.

"We have come to be baptized by the one with true authority," they said.

One afternoon beneath the blinding sun I was shocked to see Nazareth's own Rabbi Asa standing in line. He was there with two of his grandsons, familiar faces from our village. That they had come so far, in such great humility, meant much to me.

"I am very edified to see that you are here, Almon." he said.

This was the rabbi who had given me my first scroll. This was the man who had asked Joseph to grant me my freedom that I might study at the temple to become a scribe. This was the man who had testified of John in Nazareth.

He reached for my hand and kissed it as though I was not a mere servant, but a revered scribe. "You are gifted in letters," he said, "but the work you do for this season will bring you a far more lasting reward."

He then came before John, bowing, his grandsons on either side to assist their aged patriarch. "I have testified of you, John. You have not left my mind since I heard you preach, and now I bow before you and beg to be baptized by your hand."

John helped raise Rabbi Asa to his feet. Then he gave the holy man something I had not seen him give to anyone else, save Jesus.

John gave Rabbi Asa a smile.

Forty-four

The Greek word *baptizein* translated "to immerse," and that was exactly how John baptized. He immersed Rabbi Asa, his two grandsons, and every repentant and accepting soul *completely* beneath the water.

Some called John the Messiah.

Others claimed he was Moses, returned.

An Elias.

John himself tried to make it clear to all of us: "I indeed baptize you with water; but one mightier than I cometh, the latchet of whose shoes I am not worthy to unloose: he shall baptize you with the Holy Ghost and with fire."

He spoke of Jesus. Everyone did not understand, but now I did.

Jesus loved John. He revered John as the great prophet he was. Jesus baptized in the same manner, by total immersion. He taught John's disciples with the same understanding and skill that he had practiced so many times in Nazareth.

I was not the only one enthralled.

Jesus now had a growing discipleship of His own. I believed Him, but I did not always understand what He was teaching. For nearly twenty years Judaism had instructed me about repentance, and yet hearing Jesus preach about it, I asked myself, *What does it really mean to repent?*

I knew the steps: Feeling godly sorrow for sin, confessing and forsaking those sins, making amends where possible. Keeping the law from that time forward.

But, though I knew the steps, I felt that the act itself was out of my reach. I couldn't make amends for the wrongs I had committed so long ago. It seemed that every time I put my past behind me, it circled back like a hungry wolf and sprang at me when I least expected it.

Joseph was dead and buried. If I now confessed the sins of my past, what would be my penance? The level of my deceit alone was my greatest sin. I had kept the truth from Joseph; I had let him think the best of me. I had deceived the elders who supported my education as a scribe. I had kept the truth from Deborah and her family. I was certain that Joel would prefer to have his daughter remain a maid rather than to have her wed a man whose childhood was so foul, whose manhood had kept so much hidden.

What purpose would it serve to divulge my past now? Ever since Joseph rescued me, my life had changed completely. Wasn't that full and true repentance?

The advent of the kingdom of God was at hand, and I served in the shadow of the Chosen One, yet I did not take my place in line. I did not seek baptism. I served in silence and witnessed others come into the fold.

The rain came and the river rose. We took cover under tents and waited out the storm. When the sky turned pink and the birds shook the dew from their wings, Jesus rose and went for a walk in solitude.

John sat on a fallen log by the water's edge.

Normally, there would have been a crowd, but the rains had discouraged the numbers. I stoked the fire and took a place across from John, so I was there when Jesus returned and approached His cousin.

The request He made brought John to his feet.

Jesus asked to be baptized in the same manner, in the same river, as everyone else. But they were mere mortals . . . and this was Jesus.

Jesus.

I remembered how His brothers had taunted Him at Yom Kippur. "Jesus is a lunatic. He is the only one among us who has no need to repent," they had said. I could still hear the laughter echoing derisively.

I could still see the pain in Mary's eyes.

I had never known Jesus to disobey a single law. I had never witnessed Him perform an unkind act. And yet there, on the muddy banks of Yored-Dan, Jesus stood before John imploring the Baptist to immerse Him.

I stood back with some of the other disciples and watched.

No, was John's answer. "I am not worthy to bear your shoes."

Jesus smiled. He looked like He knew something—a great truth He had not known the day before. Jesus was continually changing and growing.

John's voice was low, yet strong. He slowly slipped his sandals from his feet and backed carefully into the water. His eyes did not leave Jesus. The river was high but not swift. John moved out into the water until it reached his waist.

I could see the reflection of Jesus' face in the surface of the water. The smile had not left His face.

John raised his hand into the air, and water dripped from his fingers. His chin quivered. "I have need to be baptized of thee, and comest thou to me?"

"Suffer it to be so now," said Jesus, wading into the river, "for thus it becometh us to fulfil all righteousness."

All righteousness. Jesus would leave no commandment unfulfilled.

Much later, a chosen Apostle of Jesus would pen the picture: *"And Jesus, when he was baptized, went up straightway out of the water: and, lo, the heavens were opened unto him, and he saw the Spirit of God descending like a dove, and lighting upon him:*

"And lo a voice from heaven, saying, This is my beloved Son, in whom I am well pleased."

All the scriptures I had studied, all the stories I had learned, all the laws I had lived became clasped like hands joined. The dove was the same sign God had given at the baptism of the earth. Now it was given at the baptism of His sinless Son.

It was the holiest sign—God's sign.

It is impossible for human words to speak or write the joy of that experience, and yet I wanted to engrave them for then and forever.

If I had possessed any doubts, any doubts at all about Jesus, they left me at that holiest of holy moments. I was there when the heavens were rent. I saw with my own eyes and heard with my own ears, and my heart knew on a clear and undeniable level: Jesus *was* the Son, the Promised Messiah. I knew I would follow Him and never leave Him.

Never.

Never.

Never leave Him.

Forty-five

And yet I left Him.

Rather, *He* left *me*.

He left us all.

Jesus was baptized. His divine Sonship was announced by God, His Eternal Father. His work at the banks of the river had concluded, and it was time for Jesus to move on.

I had every intention of going with Him.

There was a chill in the night air, and Jesus sat in front of the fire, holding His palms to the flame. His very face was illuminated—not from the flickering glow, but from an unmistakable light within. I stood back in the shadows and watched as He and John said their good-byes.

The kinsmen shared a bond I could not fathom. The time that they had spent together had brought both joy and sorrow, heights and depths beyond measure. I knew that I had been witness to something so divine no words could convey it. I knew that my own mind had been opened along with my heart. I also realized that my mortal mind and lowly station did not allow me even a glimpse into the smallest part of the whole. This was God's great work, and I was a mere mortal.

This day my duty was to join the other disciples in holding back the throngs, allowing Jesus and John some private time. It was no small task to keep John's followers at bay; they camped in great numbers by the riverbank. Caught between the river and a starless black sky, their orange campfires glowed.

Voices cried out. Prayers went heavenward.

I thought that John would go on crying repentance and baptizing people. But what of Jesus? What would He do now that He had been immersed and filled with the Holy Ghost?

The sound of horse hooves broke the calm of the night. I turned toward the sound but saw nothing other than moving shadows.

A voice growled. "By the order of King Herod, I command the Baptist forth."

Torches flared and then I saw them: four soldiers, armed and angry.

I rushed to the campsite of John and Jesus.

"Do not be alarmed," John said. "I will go before them. I fear only the one true and living God."

Jesus placed a hand on my shoulder, the way Joseph used to. I felt a calm and peace go through me.

The campfire was snuffed out and John stepped forth, looking part man, part animal—but I knew he was something more. Immediately, he was surrounded by his disciples, men willing to sacrifice their own lives to protect their prophet's.

Voices rose in anger.

"Be still," said John, and his words placated the crowd. The horses moved forward, Herod Antipas' soldiers riding tall and strong.

The calm of Jesus' touch dissipated and was replaced by cold fear surging through me from my heels to the crown of my head. My allegiance was to Jesus, and I squinted in the dark to bring His silhouette into focus. Even in the pitch of night I saw His face and believed He was a living light. It glowed.

He stood from the rounded rock that had been His bench, His leathern bag strapped over His arm. I went toward Him, and our eyes met.

My knees suddenly buckled beneath me. I bowed before Him.

He was my Master.

Jesus smiled slightly and turned to step over the last dying coals of the fire. He headed up the bank, away from the throng, away from the soldiers. I hurried to follow, pushing my way through the reeds, crouching beneath the drape of hanging branches. I kept the appropriate seven steps behind.

At first I thought He was running from the soldiers, but I was wrong. He was not retreating, but moving steady and certain toward something.

I followed Him through the darkness until the night sky became streaked with pink and orange. Birds rose from the grass in great flocks.

Jesus paused to look at them, to see wings spread wide and birds lifted up, up with the morning breeze.

We were headed away from the river, toward the desert.

Finally, we came upon a small desert well where we paused to refresh ourselves. I was out of breath and my throat burned.

I held the waterbag out to Jesus first.

He declined and told me that He was being led on a journey— one He was required to make *alone*.

My eyes glanced down at His feet, thinking how worn His sandals were. When mine had broken, He had taken His needle to repair them.

I sat and quickly unloosed my sandals; they had been a gift from Joseph. His skill with leather had been as keen as his skill with wood. Jesus should take mine; they were newer, and the soles thicker. The leather on His sandals was worn thin, and the stitching had come loose. How could He make any journey with such weary sandals?

Jesus was headed straight into the desert. The desert was dangerous; if anyone knew that, I did. Surely, Jesus could not go into the barren hills alone with no better sandals than His.

Then it hit me. The sandals Jesus wore were made by the same hands as the sandals I wore. They were Joseph's craftsmanship. Of course they were worn, and of course He would continue to wear them.

My hands shook. My eyes turned to the slack bag strapped over Jesus' shoulder. He needed food and water to head into the desert. He could not go so unprepared. I could not allow Him to go.

And when would we meet up again?

I didn't understand, and I feared what might happen to Him.

Again Jesus smiled and spoke the words that I had heard from His lips so many times.

"Fear not."

My hands relaxed. My heart slowed.

I will wait, Master. Though I do not understand, I will wait here until you return.

No, Jesus told me. He wanted me to care for myself. He wanted me to take refuge in the nearest village. If I must wait, He wanted me to wait in comfort.

I did not want to leave the spot where we stood.

No matter how long He needed to fast, to pray, to commune with God . . . I would be waiting when He returned.

Jesus thanked me and began His journey without once looking back. He walked across the sand, across the rugged red rock, until He was swallowed by the vastness of the barren Judean desert.

I said my standing prayer, but found no comfort in the prescribed words. I longed to pray the desires of my heart as I had heard Jesus pray. And so I did; I begged God to watch over my Master, to keep Him safe from beasts and animals and desert bandits like I had once been.

Forgive me, God, I prayed.

I sought shade and began my wait.

I waited.

The sun rose, and the backs of my hands burned.

I waited.

I drank from the water bag. I thought of Jesus, now gone for hours. How long could a man fast in this unrelenting sun?

Jesus gave no indication how long His journey would last. I did not know if He knew.

Still I waited.

My eyes thought the desert had turned to sea, one rolling wave after another, rising and falling. But the desert was made of rock, and the waves were solid, baked hard by thousands of years under the scorching sun.

In the far-distant hills I could see oval black hollows—caves, great and small. Jesus could take refuge in any of them, but they often sheltered desert cats and snakes and scorpions.

I waited.

It seemed to me that the sun stood as still as it had at the prophet Elijah's hand. Would He ever come out of the desert?

A red-tailed lizard scurried out from the shade of a rock, its black tongue flicking out and back in. It cocked its flat head and looked toward me, then darted back into the shade.

I waited.

At the bottom of my bag were some dried figs. I put one into my mouth and let it sit there. I savored its sweetness and welcomed the relief it brought to my empty stomach.

Jesus was out there hungry, thirsty, and alone. Guilt filled my belly.

I knew Jesus. He would not want me to feel guilty that I had eaten; He would want me to enjoy the fig. He had asked that I take refuge in the nearest village.

I stood and looked from east to west, from north to south. There was no other sign of life. I saw mostly only sand and rocks, a few bushes and trees. The heat rose in shimmering sheets over the rolling rocky hills.

I filled the bag again from a well that was deep and barely damp.

I waited.

I unrolled my mat and laid it in the shade of a palm. My eyes gazed up at its fronds and I thought how the palm was a symbol of royalty in Palestine. I knew that Jesus was more than royal . . . and yet His robes were common, His sandals worn, and He was alone in the vastness of barren sand and rock.

Exhaustion overtook me and I slept. When I woke I was tired and my hunger bit like a snake. My mouth was parched.

There was no sign of Jesus.

The nearest village had to be at least a half-day's journey. It would be late night before I arrived. Any wise innkeeper would have his doors bolted and refuse entrance to a stranger. The risk of thieves and rebels was too high.

Jericho was also within a few days' walk. It was large and lush. I had been there with Father, but I was fearful that was a journey that would separate me too far from Jesus.

I could stay where I was, but that did not seem right . . . or safe.

I would go to the village. But what of Jesus?

I had to believe that God would watch over Him. God had provided water from a rock for Moses and our wandering fathers. Surely, He would do no less for His Beloved Son.

The next morning I found myself at the village courtyard of a place called Kohl, which meant "sand" in Hebrew. It was small and humble, overgrown with wild, brittle vines. In the courtyard there was nothing more than a small, broken canopy that offered little relief from the sun.

I had water, but my stomach burned with hunger. There was no bakers' street in a village so small.

What of Jesus? How was He? Would He find me here? Would He know that I was waiting faithfully?

My head ached with concern.

Once again I found myself in a strange place without the ability to communicate. I walked the dirt-packed streets and marveled at how many people inhabited such a small village. Arabs and Africans. Egyptians and Syrians. Jews.

There had to be a synagogue in the village. I would find it, and would there find hospitality.

I discovered that I was not as lost as I had thought. The village was within days of the main thoroughfare from Palestine to Egypt—the same road where Joseph and Mary and Jesus had first come upon me.

Oh, that had been so long ago.

I relatched my sandals and continued to walk the village streets. Memories of my father came back to me. I swear I could hear his laugh in the morning wind. I remembered his smile, how he would scoop me up in his arms and carry me when I grew too weary to walk.

An unexpected sorrow struck me like a fist to my belly. For years I had only thought of my father as a man who had stolen and lied. He had sold me and then stolen me back. Still, he was my father, and though I was a grown man I was not done missing him.

I came upon the village synagogue, a small and dilapidated edifice. It was made of packed sand, not stone, and was badly in need of a new whitewash. The courtyard garden had been neglected and grew nothing but thistles. The menorah above the door was worn to only a faint image. The rabbi who emerged looked as ancient as the building.

I approached him humbly, holding out a small note on which I had written my request for food and shelter. I explained that I was mute and waiting here for the return of my Master. How long He would be gone, I did not know.

The man was kind enough and called for a servant boy at once. I was given bread and allowed to stay in a small back supply room. I was most grateful to be out of the beating sun.

I rolled out my mat and slept. I slept and dreamed of days long gone. I saw my father, his dark eyes and beard, his chapped lips left too long in the sun. I heard his voice clearly in my head. He was telling me how sorry he was . . . sorry for all the bad times and all the bad things that had happened.

Would I forgive him?

Would I forgive *myself?*

Next my dream brought a young Jewish woman sitting on a small gray donkey. Her long, dark hair flowed like liquid down her back. Her veil was thin, and when she turned to face me I saw her eyes.

Mary.

My memory brought Mary back the way she'd been that first day I had seen her. Young and pure. Perfect. I recalled the peace her smile had sent through me.

Then I dreamed someone was tugging on my hand. It was the boy Jesus. His curly little head bobbed. His pale eyes shone like gems. He was so small—so weak and vulnerable.

Next I saw Jesus standing in the Yored-Dan, dripping from a baptism He did not need in order to wash away sin—for He was sinless. The boy had grown into a man so powerful, so pure and perfect, He would save a nation. I saw Him walking, and I heard again the words I had heard John say, "Behold the Lamb of God!"

Jesus was that Lamb, come to free us all.

Then an image of Jesus in the desert appeared before my mind. He wore the same robes, the same thin sandals as He had been wearing when He left me. I saw Him kneeling on a smooth plateau. I saw the azure sky and the billowy clouds casting shade on my Master's sunburned face.

I awoke to find my fears vanquished.

Jesus was not alone. He was not forsaken.

God would never forsake His own Son.

Forty-six

I waited, and still Jesus did not return.

Life in the desert village was much like life in Nazareth. *Shabbat* was honored with the same laws and rituals. The scriptures were familiar, though here they were spoken in Greek more than Hebrew. I found comfort in the sameness, the familiar.

In the courtyards women ground grain every day to bake bread. They tended to small, withering gardens. Water was more valued than gold.

Men worked, tending desert goats and sheep. They built and repaired homes and buildings. They taught their children the laws of God.

In the small village marketplace they hawked the same goods as they did in every other marketplace in Palestine. But here all things were shrouded in a layer of the desert, the color of the rock, the grit of the sand. Food, fabric, trinkets, pots, jugs, and even sandals held part of the desert. I could not stop myself from purchasing a fine pair of sandals I thought would fit the size and shape of Jesus' feet. He could keep Joseph's sandals, but His feet would welcome the new ones.

Carpets woven in the village by both men and women were as fine as I remembered seeing so long ago. The rugs were large and fine, made of colorfully dyed wool—red and black, green, and even purple. Traders came from Alexandria to buy them at the lowest prices so they could sell them at the highest.

Joseph had loved the writings describing Solomon's temple and had told me, "If you study carefully, you will know that God's favorite color is purple." Since then, purple was also my favorite color.

One old market woman kept a fire going beneath her pot of lamb and lentils, seasoned with spices I did not know. I gave her money and ate from her dipper whenever I could.

I helped to pay my keep by organizing the synagogue scrolls. They were old and tattered. I read them and found myself studying Latin. My skills in Latin were minimal, and I determined to learn more of the language. I swept and cleaned and tended to the courtyard garden. The rabbi seemed pleased and very appreciative.

He asked few questions, something for which I was grateful.

I thought of Jesus every moment of every day. I believed that God had shown me Jesus was safe, but how long would He stay . . . *could* He stay . . . safe in the desert, even with God's hand shading Him?

My thoughts also folded around Deborah. She told me she understood my obligation to Jesus. Even Joel shook his head and told me I must honor Joseph's last request.

"Deborah will be here when you return."

When would that be? Days, weeks, months . . . years, perhaps?

My devotion belonged to Jesus, but still I could not stop images of Deborah from entering my mind, could not stop hearing her singing psalms. When I missed her most, I let my thumb and finger touch a small piece of fabric she had woven on a loom that I had helped Joseph to craft. The fabric was dyed a rich purple. Each time I touched it I found comfort and hope that my loyalty to Jesus would earn me forgiveness in the eyes of God and would lead me back home to my Deborah.

I kept track of the days by cutting marks in a small piece of scrap lumber I found. Then one day while I was tending to the synagogue garden, I heard horses approaching. I turned to see a band of Roman soldiers. They arrived in full uniform, their helmets glinting in the sunshine.

"You!"

A man pointed a long, thin sword at me.

I stood.

"Give us water!"

The request was a bitter insult. Fetching water was women's work, yet I rushed to the well and dipped for the soldiers. They climbed from their horses and followed me. They gulped greedily. Other villagers gathered, but did not come close to us.

"Do you know of a radical known among his followers as *the Baptist?*"

My blood ran cold.

They were after John! I had been so preoccupied thinking about Jesus, I had hardly given John as much as a memory.

I shook my head and pointed to my mouth.

"What are you saying?"

I was saying nothing.

The soldier with the sword came toward me. "Speak, boy!"

I was no boy. I was a man, and I felt my back go straight. Instead of stepping away, I moved toward him, an act that risked death.

"He is mute."

We all turned to see the rabbi. "The man is a simple servant. He does not speak because he *cannot* speak."

"A mute!" The soldier laughed, and the others laughed along with him.

Because I was mute, they assumed that I was also deaf, though I had fetched water at their bid. But they spoke about me like I could not hear them.

"The mute would be worthless to the rebel John."

John, a rebel? Herod's men had been after John when we had separated. Now the Romans were hunting him. That could only mean his following was growing. He presented a genuine threat.

The rabbi stepped forth with his hands behind his back, a stance of rebellion. "You are looking for John, the one they call the Baptist?"

"You know the Baptist?" the lead soldier demanded. "Stand forth and tell us!"

"I know of him. He commands a burgeoning audience."

"A rebel," the solder said, spitting at the rabbi's feet.

"A prophet, they say." His hands came forward, his fingers splayed, showing the soldiers that the rabbi was harmless.

Silence.

The soldier's fist clenched and released. He laughed again. "My king commands that I respect your faith. A prophet, you say—a man who gathers an army in the remote wilderness, we say, is surely a rebel."

"John preaches repentance and baptism, nothing against Caesar."

"And how do you know this?"

"All of Palestine knows of John."

The man spat again, this time at my feet. "Caesar knows of the Baptist."

"He is no threat to Caesar."

"You speak of John as if he is a brother."

"I have heard him preach."

I was surprised and tried to catch the eye of the rabbi. He kept his gaze on the soldier.

"And where is he now?"

"He preaches in the Judean desert."

"The desert is endless. Where is the Baptist *now*?"

"I do not know."

I knew John's favorite baptismal spot, now a site even holier than the inner chamber of the temple. I knew that if these men and other soldiers went into the desert to hunt for John, they would likely come across Jesus. They might mistake Him for John, and then what?

An old familiar fear crept up my spine.

I wondered why the soldiers, smart and trained, did not simply follow the people to the banks of the Yored-Dan. There they would surely find John . . . unless he had gone into hiding.

I had so many questions. So many fears. Jesus could alleviate them all if He would only return.

After those soldiers departed, more came in search of John. There were not only Romans, but Herod's hated men. In my mind they were worse than bandits. One afternoon they galloped into the village and disrupted a wedding. Just when everyone was celebrating—the men dancing, the women gathering beneath the canopy, the flutes and lyres playing—the soldiers rode in, shouting and threatening anyone supportive of John.

Everyone cried out in surprise and fear. The mother of the bride fainted. No one was unfamiliar with the level of cruelty Herod's men were capable of inflicting.

Again, it was the old rabbi who stepped forward. "John is not in our village."

"Where is he?"

I no longer knew. So many days had passed. John could be in Egypt, Africa, Asia Minor. He could be in Rome.

The soldiers dismounted, demanded to eat the food from the wedding feast, demanded to drink the finest wine. The mother of the bride had been fanned out of her swoon, and now she wailed and flung herself at one of the men. She was an ample woman, her shoulders as broad as a man's, her fingernails sharp as blades. She had to be pulled back and a twist of fabric was stuffed into her mouth to keep her quiet.

The distraught bride disappeared into a tent, and the groom was struck by one of the soldier's beating sticks. Blood gushed from his head and he had to be carried away by his father and brothers.

I hated the soldiers. Yet there was no room for hatred in my heart, not if I truly loved my Master. And I did.

So I joined the guests, who did nothing but watch and seethe. We cheered when the soldiers finally rode out of the village, but by then no one from the wedding party felt like celebrating.

Some nights after that while I was stretched out on my mat in the synagogue courtyard, I heard the sound of feet on stone and a jingling of women's jewelry. I couldn't be sure whether the sound had come from one of my many nightmares or was real.

"*Pssst.*"

It was a woman's voice, but it was not light and pleasant like Deborah's or Mary's.

"You . . . mute man!"

I sat up and squinted to focus on the source. An unveiled face peered over the wall.

I went to her, thinking she might be injured and in need of help. What I saw was a woman, aged and wearing flowing black robes. I saw a face I had not seen in ages: a face with yellow eyes. In a flash, my mind raced back to the bandits who had robbed Father and me.

The woman's guttural laugh was low and deep. "Do you not feel it?"

All I felt was the caress of the night breeze and a chill from the memory that passed through my head.

"Do you not feel the evil in your bones?" The bracelets on her wrists danced, making the jingling sound I'd heard. Her voice was more of a growl, and I felt an uneasy fear overtake me.

"He is near."

Who? I wanted to ask.

"Almon?"

I turned and saw the rabbi come through the door. He wore his sleeping robes and his head was uncovered; his long white hair glowed in the moonlight. When he saw the woman he flicked his hand, dismissing her. "Go now, Miriam. We have no need tonight of your prophecies."

"*You* do *not* feel it," she said to the rabbi. "You, teacher, are past feeling."

"I am past my hour of retirement. Go now, Miriam. Leave Almon to his rest."

The woman disappeared behind the wall, and we waited until the sound of her jangling bracelets could no longer be heard.

"Miriam is harmless. She meant you no evil. Rest well."

He went back into the synagogue, toward his own sleeping chambers, and I laid back down on my mat. Sleep would not come. There *was* a feeling around me—a dark mist so real my skin felt heavy. I prayed again the same prayer of protection for Jesus.

Had some dreadful thing happened to my Master?

He did not appear the next morning or the morning after that.

I waited.

I watched.

I prayed.

Then one day when I had notched forty marks on my wooden counter, my hand held the dipper to my lips, and my feet occupied the very spot where I had last seen Jesus. I looked across the way and saw a thin figure appearing out of the shimmer of the desert sand.

Every dark thought, every crushing fear, vanished.

Jesus was returned!

Forty-seven

The water was blue—so blue and deep it made me think of Jesus' eyes.

Those eyes penetrated souls now, seeing into hearts. And people were seeing in His eyes a light that brought them out of darkness. As Esaias the prophet said, " . . . to them which sat in the region and shadow of death light is sprung up."

Jesus was that light, and His cry—"Repent: for the kingdom of heaven is at hand"—sounded new, though it was not new. It was the same mandate John had preached in the wilderness. But John had never said, "Come, follow me," the way Jesus did.

Jesus was the way, and people followed Him eagerly. My servitude commenced in earnest.

Once Jesus had come out of the desert after forty days of fasting and prayer, after forty days of utter devotion to His Father, there was no mistaking His majesty or His mission.

It was a dangerous business, saving souls. John, who I knew was a true prophet, was hunted like a wild dog. I shuddered to think what might be happening to him, and wondered if God's power would always protect him. Those faithful to John were now scattering like frightened sheep. Jesus welcomed them into His own growing flock. What would become of Jesus when Herod discovered a new prophet was risen—one even greater and more powerful than John?

In spite of everything I knew of Jesus, I still feared for Him. Rumors of His power made it impossible for Him to go anywhere without a flock of followers. Some were there out of genuine faith in His words and works. Others followed Him out of sheer curiosity;

they saw Jesus as a spectacle. Still others lay in wait, ready to spring at Jesus to prove He was a fraud.

I appointed myself the divider. It fell to me to separate the sheep from the wolves.

That was one of the reasons we were now in the borders of Zebulun and Nephthalim, along the sea coast of Galilee. It was safer here, and Jesus had friends in Capernaum. Jesus was gathering both old and new friends in every town, every village, along every scallop of the water's edge.

I stood on the shore and looked out at the Sea of Galilee. A warm breeze rippled the water—not enough to make white caps, but enough to stir up the endless shades of blue. When I looked out far enough, past the fishing boats and larger ships bobbing on the surface, I saw the line where water met sky. It was as if the white wool clouds sat atop the waves.

I stood there knowing that I had embarked on a journey from which there would never be a return. Serving Jesus had already led me to places and experiences I could not have imagined. I did not know what lay ahead—I only knew that those words I had heard whispered so long ago by Mary and Elisabeth, those words that had floated up to me on a rooftop in Nazareth, the words I'd questioned, were now proven true.

Jesus was who they said He was.

His work had commenced, and I would be with Him until it was completed.

What had happened in the wilderness during those forty days and nights?

Cephas, a mighty man who had walked with John but who was now devoted to my Master, was bold in telling me, "Jesus communed with both good and evil. He overcame."

Cephas explained that Satan himself had approached my Master, trying to make Him doubt His identity. *"If* thou be the Son of God . . ." He had tried to tempt Jesus with riches, vanity, and appetite.

Jesus had refused to yield.

At night around our fires the disciples whispered that only *after* Jesus had proven Himself did angels sent from heaven come to minister to Him.

The mention of angels did not seem far-fetched to me now.

Among the inner circle were Andrew, the fisherman; Cephas, his brother, more often called both Simon and Peter; and Jesus' old friends from the fishing shores, James and John, the sons of Joel's friend Zebedee.

None of them knew Jesus like I did. Yet I knew they shared my conviction that Jesus of Nazareth was the Christ, the rising King of Israel.

Part of me rejoiced that I was no longer the only one walking in the shade of His holy shadow. But another part of me—a tiny, black part of my heart—resented all the others who were now taking all of Jesus' time and attention.

The tide was coming in, and the waves lapped at my bare toes, cold and refreshing. Sand gathered in the grooves of my sandals. I looked down the shoreline and saw my Master gathered with His new and closest disciples. I stayed back to give them privacy for Jesus' teaching, though I longed to be included.

My longing was futile. I was a mute. The men Jesus gathered were called to *preach* God's word, and how could I do that without a voice?

Whenever I felt jealous, I told myself that it was enough for me to stand and wait in silence. Whatever Jesus wanted, whenever He wanted it . . . I would be there to serve.

I was not the only one who felt such devotion.

I had been on the very shore where I now stood when Andrew and Peter were summoned. They had been casting their nets when Jesus had called to them, "Follow me, and I will make you fishers of men."

They did not hesitate, but left their all to follow Him.

John and James had been on their family ship, mending nets with their father. They left their nets in disrepair and followed my Master.

He became their Master, also.

A hand touched my shoulder, and when I turned, I saw the face of Jesus.

He smiled and told me it was time to leave the calm of the shore. He asked if I had made all the preparations He had requested.

Yes. Everything was packed and ready.

His smile broadened. "Fear not."

He told me to put away my long face and to share His merriment. This was a time for celebration, He said. We were on our way to Kfar, Cana, for a joyous occasion—a very special *simcha*.

It was time to lay my concerns aside. It was time to rejoice.

Jesus walked ahead of me, and I saw that He wore the sandals I had given Him as a gift. I smiled and rushed to keep in step with His quick strides.

For the moment my worries were gone, and I thought of Mary and all the familiar faces we would soon see. Deborah would be there. In my bag I carried a beautiful veil, trimmed in gold. My heart pounded, and I could not stop myself from smiling.

Jesus had caught up with Andrew and James. I heard them laugh.

This was no time for concern, but for sheer celebration.

We were on our way to the wedding!

Forty-eight

We first came to a small house where Mary was staying. I did not know the woman who greeted us, but when she called to Mary, telling her that Jesus was come, I heard the cry of happiness that rose from within.

Then there she was, her face glowing, her arms spread wide.

"My son."

To me, Mary was just as beautiful and flawless as she had been on the first day my eyes had taken her in. Perhaps the loss of Joseph rode on her shoulders. Her hair was streaked with gray beneath her veil, but her beauty remained. I wanted to run to her and embrace her as my own mother.

Instead, knowing my place, I backed into the shadows of the overhanging vines, waiting and watching.

Jesus greeted His mother with a bow and an embrace. "Woman," He said, as He so often did, extending her a term of high reverence.

They caught up on the good news of the family and the sad news that John was the target of Herod's insanity. Mary told Jesus that Anna was back in Nazareth, too old to make the trek, but she had sent her best wishes. They discussed the workshop, and Mary gave a quick update on James, Jude, Joses, Simeon, Mary, and Salome. As she spoke of each child, obvious joy shone in her eyes.

"They are all near," she said. "None would miss this wedding. You will see; the hand of God is mending our family, even now. Your brothers' hearts are softening, and they are beginning to understand your . . ."

Mary's voice suddenly broke, and she reached up and took Jesus' face in her hands. He stooped to equal His height to hers. "Oh, son, what of you, Jesus? Tell me of your work and *your* heart."

Jesus walked with Mary, out of the courtyard and up the path leading to a small olive orchard. The air was chill, and I saw Him adjust the shawl around His mother's shoulders.

They were alone, and I could only imagine His words as He told her of His baptism and the voice, the Spirit that rested down on Him with the beauty and gentleness of a dove.

Did He divulge to His mother His days and nights in the desert? Did He tell her more than He had told Peter, Andrew, James, John, and the others whom He had called to train? Did Jesus describe to His mother how Satan himself had appeared when He was weakest and had tried to destroy Him? Did He tell her how He quoted scripture to the evil one? "It is written . . . "

Jesus learned those scriptures at her knee, at the workbench of Joseph, and in the Nazarene synagogue that was like a second home to Him. Because He had learned them as a child, they came to Him whenever He needed them as a man.

What did Mary think of her son now?

Oh, I longed to be privy to their conversation, but it was not my right and not my place. Instead, I tended to the donkey that carried our load. I readied Jesus' things for the upcoming *simcha*.

When I reached into my bag, I felt the softness of the veil I had purchased for Deborah. The thought of her took my mind in a different direction, away from Mary and Jesus and their moment of solitude.

Deborah!

I knew she was near; there was no way she would miss this celebration. What would she think of me as a dust-covered servant, a scribe returned to servitude?

I looked for a way to freshen myself, to wash away the dirt, to change my clothes. I did not want Deborah to see me in such disarray. At the back of the courtyard I hoped I would find a *mikvah* deep enough that I could cleanse myself, but I found only a cistern with a small hole in the bottom to keep the water living.

Cupping my hands I washed my face, my arms. I rinsed my mouth and chewed leaves of the mint that grew thick and green at the base of the cistern. Then I went into the stable and changed into a set of clean robes. I washed my feet myself and wondered if I could ever count the others whose feet I'd washed. No matter. To do so was the duty of a servant.

As I emerged from the stable, Joel and Naomi entered the courtyard. "Almon!"

I walked to them and bowed my head.

Joel was in a jovial mood. "Lift up your head and be happy. Tell me of your journeys with Jesus. Where have you been during this time, and where is my nephew now?"

I pointed to the orchard on the slope, I then pulled from my robe pocket a small book of parchment I had purchased long ago in Jerusalem. With a tiny quill and a blotter, I wrote simple answers to Joel's questions.

Naomi stood by his side for a long moment, then excused herself and went toward the home where they were staying. Was Deborah inside the home? Where was Malik? Surely he would be here for this long-awaited wedding. Malik, married for years, was helping in the lumber business.

What had happened to the years God had given me?

What had I done with them? What, indeed?

"My daughter will be pleased to see you," Joel said, and I saw the sides of his mouth rise in a smile. "You are the man her heart beats for."

My ears felt as though they were on fire.

His smile turned into a hearty laugh. "And though you are both advanced in years, you are still children." His laugh grew so loud I feared he would attract attention from the other people who were filling the courtyard. "You do still wish to complete the second ceremony of your wedding, do you not?"

I nodded my head. *Yes! Yes! Yes!*

I hurried to my bag and pulled from it the gold-trimmed veil I had purchased for Deborah. I had paid more for it than I should, but the look on Joel's face was worth the expense.

"For Deborah?"

It was impossible for me to write rapidly because I had been trained to make each stroke perfect. *Yes, I long to complete the contract of our betrothal. This veil is a token of my love.*

I thought Joel might break into a dance right there. Instead, his feet stayed firm and his smile fell. "Almon, Jesus' work has only commenced.

I am a member of His inner family, and yet I do not completely understand His calling and all that lies before Him. Tell me, Almon, how long will you follow Jesus from village to village?"

I am committed for as long as my Master needs me.

"Jesus has become your Master?"

I nodded and looked Joel squarely in the eye. There could be no room for doubt or fear. It was Joel who seemed to waver. At times he was firmly supportive of Jesus; other times he almost mocked Him. But Joel had not heard and witnessed the miracles I had. And I knew that if I remained true to Jesus, God would remain true to me.

"You expect Deborah to wait also, or do you wish to marry her and have her join you?"

I long to marry her and have her at my side—but no, she cannot follow where Jesus leads. It is not safe.

Joel frowned. "John. Yes, I have heard how Herod's henchmen hunt him. It seems Antipas is infatuated with John's power."

I trembled to think what Herod would do once word of my Master's power spread throughout Palestine.

Joel coughed into his hand and glanced around. He then leaned toward me and whispered, "I grieve for the loss of Joseph. My brother was more to me than kin; he was my favored friend. I understand your devotion to him, and I understand your commitment to Jesus, but Almon . . . though He may be called to a station higher than the rest of us, my nephew is a lunatic. His preaching invites trouble."

I stood staring at Joel, unblinking, trying to understand what he said.

"You now look at me as if *I* am the lunatic."

I wrote so fast my marks were more scratches than letters. *No! I simply do not understand . . . do you believe in Jesus or do you not?*

Joel sat down on the courtyard bench, a small stone structure hardly big enough to hold him. He lifted his arms and faced his palms to the sky, and I could tell he was offering a prayer.

I waited, barely daring to breathe.

"Since before His birth, our family has known that Jesus would be no ordinary child. It is true . . . he is not ordinary. He is odd. We have pacified Him all these years. We have loved Him. But none of us understands Him."

That was an honest reply, and I respected Joel for his forthrightness, even if I did not agree.

He stood. "Give me the veil. I will present it to Deborah."

I hesitated only for a moment.

"Very well," he said, smiling again. "You present it to your betrothed."

He cleared his throat again and patted my shoulder, not with the warmth of Joseph or Jesus, but his touch meant much to me. "I nearly forgot to tell you . . . my daughter waits for you behind the house where Mary stays. Hurry, now—don't keep Deborah waiting any longer."

He didn't need to urge me. My feet were already out of the courtyard.

Forty-nine

It was forbidden that Deborah and I be alone, so Naomi and a distant aunt, also named Mary, sat on a log and pretended they were not watching as I presented the veil to Deborah. Nearby, a passel of children were at play.

Deborah accepted the veil with both hands, and as she did our fingers brushed. That small contact with the woman I so loved made me want to take her in my arms and hold her forever.

"It is beautiful, and I shall wear it always."

I smiled and wrote on the same page I had used to reply to Joel's questions. *There is no need to wear it always. I will buy another veil if you so like it.*

"Oh, Almon, I do like it, but in all the preparation for the wedding, I neglected to make you a gift."

Your being here is gift enough. How I have missed you!

The gate opened and a man as tall and broad as any man I had seen hoisted a large platter of roasted lamb. He waited for Mary to grant him permission to speak.

"The Master bids you direct the procession of food. The meat is grilled and the wine is ready."

"Very well," Mary responded. "Take the meat to the center table in the courtyard. Be certain there is plenty of wine. I will gather the rest of the food and sound the gong to summon the guests."

The servant in me wanted to help the man tote his cargo, but Deborah's eyes held me back. More than anything, I wanted to be near her as long as I could.

Our moment did not last. A knee-high boy with wild red hair the same shade as Deborah's streaked toward her like an arrow. She knelt and scooped him into her arms.

"Malik's youngest son," she said to me. "He is called Nathanial." Deborah hugged him and kissed his cheeks until he squirmed free.

I knelt to greet him.

"Do you know the game of chase?" he asked.

I nodded.

"Will you play with me? I will run, and you chase."

I nodded again.

Nathanial's smile turned to pure suspicion. "What is wrong with you?"

"Almon does not speak," Deborah explained.

"Why not?" Nathan asked.

"Because he can't."

"Why can't he?"

"He just can't!" Her voice grew impatient and brittle.

I felt ashamed of my muteness and embarrassed for Deborah. A flash of a vision passed before me. If she and I were to have a son, he would want to know why his father did not utter a sound. What if our son inherited my muteness?

The thought went through me like a dagger.

Deborah looked up into my eyes. "You appear ill, Almon. The color has drained from your cheeks."

I smiled at her as if nothing was wrong. Then she took hold of one of Nathanial's hands while I took the other. We went to the door and Deborah asked if there was anything we could carry to the courtyard.

Mary, the Canaanite, brought a basket of dried apricots for me to tote. I was glad for the task and grateful that Nathanial did not ask me any more questions.

Soon the courtyard drew a crowd of kinsmen, all of whom seemed happy to be reunited. The women spread out the food and talked without ceasing while the men drank wine and slapped each other on the back, laughing and joking.

"I smell the rosemary," Deborah said. "My mother's recipe was used to grill the lamb. She is very proud."

I rubbed my stomach to tell her that the savory smell made me hungry.

Joel approached us and introduced me to his friends as his future son-in-law. There was more relief in his tone than joy; still, I stood a little straighter and a bit closer to my betrothed.

Nathanial darted away from us and ran toward his father.

"Almon!" Malik said, lifting his son onto his shoulders.

I grinned like I'd seen my own brother, and we embraced.

"How are you, my friend?"

I nodded toward Deborah and smiled.

Malik threw his head back and laughed. "It is good to see you well. I fear for you as you journey in the shadow of my cousin. If Herod is fixated on John, what will he do when the power and popularity of Jesus threatens him?"

"Malik! Not today. Please, no talk of anything but joy." Deborah's words were quick and sharp. "Please, brother."

"Very well, sister" he said, grinning. "I am hungry, and the thought of food will bring me joy." He laughed, and I noted how time had thinned his face but not his stomach. Even beneath his robe and tunic, it bulged.

"Join us, Almon. Sit with me at our family's table."

Deborah seemed delighted at the invitation. She left me to join the women while I walked with Malik to the table. Tonight was a simple feast of grilled meat, dried fruit, and wine.

When Jesus entered through the gate, His very presence drew my attention. Already, He was surrounded by friends and family. Joses stood beside Him. Across the way James motioned for Jesus to take His place opposite us.

I sighed, relieved that His brothers showed such kindness. But my eyes looked around carefully. I saw Peter do the same. Whenever we were in a crowd, there were always those present who wanted to cause Him harm or embarrassment.

Jesus seemed occupied only with the people He so loved. He laughed easily. The stories He told enthralled his listeners, and He dined with eagerness.

Malik leaned toward me. "At least John *looked* the part of a prophet. Jesus appears so common."

It was true. To someone who did not know or feel His spirit, Jesus appeared no different than anyone else gathered around the table. Yet I knew there was nothing common about him. Malik knew that also.

"People will grow tired of His preaching," Malik whispered. "*Repent and be baptized.* It's the same message we've heard for centuries. Once Jesus loses favor with the crowds, you will be able to return to Nazareth and finish your home. My sister talks of nothing else."

The blessings were said by a rabbi with a thin black beard, and Malik took his share of the lamb before holding the platter to me.

I accepted a piece of meat dripping with oil and draped with the green sprigs of rosemary. I put a piece in my mouth but hardly tasted it.

How could Malik know that Jesus had only commenced His work? I could be out there following Him from village to village for months, years—even a lifetime.

After his stomach was satisfied, Malik went to Jesus and embraced Him boldly. I felt resentment crawl across my skin. Malik whispered of Jesus behind his back, but to His face Malik pledged His favor.

Jesus did not seem bothered. He seemed happy.

As the night wore on, the wine went round and round. The players came out with their flutes, lyres, and cymbals and gave us music. Men danced.

Jesus danced.

I did not dance. I slipped away from the throng and went to the wall where the servants were. It was the place I felt most comfortable.

"Almon?" Mary stood beside me. "My niece seeks your company. She is back at the garden with the children. I will walk with you."

I left the music and merriment of the courtyard and followed Mary down the road to the house where the family was made so welcome.

The night gave half a moon's glow, but it was enough to see through the fabric of her veil and take in Mary's face. She looked peaceful and yet tired.

"The wedding is tomorrow, and I may not have the opportunity to say what my heart feels." Mary stopped and reached up to touch my shoulder. "Almon, what you have done for Jesus means so much to me. You have been His older brother. You have been His keeper.

When you are near Him, I know He is safe."

Even if I had been able to speak, no words could have said what I felt.

"Your sacrifice has been great, but it will not be permanent. I believe in my heart that one day you will return to Nazareth to Deborah and to a life of your own. Until then . . . thank you."

At that point I heard music, but it did not come from the instruments in the courtyard. It came from the lips of Deborah . . . sweet and melodic. She was singing the children to sleep. Mary left me standing there in the road. She went inside, and I closed my eyes and listened to the sweetest sound.

I was not a young man. Deborah was not a young woman. But one day I prayed that her melodies would soothe the cries of our own children . . . and they *would* cry. They would cry, and laugh, and speak all the words their father could not.

Fifty

I went early to the courtyard, and already it was transformed. I had never seen anything like it—not in Nazareth, and certainly not in the desert. Flowering pots had been brought in and hung; green and pink and purple flowers draped from the top of the canopy and brushed the ground. It gave the appearance of an oasis.

The night before I had not paid attention to the surroundings, but now I saw that the courtyard was laid with some of the finest stonework I had ever seen. The ground tiles were huge and set in a pattern of alternating light and dark. Eight massive columns ran down the center, supporting three canopies to provide shade and shelter. The walls were of gray and white stone, cut in great rectangles and laid opposite to match the stone floor.

The *Magen David,* the sacred star, was engraved around the crown of each column, a reminder that life is eternal—one unending round. I thought of my Deborah and tried to imagine how we would set the courtyard at Nazareth for our wedding. Surely Joel would see to it that everything was elaborate.

When would that day arrive? Mary's words had brought a calmness I hadn't felt before, an assurance that our wedding day *would* come. *When* . . . I did not know.

I spent my time with the servants, helping to lay out goods, to order all things.

Mary came through with Naomi at her side. They wore their finest robes and checked out the supplies and settings. I fell in behind them, but they were so occupied they didn't realize my presence.

Mary raised her hands. "Oh . . . I fear we may run short of wine."

Naomi shook her head. "Sister, you worry too much."

"And meat. Is there enough meat?"

"Yes, and lambs ready to slaughter should Malik eat the whole flock."

Mary laughed, and the women went on to admire the flowers and to talk with the other women who milled around, checking to make sure all things were in order.

I went to check on Jesus and found Him by a small stream, talking with His brothers and those disciples who had accompanied Him to Cana. The scene gave me great peace. Jesus was safe, surrounded by people who loved Him.

As the day wore on I felt increasingly out of place. The servants did not accept me as one of them, though they allowed me to help. The guests looked at me as something less than one invited. And the family knew I was kind, but not blood.

I heard the laughter of children and looked up to see Deborah come through the gate. At the trail of her robes was a string of children. A baby I did not recognize sat on her hip. The sight of her made my heart pound.

She sensed me there also, and came to my side.

"Any wedding day is a blessed day," she said, organizing the children as naturally as any mother.

I gave her hand a squeeze. Deborah was right. We were gathered for a wedding, and it was my right and my duty to celebrate. With her beside me, it felt like a festival.

Nathanial rushed to me like we were seasoned friends. His little arms went around my neck. "I am sorry you don't speak, but I will speak for you."

Deborah and I laughed.

The next hours were spent playing with the children. We fed them and chased them and tended them. Only when it was time for the wedding to start did we portion them back to their parents.

I sat with the household of Joel and felt honored. As the wedding began I barely saw the bride and groom, but pictured myself and Deborah instead.

The bridal canopy, the *chuppah,* was made of embroidered cloth. It billowed in the breeze, attached to four poles that were held by James, Jude, Joses, and Simeon. The *chuppah* was a symbol of the groom's house, which the bride was to enter. It also was a reminder of the tents of our Hebrew fathers.

The flutes began to play, then the lyres and the cymbals. Then came the wedding party and the procession. All were dressed in their finest robes and tunics.

The bride began her slow circular walk around the groom—once, twice—until she had circled him seven times. I remembered how at our betrothal ceremony I had kissed the coin seven times, then presented it to Deborah. I pictured the day she would circle around me, symbolizing that I was the center of her existence, that she would be there to protect me from harm and evil.

As the recitation of blessings began and the bride and groom drank from the two cups, I imagined how the rabbi would speak on my behalf: "Almon is without voice, and yet the Lord God Almighty hears his heart. These are the words he would say to you, Deborah, if he could: You are consecrated to me according to the laws of Moses and Israel."

My mind was brought back to the present as the rabbi read from the *ketubah*, the marriage decree. It addressed the trousseau and the dowry and outlined the legal obligations of the bride to the groom and the groom to the bride.

Deborah seemed to understand, and she offered me a gentle smile beneath her veil.

As the remaining praises were recited, I said a silent prayer of my own . . . that God would find a way for me to serve both Jesus and Deborah faithfully and completely.

During the few moments of the *yichud,* a time of seclusion for the privacy of the bride and groom, I looked at Deborah and found her looking back at me.

Then James and Malik came by, slapped me on the back, and said, "You've never seen such fine food. Come now, Almon, or you'll go away hungry."

"Go," said Deborah, "it is time for me to join the women."

The courtyard burst with people, music, and food. Everyone had a story to tell of the bride or the groom. There was laughter and dancing and great joy.

Wine flowed freely. Men drank from the wine-skins like they were drinking cool spring water. It was a good sign, because a wedding without wine would bring misfortune to the union.

Tables were laden with roasted meat and vegetables. Saucers of porridge steamed. Figs, dates, and nuts spilled over the rims of their bowls.

Malik surely had his fill.

Musicians played. Kinsmen caught up on years of news. Even my own feet danced.

When it came time to rest, if people did not have a house to go to, they laid mats in the courtyard and slept beneath the shade of the trees.

The celebration continued into the night. More wine. More food. More music.

I slept with Peter and Andrew on the rooftop and woke to find people still celebrating. Even the governor of the land came to dance and drink and offer his best to the bride and groom.

Deborah and I kept the children occupied. It felt easy and right to be with her. I felt complete beside my betrothed.

Jesus, too, was happier than I had seen Him. He was always surrounded by people, holding them mesmerized.

As I walked the courtyard wall I saw Mary and realized right away that something was wrong. Hers was the only face not smiling. She rushed to me and took me by the shoulders. "Where is Jesus?" she asked me.

I pointed to the far corner of the courtyard. He was talking with the governor. Others had gathered, too—His disciples and wedding guests, eager to hear what Jesus had to say.

"Fetch Him with haste," Mary asked. "Please."

I could not imagine what was wrong, so I went right away.

Jesus excused Himself and followed me to the station where food was prepared, where Mary met Him. Peter came along, sensing that something was amiss.

"They have no more wine," she said.

Peter looked at me and we both understood her concern. There were still many thirsty guests. Water would not quench their thirst, nor would it bless the wedding couple as would the fruit of the vine. No Jewish wedding could run short of wine.

Jesus lowered His voice and spoke with kindness. "Woman, what have I to do with thee?"

Mary sighed. Her eyes implored Him to do something about the shortage, but what was He to do? What *could* He do?

Jesus stood before His mother. "Mine hour is not yet come."

She laced her fingers and waited.

No words were spoken between them, and yet mother and son were communicating, and I could not understand their sentiments.

Finally, she turned to me and to the other household servants waiting for her command. She told us, "Whatsoever he saith unto you, do it."

I nodded. Surely, if Jesus said to do something, we would do it.

Jesus lifted a finger, pointing to a set of large stone vessels on the landing. "Fill the waterpots with water."

Peter stayed, but the servants and I *ran* and did as my Master bid. We filled them up to the brim.

I sensed something powerful and wonderful and mysterious going on.

"What are you doing?" Malik and Joel were at my side, curious. "What are you doing with the huge pots?"

Jesus.

It took all of us to carry them once they were full. We set them before my Master's feet.

Mary stood beside Him, looking excited, her hands clasped in front of her.

"What is He going to do with all this water? It cannot be wasted." Joel posed the question to me instead of Jesus.

I had an inkling of what was about to occur, but it was impossible. Utterly impossible.

Joel put his arm around my shoulder and whispered into my ear. "You might believe all that He claims, but my belief is shallow. It wavers with the wind."

Then Jesus said to me, "Draw out now, and bear unto the governor of the feast."

I did, and when I lifted the dipper it held not water, but rich, dark wine.

My eyes were not the only witness to the miracle.

Some gasped, including Malik.

Mary wept along with Peter.

Joel stood without moving.

Surprise struck me, but did not overtake me. I served the ruler of the feast first. He tasted, and then called the bridegroom. "Every man at the beginning doth set forth good wine; and when men have well drunk, then that which is worse: but thou hast kept the good wine until now."

I smiled and looked to Peter. His cheeks were streaked, and astonishment shone on his face.

Joel sat on the stone step next to the pots, now filled with the richest, sweetest wine.

He looked up at me, and though his eyes were dry, they were full.

"I believe," he said.

Fifty-one

A giant dragonfly captured my attention. Its wings held so many fluttering colors I could not count them all. I watched as it hovered in the air, darting from one green leaf to another.

It was a miracle. Since seeing water turned into wine at the wedding, my life had been surrounded by miracles.

My eyes looked out at the water, as gray today as was the sky. I thought of Deborah and her gray eyes. How I missed her! Though Mary and her children had chosen to follow Jesus for a season, Deborah had elected to return to Nazareth with her parents. She gave Mary her word that she would care for Anna.

And though I had made my decision, my heart still felt divided. As Deborah's betrothed, I should be building a home for her, preparing for our future. Instead, I was here in Capernaum by the lakeside, waiting.

Beyond the water rose the hills and mountains in the far distance. They melted from shades of blue to green, then back to blue. Above the highest peaks was the sky. Above the sky were the heavens. My Master, the one on whom I waited, was Lord of them all.

I had been witness to His power. It was power enough to quell Caesar's mighty armies, to stomp on his soldiers like ants beneath His sandals. Jesus had power to set our people free from all oppression. I had seen that power as He called forth disease, as He healed the lame, as He gave the blind eyes to see.

I had been witness to miracle after miracle.

Was it any wonder people sought out Jesus and clung to Him?

He could heal their hurting.

He could mend the broken.

He was Master to the masses.

I hardly slept now, worried that Herod would get word of His power and try to take Jesus captive. My ears were always catching rumors that John had been taken and imprisoned . . . or worse. It was difficult to discern the truth from rumors.

Jesus responded with the words He often used: "Fear not."

It was His mantra.

His unbounded compassion for the wounded and the weak made it harder and harder to protect Him and to give Him any time and space for the solitude He so loved. Jesus now rested in the house of Peter, a man who had proved his loyalty to Jesus. He was not just a friend—he was a true disciple. Though Peter was strong and quick-tempered, I liked him very much. He made a perfect guard to keep Jesus safe from those who constantly wanted to defraud Him or bring Him harm.

I also favored the new disciple—Judas Iscariot, the one who kept our purse. He heralded not from Galilee like the other disciples, but from Kerioth of Judea. He worried too, like I did, about the welfare of our Master.

It fell to Judas to fill the purse. Often the coins came from the alms of followers, though there were times property was sold by the disciples, or work was done and the wages given to sustain us. Somehow, the Lord always provided for our needs.

Judas, who was as willowy as Peter was wide, was also given charge to pay our debts and to meet our day-to-day obligations. How many times did I see Judas tie and untie the purse? He counted the coins with thin, shaky fingers and snorted like a ram. "How are we to live on so little?"

Our Master simply replied, "Fear not."

And for a time Judas always smiled a broad and bright smile. He was always eager to please Jesus.

At first, I kept my feelings toward Matthew reserved. He, too, knew about money because he was a tax collector. Each time I saw him I remembered the loathed Jews, men who turned on their own people, men who came into Joseph's shop demanding money when money was so scarce. They preyed on the shopkeepers in Jerusalem, taking from many what they did not have to give.

How could Jesus have chosen such a man?

Matthew did not fit my image of a tax collector. He seemed kind and intelligent. He understood all people, especially the foreigners who had made their home on soil belonging to Israel. Peter and many of the others resented the Syrians, Greeks, Romans, and all foreigners. Matthew had the ability to converse with them. I could not help but think of my own father, the way his training as a money changer had made him acquainted with so many different peoples and cultures. It was fascinating to me to hear Matthew talk of their ways and their worship.

My memories of all I had learned as a nomadic child of the desert were fast fading. Though I knew Galilee well, I realized my world was small, while God's world was without end.

Weren't we *all* His children?

I thought Matthew was better equipped than was Judas to handle our funds. He was patient and calm, where Judas was edgy and nervous. I eventually discovered that money was not Matthew's only talent. He was skilled in writing, which led to a fast-forged friendship between us. We spent many hours reading and recording the events that transpired, the people, the miracles surrounding Jesus.

Matthew was patient with my muteness and showed me a few new hand signs for communicating. For the word Master, he kissed his fingertips and touched his heart, much like touching the *mezuzah*.

I heard someone call my name and turned to see Judas coming down the shoreline toward me. "Jesus has called us to go into the marketplace and purchase supplies. He says we will all be going to the Holy City to celebrate the Feast of the Passover."

I was glad, but I was also fearful. I had not been back to Jerusalem since Joseph had died.

Fifty-two

The pilgrimage was immense, grander than in past years. Now that there was relative peace in Judea, people from all over Galilee felt safe to take leave and journey to the Holy City. The roads were crowded. Women and the elderly rode donkeys. The rich rode horses. Most walked, as we did.

It was spring, and Passover was upon us. Jews from every quarter of Palestine were headed to the same destination. Inns along the way were full. Tents dotted the landscape and campfires burned at night. We stopped along the way to cleanse ourselves in the streams and rivers. There was no privacy there, either.

Jews weren't the only ones occupied at this time. The soothsayers and fortune-tellers were the busiest ones in the bustle. One old man stepped in front of our assembly. He held a ball of white soapstone. I had seen Joseph carve pieces of the soft stone from Africa, and I knew it was precious and rare.

"Come to me," he said, pointing at Andrew. "Come to me and I will tell you what tomorrow holds."

Andrew's eyes went wide, and he looked to Jesus.

A sadness shadowed my Master's face.

"Let us pass," said Andrew. "We take no thought of your business."

The man's beard was long and braided into one thin, gray rope. He had used some sort of charcoal to circle his eyes and darken his lips. His robes were full and black. They made me think of the robbers, those who had murdered my father. In a blink, I remembered the yellow eyes.

Suddenly he shouted out in a tongue I did not recognize. I wanted to run, but stopped to see as the teller spun the sphere in his palm. It danced from one hand to another. It then rolled, as if by an unseen power, up his arm and then back down into his palm. It vanished.

Many around us murmured, impressed by the magic.

The man threw back his head and sniffed the air like a wild animal. Then he looked toward Jesus. "There is one among you," he said, "who is no ordinary man."

I immediately stepped in front of Jesus, making of myself a shield; it was something I'd seen Peter do many times.

But Jesus was not intimidated. He nodded His appreciation, but kept walking.

"I know *you!*" the man cried. "I know who you are."

Jesus continued on, pausing only to help lift a child who had stumbled in the press of the crowd.

The soothsayer followed, shouting in an unrecognizable and terrifying tongue. Jesus did not seem bothered, but I was. So were Peter and Judas and the others closest to Jesus. We formed a sort of ring with our bodies. If the man wanted to get to Jesus, he would have to pass through us first. I feared the teller would throw the heavy soapstone ball and hit Jesus, injuring Him. Instead, he hurried after us calling out in Aramaic, "Son of David! Son of David! Son of David!"

Jesus did not turn to the right or to the left, but moved ahead, neither shortening nor lengthening His stride. Eventually, the man fell back and away.

Others came forward to taunt the Master. Still others cried out for relief. He responded *only* to those who believed. An hour did not pass without the hand of Jesus touching someone for the better.

Andrew once asked me why I did not seek the hand of Jesus to touch me and give me speech. I had no reply, not even on parchment. Since I had first seen Jesus lay hands to heal the sick, I had thought to ask Him for such a blessing. I believed He *wanted* me to ask Him.

But I couldn't. My sins were old and hidden. To bring them to light now would put everything I valued in peril. I could live with my muteness; I could not live without Deborah.

As we approached Jerusalem, the roads became even more crowded. It wasn't just crowded with people now, but with animals. Faithful Jews were bringing their firstlings for sacrifice. Many tried to lead lambs; others carried birds in cages.

I knew what to expect when we reached the city walls and gates. As at every other Passover, thousands of lambs, goats, and birds could be purchased on Temple Mount. The hawkers were no doubt there, lined up like I'd seen before. It was a strange sensation: how my mind could still picture the beauty of the temple, with its white and gold, while my nose could still smell the stench of all of those animals, and my ears could still hear the cries of so many merchants selling the sacrificial beasts.

To me, there was nothing holy about the scene.

At night when we camped, Jesus taught us of the temple. He taught us how sacred His Father's house was, how it was the one place on earth that was truly holy. He talked of Solomon and the first temple.

I remembered all the times I had studied the Torah with Jesus at the synagogue in Nazareth and at Joseph's workbench, how we had quizzed each other on the law and the prophets. The teachings He taught now were far beyond anything recorded in those scrolls.

Where had He learned such truths?

He still quoted Isaiah. He still brought to His tongue the commandments. But Jesus taught with a newness—He taught of God's unfolding kingdom, and we did not have to ask Him. We knew we were blessed witnesses to prophecy fulfilled.

When we arrived in Jerusalem, I would find the post and send a letter to Deborah. I would tell her of the good news that Jesus taught. I would tell her of His miracles. I would tell her of my devotion.

The Holy City was packed with pilgrims, just as I knew it would be. No street, no alley, no porch was vacant. Jews, along with a fair share of Gentiles, pushed and shoved and shouted. Soldiers sat atop horses, stomping and even trampling people. Some were Roman soldiers, but the majority were Herod's men, claiming they were only there to keep the peace.

If reports were true, I could not help but picture John suffering in Herod's dungeon, taken there by the force of these men.

Peter scowled. "This is our land. Only our people have a right to be here."

Andrew quieted him. This was no time for insurrection. It was a time to celebrate and honor God by remembering His hand in bringing our fathers out of Egypt.

Jesus seemed preoccupied, heartsick at the sights around us. I stayed close to Him, ready to shield Him again, eager to fetch Him anything He needed.

What Jesus needed was to leave the crush and craziness of Jerusalem. That first night we stayed just outside the city at Bethany, where Jesus had loved ones to bring Him comfort and peace.

Mary was there, as was her sister Martha, as well as Lazarus, a friend who could always bring a smile to Jesus' lips.

The days of *Pesach* had already commenced, so the diet we were offered was more strict than ever. Nothing that was leavened or fermented was allowed to enter our mouths. Nor could we eat anything that could sprout—no peas, beans, legumes, or corn. The merchants on the corners and in the marketplaces offered no bread, no cakes, no sweets, and no liquors made from wheat.

There was plenty of wine; Passover was a time of wine-drinking. We also had plenty of matzo, the unleavened bread, to remind us that our fathers had no time to bake before their escape from Egypt.

I remembered how Joseph used to gather us all around the big wood table he would set up in the courtyard. He would tell the story of the slaves in Egypt, about their burdens and the ten plagues. His voice still rang in my ears: "Let my people go!" I could see his expressions. I could feel his passion. His face became the face of Moses.

My lips drew back in a smile as my memory returned me to those happy times. I had been part of a family, even though I had been a servant. Joseph had allowed me to participate in asking the four questions. I recalled how Simeon would cry unless he was the one to find the *afikomen*.

Did Jesus ever think back to those times and feel the way I did?

I thought back to how Mary would clean the house, scouring it from top to bottom. Any trace of leavening would be gone. The seder had been a sacred time in the household of Joseph.

During those years when we had been forced to celebrate in Nazareth, we had all shouted with excitement and commitment: *Next year in Jerusalem!* And now we were here . . . and I sensed that this was no ordinary year.

Fifty-three

We were on Temple Mount, and every walled divider was crammed with merchants. I had studied here for years and yet it was difficult even for me to discern the order of the holy courtyard. Stalls were filled with sacrificial doves and pigeons. Lambs were packed so tightly they were climbing on top of each other, bleating out of confusion and terror. It was impossible to hear the voice of the person next to you.

The white stones we walked on were stained with dung and filth. The air reeked.

It was worse than I had remembered.

The look on Jesus' face was one I had never seen.

He was *angry*.

With determined step, He led our party up the stairs, through the masses. I had seldom seen Him rush, but now He was in a hurry.

A merchant stepped out in front of Him, blocking His way.

"Look, look at my doves. They are the finest. Surely, they are worth any price I ask."

"No! Look here." Another man held up a reed cage stuffed with birds. Droppings fell like splattered mud.

Jesus stepped back and I saw His eyes. His anger was increasing.

"I will change your coins," another man rose from his sitting position on a cross-legged stool. He was a money changer. This time my thoughts did not return to my father—I thought only of how to clear the way for Jesus to pass unhindered. It was impossible. People were shoving and pushing, not realizing who their hands touched.

It was Judas who forced his own way to the front. He went to the money changer and spoke to him. Whatever he said made the man stand back so Jesus could walk freely. The merchant had already turned his attention to another.

We had brought no animals for sacrifice, but within the purse that Judas held was enough money to buy the finest lambs. There were 260,000 lambs to choose from. That was the number of throats to be cut—of lives to be sacrificed.

I had never said anything to anyone, but I held a disdain for sacrifice. I knew it was the law, and I kept the law, but I did not understand how killing an innocent animal honored God.

Similitude. That was the explanation Rabbi Asa had provided me. I did not have to understand completely to obey.

"Half-shekels! Half-shekels here!" the money changers cried out, offering the only denomination accepted by the temple priests.

I saw the familiar faces of the high priests, men who had instructed me. Behind them walked scribes. It was a group I would have been included in had I stayed to finish my education. They walked past without acknowledging me.

A lamb ran wild in front of me, bleating for its very life. I nearly tripped over it, and the man next to me did. He toppled and fell and broke the front leg of the animal. It struggled to get up, but its leg had clearly snapped. The lamb could no longer stand and was no longer worthy to be sacrificed.

I felt sick.

When I looked up my stomach lurched. I could not see Jesus. He was lost in the crush. Way up ahead I caught sight of the broad shoulders of Peter, surrounded by the throng, but he too quickly disappeared.

I could not call out. All I could do was try to push my way through the press in the Court of the Gentiles. Which way should I turn? I did not know. How could I?

My heart thundered. I was the servant who would never leave Him, and yet in this very moment when Jesus was given to anger, I had allowed my attention to waver.

Where was He?

And then I heard—above the cries of the merchants, above the bleating of the lambs, above all else—I heard a voice I knew. It was the voice of my Master, but it was not His usual tone. This was a commanding voice so enraged I stopped and stared in wonder.

This was a voice that quelled the chaos.

Suddenly a sharp slap hit the air. Then another. And another.

I was not sure what made the sound, but its effect was immediate. Men and beasts stumbled back and cleared the way. In the center of the Court of the Gentiles came Jesus, wielding a makeshift whip of cords. His anger had exploded into rage. He seemed to me to be twice as large as He was. He lashed out with unmatched power and authority.

He was determined to cleanse the holy temple of unholiness.

Most people stood in shock. Some were angry.

Up and down He went to those who sold salt and oil for sacrifice. Their tables and chairs flew into the air along with their wares.

Wineskins were knocked from shelves, and the rich, red sacrificial liquid ran across the filthy marble like so much blood.

Jesus was enraged, yes—but most apparent, He was in charge.

Again the whip swung and snapped.

I heard someone cheer and turned to see Ovadya. He stood with a group of Pharisees, the hems of their fine white robes stained from the filth on the floor. His fist was held high as if he was hoisting the Torah. "Master!"

Other Jews joined him in urging Jesus to continue.

The cries rose. "Master! Lord! Jesus!"

Two merchants lunged toward Jesus but were stopped cold by Peter. He knocked a third to the ground.

I moved in closer.

Jesus turned to the man who had shoved at Him a reed cage filled with birds. "Take these things hence," He commanded. "Make not my Father's house an house of merchandise."

He overthrew a long table and coins rolled in all directions; the weights and measures slammed against the stone floor, breaking into pieces. The red-faced money changer shook his fist at Jesus and screamed curses, but it was like a whisper in a storm—and Jesus was the hurricane.

Now oxen were bellowing, men unable to curb them. The terrified beasts slid in their own dung and ran through the press, along with sheep and goats. I had never seen such chaos.

I tried to make my way to Jesus, but kept getting pushed back. A woman screamed, and I grabbed her hand to keep her from being trampled. Her veil was yanked off, and she hid her face with her hands.

More cries.

Jesus toppled another table, and another. His whip cracked the air.

Doves flew free from their cages. One fluttered so close to me I reached out to keep it from flying into my face. Its wing was broken.

A hand shoved me forward, and I turned to face the uniformed height of a Roman soldier. He was not alone, but was flanked by others in their shining helmets and armbands. They held their shields.

My heart stopped. What would they do to Jesus? Jesus, who had overthrown tables, set penned animals free, scattered money in every direction. Jesus, who still held the whip in His hand.

I looked at Him. There was no fear in His face, only contempt. And courage.

Within seconds, the Roman soldiers were joined by several of Herod's men.

I pushed around them, trying to reach Jesus before they did.

There was no need. Already Jews were heralding my Master's bold actions. Jews were stepping forth in throngs, grateful for one man's courage to defend their holy ground from the defilement of the Gentiles.

Judas stood at the head of the cheering crowd. Andrew was there too, and so were John and James. Peter held his arms out straight, keeping back anyone who would harm Jesus.

I pushed and shoved my way through the press.

Judas saw me and waved me forward, giving me one of his signature smiles.

I was grateful. I felt proud to stand alongside them. If the soldiers raised their swords to strike our Lord, they would have to strike us first. In so doing, they had to know they would incite a riot.

The soldier in charge broke through and demanded of Jesus, "What sign shewest thou unto us, seeing that thou doest these things?"

Jesus answered, "Destroy this temple, and in three days I will raise it up."

A man behind me scoffed.

I knew Jesus. His words always said more than they seemed to say.

"Forty and six years was this temple in building, and wilt thou rear it up in three days?"

I did not understand then what I would come to know later. Jesus was not talking of a temple built of stone and mortar, but of His body—the holiest of all temples.

A man of authority, a Pharisee in colorful robes, stepped out into the open circle. "I am called Nicodemus," he said. "This man has done no wrong, but stood for right today."

More cheers erupted.

Our people had found in Jesus a leader capable of standing against greed and filth. I had seen the eyes of those watching Jesus as we made our way into the Holy City. He was recognized. Already many had been blessed by Him, cured and made whole. Some had tasted the water turned into wine at the wedding in Cana. Others had been at the waters of baptism with Him. Many recognized Him as more than the man He appeared to be.

I thanked God that Jesus was not as alone as I had feared. His Son was surrounded by people who revered Him, as well as those who reviled Him.

The cattle were still bellowing, the doves still beating their wings against the wicker. Jesus had not finished cleansing the temple, but the merchants had become still, silenced by their own guilt.

"Fear not." I heard my Master's voice and knew His words.

In the end, the soldiers backed away. The merchants and money-changers grumbled and breathed out threatenings, but did nothing more.

And in the end, Jesus drove the vile from the holy. His actions made a statement bolder and bigger than any priestly words could have.

Many who saw and felt His power came to believe what I already knew. This holy temple Jesus had cleansed was indeed *His* Father's house.

Fifty-four

He came like a thief in the night.

Nicodemus.

We were breathing the fresh air from John's rooftop, a place where Jesus preferred to teach. The stars were out; the sky was like a black blanket sprinkled with gold dust. Below us the city glowed with torchlight. The temple itself was outlined by burning torches positioned around the walls.

It was late, but not so late that we could not hear voices calling to one another. Still we could hear the clopping of animal hooves on the stone roads below.

My blood continued to run chill from the fear that someone, soldier or priest, would come for Jesus. Yes, they had allowed Him to leave Temple Mount unharmed. But it was clear to all that He had used His whip and His words to draw an invisible line, dividing those who believed from those who belittled. Among the most disparaging were not the Roman soldiers, but our own leaders, especially the reigning body of authority—the Sanhedrin. They had come out of their holy places to witness the commotion, to watch as Jesus set things aright.

So was it a wonder that one of their own should seek my Master?

Of course, he came cloaked in darkness. A slave arrived first, announcing the honorable member of the Sanhedrin, Nicodemus. We all turned from where we sat in a circle to see the man.

He was familiar to me.

John greeted him and inquired, "What is the purpose of your presence here? This is my home."

Nicodemus spoke with a voice both low and faltering. "I seek the one who is called Jesus. The man who did what many Jews wished to be done."

"Why come shrouded in darkness?"

Nicodemus let down his hood, and I saw that it was indeed the same man who had spoken to Ovadya. He was not young, but not nearly as old as the holiest rabbis at the temple. I had not known him in my days of training as a scribe, but I knew him now.

John recognized him also. He hurried to him and kissed the man's hands, holy hands. "Rabbi, the streets of Jerusalem are not safe at night. Thieves and robbers lay in wait."

"I have my torchbearer," Nicodemus replied, gesturing to his slave, who stood close to me at the top of the ladder.

John offered Nicodemus the wine-skin, but the man refused.

"I have come but for one purpose, to seek out this man many call the Messiah."

The word *Messiah* brought back the words that Andrew had first spoken to Peter about Jesus: "Come, see, I have found the Messiah."

How many times had my pen inscribed that word? How many times had I translated it from one holy script to another? I had written of prophecies to be fulfilled, and now I was seeing them come to pass.

Jesus rose and greeted Nicodemus.

"Rabbi."

The two of them went off a little way, toward the far corner of the rooftop, near a small room where we gathered when the rain fell or the winds blew or the sun beat down too hot.

They sat on mats and Jesus beckoned to me to bring the towel and bowl. The rabbi's feet must be cleansed as an act of honor.

At their feet, I listened as Nicodemus referred to Jesus as a Galilean. He was direct and open as he admitted that had he never witnessed anyone from Galilee so powerful, so eloquent, so obviously educated. He told Jesus that most of the members of the Sanhedrin who had heard of Jesus—even those who had witnessed His power—considered Him a man possessed of evil.

Jesus seemed saddened, but not surprised.

Nicodemus was quick to make clear that not all of the Sanhedrin were opposed to Jesus. "We know that thou art a teacher come from

God: for no man can do these miracles that thou doest, except God be with him."

He was more than a teacher! I knew that.

Nicodemus spoke of John's disciples, men who had reported to the Sanhedrin that a voice had been heard from heaven when Jesus had been baptized.

"One of my fellow priests has a kinsman who claims you turned water into wine at a wedding in Cana."

He did! I wanted to shout. He made gallons and gallons of wine from water. It was the first of so many miracles.

"I have heard your own disciples testify that you are the very Son of David."

It all made sense to me—Son of David, heir to the throne of Israel. Joseph's lineage went back to the mighty king.

Jesus was patient in hearing the concerns and questions of the holy man. Nicodemus talked of many things: teachings and traditions, concern that the law seemed to lead so many in different directions. "This dissension is tearing our very own apart, like the teeth of a wolf."

Jesus nodded and pulled His shawl around His shoulders. A gentle breeze began to stir, soft yet cold. I shivered and pulled my own robes tighter. James brought a blanket and offered it to the man, but he declined.

"I am not cold. I am only concerned with answers. My brethren must not discover where I am. It would only lead to further division."

Nicodemus brought up many of the concerns I had, taking me back to Nazareth and the battles between our Nazarene rabbis and visiting teachers. I remembered great dissension over questions as simple as, "What does it mean to be Jewish?"

All of the disciples, even the newest ones, gathered around now and listened as Nicodemus asked and Jesus answered.

Finally, Nicodemus asked Jesus, "How can one enter the kingdom of God?"

Jesus leaned forward. "Verily, verily, I say unto thee, Except a man be born again, he cannot see the kingdom of God."

Nicodemus rubbed his graying beard. "How can a man be born when he is old? can he enter the second time into his mother's womb, and be born?"

Peter laughed, but it was no light matter.

Always Jesus spoke more than He said.

"Except a man be born of water and of the Spirit, he cannot enter into the kingdom of God. That which is born of the flesh is flesh; and that which is born of the Spirit is spirit. Marvel not that I said unto thee, Ye must be born again."

The wind kicked up, and Jesus raised His hand into the air. "The wind bloweth where it listeth, and thou hearest the sound thereof, but canst not tell whence it cometh, and wither it goeth: so is every one that is born of the Spirit."

"How can these things be?" Nicodemus asked.

"Art thou a master of Israel, and knowest not these things?"

Again, Peter laughed, this time joined by many of the others.

But Nicodemus would not be deterred or offended. His questions kept coming.

Jesus finally asked, "If I have told you earthly things, and ye believe not, how shall ye believe, if I tell you of heavenly things?"

Then Jesus bore testimony of Himself. It might not have been clear to all, but it was clear to me. The very Son of Man sat before Nicodemus, trying to help the priest understand his own scriptures. Moses and every other ancient prophet had testified of His coming, and now He was before us.

Of all people, Nicodemus should not have struggled with that fact.

"Whosoever believeth in him should not perish, but have eternal life. For God so loved the world, that he gave his only begotten Son, that whosoever believeth in him should not perish, but have everlasting life."

Whosoever.

I thought of myself and my own struggles, but they seemed simple compared to the struggle expressed on Nicodemus' face.

I could see the agony in his twisted expression. He wanted to believe.

He asked, "Does God send His Son to condemn us?"

Jesus smiled and shook His head. "God sent not his Son into the world to condemn the world; but that the world through him might be saved. He that believeth on him is not condemned: but he that believeth not is condemned already, because he hath not believed in the name of the only begotten Son of God. And this is the condemnation, that light is come into the world, and men loved darkness rather than light, because their deeds were evil. For every one that doeth evil hateth the light, neither cometh to the light, lest his deeds should be reproved. But he that doeth truth cometh to the light, that his deeds may be made manifest, that they are wrought in God."

God knew my darkest deeds. I could not hide them from Him.

When Jesus talked of spiritual rebirth, His teachings were deep. They required keen ears and an open heart.

Even as Jesus testified of the light, the flame from the torch in the slave's hand flickered in Jesus' eyes. The reflection of light was there, but it was something more: the man who taught us was a living torch. We need only open our eyes to see that truth.

Fifty-five

We tarried in Judea for a season; Jesus had added more faithful ones to his inner circle, choosing carefully the men who were most believing and sincere. These were those who would carry His word to the masses, who would go into the lands where He would never go.

My feelings of jealousy vanished as I grew to love these men. They were good men, and each was as devoted to Jesus as I was. Our lives had been changed forever, and before us spread a work so great and powerful we could see no end.

Every where we went, people sought out my Master; all wanted favor from Him. The lines of people wanting to see Jesus wound through all of Judea. Every person came with a need and a story. Jesus heard them all and helped the ones who believed on Him.

They went away, some weeping with gratitude, some cured but ungrateful. Others were angry because the power of Jesus did not work in their lives.

"Why?" Andrew asked James. "Why does our Master's touch not cure all?"

I knew that answer. So did James. "First they must believe, and then cometh the miracle."

Many claimed to believe, but did not. Those people frightened me because they directed their rage toward my Master. They made accusations and threats of revenge. There were times when that old fear of losing my father crept up like a strangling snake from my childhood and choked the air from me.

My greatest fear was that I—that all of us—might lose Jesus. Some insane person might harm Him. An angry mob might stone

Him. More and more, there were men who followed us, accusing Jesus of blasphemy.

They were the nonbelievers.

The ones who believed, though, were made well. I saw it every day. Jesus touched the lame, and they rose to their feet. He blessed the blind, and film was peeled from their eyes. Lepers were cleansed and made well at His command.

Word of His power and might and unlimited mercy spread through the whole of Judea. I wrote home to Deborah and told her of the miracles her cousin performed. She did not reply, but I did not expect her to; we did not stay in any one place for any real length of time, so exchanging letters was often not possible. Jesus was always anxious to move on to the next village, to reach as many people as He could.

Thoughts of Deborah never left me, but there was no time to pity myself, because Jesus kept us occupied. I might have been a servant, but it was He who taught me by His example of service. He found every person worthy of kindness and time. *Every* person.

Rumors of John's imprisonment proved to be exaggerated. To my utter joy, John was in Aenon near Salim, baptizing still. John sent on to us the disciples who came to him and believed on him. There were many. They arrived almost daily, humble and anxious to serve the One even greater than John.

I feared because of the expectations of so many. They wanted Jesus to bring down the Roman soldiers. They wanted Herod's men killed. They wanted Jesus to rise up and cleanse all of Palestine the way He had cleansed Temple Mount. They wanted their kingdom back.

Didn't they understand that Jesus came to establish a higher kingdom? Had they not read their own scriptures?

One night I sat outside the house in Bethany, a place of love and peace. I sat beneath the canopy of a gathering storm; the clouds were black as ash and ready to spill. I had made a small fire to warm myself, and I sat close to it. Judas came to me after the flames had burned and become no more than red embers.

"You are alone?"

I nodded.

"Forgive me for asking, but why . . . " he paused, and I could tell the question on his tongue was bitter.

"Today we have seen our Master do mighty miracles. Today He restored a child's burned face to innocence. Today He cast a devil from a man. Today He taught us as one with authority only God could give Him."

I nodded my agreement.

Judas gave me the smile of a friend. "Almon, you know Jesus best. You have been His servant since He was just a boy."

I nodded again.

"Why then do you not have the Master lay fingers to your lips and heal your muteness?"

That question again!

I had no reply for Judas. As always, my deepest feelings went unspoken.

"Almon, you are a good man. Your dedication to Jesus never tires. Your pen is seldom dry; you are willing to make letters for those who cannot write. Though I wish you would, you do not always take the money you have earned.

"All you have to do is ask our Master. With a word, He can give life to your tongue."

He added more wood to the fire and watched as orange flames lapped at the black night. Red sparks rose into the air and quickly cooled to black ashes.

"Almon, you are more than a servant. You are a man of value. I know that you believe in Jesus, but you must also believe in yourself."

I stared into the flames and gave silent thanks for Judas. He was my true friend and always had a way of lifting my spirits. I wondered if I could tell him the truth . . . that despicable sins from ages ago kept me from asking for what I knew Jesus could and would give me.

No. I couldn't tell anyone. All I could do was live my best life. God knew my heart, the good and the bad. I had no secrets from Him.

Judas yawned and stood. "I am weary. Tomorrow is another long day. Our Master never slows, never quits giving. Do you realize what a wealthy man He would be—we would *all* be—if He charged just a half-shekel for His miracles? I think about it often. I calculate the figures in my head."

His words did not surprise me. Judas was always thinking of money.

He yawned again. "Oh, well . . . rest well, my friend. The Lord's mercy is new every day. It is a blessing I have come to count on."

He patted my shoulder and walked off into the darkness.

I sat before the comfort of the fire, my thoughts flickering like the last of the flames. And then I closed my eyes, curled up on the warm ground, and began to dream.

I dreamt I was back on the shores of the Yored-Dan. John was beckoning me to come out into the water. His smile was as wide as the river. Jesus' voice echoed around me. I recognized His voice but could not make out what He was saying.

Then I realized He was talking about being born again—the same thing He had taught Nicodemus. I tried to understand. Words and gauzy images came one at a time: *repentance . . . immersion . . . spirit . . . obedience.*

Being born again was a process, not a plunge.

I saw myself baptized only once, but I saw myself being born again with every kept commandment, every act of service.

Being born again was a process, not a plunge.

I shivered when I woke. My dream was so real that I expected my robes to be wet. The smell of the river was thick around me. I felt clean and happy. Hopeful.

A hand touched my shoulder, and I turned to see the smile of Jesus. He was there to stoke the fire, to help fry corn cakes for our morning meal.

Service was His way.

That way garnered great crowds. Each day the masses grew. Since Nicodemus visited, the Sanhedrin paid particular attention to Jesus and His burgeoning ministry. They sent spies to gather evidence against the Master.

They attributed His miracles to the power of Satan.

Satan!

They accused Jesus of blasphemy, but could not prove their claims.

Jesus *was* who He claimed He was.

He was the Son, the One, the Master.

We were in Judea when indisputable word came that John had spoken out against Herod Antipas. *Our* John. The great, wild Baptist. The man who had baptized my Master.

His testimony resounded throughout all of Palestine. "He that believeth on the Son hath everlasting life: and he that believeth not the Son shall not see life; but the wrath of God abideth on him."

There was more trouble involving Antipas, the vile coward, insane with jealousy. Antipas, who had married his brother's wife and defiled the law. John had condemned him, and now John was in chains and lay suffering in the fortress at Machaerus.

I knew Machaerus; just east of the Dead Sea, the fortress stood on a slope. It was an edifice fit to house demons, not a holy man like John.

The news frightened and sickened me.

I saw agony in Jesus' eyes when He heard the news. He laced His fingers and put them behind His head, then tipped His chin to His chest and wept.

Andrew, who knew John so well, sobbed audibly. "John will surely die. He is a man of the wilderness. His days have been spent beneath the sun and stars; he has never known confinement. Surely, my friend will suffer."

I thought of the nights Jesus and John had slept on the rooftop in Nazareth—how John had pointed out all the constellations to us.

I remembered the last time I had seen John. Herod's soldiers had been after him during Roman fourth watch, the earliest hour. He and Jesus had parted in soberness and love.

Jesus' disciples tried to comfort Him, to assure Him that John was a mighty man and that he could fight Herod and his armies. He was God's faithful servant. Surely he would be set free.

Jesus expressed gratitude for the kind words, but left to go on a walk. Alone.

What I knew of Antipas was this: his father was Herod the Great, the one who had rebuilt most of our holy land—including the temple named in his honor. Herod's temple was really God's temple, but people had forgotten that. Appointed by Caesar Augustus, he had ordered the slaughter of babies. Their innocent blood stained his hands. He claimed to be a Jew, but lived the life of a pagan.

Since his father's death, Antipas now governed Galilee and Perea. In his position, he used women for pleasure and lust. He had recently divorced his wife to marry the wife of his half-brother Philip. (It was nearly impossible to keep an accurate record of the household of Herod—it twisted and turned and grew like a noxious vine.) Jews everywhere were appalled by such blatant sin.

John spoke boldly, calling the sin a sin. His followers grew, too, threatening Herod until his soldiers came to take the prophet of truth into chains.

I felt heartsick for John, but fearful for Jesus.

If Antipas was threatened by John, a man who did nothing but cry repentance and baptize, what would he do to Jesus—a man who performed undeniable miracles daily?

I felt certain that Jesus would rally us. I felt certain we would go to John and help set him free. I believed Jesus would command the fortress walls to crumble, just as Joshua had done in Jericho.

I was wrong.

Jesus returned from his walk and asked me to fetch His bag. In it He carried His old sandals, tooled by Joseph, a clean change of robes, and a number of personal items.

I packed my own bag, including dried meats and fruits. I filled both water-skins.

Jesus thanked me, but then dismissed me. This was another journey He had to make on His own.

I thought of the forty days he'd spent in the wilderness. I had waited, nearly going insane with worry. This would likely be the same, but there was no time to ask questions.

Jesus turned and walked toward the nearest ridge.

Just like that, He was gone.

Fifty-six

Angels.

Jesus had gone to send angels to His cousin.

I don't know how He did it, but when I knew that it was done, I felt relief. We all did. John was still in prison, but we did not need to fear that he was alone or forgotten. His cousin, the Master of all, had sent angels to comfort and give strength.

After that, Jesus announced that we were leaving Judea for Galilee.

I was ecstatic. I would be that much closer to Deborah.

Instead of traveling through Perea as we always did, Jesus told us He needed to travel through Samaria.

"Samaria!" Matthew said, shock on his face.

He was not alone. All of us were stunned at the prospect of traveling through Samaria.

Judas stepped forward. "Master, Samaria is peopled with pagans. The road that runs along the hill of Akrabbim, leading into the land, is wet with blood. The rebels breed there."

Jesus knew but would not be deterred.

John begged, his voice cracking with emotion. "The climate is unsafe, Lord. Antipas has imprisoned your cousin. He would do the same to you, Master." John turned away.

Peter surprised me by standing with boldness to support such a route. "Samaria is the land of our ancient fathers. Yes, it has been overrun with half-heathens. Yes, it is unsafe. But we travel with One who is protected."

We all looked to Jesus.

I knew the Samaritans were a mixed people. They held on to pagan superstitions, but combined them with sacred Jewish doctrines. Like Jews, they waited for a Messiah. They had once built a temple of their own on Mount Gerizim. They appointed their own high priest, like Herod had appointed ours. I hated them, but Jesus did not.

Some believed the land of Samaria was haunted.

Others simply refused to step on idolatrous ground.

It was just a three-day trek, even allowing time to stop along the way and help those who came to Jesus. I could not help but note how our throng thinned the closer we came to Sychar, the land of Jacob's well.

The country was hilly and the sun hot. Everything around us looked baked and brown. It was the first time I had seen Jesus look so worn.

"Are you ill, Master?" John asked.

Jesus explained that he was not ill, but weary.

We approached the hallowed ground of Sychar by first praying. It was here that Jacob gave Joseph the land. The well itself was dug to the depth of twenty men, ten men across. How many lives, both human and animal, had it saved?

It might have been inhabited by Samaritans, but the ground felt sacred to me. I was glad to be there.

On one side of the worn stone well rose Ebal, on the other, Gerizim—both holy mountains. Close by, but out of view, was the tomb where Joseph's bones were carried from Egypt and laid to rest.

As we approached the well, Jesus asked Judas what was in our purse.

Judas didn't have to open it to know the exact change. "Enough to purchase food and lodging, Master."

He asked us to go ahead into the village, to purchase what we needed, and to allow Him some solitude at this hallowed place.

I did not want to leave him, but Jesus and I had developed a look that we exchanged. He told me with His eyes to go ahead into town. He would be all right.

And so we left Him.

"What food can we purchase in Sychar?" Judas asked, clearly disgusted.

"To eat the bread of a Samaritan is equal to eating the flesh of swine."

Samaritans looked at us with the disdain we felt for them. The faces were unfriendly. We drew looks as deadly as daggers. The marketplace was unsettled and unfamiliar.

All the disciples were anxious.

"Let us move with haste," said Judas. "To give our money to these people is a difficult task for me."

"We must hurry to return to Jesus," John said.

Peter snorted. "Jesus is Lord of all. He can tend to Himself."

The ever-present friction between Peter and John was something we all felt. The men were so different—Peter with his bold, brash ways, and John with his thoughtful, almost tender approach. Yet Jesus valued them both.

"John, if you are so worried about Jesus, pick up your sandals and advance a little faster," Peter said, moving ahead of all of us.

John put on his wounded expression, but said nothing. Andrew looked at me and rolled his eyes. We all felt anxious, tense, and confused.

Judas refused to pay with the prices the Samaritans were asking, not even for bread. As he bickered—and as the marketplace grew increasingly more crowded with us as the object of mounting curiosity—the tension between Peter and John grew.

Finally, Peter thrust a finger in Judas' face. "Our Master waits. He is hungry. Pay what is asked, and I will return to Him. You can linger as long as you wish."

"I will return with you," John said.

"You *all* go back. Almon will stay with me," Judas said, showing the frustration we all felt.

It took more coaxing, but finally Judas opened the purse strings and purchased enough food to help sustain Jesus.

Peter and the others fled from the city like they were being chased.

I stayed beside Judas, listening to him drive down every price that was set.

"Once we leave here we are headed to Cana," he said. "We will need supplies. My brethren fail to understand . . . each coin must count."

We had been there bargaining for a while when a woman came running down the market path. She was shouting. "Come and see! The Messiah drinks from our father's well!"

"What did you say?" someone asked.

The woman was out of breath. She wore no veil and carried no waterskin or jug. Her hair was long, dark, and wavy as the sea. I looked away, ashamed that I had gazed upon her.

I could still hear her words. "I have just come from Jacob's well. There sits a man, a prophet, who said, 'Give me to drink.'"

Judas looked at me, his eyes wide. "Jesus. She speaks of Jesus."

I nodded.

"Come!" the woman cried, bringing a crowd of the curious to her. "Come! There sits a prophet at Jacob's well."

Judas pushed through the people and approached her with humility. "Tell us. Tell us of your encounter."

I stayed at his heels.

She looked at Judas and then at me. "You are Jews."

"Yes," said Judas. "We are Jews. Tell us of your encounter with this prophet."

"He, too, is a Jew," the woman said, "a Jew like you. He asked water of me, a Samaritan. He had no dipper. He told me that He could provide living water, that if I drank of the water He provides, I will not thirst again." Her smile was so wide I could see all of her teeth.

She was a beautiful woman, and I did not try to look away. I no longer felt guilty for looking at her. I only saw her enthusiasm for Jesus.

I understood the meaning of *living water*, but those who had gathered did not. How long had they lived in the desert? Their mouths were dry. Their spirits were dry. These Samaritans had not drunk from the well of truth for generations.

"This prophet knew my heart," she said, tears now dribbling down her cheeks. "He spoke to me of things He could not know without divine revelation. I tell you, the man who now sits by the well is a prophet. Come! Come see, one and all."

We came. We saw. We heard.

For days our Master taught starving Samarians that a new and better way had come to their old and parched world.

He brought them living water.

He was *Jehovah*, the one both Samaritans and Jews awaited.

And the Samaritans, those unbelieving pagans who Jews had loathed for years, the very people we had urged Jesus to avoid, opened their withered hearts and minds and accepted Jesus.

They believed.

Fifty-seven

Cana was the same peaceful, lush town I remembered. It had been nearly a year since we'd been there for the wedding—a year since Jesus had turned the water into wine, His first miracle. A year since Deborah had been beside me.

The place was the same, but we were changed.

Twelve months ago, Jesus had a small but growing following. Now we could not go anywhere without people calling for The Healer, The Messias. They had forgotten that He was a scholar, a skilled carpenter. He was now the Son of God.

Of course people sought Him.

We were just outside the common courtyard, near the main well, when a man came through the press. I recognized him as an official of Antipas.

My heart went cold. John was still in prison. Had the time come that someone would attempt to take Jesus into custody?

"What is it you desire?" Peter asked. We were all tired; it was hot, and we had not yet eaten. Peter was in no humor to tolerate any harassment, not even from a nobleman.

I kept my eye on Jesus. He was occupied with a small child, a girl who had been brought to Him in her mother's arms. The child's hand was bandaged and the linen was soaked red. She had sobbed herself limp. Her dark curls clung to her face.

Gently, Jesus removed the rag.

I saw that an accident had taken off two of the girl's fingers. They were the same two fingers Joseph had lost.

Jesus tipped His head skyward. He always gave thanks before performing any miracle.

Voices rose. I turned back to the nobleman. He was begging for an audience with the Master. I took heart in the fact that he wore no armor, rode no horse, and did not use a voice of authority. Instead he was pleading.

When I turned back to Jesus, my mouth fell open.

The girl's hand was whole. Her restored fingers reached up to touch Jesus' beard. They both smiled. The grateful mother knelt at Jesus' feet, bathing them in tears.

Now I understood. I grasped why James and the other brothers had been so distraught, so upset with Jesus. They knew He had power to restore and to save, and yet Joseph had died.

But His time had not yet come.

So much was finally beginning to unfold in my mind.

Nathaniel approached Him. "Master?"

Jesus turned.

Peter motioned for His attention. The nobleman looked absolutely desperate. Jesus kissed the child and returned her to her mother's arms.

I overheard the nobleman cry out to anyone who would listen. "I reside in Capernaum, where my son lies sick."

I thought of Matthew and James, who were on the road between Cana and Capernaum. If they knew of this man's son, they could aid him—but there was no way to inform them.

Jesus went directly to the nobleman, who bowed in His presence. "Rabbi, I beseech thee, heal my son, for he is at the point of death."

Jesus paused, looking worn yet compassionate. "Except ye see signs and wonders, ye will not believe."

I knew what Jesus was doing—He was testing the faith of this father. I had seen Him do it many times, but this father, unlike many others, was sincere.

I said a silent prayer that Jesus would not only heal the dying son, but would also grant the father enough faith to meet his request.

The man shook his head and kissed our Master's hands. "Sir, come down ere my child die."

Jesus still looked weary—too weary to make the journey from Cana to Capernaum without rest. I sensed we all felt the same way. Yet weariness had never stopped Jesus from doing good.

He touched the man's shoulder. "Go thy way; thy son liveth."

No one dared to breathe.

Slowly, the father looked up into the blue eyes of Jesus. "I believe," he said. "I believe that my son liveth!"

It was the first time I had witnessed Jesus healing from afar. Always before, we had gone to the home of the sick, or the sick one had been brought to us. I don't know why it surprised me, but it did.

Judas came to my side. He did not look astounded. "God governs all things in all places. Blessed be the Lord God Almighty."

The father left gratefully.

Judas wanted to ask for payment, but knew better. Jesus would not tolerate such a request. Judas turned to me and lowered his voice. "Imagine the wealth we could take in with such power. Imagine!" He opened his purse to show that we were nearly devoid of funds.

Later, when James and Matthew arrived, they told of an encounter they had experienced along the road. James asked, "Did the Master heal a dying boy?"

"A boy," said Judas, "the son of a nobleman. He could have paid a great deal, but I could not even ask for a—"

James held up his hand to cut Judas short. "We met him. We met the nobleman. His servants, also. They had come to tell their master that his son was mending!"

"It is true," Matthew said. "The man asked at what hour his son began to improve. When they told him, he said it was at the very same hour that Jesus had declared, 'Thy son liveth.'"

James did a dance, and his sandals kicked up the dirt. "And now the nobleman and his entire household believe. They all believe!"

"If our Master continues on with such miracles, soon all of Palestine will believe," said Peter, joining the conversation.

Judas rubbed his chin. "Imagine if we charged a mere . . . "

We all turned to glare at him. He sighed and shook the purse that barely jingled.

"Poor Judas," John said. "You don't understand. We have faith. We have Jesus. We are already wealthy beyond measure."

Fifty-eight

We were home!

Nazareth was everything I remembered, quaint and ordered. The steep streets were welcome paths after all of the flat, dusty roads we'd traveled. The faces were not all unfamiliar, though time had altered everyone. I was anxious to see Jesus accepted by those who knew Him, revered now that His fame had arrived before we did.

Finally, He was among people who knew and understood Him.

The marketplace was busy and smelled of fresh bread. It brought back many memories, almost all of them fond.

I excused myself from Jesus, wanting to give Him privacy as He rejoined His family. Though Mary and her sons had recently been in Capernaum, they were now back in Nazareth, readying for Jesus' return to His home village.

The disciples also divided, feeling as I did.

Before I sought out Deborah, I went to our house—the abode I had left only half complete when I was called to follow Jesus. The sight of the house left my knees unsteady. Someone had finished the entire structure. It was even whitewashed and had a terra-cotta roof.

In awe, I walked around the two rooms that were meant to be a home for Deborah and me. The more I saw, the more assured I became that those rooms would one day still be our home. I recognized the quality wood door and knew that Joel had contributed it. The fine craftsmanship led me to believe that the brothers of Jesus had worked on my behalf.

When I considered how blessed I was, I bowed behind the building and silently poured out my gratitude; it flowed like water from a pitcher. *Hear, oh Lord, the words of my heart . . . the words my tongue cannot speak.*

If I had been given a voice, it would have filled the hill country, a land that I had not realized how much I had missed.

I was so happy to be returned.

But I had not returned with Jesus, the carpenter, Jesus bar Joseph. No.

I was in the shadow of Jesus the Christ, the Promised Messiah. I knew I could walk to the synagogue, go to the ark, and find scroll after scroll prophesying of the very man who called Nazareth home.

How would the people here accept Jesus now that His true identity was known?

I washed myself at the top of Market Street. The spring water was just as cold and sweet as I remembered it.

Before I even reached Mary's house, I heard the sound of voices and smelled her bread baking.

Home.

Salome was the first to greet me. When had she grown into a woman?

She stood at the gate, watching a red-breasted bird hop from branch to branch. Seeing her took me back to the days when, as a boy, Jesus had spent hours watching birds and animals. He still loved everything God's breath had given life to.

Because she was the youngest, I did not know Salome as well as I knew the others. But she wore her mother's smile and bade me welcome.

There was much rejoicing at the house. Mary took me in her arms and held me like she would her own son.

"Oh, Almon. It is good to see you safe and looking well." Mary, too, looked well. "Your Deborah is in the kitchen."

I hurriedly moved to the other side of the house and peered in through the window. I saw Deborah's red hair flowing around her veil. When she saw me she hurried outside.

"Oh, Almon!"

There was something different about Deborah—something I felt but could not discern. She seemed lighter, happier. I sensed it was more than my return.

"Have you been to our home?"

I nodded and fought to hold back my tears of gratitude.

"My father and Malik have worked so hard. Joseph's sons, also, labored to surprise you."

It was as I had suspected, and my gratitude filled my heart to overflowing. My arms reached out for Deborah, and though we could have been condemned for it, I embraced her and pressed her so tight that I felt her own heart pound next to mine.

Carefully, she took my hand and guided it to her face. She lifted her veil, only a slip, so my hand could touch her cheek. I remembered what her skin felt like . . . all those years ago I had touched it. It felt like barnacles on the back of a giant fish.

But now Deborah's cheek felt smooth and unblemished beneath my fingertips. I was so shocked I quickly pulled my hand away.

She began to sob.

Immediately, I tried to apologize.

"No!" she cried, "No! I am joyous. You do not understand. When Jesus arrived today, I went to Him in faith. I begged Him to heal me, and with a simple word, He did." Her voice was choked with emotion so deep it made my own knees buckle.

I fell to the ground before her and did not even try to stop my tears. My Deborah had been made whole. No wonder the household was rejoicing.

Deborah touched my own cheek with her hand. "My cousin can do the same for you, Almon. He can give you voice."

No.

"All you have to do is believe and ask."

No.

At that moment Naomi's head came out of the open window. "Deborah! It is not proper for you to be alone with Almon."

Quickly, Deborah made her own apologies. "Mother, I have shared my miracle with Almon."

"Then there is no reason to stay with him longer. You are needed in the kitchen." Naomi's words were stern, but her tone was gentle. I knew she felt the same overpowering joy Deborah and I did. How could she not? She was Deborah's mother.

When Deborah went inside, I went in search of Jesus. I found Him in the same hills He had wandered so often as a boy. Sheep were scattered among the rocks, and He sat on a boulder, looking down on the rows that made up Nazareth.

I bowed before Him. There was no need to search for words I could not utter. Jesus understood my heart.

I was thrilled, but my Master appeared saddened. I took His mood for weariness and walked away, allowing Him the solitude He enjoyed so rarely.

The time spent in Nazareth was pleasant, but short. Jesus did not perform the mighty miracles He might have, though to those of us who loved Deborah, there was no greater miracle than her healing.

The *Shabbat* came upon us as it did every week. Mary set to cleaning the house, preparing the food, setting out the candles. It was my favorite day, and I felt great joy as we all walked together to worship.

Rabbi Asa met us in the synagogue courtyard. He wore the same shawl as he had all those years ago. He greeted Jesus with the respect due a fellow rabbi.

"How is John?"

The smile melted from Jesus' face.

"He languishes still at the cruelty of Antipas," Peter said, practically spitting the words at Rabbi Asa's feet.

Nazarenes came in numbers I did not recall, but I suspected they crowded to worship this day, hoping to hear from the man who was rumored to have turned water into wine and whose very touch had taken the deformity from Deborah's cheeks.

We separated, the women from the men. Inside it was just as I remembered—the Most Holy and Holy areas divided. I was surprised to see rabbis who I had never seen there before.

I took my seat at the back with Joel, while Andrew, Peter, John, James, Nathaniel, and Judas sat near the front, close to the lectern.

All eyes were fixed on Jesus, especially those of Rabbi Zeev, a man who had not aged well. His face was rough and withered, and the whites of his eyes were veined red. Even after all the years that had passed, his presence made my heart go cold.

But this was not his moment; it belonged to Jesus. Jesus was a man they knew, and yet they had heard so many things about Him that seemed unbelievable.

I kept watch over Deborah, but her veil was thick and I could not see her face. I did see people stare at her and whisper.

Mary seemed content, pleased to have her family gathered around her in such a sacred setting.

Jesus was friendly as always, but focused. He seemed to be looking above the lintel at the candlestick, with its seven sacred branches. I wondered what thoughts filled His mind.

When the service commenced, my own focus fixed on the prayers. I mouthed *Shema,* even though no sound came from my lips. I listened especially for Deborah's song during the music. I couldn't imagine an angel sounding any sweeter.

More prayers, the seventeen benedictions, and finally the unrolling of the scroll. Seven men were called to read. First a son of Aaron, then a Levite, and five other Israelites in no particular order. I thought of how many times I had heard Joseph read. A searing pain sliced through me; how I missed him! I looked around at his family and knew I wasn't the only one feeling sorrow at his absence.

Nazareth without Joseph was not Nazareth to me.

Jesus was chosen, as we all knew He would be, to read from the Prophets. People sat forward, anxious to hear this man they knew, but did not know. I heard the whispers rise around me. Were the rumors true? Had He really saved a child from the grip of death? Had He really gone mad and cleansed the temple? Beneath Deborah's veil, was her face really smooth?

I hated the murmuring. I hated the disbelief that went through the synagogue as sure as a disease.

I looked up when I heard a murmur rise from the packed crowd. Jesus had stood to read from the prophets. To Him was delivered the book of Esaias.

He read, and my thoughts again turned to Joseph. I felt sad that he could not see Jesus now—so eloquent, so powerful.

How could anyone hear Him and doubt?

His voice was gentle, yet full as a warm day, as He began to read the prophecies about Himself. I looked at Him with eyes that wept. A burning filled my chest and drove its way from the center out until I thought my ribs were on fire. It was a feeling I welcomed and bid stay.

He who stood before us reading the words of Isaiah was God's Son.

He read in perfect Hebrew. Then came the *targums,* the oral translations into Aramaic.

"The Spirit of the Lord is upon me, because he hath anointed me to preach the gospel to the poor; he hath sent me to heal the broken-hearted, to preach deliverance to the captives, and recovering of sight to the blind, to set at liberty them that are bruised. To preach the acceptable year of the Lord."

I wanted to stand and shout. I ached to open my mouth and testify that Jesus was He of whom Isaiah wrote.

Jesus then closed the book, gave it back to the attendant, and quietly took His seat. The entire synagogue went still as stone.

All waited. Even the children were silent.

Jesus did not need to raise His voice to be heard of all. "This day is this scripture fulfilled in your ears."

I looked around. It was difficult for people to stay seated. I was certain they felt the same power and glory I did—that fire burned in their hearts.

Jesus was the Promised Messiah. Here in His own humble Nazarene synagogue was the very God we all claimed to worship.

I half expected the stone walls of the synagogue to come tumbling down in joy and power. Instead, to my sorrow and utter dismay, I heard Rabbi Zeev say, "How can He be the Son of God? He is one of us. We know Him."

The fire in my heart was doused by the ice that filled my chest.

Peter suddenly leapt to his feet. Then it was as if the synagogue was struck by a hurricane from within. People were shouting, saying things like "Is this not Joseph's son?"

Jesus stood, and I saw the joy drain from His face.

He had so much to give to these, the people He knew and loved so much. Yet they were rejecting Him because they thought they knew Him.

Even James, Joses, Jude, and Simon appeared ashamed at their elder brother's brazen declaration.

Joel, who had witnessed for himself the power of his nephew, kept his head down. Malik took his son by the hand and headed out the door.

My heart broke. Jesus' own family could not stand up for Him.

A man in front of me turned to face me. His eyes were hard as baked earth. "Are you not one with Him?"

I raised and lowered my chin slowly, so there could be no mistake. Yes. I was with Jesus.

The man sneered. "I know you. You are the mute. What good are you?" He then pushed forward, crossing the divider between the Holy and the Most Holy areas. He stopped at the barricade Peter made with his body, but shouted at our Master anyway. "Jesus, they say you have performed mighty miracles for others. Perform them for us now!"

Others joined in the chaos and cruelty.

"Show us a sign!"

"He is no prophet—He is but a carpenter."

"A lowly carpenter."

"His miracles are only rumors."

I looked to Mary, but saw that Naomi and Deborah were guiding her toward the door for the women. I was glad. I did not want any of them to witness how the dogs of Nazareth had turned on their own.

Jesus moved to the lectern and the chaos quieted.

"Look at Him! He is going to bring about a miracle!"

"Bring Him water; let us see if His wine is as sweet as they say in Cana."

"Stand, Rabbi Asa, let Jesus lay hands on you to make your bent back straight."

"What of His mute?"

"Yes, what of His mute, the servant, Almon? If Jesus works miracles, why is Almon still silent?"

"Speak, Almon. Tell us that your Master is the Messiah!"

My head felt crushed. I could not think.

I looked to Jesus. There was a sorrow, deep as Jacob's well, in His eyes. The warmth had turned to cold, and I felt the heart of Jesus break in my own chest.

Jesus quietly said, "No prophet is accepted in his own country."

The cry went up in disappointment and vengeance. Though He had much to say, His own people refused to hear Him.

"Blasphemy!" shouted an angry man near the back of the room.

Master. I said the word, but no sound came forth. My body moved through the crush with irreverence. I pushed my way to Jesus with a force I had never known. I even made it around Peter.

I knew these people. They were neighbors, lifelong friends, the family of Jesus.

They were His own.

What right did they have to curse Him like this? Why could they not see who they were rejecting? *Why?*

In an instant the crowd became a mob.

"Stone him!" cried a voice. I looked to see a neighbor who had grown up and studied with Jesus in the synagogue.

Peter and I were beside Jesus, but He did not require our strength. He stood on legs of His own. I felt His power. Why could they not feel it, too?

Rabbi Asa stood, gripping the lectern, trying to get to his balance so he could speak. But a young boy hollered, "Sit down, old man. Stay steady."

These were religious people. They had spent their lives reading the Law and the Prophets. They should have recognized who stood before them. But their rituals were empty and hollow, their hearts filled with blackness and evil.

Rage spread like flames.

Hands pushed and pulled at me. Someone tore my cloak and shoved me to the ground.

I heard a man cry out in pain and saw that Judas had also been knocked to the stone floor. He looked at me with sheer terror on his face.

Where was Peter? The other disciples? Where was Jesus?

All I could see were legs and feet—feet I had washed when they had entered the household of Joseph. Now those feet kicked at me, kicked at my Master.

Jesus was being led, driven like a beast out the door.

The mob was hot and vicious. They tore at Jesus, shoving and pushing.

I managed to stand and tried to follow Him.

"Headlong!" I heard someone shout.

No.

No!

Surely, they could not mean . . . a rebel's beating.

These men of faith, men who sat on chairs and ate at tables crafted by Jesus, circled their Savior to kill Him. They were the complete definition of hypocrisy. None of them was willing to lift a fist or raise a stone—instead, they intended to crowd Jesus over the edge of a cliff. If the mob moved as one body, no individual could be held responsible for murder.

Yet it *was* murder.

Cowardly and brutal.

It could not happen. Jesus could not meet His end like this.

I had known fear so many times, and yet nothing seized me like the hands of fear now seized me over what was happening.

The mob screamed and cried and men's cheeks grew red with rage, their eyes black with hatred. Their faces were the faces of demons.

I caught up with Jesus and grabbed hold of His robe.

He looked at me and whispered simply, "Fear not."

Jesus did not die that day, crushed on the red rocks of Nazareth. Instead, while the mob raged, He simply passed through the crowd unharmed and unhindered. The hand of His Father guided Jesus to safety.

When I saw Him next, outside the village that had once been His home, Jesus marveled at the disbelief of those He knew and loved.

He did not tarry in sorrow. Instead, He turned His back on Nazareth and began a new path. I rushed after Him, anxiously wondering where my Master would lead me next.

Fifty-nine

A sense of relief washed over me. Jesus made Capernaum His base because it was a place of believers. Matthew had family here, and along the shores of the lake Jesus had summoned His "fishers of men." Peter, Andrew, James, and John had not only fished here, but had worshipped in the synagogue where Zebedee held a place of honor. Jesus' aunt and Zebedee's wife, Salome, enjoyed preparing abundant meals for us.

Unlike those in Nazareth, the people here listened with open ears and open hearts.

Even the rabbi proclaimed, "We are astonished at His doctrine; for He teaches as one with authority."

Just as I began to feel secure in His safety in Capernaum, something happened that made me fear a repeat of the horror in Nazareth. While Jesus was teaching in the synagogue, a man began to scream.

All heads turned at the outburst. All were confused, including me. I had no idea what Jesus had said to cause such a reaction.

Until the moment he started to scream, the man appeared to be normal, no different from the men who sat on either side of him. Now his eyes bulged red and a fat blue vein pulsed in his forehead. Saliva spun from his mouth like spider webs.

Jesus seemed unaffected.

The man lunged and had to be pulled back. "Let us alone; what have we to do with thee, thou Jesus of Nazareth?"

Jesus did not flinch.

The man ranted. "Art thou come to destroy us?"

Mothers pulled their children back into their protective arms. Men sat forward, not sure if they should go after the crazed man or Jesus.

Then in a voice not his own but that of a growling, foaming animal, the man announced, "I know thee who thou art, the Holy One of God."

A collective gasp rippled through the chamber.

Jesus held up His hand. "Hold thy peace, and come out him." He did not ask. He commanded, in a voice that was also changed. I thought of Moses come down from the mount.

I knew then that Jesus was not speaking to the man, but to the unclean spirit dwelling within the man's tabernacle. I'd seen it before—the miracle of exorcism.

Peter and a half dozen other disciples stood ready for whatever would happen next. I positioned myself ready to spring in case the man attacked Jesus.

The possessed man writhed like he was torn apart, but the evil spirit could not disobey Jesus. One minute it was torturing the man's body, using the man's voice to fling insults at the Master. The next, the spirit was gone. The man was so limp and weak that he had to be helped back to the bench.

We were all witnesses—not only His disciples, but Zebedee, the rabbis, the scribes, the holy men, and the women. Even the children who sat on the floor saw it.

"Glory be to God!" Peter praised God with might and glory. This was his family's synagogue, and many of the people there were Peter's kinsmen.

Most people were still too confused to realize what had happened.

The rabbi asked, "What thing is this? what new doctrine is this? For with authority commandeth he even the unclean spirits, and they do obey him."

Unlike the Nazarenes, the people in Capernaum were willing to let Jesus answer them.

They listened. They learned.

And they left edified.

Every person who went out from the synagogue that day departed with a personal testimony of Jesus' power.

Even the demons of hell had cowered at His command.

The fame of my Master spread up and down the shores of Galilee. There were so many miracles, so many needy.

I kept a record of the places where Jesus preached, the memorable people He touched, the miracles He wrought.

At night when the masses finally allowed Jesus time unhindered, I went out by myself and wrote the day's events in my book of papyrus. There wasn't room to write all that I wanted to, and it was a simple record, but it was a record—and records were important to Jesus.

The book I wrote in now was a gift He had purchased for me.

Jesus showed no fear of the diseased or the demonic. The truth was, He sought them out. Leprosy was rampant in parts of Galilee, and was a disease "holy" men attributed to sin. Lepers were shunned, sent to live in colonies apart from the whole and healthy part of society. But they were not shunned by Jesus.

I thought of Deborah and how her face had been destroyed by a disease not unlike leprosy. Now, though, the hand of the Healer had touched her. No day passed when my thoughts did not center on Deborah. How I missed everything about her! We had left Nazareth so abruptly, only my letters could explain my feelings.

I worried about Joel. He had shown shame; even though he knew Jesus was the Christ, Joel had failed to stand in His defense. My respect for my future father-in-law had plummeted in that telling moment. I worried about how our relationship would be affected as a result.

Judas was glum about his duties as treasurer. The purse was nearly empty, and he asked that we all work to fill it. So I hired myself out to the lord of a vineyard in Capernaum. I picked clusters from the vine and put them in baskets for others to carry to the press.

One day as I worked, I suddenly heard a voice. "Is your Master nearby?"

I turned and saw a sight that stole my breath.

A leper stood before me. The skin on his face was eaten away as if by worms. His bare arms, even the tops of his feet, were gray where the flesh should have been pink.

Even if I could have spoken I don't think I could have found words. To look upon the man was to see walking death.

I wasn't the only one who backed away, afraid that this man's disease would spread to my own skin. The scent of rotting flesh was enough to make me and my fellow workers lunge away in horror.

Jesus came forth out of the group and approached the man.

The leper begged. "Lord, if thou wilt, thou canst make me clean."

Jesus showed no fear. He put forth His hand and touched the man at the very spot where the flesh was vile and putrid.

By now a crowd had circled around the man. People were curious to see what Jesus would or could do.

"I will; be thou clean." Jesus spoke with resolve.

Before all the watching eyes, the man's rotten flesh repaired itself. What had been putrid was now whole and clean.

The near-dead now lived.

It was no wonder that word of Jesus and His healing power went through the land like fire fanned by wind. Every leper, every lame man, everyone who loved anyone in need of healing came to seek the hand and heart of Jesus.

I sat outside a home one afternoon, cleaning up the spot where we had roasted quail for our midday meal. Inside, the people crowded around Jesus, listening to His teachings, reaching for His healing.

A gentle breeze carried the scent of the sea. I breathed deep, filling my lungs with the air I so loved. But I did not enjoy peace or quiet: not only was the house packed so tightly that not even one more soul could enter, but the courtyard was also filled to overflowing.

Then came four men carrying a mat. On the mat was a curled-up man, shaking and sobbing.

I had seen many people crippled by disease or deformity, but this was different.

Judas rushed to the men. "The Lord cannot accommodate you."

One of the four men smiled desperately. "Our friend is sick with the palsy. Your Lord can heal him. *Only* your Lord can heal him."

Judas looked over at me and frowned. I knew what he was thinking. These men were dressed in tattered robes; two of them walked on unshod feet. They were poor. Judas was not interested in accommodating poor people.

"There is no room to receive others," Judas said, firmly. "The house is full. The Lord is occupied."

Another of the men begged. "But he that lies tormented is our friend."

Judas sighed. "Yes, but our Lord is besieged with friends."

I watched the sick man. He was extraordinarily thin. His feet were bare and shaking. His hands, too, could not be stilled.

I felt sorry for him, but Judas was right. Jesus had dozens of others to attend to before this man. People were crowded in and around the house, thick as reeds along the shoreline. Judas forged his way back inside to be near our Master.

I turned my attention back to my writing, and then I heard the sound of wood breaking. I stood and ran to where the people were flocking.

The four men who had carried their friend on a mat were taking the roof off the house—lifting it off in pieces. Others quickly joined them, prying the awning loose so they could lower their friend on his bed into the house where Jesus was. The crowd went quiet, and I heard Jesus tell them to be about their business.

"Master," one of them said.

There was honor and faith in the way he pronounced the title. I felt it.

So did the crowd. They rushed to help the men bring their palsied friend to Jesus.

I went to do what I could and saw Jesus through the open window. I recognized the compassion He felt. His heart was always softened easily when people asked favors not for themselves, but for others.

"Son," said Jesus, "be of good cheer; thy sins be forgiven thee."

The power of His words surged through me, and I imagined what would become of me if Jesus spoke those words to me—if the sins that held my heart down were forgiven.

"Arise, take up thy bed, and go unto thine house."

The man quit shaking. His curled legs straightened. His feeble fingers stretched strong. He stood, picked up his bed, and walked on legs that had refused to hold him upright for years.

The crowd marveled.

I kept an eye on the Pharisees among the crowd. Pharisees were always there. Three hunched together, whispering. While the rest of the crowd was impressed by the miracle, the three Pharisees were angry and fearful.

"Why doth this man thus speak blasphemies?"

Their own eyes had seen the lame restored. Did they not realize who Jesus really was? How could they not?

Jesus was unaffected both by the accolades of His believers and by the accusations of His critics.

Jesus went to the healed man's friends and blessed them also.

Next, He approached the trio of Pharisees, huddled among themselves.

The boldest of the three asked, "Who can forgive sins but God only?"

Jesus' answer left no room for anything but the truth. "Why reason ye these things in your hearts? . . . That ye may know that the Son of man hath power on earth to forgive sins."

They left before the others, angry and offended. But I saw that one of them looked back at Jesus, and I thought I read his heart.

How would his life change if Jesus said those words to him?

Sixty

The Hebrew word for sin means to "miss the mark."

As in archery.

As in life.

Jesus forgave the sins of all those who came to Him asking and believing.

"Can you pay?" Judas questioned them, always in the shadows, always when he thought none of the disciples was aware.

At the Roman fourth watch, when the sun was just coming over the horizon, Judas came to me excited. "Look at this!"

He held out a flat palm covered with coins.

My eyes squinted to question him. For weeks, our purse had been empty. Now suddenly it was full?

"A man desperate to sell his sins paid all this. I believe he has more!"

Judas! A man could not *sell* his sins. What spirit of greed and fear had motivated my friend?

"Do not look at me with such harsh judgment, Almon. Jesus is the Christ! He should not have to camp out in the open, to glean from the fields. He is entitled to stay in the finest inns, to know the luxuries of life. We are all entitled."

I did not feel entitled to anything. And I knew no more humble man than our Master.

Oh, Judas! What dark road are you traveling?

"The people He blesses *want* to pay."

But not all *could* pay, and Judas knew that.

The man who had paid Judas walked out of the shadows and approached me.

"Sir," he said quietly, "I seek the one they call the Forgiver."

I had heard Jesus called many things, but never the Forgiver. The term made me uneasy. Was Judas promoting Jesus for money?

No. It was unthinkable. We were not desperate. We never would be desperate with Jesus as our Master.

I looked at the man. He seemed older than me by years, broader across the shoulders. His head hung down, so I could not see his face. He had no hair, and his robes were not the robes of a rich man.

I gave Judas another hard glare and pointed toward the hill where Jesus had gone for a private walk.

Philip was by my side. "Judas?"

Judas' laugh came out as a rapid stutter. He was nervous.

Philip turned to the man. "What do you wish of my Master?"

"I am a sinner."

"You wish to confess your sins to Jesus?"

"Yes."

Now I could tell the man was not Jewish, but Arabic. If I had to speculate, I would say he had suffered a tragic life. Deep lines were etched across his forehead and down his cheeks. His shoulders were sloped, as though they carried great weight.

I was shocked by the harsh tone Philip took with him. "Jesus has come to save His own."

The man looked desperate. He searched for Judas, but Judas had vanished.

"I know that, lord. I am unworthy, and yet I am desperate to be clean. Please, sir. I have paid my dues."

"What dues?" Philip expected me to have the answer. I looked to see where Judas had gone.

Realizing what had happened, Philip's lip curled back in anger. "Almon, see to this man. Make him welcome while I go seek Judas."

All I could offer was a piece of dried fish and a half-empty wineskin.

He accepted the offer gratefully.

When his eyes met mine, I was suddenly nine years old again.

Yellow!

The man's eyes were the color of an Egyptian cat. His skin was dark. My nostrils filled with a scent that I had not smelled in years—the sickening scent of a body aflame.

Father!

If this was the man—now grown—who had robbed my father and me, he had to know everything that had happened. He had to know what had become of Father.

Of course he was laden with sin. He was a murderer!

I tried not to alarm him, though my heart beat in my head like a gong. Sweat beaded on my lip. He sat on a log by the ashes of last night's fire. I sat across from him, desperate to ask the questions I could not.

We waited in tense silence until Jesus came back to camp.

Immediately, the man fell on his knees.

"Jesus. I am a sinner."

Jesus did not raise the man, but instead knelt down beside him. They spoke so softly I could not discern their words. I was desperate to hear the man's confession, but I stayed back where I knew Jesus would want me.

Time shifted as slowly as sand on a windless day. When the man finally stood, Jesus embraced him like a brother.

"Go thy way and sin no more."

The man came to me. The dirt that had been on his cheeks had been washed away by his tears. He knelt before me and looked deep into my eyes. Then he took my hands in his and kissed each one, a sign of the deepest gratitude.

I had done nothing but silently condemn the man. If he was the boy—now a grown, worn man—who had taken the life of my father, I would not forgive him.

I was not Jesus.

My hand gripped his tightly. I had no way to ask him the questions that burned inside me. I looked to Jesus for help, but Philip had returned and was frantically telling Jesus of Judas.

The man pulled his hand from mine. "My sins are forgiven. My sins are forgiven! Jesus forgave my sins."

No! Your sins cannot be forgiven if you had a hand in killing my father. They could never be forgiven.

The other disciples came into camp . . . without Judas. They were hungry and anxious to start the day. I grabbed my writing parchment and implored Matthew to question the man.

I suspect he killed my father, I wrote.

Matthew's brows rose in surprise. "Your father? He has been dead since you were a child."

I jerked my hand toward the man. I had to make Matthew understand. He knew the story of my childhood, how bandits in black hoods had robbed us and left me for dead. How Joseph and Mary had saved me. How there was no answer about my father's fate.

Ask the man, please.

Matthew was hesitant, but did as I requested. He took the man aside and walked the same hill that Jesus had walked earlier. I wanted to come, but Matthew motioned for me to stay behind.

Out of the bush a white crane pumped its wide wings and rose above us as if this was any ordinary dawn. My heart refused to slow.

If this man had taken so much from me, he could not bow before the Master and be forgiven so easily. I would not allow it.

I helped with morning chores, but my mind was not on anything but the memories I had buried so long ago. It *had* to be the man. How many Arabs had the eyes of a cat? It *had* to be him, and if Jesus had forgiven him, it was because Jesus didn't know the depth and breadth of the man's sins.

I almost asked Jesus to tell me what sins the man had confessed, but knew that was a line I had no right to cross. Besides, I saw that Jesus was disturbed by what Judas had been doing—extracting fees for forgiveness. Jesus did not eat, but went in search of Judas. Philip and Peter went with Him.

I feared for Judas. But more than that, I feared for myself if the man turned out to be my father's murderer.

And he was.

As he and Matthew walked over the ridge toward us, I saw the sorrow and guilt written on the Arab's face. He ran to me and collapsed at my feet.

"Forgive me, sir. Long ago, I was the one. I was there with my father and brother. I was there when the shovel came down upon your father's head. He died, and my father forced me to dig a hole in the sand to bury him. I am guilty."

The man sobbed. All the disciples stared with disbelief.

He spoke with his head down. Tears fell from his eyes, moisture from his nose. His tears bathed my feet. "My father commanded that I kill and bury you, but I could not. I put you on your donkey and led you to the road. I deceived my father. I was a foul and vile sinner!"

I hardly believed it. Palestine was a large land. It had to be God's hand that had brought this man forward now. God's hand that had brought him to me for punishment.

"All these years I have carried those sins and so many others. They have weighed me down and cost me more than I can tell. Only when I heard of your Master, the Forgiver, did I feel hope for a new life."

His words were too much for my spirit to bear. My mouth filled with blood and I spit red on the man's bald head.

"I beg your forgiveness." He looked up at me with those yellow eyes. They burned into my soul like fire, and within their reflection I saw myself.

I spit again. My body almost lunged at the man. I wanted to rip open his throat and drain the very life from him. I wanted to defend my father now because I had failed to defend him then.

Matthew stood between us. "Almon, I do not know this side of you. You must stop now!"

I heard sobs.

"Almon, this man has shown great faith in our Master. He has beseeched Him for forgiveness. That plea has been granted. You, too, must forgive."

I cannot. The sobs were coming from my own shattered heart.

"Forgive me," the man said, still at my feet. "I was not much older than a child. I make no excuses, but I was at the mercy of my father's hand."

The story he told was *my* story. I was a child sinner who still carried those sins, sins that weighed me down like so many stones. How could I hope to be forgiven when I refused to extend forgiveness?

My knees collapsed and I fell beside the man.

I was a child again, silently sobbing so hard my breath was gone.

God had brought this man into my life, not so I could punish him, but so I could forgive him. And so I could begin to forgive my father . . . and myself.

Sixty-one

It had been a year since Jesus had cleansed the Court of the Gentiles.

Now all of us were back on the *Shabbat* of Passover.

Our journey had taken us to the district of the stockyards. The smell and noise of ten thousand sheep was overpowering. They were penned, hungry, thirsty, scared, and lined up to be sacrificed. The shepherds were still there with them, sorting the unblemished from the blemished.

Jesus and Andrew stopped to help lift a stray lamb back into the pen. An image, powerful and painful, flashed through my mind like lightning over a black sky: I saw Jesus offering Himself as a sacrifice at the altar. I *saw* Him. His body was bruised, His head bowed. He walked as a man condemned.

I shut my eyes and kept them shut until the image vanished, until I saw nothing but blackness. Jesus as an unblemished sacrificial lamb was an image so real I could not bear it.

As we approached the twin pools of Bethesda, the house of mercy, it seemed all the impotent had gathered there beneath the cloisters: the blind, the halt, and every withered folk. Young and old lay suffering under the porches.

Thaddaeus must have seen the expression on my face because he stopped to explain, "This is the day superstition dictates the water in the pool will move."

It looked stagnant to me.

"All these people believe it is stirred by an unseen angel."

It was impossible to live in Palestine and not know of superstition. The poor people, unable to pay high prices for sacrificial lambs and doves, used amulets, charms, magic powders, and curses to bring about favor.

Whenever I saw them I thought of my childhood with Father. In the desert where death is the ruling hand, it was not uncommon to see sorcerers and all their fares. Back then, I was mesmerized. But now that I knew true power from on high, the trinkets were just that—trinkets and nothing more.

Thaddeus went to Jesus. "See that man there by the edge? He has had his infirmity for thirty and eight years."

My mind counted the years. It was almost as many years as our fathers had wandered in the wilderness. It was longer than either Jesus or I had lived.

The Master raised His eyebrows. He asked Thaddeus to explain the superstition.

"Whosoever enters the water first after it has been troubled by the angel, he is made whole of whatsoever disease he has."

There was little room to maneuver. The press was tight and had swelled to hundreds. All eyes, as always, were fixed on my Master.

Jesus sighed and walked to the man, casting His shadow over the man's thin and filthy mat. The stiffness of the man's neck did not allow him to turn to see Jesus, who had cast a shadow over him. At least twenty people knelt around the man.

"Wilt thou be made whole?"

The withered man responded in a whine. "Sir, I have no man, when the water is troubled, to put me into the pool: but while I am coming, another steppeth down before me."

Jesus said, "Rise, take up thy bed, and walk."

The Pharisees and infiltrators, those who sought to injure my Master, laughed softly. Rabbi Zeev, the Nazarene who kept turning up, had seen Jesus perform miracles. He had no right to scoff.

The miracle Jesus called for now was to restore a man who had lain almost motionless for thirty-eight years. His body was a skeleton covered in leathered skin. His very bones twisted in unnatural directions.

Sheep bleated in the background.

The disciples held their breath.

Traitors waited.

Jesus smiled.

The man's limbs shook as life coursed back into them. The man was made whole. He took up his bed. After a moment of shock and elation, the man did as he was bid. He walked.

When he looked to thank Jesus, he realized the assembly was large and the faces many. He could not be sure of his benefactor.

The disciples praised God. They rejoiced at the man's good fortune.

The Pharisees burst into bitter accusations. They huddled together and then decided to follow the man.

Jesus frowned when He saw and understood their dark intent. With an expression in His eyes, a look I knew well, He bid me follow the man also.

I did. We headed toward the heart of the Holy City.

The man who hadn't walked in nearly forty years now walked with haste. When he approached the archway, a Pharisee stepped in front of him, cutting him off like he had some kind of royal right to do so. The blue tassels on the Pharisee's tunic moved like soundless bells. He looked holy, but did not act the part of one possessed of God's spirit.

He pointed a twig of an accusing finger at the mat the man held tucked beneath his arm. "It is the sabbath day: it is not lawful for thee to carry thy bed."

How could they focus on a simple infraction of the Sabbath rule when they had just witnessed a true and mighty miracle?

The healed man stepped back. "He that made me whole, the same said unto me, take up thy bed, and walk."

The Pharisees sneered. They knew, but asked anyway, "What man is that which said unto thee, Take up thy bed, and walk?"

The man turned and looked back toward the pool. I looked also, but knew there would be no sign of Jesus.

The Pharisees called Jesus a rebel, an accusation that could bring both the Roman soldiers and Herod's soldiers after my Master.

I went back in search of Jesus and found Him near the temple. As always, a crowd encircled Him.

This day He taught of His own divinity.

He testified of His Father's unlimited power.

To those who accused Him of breaking the Sabbath laws, He said, "My Father worketh hitherto, and I work."

The Pharisees turned red with anger. Their faces swelled. The hands they were forbidden to raise on the *Shabbat* were raised in fists.

When Jesus noticed the man whom He had earlier healed, He approached him. I stood close enough to hear the exchange between the men.

The one who had been healed said, "Thou art Jesus. Thy power has given me new life."

"Behold," Jesus said, "thou art made whole: sin no more, lest a worse thing come unto thee."

He made his vows and then ran through the multitude, telling those who would listen that Jesus was the one whose touch had healed him.

The multitude grew, and so did the animosity toward the Master. But He would not be deterred from His message. They shouted their threats, but He only preached louder.

"For the Father loveth the Son, and sheweth him all things that himself doeth: and he will shew him greater works than these, that ye may marvel. For as the Father raiseth up the dead, and quickeneth them; even so the Son quickeneth whom he will. For the Father judgeth no man, but hath committed all judgment unto the Son: that all men should honour the Son, even as they honour the Father. He that honoureth not the Son honoureth not the Father which hath sent him."

Rabbi Zeev shook his fist. Hate burned in his dark eyes. "Jesus speaks of Himself. He claims to be the Son of God. He claims to be equal to God!"

A roar went through the crowd. A few rose their voices in praise, but most swore to kill Jesus.

"I can of mine own self do nothing . . ."

Those whose ears were shut would not hear. Instead, they cried for the blood of Jesus.

Peter came to me and asked that I walk the perimeter of the crowd with him. Andrew and enough of the others were inside, close enough to the Master to keep back the crazed and all those who wanted to bring Him harm. I felt secure enough to follow.

The hand of Peter bore a bandage, brown with dried blood. I pointed to it, asking of his injury.

"A woman with a dagger lunged at Jesus. She claimed He was the devil."

I shook my head. My own face bore the mark from where a man's fist had struck me, claiming I was employed by the devil. The man was a famed healer in Jerusalem. For a fee, he would utter words, burn incense, and give a promise that in time his power would cure even the most advanced diseases.

Judas had spent much of the day observing the man's work.

When the man realized that I was a servant of Jesus, a healer who charged no price for giving legs to the lame, he simply struck me.

I was tired and hungry. My body ached. I longed to leave the city for Bethany, where the household of Lazarus waited with clean beds and plenty of meat.

Jesus continued teaching. He went on until the night guards told the crowd they had to move. By that time I feared my own legs would go lame.

As we walked out of Jerusalem by torchlight, I was so weary it was difficult to put one foot in front of the other. I could scarcely keep my eyes open. Judas walked next to me, his hand heavy on my shoulder. He looked more worn than I felt.

Not Jesus.

Jesus moved at a clip, leading us all. He held a torch in His hand and had a look of urgency on His face. He had lessons to teach, and He knew what we did not—that His time for teaching was draining like sand through an hourglass.

Sixty-two

Our rest in Bethany was never long. Soon we were back at work, preaching and teaching and ministering to those who believed in our Master.

At least for a time, the Pharisees and Sanhedrinists were left behind. I knew them. I knew they plotted and planned how to convict Jesus of crimes He would never commit.

And though Jesus repeatedly told me "Fear not," I *was* afraid. I feared for the future that would surely come if the mounting hatred of Jesus was not halted.

The question His critics raised over and over was, "How can this man be a true prophet if He and those who follow Him do not keep the sacred laws of *Shabbat*?"

Their accusations only grew more vile when spying eyes returned to follow us, reporting what they witnessed on a particular Sabbath day in Galilee. We had followed Jesus as He had taught and healed and consoled the sorrowing. We had been worn and hungry, as we usually were.

Judas had sworn that he was about to faint. Andrew had laughed at him and had grabbed at his pack. In it Judas had hoarded a thick slab of jerky. It had not lasted long—not once it had been passed among all of us. Jesus was the only one who had not eaten.

Judas had been outraged.

The barley harvest had recently begun and we had walked through a corn field. We had plucked the ears, rubbed them, and eaten the grains that we had managed to gather. It wasn't much, but it had been enough to calm the pangs of hunger.

It was also enough of a Sabbath violation that spies had emerged from the stalks to attack us with their accusations. They had not attacked Jesus, but they had attacked *us*—and that had infuriated Jesus.

He had countered their accusations with their own scriptures. "Have ye not read what David did, when he was an hungered, and they that were with him; How he entered into the house of God, and did eat the shewbread, which was not lawful for him to eat, neither for them which were with him, but only for the priests?"

They had stood defiant, but had been unable to defend themselves. I knew they were most dangerous at this stage, and I had hoped that Jesus would fall silent. But He had gone on testifying, finally announcing one thing that only sharpened their poisonous arrows: "For the Son of man is Lord even of the Sabbath day."

To them, this blasphemy was a sin that even the great altar in Jerusalem could not consume.

After that, Peter and a young man named Mathias determined that Jesus needed constant guarding. His life was no longer safe.

Spies were everywhere we went, pretending to be faithful, needy, and worthy.

But their pretense was useless. Jesus was Jesus, and He saw the blackness in their hearts.

One Sabbath He went into the synagogue, where a man with a withered hand approached Him. Peter looked at me to let me know he thought the man had been put there as a trap. I only knew that Jesus accepted him for what he was . . . whatever that was.

"Is it lawful to heal on the Sabbath day?"

He posed the question that he might accuse Jesus.

With every eye focused on Him, Jesus gave His answer: "What man shall there be among you, that shall have one sheep, and if it fall into a pit on the sabbath day, will he not lay hold on it, and lift it out? How much then is a man better than a sheep? Wherefore it is lawful to do well on the sabbath days."

The afflicted man trembled. He was caught between Jesus and the Jews who would see Him dead for doing good.

Always compassionate, Jesus told the man, "Stretch forth thine hand."

The synagogue went silent. Even the Pharisees stepped back, not sure what was going to happen. I saw fear on Rabbi Zeev's face, and I felt glad.

Jesus also saw the fear on the rabbi's face and turned to the holy accusers. "Is it lawful to do good on the sabbath days, or to do evil? to save life, or to kill?"

I thought Rabbi Zeev would choke on his own spit. All of them had to hold their peace; any reply they gave would surely condemn them.

Hatred rose like deadly smoke.

The man stretched forth his hand, and the miracle came. The hand that was malformed and short was made equal to the other.

All eyes were witness to the miracle. The grateful man fell on his face and wept.

The Pharisees went out of the synagogue to plot how they would kill Jesus for healing on the Sabbath. Peter said they were gone to meet with the Herodians, the most despised sect in all of Palestine. They were the torturers, the half-apostates who defiled the laws that the Pharisees claimed to uphold. It made no sense. How could these men who knew so much, know so little? How could they so hate the very God of love?

Sixty-three

A sadness fell over Jesus that stayed with Him no matter how we tried to cheer Him.

He had been rejected by His own.

We all felt it, but not with the intensity that scarred Jesus.

"Why doesn't He just give up?" Judas asked one day while we were on a shopping errand. "He could settle in Bethany and let the people come to Him. If Jesus just agreed to charge a small fee, nothing great, it would be enough to build His treasure."

I shook my head. I was tired of hearing Judas talk of money.

"Instead of taking coins in, I'm charged with dispensing them to the poor. Did you see that old woman with all of the children? Jesus told me to give her a full shekel. He would have given more if we had had more."

The Gentile community of Decapolis proved fertile ground for the Master's teaching. There, the people received Him with open hearts. And Judas was right . . . people *were* willing to come to Jesus. They came from Galilee, Judea, Jerusalem, Idumea, from Tyre and Sidon. Gentiles, Jews, and Greeks sought Him. It was important to Jesus that His chosen learn to communicate in Aramaic, Greek, and Hebrew so that everyone could be taught.

Even in His sleeping hours, people sought the Master. There was no peace.

He did not want to depart from them, but He had to find a way to separate Himself from their constantly reaching hands. One morning He asked Andrew, James, and me to secure a small boat. Jesus sat in it and went a short distance into the water. He left the people on the shore, but faced them so He could preach and be heard.

When He wasn't preaching, Jesus was touching, lifting, and edifying. He healed the sick, cast out devils, and listened to the woes of those who would be heard.

Every day Jesus gave more and more of Himself until He was eventually whittled away like one of Simon's little wooden creations. I did my best to serve Him well, meeting every need I saw, filling every request He made. But it wasn't enough.

The help He needed most was help I could not give. The men who were most loyal to Jesus became more than mere disciples; they were His inner circle, His envoys. I was His shadow and His ever-ready servant. I hoped I was more to Him than that . . . but if that was all I was, it was enough. I felt grateful that Jesus had others to help shoulder the burdens He bore.

Jesus left to go to the mountain, where He could be alone with God. The sky was filled with dark gray clouds, but no rain fell. We did not know when to expect the Lord's return, so we waited. We were great in number now; even James, the brother of Jesus, occasionally came to be with us.

It was the first light of morning when Jesus returned. He wore a mantle of peace like He had not worn in so long. He called for all of His disciples who would follow Him.

Of all who followed, He selected twelve.

Twelve gates of the Holy City's temple.

Twelve tribes of Israel.

Twelve of His own.

Peter was first—the Rock. His strength was both physical and spiritual. His brother, Andrew, was just as valiant, but showed more patience. Then came the Sons of Thunder, James and John—men who would give their very lives for Jesus. They were kinsmen of Jesus and also of John the Baptist. Philip brought Nathaniel, sometimes called Bartholomew.

Matthew had been the Lord's friend for some time. Though the others resented him because he collected taxes for the empire, Jesus loved him for his kindness and intelligence, and he was faithful in the record he kept of Jesus' doings. Thomas, a twin, was a man whose testimony of Jesus shored up my own weakness. He knew without doubt that Jesus was the Christ. James the lesser was young, but bold in his witness and eager to learn. Thaddeus, also called Jude, was a man of mighty spirit whom the Lord often allowed to preach from the same lectern where He taught.

Simon, the Zealot, knew much about the people and the government. His knowledge and skills saved us hardship as we traveled from one region to the next. My friend Judas, a descendant of Judah, had great ambitions and first came to Jesus expecting a miracle of prosperity. I knew he loved Jesus, but I worried that he was torn between his desire for wealth and his desire to serve the Master.

Most of the men had families. James the lesser was betrothed like I was.

Before, these men had been disciples . . . those who *followed*. Anyone who followed Jesus was His disciple. Now they were set apart at the hand of Jesus as Apostles . . . those who were *sent*.

The smallest part of me felt envious. I wanted to be among those Jesus most trusted, but these men were called to preach and to testify. How could I do that with no voice?

I wasn't the only one with such feelings. Jesus' choice of those particular twelve brought out squabbles among the inner circle. Some men grew angry and left. Others stayed, but murmured.

Jesus seemed relieved and grateful to have help in reaching more people. The Twelve now had authority to heal, to teach, to expound. None was Jesus, yet each was given His power.

And our numbers grew again.

Sixty-four

I sensed that our mission was more urgent than ever. Our days seemed longer, and the crowds grew larger. Jesus seldom rested. This day the throngs approached because the Master was preparing a particularly important sermon.

The poor and the sick were always among us. So were the groups of spies, the holy men with unholy intent. They followed us like hungry dogs. I hated them, though Jesus told me a heart dedicated to God held no room for hate.

There were times when I knew that Jesus could see into my heart. He knew my sins, and allowed me to serve anyway. One day I would bow before Him; I would pass Him the long list . . . every sin I knew I'd committed. At that point He could excuse me or expel me. But I was not yet ready for that moment of truth.

My dreams had changed. Ever since the Arab with the yellow eyes had come and gone, I no longer woke from the memory of the desert. Now I only dreamed of Deborah and the day she would become my wife.

She was my only thought as I looked out at the waters of Galilee. This day the surface was blue on blue.

"Almon."

It was Andrew. "The Master wishes your company."

I went in haste up the hillside, over boulders, to the flatland where flowers bloomed and waved like old friends. Judas sat on a rock, counting coins in his hand. He did not even look up as I hiked past him.

The day was perfect. The sun, the sky, the shade of billowy white clouds.

The Twelve were scattered around the Lord. Each had duties of his own, though Peter and John were having another argument. They disagreed over trivial things, like who should be allowed to assist Mary up the hill. She had come with Simon and the twins, so she needed no assistance from anyone other than her son.

It made me sad to know that since the rebel's beating incident, Joel and Naomi no longer came to visit Jesus, not even to hear Him preach. I imagined how Mary missed her sister-in-law. But over the months, others kinswomen had joined her: Salome, the mother of James and John, as well as Joanna and another relative named Mary. I knew it brought comfort to Jesus to know that His mother was surrounded by love and support.

James and Jude carried a palsied man up the mount, their arms intertwined to form a chair for his comfort. James, who still oversaw the workshop in Nazareth, brought me occasional notes from Deborah. She wrote of her father's shame—and of Malik's shame, too. She told how people shunned her now more than ever, now that Jesus had touched her face and restored it. They claimed she had been healed by Satan.

Deborah wrote of her heart's empty place, a void that would not be filled until we were married.

I kept her notes in my pouch, bound with a scrap from the fabric she'd given me years earlier.

Jesus smiled when He saw me.

I brought Him the waterskin. He took it and then held it out for me to drink first.

It was a kindness He often showed.

From my bag, I also offered Him the juicy red seeds of a pomegranate that one of the disciples had brought as an offering.

Jesus ate and seemed to savor the sweetness of each seed. That was His way; every detail of every day belonged to Him. While I *gulped* the water, he *felt* it wet His tongue and drain down His parched throat. While I chewed the pomegranate seeds and swallowed, barely tasting them, He let each seed feed Him.

Jesus lived fully and I learned from His example. I wanted to be more, to know more, to do more, to give more.

Hundreds of His followers came now to the mount overlooking the sea. I saw the blue of the water reflected in the Master's eyes, and felt embarrassed when He caught me staring.

Thomas reached out for the water-skin. "The Master preaches today, a sermon worthy of recording."

I reached into my cloak pocket to show both Thomas and Jesus that I had my pad and coal pen. I also had my wax tablet.

Matthew was behind me, and he also produced a pen and paper. "What you miss, Almon, I'll be sure to record." He smiled and went to join up with a group of people he recognized.

Another man, thick through the chest with a mane of sun-bleached hair, opened his arms to embrace me. I didn't recognize him for a moment, but then the face came clear. It was Luke, the physician who often came to hear Jesus preach. He was a kind man, generous in helping others.

"I saw Judas down the mount a way. He is collecting quite a purse. I put in a coin or two myself."

Peter heard. Andrew did, too. They both rushed to deal with the matter. I felt a wave of pity for what they'd do when they caught Judas charging to hear the words of Jesus.

I watched as Luke and Jesus greeted one another. I looked again at Jesus. The words of Isaiah and Jeremiah rushed to my head—prophecies I had long ago memorized. They were words I tried to chase away, for they foretold of the Master's imminent death.

The time was drawing nigh. I could feel it, but I did not want to accept it.

Jesus spread His arms wide and lifted His voice. "Come, follow me," He said, and we all climbed higher until we had scaled the mount, passing through the summer grass and wildflowers that tilted this way and that, urged by the breeze.

The sea moved below like a billowing blue blanket. A pair of eagles soared above us, and even Jesus watched them for the longest time.

The salty smell of the sea hung in the air. I breathed deeply, always glad for the way sea air refreshed me.

I looked at Jesus as He looked upon the Twelve. Judas stood between Peter and Andrew; all three looked sour.

Jesus sat on a speckled boulder, and everyone else found a sitting spot—some on rocks, others on the grass. A few brought blankets they spread out.

Jesus indicated that He wanted me to sit to the right of Him, close by, in case He should need me. Then He began speaking.

"Blessed are the poor in spirit: for theirs is the kingdom of heaven.

"Blessed are they that mourn: for they shall be comforted.

"Blessed are the meek: for they shall inherit the earth.

"Blessed are they which do hunger and thirst after righteousness: for they shall be filled.

"Blessed are the merciful: for they shall obtain mercy.

"Blessed are the pure in heart: for they shall see God.

"Blessed are the peacemakers: for they shall be called the children of God.

"Blessed are they which are persecuted for righteousness' sake: for theirs is the kingdom of heaven.

"Blessed are ye, when men shall revile you, and persecute you, and shall say all manner of evil against you falsely, for my sake.

"Rejoice, and be exceeding glad: for great is your reward . . . "

Judas jerked away from the grasp of Peter and Andrew. But Jesus would not be disturbed. He continued on, blessing all people.

I fought the urge to throw my head back and laugh at my blessed fortune. How could a thief of a boy with no voice, no home, no family end up at the feet of the Lord of all?

Gratitude burned in me and I felt it drench me, from the crown of my head to the tips of my toes. It filled my heart, and I *did* throw my head back. I squinted into the blue sky and bright sun and I prayed. *Hear, oh God, my prayer of thanksgiving.*

Jesus held His arms wide as He explained a new way of living. "Think not that I am come to destroy the law, or the prophets: I am not come to destroy, but to fulfil."

I understood, but could see from the faces of the multitude that many did not.

"But I say unto you, That whosoever is angry with his brother without a cause shall be in danger of the judgment . . . "

Judas snorted, and Peter took hold of his elbow. I imagined I heard him threaten to take away the purse if Judas did not comply.

Jesus continued on, talking to every sin and sinner.

"Ye have heard that it hath been said, Thou shalt love thy neighbour, and hate thine enemy. But I say unto you, Love your enemies, bless them that curse you, do good to them that hate you, and pray for them which despitefully use you, and persecute you; That ye may be the children of your Father which is in heaven: for he maketh his sun to rise on the evil and on the good . . . "

I felt a conviction in my own heart. Not long before, I had wanted to kill a man. Now Jesus commanded that I should pray for him.

I thought the old law was backbreaking, but Jesus' laws were harder still. They had to be kept from the inside out. Appearance meant little to Him. He wanted the heart to be set right. These new laws would not be easy to obey, but the reward would be great.

"And unto him that smiteth thee on the one cheek offer also the other; and him that taketh away thy cloke forbid not to take thy coat also. Give to every man that asketh of thee; and of him that taketh away thy goods ask them not again. And as ye would that men should do to you, do ye also to them likewise.

"For if ye love them which love you, what thank have ye? For sinners also love those that love them . . . "

It was a higher law that came from the mouth of Jesus. No longer was an eye required for an eye. Just as the mountain lifted us, so did the beatitude that Jesus spoke.

" . . . love ye your enemies, and do good, and lend, hoping for nothing again; and your reward shall be great, and ye shall be the children of the Highest: for he is kind unto the unthankful and to the evil. Be ye therefore merciful, as your Father also is merciful."

I thought of the multitudes. Jesus not only blessed the people, but He insisted that *we* bless them as well. How many times had I fetched water for the thirsty, washed the filthy feet of strangers, carried the burdens that had grown too heavy for the weak to carry themselves? He did no less. Now I understood that those burdens were actually blessings.

Jesus had beckoned me to serve . . . and in so doing, I was following Him in a different way than merely shadowing Him. Was it possible for someone as simple as I to become like Jesus? How I wanted to possess His mercy, His compassion, His peace.

Sweat trickled down the cheek of Jesus. He wiped it with the back of His hand before continuing.

"Ye are the salt of the earth: but if the salt have lost his savour wherewith shall it be salted? it is thenceforth good for nothing, but to be cast out, and to be trodden under foot of men.

"Ye are the light of the world. A city that is set on a hill cannot be hid.

"Neither do men light a candle, and put it under a bushel, but on a candlestick; and it giveth light unto all that are in the house.

"Let your light so shine before men, that they may see your good works, and glorify your Father which is in heaven."

The crowd sat still and peaceful. There was no murmuring, no shouting out.

His words were so plain and simple, how could they be twisted into anything ugly?

While the commandments Moses gave were written in stone, the commandments Jesus set forth—there on the grassy mount, before a multitude of believers and nonbelievers—were etched forever across the face of my heart.

Sixty-five

I thought the sermon was finished, but it was far from complete.

Jesus shifted as the cool morning breeze turned from gentle to hot.

"Take heed that ye do not your alms before men, to be seen of them: otherwise ye have no reward of your Father which is in heaven. Therefore when thou doest thine alms, do not sound a trumpet before thee, as the hypocrites do in the synagogues and in the streets, that they may have glory of men. Verily I say unto you, They have their reward."

Someone made a disgruntled sound, and I looked to see Judas moving through the multitude. When he caught my eye he came toward me and knelt down next to me, enraged.

"The Master refers to *me.* He calls me a hypocrite!"

I shrugged. Jesus had tried to teach all of us, not just Judas, that we were to give our alms in secret—but Judas was the one among us who still counted the cost of each sacrificed coin. He enjoyed announcing the money he had given as alms. Now he was offended by the sermon, and I could not console him.

Instead, I turned back to my tablet, and tried to write each word Jesus spoke. This was no ordinary sermon. He taught us how to live, to give, to pray . . .

"And when thou prayest, thou shalt not be as the hypocrites are: for they love to pray standing in the synagogues and in the corners of the streets, that they may be seen of men. Verily I say unto you, They have their reward.

"But thou, when thou prayest, enter into thy closet, and when thou hast shut thy door, pray to thy Father which is in secret; and thy Father which seeth in secret shall reward thee openly.

"But when ye pray, use not vain repetitions, as the heathen do: for they think that they shall be heard for their much speaking.

"Be not ye therefore like unto them: for your Father knoweth what things ye have need of, before ye ask him."

A voice I knew as the Apostle John's rang out. "Teach us to pray, Lord."

And Jesus did.

His prayer took me back to the vineyard so many years earlier when we had gotten lost between Nazareth and Sepphoris. It was the first time I had heard anyone really commune with God in prayer. The words Jesus uttered now were even more powerful.

"Our Father which art in heaven, Hallowed be thy name.

"Thy kingdom come. Thy will be done in earth, as it is in heaven.

"Give us this day our daily bread.

"And forgive us our debts, as we forgive our debtors.

"And lead us not into temptation, but deliver us from evil: For thine is the kingdom, and the power, and the glory, for ever. Amen."

The Spirit went through the multitude as gentle as the breeze, as powerful as the sun.

He taught us to fast . . . and to treasure that which lasts.

Judas squirmed beside me. Every word Jesus spoke seemed to give him offense.

"Lay not up for yourselves treasures upon earth, where moth and rust doth corrupt, and where thieves break through and steal: But lay up for yourselves treasures in heaven, where neither moth nor rust doth corrupt, and where thieves do not break through nor steal: For where your treasure is, there will your heart be also."

At that moment Jesus turned and gazed into the eyes of Judas. But Judas tucked his head to hide his eyes from the Savior.

"The light of the body is the eye:" Jesus' voice rang clear and strong; "if therefore thine eye be single, thy whole body shall be full of light.

"But if thine eye be evil, thy whole body shall be full of darkness. If therefore the light that is in thee be darkness, how great is that darkness!

"No man can serve two masters: for either he will hate the one, and love the other; or else he will hold to the one, and despise the other. Ye cannot serve God and mammon."

Jesus continued, but Judas did not. Grunting and grumbling, he picked up his walking stick and made his way down the mount, weaving his way as quickly as he could through the listening multitude.

I felt sorrow for Judas' conviction, but I felt a greater drive to record the words of truth that Jesus spoke. The point of my reed went into the wax, but the sun was hot and the wax soft. I wanted my heart to be soft, the words to sink deep.

I sunk down into the grass about me and *felt* the earth. I smelled the growing plants around me. Wild flax, with its blue flowers, looked so pretty, and yet I knew it had a purpose—woven, it became clothing and sails. The clouds above gave shade. The sun offered light. Jesus brought salvation.

I wanted my life to have purpose.

I longed to matter.

How could I know with certainty that my life was pleasing to God? I had hardly asked myself the question when Jesus provided the answer.

"Ye shall know them by their fruits," Jesus said. "Do men gather grapes of thorns, or figs of thistles?

"Even so every good tree bringeth forth good fruit; but a corrupt tree bringeth forth evil fruit.

"A good tree cannot bring forth evil fruit, neither can a corrupt tree bring forth good fruit.

"Every tree that bringeth not forth good fruit is hewn down, and cast into the fire.

"Wherefore by their fruits ye shall know them."

That day Jesus' message was impossible to misunderstand . . .

"Not every one that saith unto me, Lord, Lord, shall enter into the kingdom of heaven; but he that doeth the will of my Father which is in heaven.

"Many will say to me in that day, Lord, Lord, have we not prophesied in thy name? and in thy name have cast out devils? and in thy name done many wonderful works?

"And then will I profess unto them, I never knew you: depart from me, ye that work iniquity.

"Therefore whosoever heareth these sayings of mine, and doeth them, I will liken him unto a wise man, which built his house upon a rock:

"And the rain descended, and the floods came, and the winds blew, and beat upon that house; and it fell not: for it was founded upon a rock."

"Almon?"

It was Matthew, come to borrow a pen from me since the tip of his had broken. I reached into my bag and felt first for the thick, crooked pen that had been presented to me when I became a Son of the Commandment.

It had been a gift from Jesus, crafted by His own hands.

"What an ugly pen," Matthew whispered, half-smiling.

Tenderly, my fingers wrapped around every twist and notch. With my other hand, I offered Matthew my finest pen, an instrument I had purchased while training as a scribe at the temple.

He turned it over and found it acceptable, thanked me, and crawled back to his place in the front rows.

I looked down at my hand, at the crude and crooked pen, and the words Jesus had just spoken rang again in my ears. "For where your treasure is, there will your heart be also."

Sixty-six

That night we camped in tents on the mountain. We had barely met with morning when a leper came searching for Jesus.

The Master's hand touched the leper and made him clean. Whether it was our exhaustion or our callousness, none among us accepted the miracle with the jubilation that it deserved. For more than a year, our eyes had witnessed miracles every day. This dawn we looked upon a cleansed leper with the same eyes with which we saw a tree or a desert cat—as if a miracle were something commonplace.

"See thou tell no man," Jesus said to the leper, "but go thy way, shew thyself to the priest, and offer the gift that Moses commanded, for a testimony unto them." Though He had brought the new law, He honored the old law, knowing it would not be fulfilled until His final Atonement.

I watched Judas. He seemed to be in pain as he observed the leper leave without paying so much as a single coin. What did I know of the burden Judas carried? It was not my place to judge him, though Peter and Andrew kept him flanked. They would not tolerate his imploring people for money.

It was not the Master's way.

When we returned to Capernaum, a centurion approached us. Simon went rigid with resentment. In spite of Jesus' teachings on love, it was a great challenge for Simon, a Zealot, to find love in his heart for a man of the empire. A garrison was located nearby, and the growing power of the empire caused Simon increasing misery.

"What is it that you wish of our Master?" Simon's tone betrayed his feelings.

The centurion ignored the Apostle's query and went directly to Jesus. "Lord, my servant lieth at home sick of the palsy, grievously tormented."

Simon was enraged. "This man is a soldier in the service of Herod, the vile tyrant," he told Jesus. "Need I remind you that your kinsman, John, still languishes in Herod's dungeon?"

Jesus offered Simon a look of compassion, but nothing else.

John approached Jesus and spoke softly. "It is true, Lord, that this man is a soldier. But he is also an adopted son of Abraham. His generosity helped to build the new synagogue in Capernaum. He seeks not for his own self, but for his servant, whom he loveth."

Jesus looked at me, his *servant*. A sense of love and honor shot through me.

"I will come and heal him," the Master said.

But the centurion looked dismayed. "Lord, I am not worthy that thou shouldest come under my roof: but speak the word only, and my servant shall be healed. For I am a man under authority, having soldiers under me: and I say to this man, Go, and he goeth; and to another, Come, and he cometh; and to my servant, Do this, and he doeth it."

Jesus marveled. He looked around at us. "Verily I say unto you, I have not found so great faith, no, not in Israel.

"And I say unto you, That many shall come from the east and west, and shall sit down with Abraham, and Isaac, and Jacob, in the kingdom of heaven.

"But the children of the kingdom shall be cast out into outer darkness: there shall be weeping and gnashing of teeth."

I thought of the child who had lain in death's grip. Jesus had spoken the word, and His healing power had crossed the distance and saved the boy.

Jesus smiled gently at the centurion. "Go thy way; and as thou hast believed, so be it done unto thee."

Another hour, another miracle.

When we arrived at Peter's house, his mother-in-law lay sick. Her face was scorching hot with fever and damp with sweat.

Peter's wife wept openly, grateful when she saw her husband and Jesus. Rushing out of the courtyard gate, she came to Peter, weeping.

His brute strength lifted her off the ground, but his tender heart whispered the same words we all heard from the Master. "Weep not."

Jesus went directly to Peter's mother-in-law. His lips moved in silent prayer as He knelt beside her pallet. When He took her hand, we all saw the fever leave. When we arrived, her hair was gray and damp; her eyelids were swollen, too heavy to lift. And yet at the Master's touch, the woman's eyes fluttered open and her health was fully restored.

It was she who came out into the courtyard and ministered to us. She carried corn cakes and stewed meat seasoned with pungent spices.

She could not stop thanking Jesus or praising Him. Peter's wife also showed gratitude and true humility. It gave me great pleasure to see Peter encircled by his family. His wife was as small as he was large. His children climbed on his lap, hung on his shoulders, and laughed at his stories.

I imagined myself in his very chair, surrounded one day by Deborah and our children. The thought made my heart swell. It was possible for me to marry now, to expect Deborah to wait as Peter's wife waited for her husband. Or I could ask her to accompany us. There were always women in our camp—kinswomen of Mary, the mother of Jesus, and wives of those who ministered with Jesus. Mary and Martha, friends who meant so much to the Master, were often with us as well.

Somehow, though, the decision did not seem right for Deborah. She did not want to leave her family, and I was concerned for her safety so I begged God to grant her patience. I knew the day was coming when we would be joined as husband and wife, not to be separated again.

After evening prayers I fell asleep and woke to find Jesus standing above me with a blanket. Not aware that I had seen Him, He put the blanket gently over me so as not to disturb my slumber. I lay silent and motionless, thinking how He whom I served so often served me.

The next day we left early to beat the sun's heat. Jesus seemed urgent. He was headed toward Nain, a village so small and remote not everyone knew of its existence. But to Jesus there was no place, no person unknown.

We walked steadily, adding to our multitude as we went. Not all of the Apostles traveled with us; some had commissions of their own.

Jesus was doing what He said He would do: sending His Apostles out to do the same kinds of things He did.

The journey took all day because we were slowed by the great number of our caravan. By the time evening fell, even Jesus no longer walked with haste. The thick, amber light fell on His profile, and I saw how tired He truly was.

We were a joyous caravan—tired, but filled with the strength and vigor of seeing Jesus work along the way. Then came the unmistakable sound of pain . . . wrenching sobs, wailing. We fell silent. Death had set us still.

We had come upon a funeral in progress. A small, lifeless body had been wrapped and spiced and prepared to be laid in the tomb. Beyond consolation, the mother's head was covered in ashes. I thought of Mary, years earlier, at the funeral of Joseph. The melancholy tinkle of cymbals and the cry of flutes added to the sadness of the funeral procession.

The poor mother was next to the funeral bier, a stooped woman as slight as Peter's wife. She was a widow in black sackcloth. Her lamentations were bitter and anguished. In grief, her upper garment was rent.

"My son!" My only son!" she cried.

Though I did not know her, I felt her pain.

Her head turned toward Jesus. Ashes fell, scattering over her veil. Her words were filled with anguish. "I prayed for him. I tended him. I trusted, and I lost."

The other women with her wailed and mourned. Townspeople followed in open support and pity.

The lost youth lay on the open bier.

My heart broke to think that we had arrived too late. If only we'd come a day earlier, Jesus could have touched the boy and restored him to his mother's arms.

But now it was too late. I wiped away a tear of regret.

John, too, wept. His cheeks were wet, but he saw what I did not.

"This day," he said, "is the day death meets life."

Jesus went to the grief-stricken mother. Her pain rent the air like her hands rent her garment. He offered a stranger's compassion.

Then He offered something more.

"Weep not," Jesus said, reaching out His hand to touch the bier.

The procession stood still, and those that bore the body dared not even breathe. Who was this man willing to reach out and touch the dead?

One of the bearers cried out, "Is this Jesus of Nazareth?"

"Yes. It is He."

The mother's eyes went wide behind her veil. She looked at her dead son and then at the man who reached to touch him.

The music stopped.

Even the wind became still.

"Young man, I say unto thee, Arise."

The corpse, dead and wrapped and ready for its final rest, arose.

The son that was dead and gone sat up and began to speak.

Jesus lifted him, unwrapped his head, and presented him to his mother.

My knees would not hold my own weight. I fell to the ground and worshipped Jesus in a way no words could describe.

From face to face the story was told. The mother's face expressed shock and gratitude. Profound joy. The expression on Rabbi Zeev's face brought a smile to mine. He was a spy, a traitor—one who could never again accuse my Master of blasphemy. And Judas wore the surprise and joy of everyone.

"Mother!" Judas cried out, rushing to the woman and her son. He then did something I had never seen Judas do. He opened the purse and pressed coins into her hands. "Glory be to God. Use this alm to rebuild your broken life."

No one could ever deny my Master again.

This miracle of miracles would shut every mouth against Him.

I felt relief. I felt overwhelming joy. I felt certain that Jesus had performed the greatest possible miracle.

What more could the Master do than He had done this day?

Sixty-seven

They came in the night to our camp in Galilee—a large group of men, walking in shadow and moonlight. It was my watch, and with my heart pounding in my throat, I hurried to wake Peter, to warn him and the others.

"Where?" Peter asked through an open-mouthed yawn. He kept his voice low, but even then it was a growl. It was his way.

I pointed to a ridge in the distance.

Peter squinted. "I see only bushes."

But then, like a billowing sea, the men rose up and moved as one. With a blue cast of moonlight behind them, it was possible to tell that their numbers were not great—twelve, perhaps fifteen. No more than that. Still, they were an equal match to us.

Peter reached for his saber. We could not be certain if they were friends or foes. Jesus had both, and friends did not usually approach under the cloak of darkness.

Quietly, Peter roused Andrew, Philip, and Nathaniel. I went to Judas and Thomas. We let Jesus and the others sleep.

"They may be Pharisees," Thomas whispered, "the same group who dogged us in Capernaum."

Philip chuckled softly. "Pharisees would be sleeping at this hour."

I looked to Judas. He held a club in his hands, but kept turning and twisting it. His eyes darted toward the oncoming men and then back to the fire where Jesus lay sleeping. I could tell he was nervous. I wanted to calm him, so I reached out to touch his arm.

He yanked away and I saw a darkness cross his face. It was a look I had never seen on Judas, and for a moment I barely recognized the man.

Just as quickly as he went dark, the light came back to his face, and Judas was my friend again. "Jesus is Lord. No harm can befall Him. His Father would never allow true or lasting harm to come to the Master."

His words were strong, but Judas did not sound certain. He had the purse girdled tightly around him, next to his heart, only half hidden by his open robe. I felt such pity for my friend; his concern for the purse weighed on him without ceasing. I would never say so, but the burden of that purse reminded me of the burden placed on Azazel, the scapegoat on the Day of Atonement. It was a bag of sins, and Judas never let it go.

I understood about carrying the weight of sin. But each day that I learned from Jesus, I learned to let go of all the things that weighed me down—not just ancient sins, but current iniquities, like feelings of jealousy and bitterness.

"Follow my lead," Peter whispered. We all took up our weapons and stepped where he stepped.

When the men drew near, we were ready. Not waiting until they reached our camp, we hid ourselves in a ravine just beyond our camp-site. We took our courage from Peter, who was always prepared and willing to die, to protect Jesus.

My heart thundered in my head, crashing like cymbals. Behind the noise of my own fear I told myself that Judas was right. Jesus was Lord, and no harm could come to Him. God would protect His Only Begotten.

If Jesus could raise a dead child and return him to his rejoicing mother, He could save Himself from mere bandits. He could save us all. Still, my hands shook as I held the knife—the knife Joseph had given me all those years ago.

The sound of brush crunching underfoot broke the still silence.

"State your business," Peter said, his voice that of a commander.

The men stopped dead. It was impossible for them to tell the direction of the voice.

"We are sent from John bar Zacharias—the Baptist."

"State your business," Peter repeated.

One of the men stepped forward and a shaft of light fell on him, revealing not a soldier or a fine scribe or a treacherous Pharisee, but a ragged disciple of John. Again he said, "John the Baptist hath sent us unto thee."

Thomas whispered, "John is in prison. How could he have sent such a group?"

"We have recently come from his presence at the fortress. He commanded that we give our allegiance to Jesus—his kinsman, his Master."

Peter stood and ordered all of us to stand with him. Our weapons went down, and our arms opened wide. We welcomed the men sent from John.

We did not have many provisions; all I had to offer was some fruit and dried fish, a few dried figs. They seemed most grateful and eager to crowd with us, all of us awake now, around the fire. Nathaniel stoked it with dried brush, and orange flames rose up, licking the darkness, sending burning embers into the air.

Andrew and John knew most of the men from their discipleship with the Baptist. They seemed both gladdened and sorrowful at their reunion. There was much to talk about.

Jesus asked of His cousin.

A man named Liran spoke. "We are come from Perea, the dungeon at Machaerus. These many months our prophet has suffered at the hands of Antipas."

"Tell us," said Jesus.

He told of the torture John had endured, the evil that had gone on within the walls of that den of darkness. The horrendous cruelty of Antipas. How John had endured it all and still stood before his captors to testify of the Messiah.

Jesus wept openly.

My own eyes dripped tears of sorrow. I kept picturing John free and strong in his natural element, the Judean wilderness. I heard again the words he had spoken to all: "Behold, the Lamb of God."

Liran spoke directly to Jesus. He leaned forward on the log and looked intently into Jesus' eyes. "Word has reached our prophet of your miracles. They say you have granted sight to the blind, that your touch has unstopped the ears of the deaf. That you cleanse lepers and send unclean spirits from the tormented."

Jesus said not a word.

Judas spoke up. "He does! He has! Jesus who sits before you is Master of all miracles!"

The rest of us agreed, and though I could not speak, I nodded with great resolve. I hoped the men could feel my testimony.

Liran's voice went low as he looked around at his fellow disciples. "Rumor reached our prophet's ears that you, Jesus, gave life back to a dead child, the son of a widow."

For a moment, we all looked at Jesus. His face glowed amber in the firelight, but His eyes were wet. He was not thinking of Himself, but of His cousin. I knew how much Jesus loved John. I had seen them together as children. I had seen them at the banks of the Yored-Dan. Jesus had the power to heal the nobleman's son a day's journey away. He did the same for the Centurion. Surely He had the power to raise His hand now and set John free.

Why didn't He do it?

"It's true!" Judas said, rising from his seat. "Jesus brought a dead boy back to life."

Still, Jesus said nothing.

"We are come to you now, at the bequest of the Baptist. We did not desire to leave him, but to stay and administer to him as Antipas allowed. It was he, John, who asked us to leave him to come to you, to find out for ourselves."

"Yes," the other disciples echoed.

Then Liran stood and looked at Jesus. He bowed before Him on the ground next to the fire. "Art thou He that should come? Or look we for another?"

We all waited for Jesus to answer. So many emotions played on His face in those moments. Sorrow. Compassion. Love.

His eyes found me, His mute servant in the shadows.

Please Father, let Jesus feel all that my heart sings.

Jesus remained silent, but His actions bid the invitation: *Come, follow me.*

Jesus, without speaking, answered those men not with words, but with works. He did not tell them He was God . . . he *showed* them. We all followed him for days, witnessing His answer.

Sixty-eight

When John's disciples had witnessed for themselves the healing power of the Master, they returned to assure the Baptist that the Lord's ministry carried authority and anointing equal to the rumors.

Jesus sent them off with the admonition, "Go your way, and tell John what things ye have seen and heard; how that the blind see, the lame walk, the lepers are cleansed, the deaf hear, the dead are raised, to the poor the gospel is preached. And blessed is he, whosoever shall not be offended in me."

After they had gone and we were out among the people, Jesus testified that John was much more than a prophet: "Among those that are born of women there is not a greater prophet than John the Baptist . . . "

Even Matthew's friends, the publicans, were affected. But Jesus' words did not move the Pharisees, the Saducees, the lawyers, or the scribes. They rejected the living prophets and clung to those who were dead.

What would have become of me if I had completed my temple training as a scribe? If I had elected to stay in Jerusalem instead of following Jesus? I dared not think how hollow my days—my life—would be without Him.

Violence grew around us. The spies of the Sanhedrin did more than whisper untruths. They beat and abused believers of both John and Jesus. Before the sincerely curious reached us, they were accosted and threatened. The Apostles themselves often showed the battle wounds of encounters with the Jews, who grew more and more violent against Jesus.

Herod's sons erected crosses on hilltops in nearly every village. Men were crucified for everything from thievery to blasphemy—any excuse to silence a threat to Herod.

We seldom saw Nicodemus, but other members of the Sanhedrin showed up regularly, slinging accusations and fanning threats. I was surprised when I saw Judas meeting with a small group of the vile traitors. Because I could not speak, a certain time passed before he realized I had discovered him. I did not hear what they said, but he assumed I did.

Judas did not look at me as his friend. "Almon! Slink back to your duties. Tend to feet washing. My business is not yours."

What had turned Judas into someone I no longer knew? How could Jesus not know that one of His chosen was so changed?

One day the physician Luke, accompanied by a Pharisee named Simon, came to visit the Master.

"It is my obligation to bid you come to a banquet at my house," Simon said, dressed in his blue-tasseled finery.

Jesus was considered a rabbi because no greater teacher existed, yet He had never received the formal training of that title. Despite His lack of formal education, He often received invitations to dine with the reigning rabbis and Pharisees.

Simon scoffed at the preaching of John. He made it clear that Jesus was a rabbi and nothing more. So I was surprised when Jesus accepted the invitation and asked me to accompany Him to Simon's home. Peter, James, and John were also invited.

I went in the capacity in which I felt most comfortable: that of a servant.

The house was ample, but could not compare to the home of Matthew. It was far too small, even with the added courtyard, to accommodate the crowd that pressed to get close to Jesus.

We removed our sandals; no servant came forward to wash our feet. I noted how Jesus carefully stepped over the mats and rugs on which the family surely offered their set prayers.

I took my place in the corner, waiting for any task my Master might require. Peter wore a look I knew well. He was disgusted and distrustful of almost everyone there. Though hidden, his saber was sheathed in his tunic, ready should he need it.

John was his gentle self and James fielded questions, quoting scripture as rapidly and accurately as even Simon, the host.

At the table Jesus and the other guests reclined on couches, stretching their feet outward from the table.

A woman came through the open door carrying a small alabaster box. She walked past me and made her way to stand behind Jesus. Peter locked his eyes on her to see what she held in the box. I was prepared to spring at her if she produced a small dagger or any other object of harm.

It was ointment.

I could smell it as soon as the box was opened. Not everyone noticed her at first, but Jesus did. The woman wept silently, her tears washing the dust from His feet. She then wiped them with her lengthy hair and wet them with more tears.

Did I know her?

Everyone looked at her now. She had become a spectacle— weeping, washing, and finally anointing.

Another man walked through the door and pressed his way inside. It was Judas.

"Who is the woman?" he asked.

I only shrugged.

But a Jew at the far end of the table answered, "She is a sinner."

"I *was* a sinner," the woman said through her tears, "until I repented, was baptized, and forgiven by my Lord." She bent to kiss His feet.

Expecting rebellion, I saw Peter reach for his blade.

But there was no need. Simon held up a hand to keep his guests in control.

Jesus, though, gave him a long, hard look. "Simon, I have somewhat to say unto thee."

Simon shifted uncomfortably. "Master, say on."

Then came the fitting parable. "There was a certain creditor which had two debtors: the one owed five hundred pence, and the other fifty. And when they had nothing to pay, he frankly forgave them both. Tell me therefore, which of them will love him most?"

Simon shifted again. He reminded me of a synagogue student, confident in his answer. "I suppose that he, to whom he forgave most."

Jesus nodded. "Thou has rightly judged."

Jesus turned to the woman, but spoke to Simon, "Seest thou this woman? I entered into thine house, thou gavest me no water for my feet: but she hath washed my feet with tears, and wiped them with the hairs of her head. Thou gavest me no kiss: but this woman since the time I came in hath not ceased to kiss my feet. My head with oil thou didst not anoint: but this woman hath anointed my feet with ointment. Wherefore I say unto thee, Her sins, which are many, are forgiven; for she loved much: but to whom little is forgiven, the same loveth little."

Then Jesus turned to the woman and said to her what we already knew. "Thy sins are forgiven."

At that point the uproar began. The murmurings, the threats. The spirit of evil rose like steam from the grilled meat. I stepped close to Jesus, making myself His shield.

"Who is this that forgiveth sins also?" the Jews asked.

Jesus stood and said to the woman, "Thy faith hath saved thee; go in peace."

On our way out into the courtyard, with the disciples still riled up by what had been done and said in the house of the Pharisee, Peter walked beside me, half-smiling. "Peace. What is peace?"

Sixty-nine

The ugly head of jealousy crept up and grinned at me. I saw it whenever Jesus held me back from His counsels with His chosen Twelve. I even fought jealousy when He spent time alone with each one, teaching each what he needed to know, because they would have to carry on when He was gone.

Didn't Jesus know by now that my heart belonged to Him? He could count on me for any task at any time. I had given up everything to serve Him—and still, He cut me off from time to time, leaving me to battle my own feelings of unworthiness. I felt so alone. I no longer had Judas as a friend, and the other Apostles had more demands than they could meet.

There were some moments when I felt so unneeded that I thought of walking back to Nazareth to see Deborah. Thoughts of her never left my mind or my heart.

The times I enjoyed most with Jesus were the simple times, like sitting in a home and listening to Him tell parables. Most favorite for me were days marked by ordinary service, times when Jesus climbed on the roof of a widow's home to help repair the thatch, or when we helped a farmer bring in his final harvest before a gathering storm.

I was happiest when I was busy doing good.

Jesus seemed happiest when He spoke of His Father. He touched people with words now; His parables testified of God's goodness. The language Jesus used was the language people best understood. To the farmer He spoke of the seed. To the fishermen He spoke of fish. To the Pharisees He spoke of hypocrisy.

This day Jesus entered the ship Zebedee brought. The shores of Galilee were too crowded, and Peter felt it was impossible to keep

Jesus safe in such a crush. Hands were always grabbing at Him, tearing His robes, pushing and shoving, claiming the right to stand next to the Master.

A gull glided effortlessly above us, and an image crossed my mind—how Jesus, as a little boy, used to spread His arms and pretend to fly. I could not stop my lips from smiling.

From the safety of the boat the Master's voice rippled out like gentle waves across the water.

"Behold, a sower went forth to sow; And when he sowed, some seeds fell by the way side, and the fowls came and devoured them up: Some fell upon stony places, where they had not much earth: and forthwith they sprung up, because they had no deepness of earth: And when the sun was up, they were scorched; and because they had no root, they withered away. And some fell among thorns; and the thorns sprung up, and choked them: But other fell into good ground, and brought forth fruit, some an hundredfold, some sixtyfold, some thirtyfold.

"Who hath ears to hear, let him hear."

I thought back to the days of my education in Nazareth. Rabbi Asa would whisper into an interpreter's ear the words he wanted his students to hear. The interpreter, who heard the message in Hebrew, proclaimed it aloud in Aramaic. The interpreter could not add or subtract a single word; the translation had to be perfect, or the interpreter faced expulsion.

To me, that was what Jesus was saying: *understand and do my will, or face expulsion from the Father's kingdom.*

After all this time, after Jesus had repeated the same teachings a thousand times, why did people still stare with blank eyes and open mouths?

" . . . blessed are your eyes, for they see: and your ears, for they hear.

"For verily I say unto you, That many prophets and righteous men have desired to see those things which ye see, and have not seen them; and to hear those things which ye hear, and have not heard them.

"When any one heareth the word of the kingdom, and understandeth it not, then cometh the wicked one, and catcheth away that which was sown in his heart."

Mary of Magdalene—who had been healed of great infirmities—was there, her arm wrapped around mother Mary's shoulder. The two Marys had become close, and the sight made me smile.

Finally, after a full day of telling parables, trying every way He knew to make the people understand the gospel, Jesus sent the multitude away. He went into the house, exhausted, but even there He was not unhindered.

More disciples followed Him, begging for more parables. Jesus taught, and was still teaching when my eyes closed tight.

When I woke I realized the house was empty. I ran outside looking for Jesus. He had once again been mobbed and had been forced to climb into Zebedee's ship to teach the masses that lined the shore.

While I had slept, He had worked on.

The oppressive heat of the day had dissipated. Dark gray clouds blocked the sun and any blue from the sky. The day was gone, but the night had not yet come on.

It was a short swim to the boat, and the disciple named Mark reached to help me onto the deck. The multitude was thinning, but three men held Jesus' attention. His voice was rough and raspy. His back was bent, and I could tell from the way He rubbed his neck that it ached.

He seemed happy but surprised to see me, awake and sopping wet.

I found the waterskins and brought Him fresh drink. I handed Him a soaked rag to rest on His neck. He smiled His gratitude, but I could tell it took great effort for Him just to raise the corners of His mouth. I had never seen Jesus so worn.

When He was done talking with the three men, Jesus turned to Andrew. "Let us go over unto the other side of the lake."

A look of dismay crossed Andrew's face. He looked back at me. "We are ill-prepared for such a journey."

"Fear not," said Peter, "the waters are placid."

"But the wind comes from the east," said Andrew.

I was still soaked and felt the easterly kiss of the sea's breath. I knew better than anyone how ill-prepared we were for a sudden sail across the lake.

Yet the Master had bid us sail, and so we sailed.

Jesus slept, finally and deeply, in the hull of the ship.

As darkness enveloped us, the squalls came. Water lapped onto the deck, and we all pitched it back into the sea bucket by bucket. But the sea spit it back faster. Soon a fear I did not know took charge—not just of me, but of all of us.

"Satan has hold of the rudder," James shouted. "I cannot steer!"

It was almost impossible to hear his voice. It was almost impossible to stay standing. Waves rocked and pitched the ship, and I worried that John—the lightest of all of us—might go over the edge with the next wash.

We did our best to fight nature for what seemed like forever.

Suddenly Peter took me by both shoulders. "Almon! Go to the Master. Wake him."

"How can He sleep when we perish?" Judas demanded. "If He is the Master, why has He done this evil to us?"

If?

Did I hear Judas right?

Jesus didn't bring on this storm . . . What storm was twisting Judas' mind?

I went down to find Jesus with John at my back. It was his urgent voice that woke our sleeping Master.

"Master, carest thou not that we perish?"

Jesus raised His head from the pillow and followed us. He seemed more sad than tired. But when He reached the deck, the ship was pitching like a bucking horse. He lifted His voice and spoke to the very elements. He rebuked the wind. To the sea He said, "Peace, be still."

The wind ceased and the water calmed.

We gathered to Him, awed.

"Why are ye so fearful? how is it that ye have no faith?" He asked.

As He returned to His rest there were those among us who sounded more like doubting Pharisees than believing Apostles. "What manner of man is this, that even the wind and the sea obey Him?" one uttered.

Seventy

We arrived on the Perean shores, the water as calm as our Master. Our spirits were quiet and humble.

"I, for one, am reminded that as Moses lifted his rod to part the great Red Sea, Jesus lifted His hand to still the waves of this great lake," Peter proclaimed. "He is Master of all . . . even nature."

Judas held a hand to his bruised cheek. In the whipping of the storm, his face had met the mast. I couldn't help but notice that his purse was intact and tied tightly to his body. I brought him water, for that was all we had on the ship. It would fall to him to purchase food and supplies among the Gadarenes.

This eastern side of the lake was very different from the soft, rolling shores of Capernaum. There were sharp peaks, and the breaking water gave way to high, sheer, jagged cliffs. The colors were not soft, but deep and hard—black-bladed rocks, azure skies, and rich green flatlands.

We docked outside the city limits in the land of tombs. Jesus had never set His sandaled feet on this ground. "There may be those here who have not yet heard of the Master," Jude observed.

"Impossible," Nathaniel said. "Word of His works has spread throughout all of Palestine. There is no soul, no corner that His spirit has not touched."

"Yes," said Jude, "yet this is a land filled with Romans."

Simon growled.

Thomas drew a deep breath and let it out rapidly. "Our Master will leave no stone unturned. He seeks out *every* soul."

Jesus never engaged in such speculation. He trekked ahead, not at the pace of a weary man. We had to climb a good distance to reach the flatlands. Our sandals slipped on the wet, mossy rock. I slipped and scraped the palms of my hands.

As we came up from the rocks, we found ourselves in the tombs of the Gadarenes. Great walls of barnacled brown rock had been hewn out for burying the dead.

Our bodies shivered.

Our voices echoed off the rising walls.

"This feels like heathen ground," Simon whispered.

Because we had docked so near the tombs, we were alone except for a group of men in a far-off field. They had stopped their task to stare at us.

"Look," said Simon with disgust. "They tend *swine*." As Jews, we regarded swine as unclean animals.

Jesus went forward while the rest of us stood still. Immediately, a terrifying sight came running at him. It was a man, but no kind of man I had ever laid eyes on. He was huge as Goliath and scarred as though he'd been repeatedly flogged. He wore not a stitch of clothes. His face, his arms, and his legs bled. His feet were bruised black; so were his hands.

My first thought was that the poor fellow had been pounded in last night's storm.

But Peter called him crazed. He went immediately to protect the Master, and though I was only half the man's size, I also went to give my all—though I would be found wanting if measured.

The man rushed right for Jesus, as if his bulging eyes recognized an old enemy.

"He is possessed!" someone shouted.

"Demonic!"

In a voice that was not human, the demand was made. "What have I to do with thee, Jesus, thou Son of the most high God?"

It wasn't the man who knew Jesus—it was the demonic spirit within him.

As though evil could command the Lord, the black tongue said, "I adjure thee by God, that thou torment me not."

Jesus stood tall, his chest filled with His great compassion. "Come out of the man, thou unclean spirit."

The man's body shook like a terrified beast. He collapsed at the Savior's feet.

Terror gripped my throat as surely as a murderous hand. It was hard to breathe. Evil addressed Jesus . . . and though I knew without doubt that Jesus would triumph, fear flashed through me.

"What is thy name?" Jesus demanded.

"My name is Legion: for we are many."

I wondered if the evil spirit was referring to the nearby Roman legion . . . but John had another explanation.

"More than a single demon resides in the man's body," John said. "The devils know that Jesus is Lord. They know His identity and His power. Almon, you are taken with fear, but your fear is nothing compared to the fear those evil spirits feel."

The vile demons implored the Lord that He would not send them away out of the country: "Send us into the swine, that we may enter into them."

We all looked to toward the mountain slope where at least two thousand swine fed. Their caregivers now looked toward us. One man came running.

While the crazed man implored the Master, shirking and writhing, the caregiver reached Andrew and pointed to the man possessed. "He presents to you grave danger. Leave him be," the caregiver pleaded.

Andrew was calm. "Our Master, Jesus, will heal him."

The man shook his staff. "No. No man can cure the evil that lives in him. For years he has haunted this region, making it unsafe for any man to pass. He is mad and fierce."

"Has no one attempted to aid him?" Andrew asked.

"Oh, the efforts that have been made on his behalf! He breaks his bindings, even chains cannot hold him. Fettered, he breaks free. He is walking evil, I warn you. He slashes his own flesh and his blood darkens the soil of this region. Satan rules this man, and has for years."

The man's howls continued. He lifted a sharp stone, and Peter stood ready to tackle him should he lunge at Jesus. But the man slashed his own chest, drawing another red river.

Thomas stepped forth. "Jesus is aware."

The caregiver cursed. "Your Master, Jesus, will die if He allows Himself to move close enough for the evil one to take hold of His throat."

Again, I felt invisible fingers choke the breath from my own throat.

"You do not know Jesus," Thomas said.

"You have been warned!" The man shook his staff again and then turned and lunged away.

The devils within the man were left without choice.

They had to obey the Lord's command.

"Go." Jesus gave them their leave. Shortly thereafter, the caregivers of the swine screamed, flinging stones and shaking their staffs, desperate to control and protect such a great number of livestock. The man who had spoken to us wailed like he was a hired mourner.

It was clear to us who watched the horrific scene unfold that the devils had taken over the tabernacles of the animals.

As an uncontrollable body, they squealed and ran in violent torment. Their caregivers had no chance of heading them off. The animals raced in terror down a steep bluff. We had just come from the shore, and I knew that at the base of that bluff was a sharp and jagged ledge.

Moving as one tortured body, the swine ran without slowing over the edge of the bluff. Those that were not dashed on the rocks choked in the sea. The squeals and cries of death filled the air.

The caregivers were shocked and terrified.

Andrew called to them, but they wanted nothing to do with us. Instead, they raced toward the city.

"Those swine were their livelihood," the man said.

We all turned to him in utter shock. He spoke in his right mind. Jesus had taken the outer cloak from Peter and had clothed the man.

Jesus sat on a limestone bench; the man sat completely sane at His feet. His bleeding wounds were healed. Even the thick scars around his ankles and wrists had vanished.

That is how the people of Gerasa and Gadara found him when they returned—healed and whole.

Two thousand swine lay dead, swollen and floating in the sea. The sight was enough to send anyone into panic. Yet the Roman townspeople and all those who had come to witness the destruction of their livelihood were most terrified of the man who sat at Jesus' feet.

The people came in groups, curious and uncertain. Jesus did to them what He did to all those who sought Him . . . He preached His Father's plan. He taught faith, repentance, baptism, and obedience.

The healed man stayed so close to Jesus that he could reach out and take hold of the Master's robe at any time. "Jesus . . . Jesus . . . Jesus."

The owner of the swine and the caregiver who had spoken to Andrew approached James and John. "We know this man . . . he is not the same."

"Our Master's touch leaves everyone changed."

"You cannot stay here," the owner said. "You and your Jesus must leave."

"Because your swine were destroyed?"

The men looked at each other. "Because you bring with you a spirit we do not understand. It fills us with fear."

I could not believe my ears. These men had lived for years, haunted by a man possessed of devils—and now they wanted us to depart because Jesus brought a spirit of truth and goodness?

The man was intent. "We beseech you to depart."

Others were furious at what had happened. They shouted that we had to make retribution for the lost swine, but the caregiver stood up and rebuked them.

"Depart and leave us as we were," he implored, directing his words at Jesus.

Jesus would never impose Himself where He was unwanted, so we turned to leave. The healed man begged to stay with Jesus, to return to Capernaum with us.

Jesus said no. "Go home to thy friends, and tell them how great things the Lord hath done for thee, and hath had compassion on thee."

We made our way back down to the shore. With James at the helm, we steered through the bloated pigs, some floating with their snouts upward and their eyes still open.

"Roman swine," Simon said. "They had no right to reject our Master."

We all agreed.

Jesus had gone back to the stern, more sad than He was weary. We sailed back to Capernaum with the wind in our favor.

Seventy-one

Great crowds waited on the shores near Capernaum. Mary Magdalene waved, relieved to see that Jesus and the rest of us were safe, since we had taken sail with little warning to anyone.

As I stepped from the ship, a hand took hold of my elbow. "Almon."

It was Jairus, the ruler of the local synagogue. I knew him to be a friend to Jesus. He looked past me. His eyes were filled with agony, and I wanted to ask him what the matter was, but he saw Jesus and ran to Him.

Falling at the Master's feet he cried, "My little daughter lieth at the point of death. I pray thee, come and lay thy hands on her, that she may be healed and she shall live."

I knew that Jesus longed for a meal and a rest on His favorite pallet. I expected Him to tell Jairus to go his way and that the girl would be healed. Instead, Jesus agreed to go with Jairus.

Hundreds of people hungry for the word of the Master followed Jesus. Peter, who was worn and quick of temper, had to push the most intense of the crowd back to keep them from grabbing the Master and ripping His robes. I ran back to the house and refilled the waterskins; I gathered grapes and a raisin cake Mary had made. She handed me a basket filled with fresh bread and dried fish, enough for a meal to feed the Apostles, but not enough to offer a bite to everyone else who refused to leave the shadow of the Master.

I fetched a clean set of robes and wondered what else I might bring Jesus to offer comfort. I did not know how long we would be gone. My last inclination was to tuck His sleeping pallet beneath my arm. I feared for Him. No man could give of Himself as Jesus did and continue without replenishment. The voyage to the other side of the lake was meant to allow Him rest, but I had been among those who had awoken Him to calm a storm when any one of us possessed the faith to do the same. We could have bid God calm the waters; instead, we had feared.

If it had been a test of faith, we'd all failed.

I ran without stopping to catch up to the throng. I couldn't even see Jesus for all the people, pressed shoulder to shoulder. I did see Jairus, and the look of anguish on his face made my heart ache for him.

The crowd stalled, and I heard the Master's voice call out, "Who touched my clothes?"

I wound my way up to Him and heard Judas speak in a voice that lacked the respect he usually used when speaking to Jesus, "Thou seest the multitude thronging thee, and sayest thou, *Who touched me?*"

A woman about the age of Mary approached Him, and the other people stepped back. Her tone was one of reverence and love. "Lord, for twelve years I have had an issue of blood. I have suffered many things of many physicians, and have spent all that I had. Nothing was bettered, but rather grew worse. When I heard of you, Jesus, I came in the press behind you. I knew if I might but touch your clothes, I would be made whole."

Jesus looked gladdened. "Daughter, thy faith hath made thee whole; go in peace, and be whole of thy plague."

Awe rippled across the throng of people, many of them inflicted themselves and hoping for a miracle. As they rejoiced, a servant of Jairus' approached. Judas grabbed his arm. "Thy daughter is dead," he scoffed. "Why troublest the Master any further?"

Jairus fell back and had to be caught in the arms of those around him. For an instant, I wondered if his heart would break with grief, but Jesus went to him and spoke the words I'd heard Him speak to me so many times: "Be not afraid, only believe."

Jesus bid me come to Him. I offered the basket, the pallet, and the drink, but Jesus would have none of it. He told me to join with the other Apostles; He was going on with only Peter, James, and John, His brother. The rest of us were to stay with the crowd and keep them from following Jesus.

I felt a swell of jealousy, but it left as quickly as it had arisen, and I did as I was asked. I served while those to whom Jesus had given authority preached and ministered, doing their best to honor the Master. But the people wanted Jesus. One man even spit on Thomas, calling him an imposter.

I washed the spittle from Thomas' face, and as I did, a new testimony surged through me. The Twelve who Jesus had chosen were more than mere men—they were His bearers. They possessed authority and power to act in His holy name. No wonder Jesus was disappointed that not one of them had raised a hand to calm the storm. They were His ambassadors, and I was grateful they were also my friends.

I was there to welcome Jesus when He returned. He was not alone. Two blind men came begging—not for bread or meat, but for the touch of the Master's hand. I realized at that moment that I had yet to see Jesus give sight to sightless eyes, though I knew He could do it . . . would do it, if the men had sufficient faith.

"Thou son of David, have mercy on us," one pleaded.

"Believe ye that I am able to do this?"

"Yea, Lord."

He touched their eyes saying, "According to your faith be it unto you."

Suddenly, their eyes were opened. Jesus charged them, saying, "See that no man know it."

But the men could not contain their tongues, and they told what had been done to them, spreading the fame of Jesus near and far.

Later, when we were all together again, Peter relayed to us what had happened at the house of Jairus. We were back at the house at Capernaum. Jesus was finally resting inside, while outside we sat beneath a makeshift canopy, well fed and alone for the time.

"The courtyard was filled with those that wept and wailed greatly. Jesus saith unto them, 'Why make ye this ado, and weep? the damsel is not dead, but sleepeth.'"

Peter's voice thundered as he said, "They laughed him to scorn. But when he had put them all out, he taketh the father and the mother of the damsel, and them that were with him, and entereth in where the damsel was lying. And he took the damsel by the hand, and said unto her, "*Talitha cumi* . . . Damsel, I say unto thee, arise.'

"And straightway the damsel arose, and walked; for she was of the age of twelve years. And they were astonished with a great astonishment."

His paw of a hand reached for the basket that contained the raisin cake. Peter broke off a piece and said, "Jesus charged her parents that no man should know it, and commanded that something should be given her to eat."

He bit into the cake and smiled at the memory of the mighty miracle.

Seventy-two

Jesus moved and worked with a new urgency. As His miracles mounted, so did the opposition against Him. Judas found it more and more difficult to fill the purse. Peter and James brought in funds from an occasional haul, and I found work as a scribe from time to time, bringing in a coin or two.

We had enough, but never more.

Yet Jesus went forward from village to village, doing only the work of His Father. The Pharisees and their spies no longer made an attempt to be subtle. They watched Jesus without blinking, hoping He would make a mistake or commit a sin for which they could accuse Him. When He didn't, they fabricated His reputation, saying He worked through the power of the devil.

It was not a new accusation, but it was heard increasingly more often. Jesus spoke of sifting the wheat from the tares, and I could see that happening as more and more followers fell by the wayside. Even some of those who had been healed turned against the Master.

A feeling of unrest and insurrection—not unlike that when Sepphoris had burned so long ago—was spreading through the land. Jews were threatening to take power from the Romans and their appointed puppets. If Jesus was not going to rise up and be the political leader they looked for, they would look elsewhere.

Yes, Jesus had come to set His people free, but not from the mortal hand of Caesar. Why could their blind eyes not open to that fact?

Antipas spread sin with every move he made. His vile life infested the people like locusts. He refused to release John, and even some of those closest to Jesus asked why we did not go to the fortress to release the Baptist.

Were angels enough?

Then came a familiar face. Mathias appeared among the crowds and asked for an audience with Jesus. He brought with him a friend from Arimethea, Joseph. No one had to guess that the news they brought was grim.

"He is dead," said Mathias.

We knew he spoke of John. Our hearts stopped at the announcement.

My throat threatened to close over. I could not swallow the lump that rose and robbed me of my breath.

Nathaniel cried aloud. Jesus buried His face in His hands as He listened to the unfolding of the murderous tale.

Mathias said, "I have measured my words again and again, that I might be accurate in relaying what I know of Antipas. His father sought *your* life, Master. In so doing, he killed innocent babes, and innocent men like John's father, Zacharias.

"The household of Herod has been one of murder. Herod the Great killed his own children when they presented a threat to his power. He slew his own wives. Now the son of his that rules Galilee has only increased his father's sins.

"That household has intermarried until it is a web of the most vile unions. As you know, John denounced the union of Antipas to his own brother's wife, Herodias." Mathias spit at the mention of her name. "Her father is also the brother of Antipas."

Judas shook his head. "I cannot keep count of all the sins of this man."

Joseph of Arimethea continued. "Herod Philip and Herodias have a daughter, Salome. She is a vixen like her mother. At a recent banquet—a heathen affair like Antipas is so fond of hosting—there were men of Rome, military leaders, and political leaders. There were Herod's closest cohorts. And I am saddened to say, there were men of Palestine, Jews . . . even holy men."

Ever since Jesus had healed the man's withered hand in the synagogue, we all knew that the Pharisees sought the Herodians' help in thwarting Jesus, even finding reason to put Him to death. It was a bond as sinful as any in the household of Herod.

Joseph's voice broke off, and Mathias continued. "Any sin imagined has been wrought at that banquet table . . . so Salome came to dance before her stepfather and his drunken guests.

"He was so taken by her vulgar performance that he offered her even half the kingdom, and the stupid girl went to her mother to see what she should demand.

"She came back demanding the head of our Baptist on a charger."

At this we all fell sick.

"Antipas, the coward, sobered up. He was fearful. He knew that John was a prophet . . . powerful. He knew that great things had transpired in the cell of his dungeon. He *knew,* and yet he sent the ax."

Joseph's face was wet with tears of anger and sadness. "That woman . . . the adultress and incestuous whore . . . rejoiced at the death of the Baptist. He had offended her, and she ordered John's headless body to be flung out over the battlements for dogs and vultures to devour."

Jesus groaned. Tears ran between His fingers and dampened the dirt. I could not see His face, but I could imagine it.

Mathias went to Jesus, knelt down, and embraced Him. "Fear not, Lord. Those of us who loved John preserved his body. We washed it, wrapped it, anointed it, and laid it to rest."

The details continued, and as they did, word spread throughout the land of the evil that had been done to one who was so good. So loved. So followed.

The Galileans were incensed. John had been executed without a trial—a legal breach they would not tolerate. The angriest among us called for the blood of Herod Antipas. They called for the head of Herodias and her sinful daughter to be fed to the dogs.

Herod's soldiers appeared in force to quell the rising rebellion. With the soldiers came word that Antipas was now fixated on Jesus.

"The man is mad," Mathias said. "He cannot close his eyes without seeing the severed head of the Baptist. In his madness, he believes Jesus is John restored to life again, come only to haunt him."

"Good," said Peter. "I am glad to hear that Antipas is tortured in his own mind."

But the news was not good. It changed the course of our work. It was no longer safe for Jesus to walk the shores of Galilee. We were forced to hide, and Jesus was not one to work in the shadows.

My old fear had come back to follow me. Everywhere we went I looked for the one who would take Jesus from me. My devotion to Him was stronger than ever.

Yet there were those among us who were resentful.

Judas made the accusation. "Jesus, you could have saved John, but you didn't." He echoed the sentiment of His brothers in Nazareth, who had raged against Him for not saving Joseph when He could have.

And through it all, I feared my greatest fear yet. *If the Master could not save John, would He be able to save Himself?*

Seventy-three

Jesus sent me away.

He sent us all away.

He sent me back to Nazareth for a season, that I should bring back those who desired to join Him. Deborah was all I could think of, and I packed my bag with haste.

The Apostles, having been given authority by His own hands, left for their own ministries, going from village to village to preach and heal as Jesus did.

We were to meet back in the borders of Judea, where Herod's son Philip ruled. There we would be out from under his crazed and tortured brother, Antipas.

Nazareth looked no different to my eyes, but it *felt* different. Here were the memories of a wonderful childhood, but here also was the memory of that day when so many had turned against Jesus and tried in their cowardly justification to kill Him.

Mary's daughters lived here now. One was married, the other betrothed. They kept the family home. Jesus' mother and brothers were close to Him, and they kept a home in Capernaum.

Joseph's workshop was busy, but not with any craftsman of his household. That left me with a profound sadness.

I washed and changed my clothes and went to the courtyard of Joel. It was a picture that stole my breath away. Naomi and Deborah sat in the courtyard at the loom. Deborah's voice filled the air with song.

I stood at the gate, feeling like a stranger—an unexpected, perhaps unwanted intruder.

Naomi saw me first and let out a short cry.

When Deborah saw me there, she nearly toppled the loom to reach me. "Almon! My Almon!"

Then she fell away in gloom. "Is it Jesus? Has harm come to the Master?"

I shook my head, touched at the obvious love and devotion Deborah still held for her cousin. Her veil was thinner than I was used to seeing her wear, and beneath its shimmer, her face was smooth and clear. Beautiful.

My betrothed!

Along the journey that had taken a full eight days and nights, I had made a written message to explain Jesus' wishes. She and Naomi read it together.

Naomi bid me sit, and I took the bench across from the loom. She offered me meat and drink, and while I partook, Naomi asked, "How is my cousin, Mary?"

I smiled and wrote quickly that Mary was among her sons and those loyal to Jesus. She was well.

"I miss her so. Yet my place is here with Joel. His business has fallen off. His health fails him as well."

I was sorry to hear that. I wanted to help, but what could I do?

"Malik is a dutiful son. He tends to both his father and the business. They will not travel with you to join Jesus."

Her words were firm, and they chilled my heart.

"However . . . " She held up a straight finger. "Deborah will join you. For two years my daughter has been betrothed. Take her now. When the wedding time is nigh, send word, and we will join you at Capernaum."

Deborah looked at me and our eyes locked. How did she feel?

"Never allow yourselves to be alone. Not for a minute. Promise me that."

We both promised, and when Joel came home and was told about the plan, he said, "I should have stood up that day in the synagogue. I should have stood and fought for Jesus."

Two days later we had amassed a small company, including Rabbi Asa and his son and family. Because so much of Nazareth was made of family, there were distant cousins of the Master who wished to come along. I knew He would rejoice when He saw so many. I knew that His heart would sorrow when He saw that Joel, Malik, and Naomi were not present.

We met the Master at a refuge near Bethsaida in the desert.

He looked well, but not rested. As I suspected, He was joyous to unite with His family and Nazarene friends. Mary took Deborah into her arms and they walked, catching up on all the things that had transpired. Mary Magdalene brought cakes and meat for everyone, and the wine was as sweet as the wine had been at Cana.

I felt like a man renewed.

Deborah was within my sight and soon would be my wife.

Peter and the others were back with their reports of individual missions. Some were more discouraged than others. Judas looked like a man with a mountain on his back. I tried to communicate with him. He was polite, but cold. I was glad he had his family with him now; perhaps they could bring him peace.

Nathaniel told me that our season of rest had to be short-lived. Antipas continued to have his night terrors, imagining that Jesus was John, come back to haunt him.

Pontias Pilate, the Roman appointee, had swung a wide and sharp sword at all Galilean rebels. Jesus took Simon on long walks, calming his rage and telling him there was a better way to battle the empire than with another sword.

In the days that followed, disciples—thousands of men, along with their women and children—followed Jesus out to the great, grassy plains.

"They look for a new king in Jesus," Simon told us. "Listen well to their sayings. They believe that Jesus will free them from oppression. They quote scriptures."

I knew the scriptures; I had heard their speculations.

Jesus was come to set them free, but from a foe far more oppressive than Pilate. Why couldn't they understand that?

As the numbers swelled and the demands grew, Judas surprised me. He would normally be eager to fill the purse with their offerings, but he approached the Master and implored, "Send them away."

Jesus refused.

Even Mary Magdalene appeared concerned. "There are thousands here, Master. They hunger, but have no food. Send them away, that they may go into the towns and country around about, and lodge, and get victuals."

By now those closest to Jesus were gathered around, trying to explain the situation. But I looked at Him and knew that He understood better than any of us.

Judas' voice rose so high it cracked. "We have no more but five loaves and two fishes; except we should go and buy meat for all this people." He shook the purse to show that we did not have the money to make such a purchase.

But Jesus said to His Apostles, "Make them sit down by fifties in a company."

We divided the people into groups of fifty and spread them over the grass in rows like a farmer plants his crops. Baskets were set before the Master—empty baskets.

"What is Jesus doing?" Deborah asked me.

A miracle. I mouthed the words, and she soon understood.

He took the five small round peasant loaves and the two fishes—not enough to feed Peter for a single meal. He blessed them and brake and gave to the disciples to set before the multitude.

The baskets were filled.

The multitude was fed.

He commanded that I gather the fragments so that nothing be wasted.

It was a miracle for the eyes and the stomachs.

"Surely, this is Christ, the King!" the people said among themselves. "He will deliver us. He will feed us. Jesus will lift the burdens from our lives."

Later, when the people had departed and Jesus was praying, He asked those of us with Him, "Whom say the people that I am?"

Andrew said, "John the Baptist; but some say, Elias; and others say, that one of the old prophets is risen again."

Jesus moaned as though His body ached. "But whom say *ye* that I am?"

Peter gave the reply we all felt. "The Christ of God."

Seventy-four

Jesus sought no praise or honor from men. He *only* wanted to serve His Father, so the accolades of those who wanted Him to wear a royal robe and crown brought Him much discomfort.

There came a time when the press grew so weighty that He sent even His disciples away—telling them to go out on the ship, to take refuge on the sea, while He went alone into the mountain.

I expected to stay there, at the base of the mountain, but Jesus told me to join the others at the shore. Deborah had already returned to the house at Capernaum with Mary and the others.

My heart hesitated. I did not wish to leave Jesus—not for an hour, not for a minute. But His eyes bid me go, and so I went.

It was my fortune that the disciples had not yet set out on the sea. Peter saw me running and separated me from the throng.

"Almon, is the Master well?"

Yes.

"Then join us. The sea is calm and the skies cloudless. Our voyage will be refreshing. John stands at the helm." He chuckled.

I knew that Peter resented John's easy manner. One was the talon of the cock, the other the feather. Both were needed to make the bird whole.

We rowed as equal forces on either side and made our way thirty furlongs out onto the water. We spoke of our experiences, our thoughts, even our fears, and then we rested.

Sometime in the night I heard a voice and looked to see the hunched form of Andrew praying. When he felt my eyes upon him he looked at me, moonlight shining down on us.

"What more can He do?" Andrew asked.

Immediately, I knew the meaning of his question. Jesus had healed the lame, baptized the repentant, preached the pure and complete gospel. He had raised the dead and fed multitudes without means.

We both felt it . . . His sacred ministry was drawing to a close.

I did not sleep again until I heard the sounds of Andrew sleeping.

Only when the early-morning winds arose did we wake.

Peter already held an oar and he tossed me another. I sat behind him and marveled at his strength. Soon we all rowed against a contrary wind.

"How will Jesus find us?" Judas asked over the wind.

"He will wait for us at the house or come to the shores of Capernaum. He will find us."

At that moment I looked across the waves and saw that the Master had indeed found us. I wanted to raise my voice, but could not, so before the others saw Him, I watched Jesus come toward us.

He brought no boat, but walked upon the waves.

I marveled only for a moment, and then remembered how He had commanded this very water to be still. Why, then, could He not command it to support Him as He walked toward us?

When the others caught sight of Jesus walking on the water, fear penetrated every heart.

"It is I; be not afraid." Fear was vanquished. Jesus was made welcome.

At the shores of Capernaum Jesus was met by a confused multitude. They knew that the disciples had departed on a ship without Jesus. They also knew that Jesus had taken no boat—and yet He arrived in the same ship with His disciples.

They did not understand, but they sought Him anyway.

Jesus saw through their souls and said, "Ye seek me, not because ye saw the miracles, but because ye did eat of the loaves, and were filled. Labour not for the meat which perisheth, but for that meat which endureth unto everlasting life, which the Son of man shall give unto you: for him hath God the Father sealed."

A rabbi cried out, "What shall we do, that we might work the works of God?"

Jesus answered, "This is the work of God, that ye believe on him whom he hath sent."

"What sign shewest thou then, that we may see, and believe thee?"

I threw my head back, opened my mouth, and wailed soundlessly. How could these people ask for a sign that they might know? Jesus *was* the sign. Many of them were signs, healed and made whole by His good works. Most had tasted of His manna; they had been fed when there was no food.

Now they demanded manna like that which Moses had provided. Only Moses had not provided the manna. God had.

They were like Judas, thinking that his endless efforts filled the purse.

Judas did not fill the purse. Jesus did.

Jesus said, "I am the bread of life: he that cometh to me shall never hunger; and he that believeth on me shall never thirst."

The murmur that rippled through the crowd was as wind on water. Standing in the midst, I felt the spirit of rejection. These people looked for a mighty soldier. They looked for meat and bread to fill the belly.

Jesus offered freedom from sin.

He offered food and water for their souls.

His words continued, and yet the crowd stepped back, one unbeliever at a time.

Seventy-five

If His own would not believe, Jesus found others. We sailed to the Gentile coastal towns of Tyre and Sidon in search of listening ears.

No opportunity to teach was lost. Jesus seldom slept. He sought out certain Apostles to teach and to testify. Peter was the one who most often sought out Jesus, asking Him to tell the same parables over and over so he would be certain he understood.

And yet none of us fully understood all that He so desperately taught.

When we landed on the coast, Peter approached Jesus with a warning. "A woman of Cana seeks thee, Lord."

Jesus said nothing.

The woman pressed through the curious, for even here among the nonbelievers, Jesus was known. "Have mercy on me, O Lord, thou Son of David; my daughter is grievously vexed with a devil."

Jesus did not respond.

Simon moved to halt the woman and Jesus continued on.

I could hear her cries above the sounds of the multitude. My heart felt pity, and I did not understand how the Master could ignore such desperation.

"Send her away," said Jude, "for she crieth after us."

Jesus replied, "I am not sent but unto the lost sheep of the house of Israel."

The woman would not be deterred. Her daughter was in need, and she sought Jesus for the one she loved.

"Lord, help me."

He turned on her with full compassion. "It is not meet to take the children's bread, and to cast it to dogs."

His words were harsh, but I knew His heart was not. He was testing the faith of the Canaanite woman.

Most people would have taken grave offense, but she said, "Truth, Lord: yet the dogs eat of the crumbs which fall from their masters' table."

The Master's eyes filled to overflowing. "O woman, great is thy faith: be it unto thee even as thou wilt."

And her daughter was made whole.

"Why, Almon, does the Master not heal you?" Deborah asked later that day. "When I sought Jesus to cleanse me of the disease that maimed me, He did not hesitate. For you, He would do the same. I am certain."

I had not been healed because I had not asked. Even *I* did not fully understand why . . . was it guilt for old sins? Feelings of unworthiness? Fear of how my life would change if my tongue came to life?

After we returned to Galilee, another multitude came bringing their blind, dumb, maimed, and demonic. He healed them all.

The multitude glorified the God of Israel when they saw His miracles. He called us to Him and said, "I have compassion on the multitude, because they continue with me now three days, and have nothing to eat: and I will not send them away fasting, lest they faint in the way."

We were far from the towns and marketplaces; one of the disciples asked, "Whence should we have so much bread in the wilderness, as to fill so great a multitude?"

"How many loaves have ye?" asked Jesus.

"Seven, and a few little fishes."

I had a sense what was coming as He commanded the multitude to sit down on the ground. Jesus took the loaves and fishes, gave thanks, and brake them. We did all eat.

He asked that I help gather all that was left and tell Him. After four thousand men, their women, and their children ate, I brought to the Master seven baskets, still full.

I felt full . . . full of the Spirit. These people, unlike the previous multitude that had tasted of the miraculous manna, did not push Jesus to be a mortal king. They ate His bread, but valued His word.

Next we went to Magdala, Mary Magdalene's hometown, along the coast.

There the Pharisees and Sadducees were out in full force. They begged from Him a sign.

Jesus lifted His hand to the sky. "When it is evening, ye say, It will be fair weather: for the sky is red. And in the morning, It will be foul weather to day: for the sky is red and lowring, O ye hypocrites, ye can discern the face of the sky; but can ye not discern the signs of the times?

"A wicked and adulterous generation seeketh after a sign; and there shall no sign be given unto it, but the sign of the prophet Jonas."

As Jesus left the Pharisees, Judas came to Him. "We have forgotten to take bread, Master. We have nothing to eat." Many of the others echoed his concern. I felt my own stomach growl.

"O ye of little faith," He said, looking like His heart was broken anew. "Do ye not yet understand, neither remember the five loaves of the five thousand, and how many baskets ye took up? Neither the seven loaves of the four thousand, and how many baskets ye took up?"

He looked right at me and, without speaking my name, chastened me like I'd never been chastened. My eyes had seen miracle after miracle. I'd tasted of His miraculous loaves and fish, yet I feared at the first growl of my stomach.

Jesus went on to preach of the leaven of the Pharisees and Sadducees, and how we must beware. Our main thoughts were still on our empty stomachs and the fact that we had forgotten to bring bread.

Seventy-six

They were gathered in the village courtyard: Jesus, surrounded by the children who followed him as faithfully as the Pharisees. The laughter sounded high above the gates. I had come to carry a boy whose legs refused to grow; his mother had bid me tote him.

Jesus opened His arms wide when He saw me, and I placed the boy on His lap. The boy's little arms went around the Savior's neck, and he held on as if his very life was at stake.

Jesus conversed with the mother and then healed the child for all to see. The children who witnessed the miracle marveled with an enthusiasm that so many of us had lost, taking for granted the powers of God at work. They cheered. They cried. They hugged and kissed Jesus, honoring Him for the Master that He was.

Then one of His disciples asked, "Who is the greatest in the kingdom of heaven?"

Most there knew that Jesus had just paid tribute to Caesar, and the Pharisees waited to trap the Master with His own answer. Jesus called the healed boy back to Him.

"Verily I say unto you, Except ye be converted, and become as little children, ye shall not enter into the kingdom of heaven. Whosoever therefore shall humble himself as this little child, the same is greatest in the kingdom of heaven. And whoso shall receive one such little child in my name receiveth me."

He drew a deep breath and His eyes filled with tears. "But whoso shall offend one of these little ones which believe in me, it were better for him that a millstone were hanged about his neck, and that he were drowned in the depth of the sea."

Jesus then took the opportunity to teach of offenses: "It must needs be that offences come; but woe to that man by whom the offence cometh!"

I watched Peter's face. He leaned forward and squinted, trying to understand all that was being taught.

Jesus said it was better that our hands and feet be gone than that we should use them to hurt another.

His arm swept over the group of children. "Take heed that ye despise not one of these little ones; for I say unto you, That in heaven their angels do always behold the face of my Father which is in heaven."

With so many children looking to Him, Jesus taught in parables. "If a man have an hundred sheep, and one of them be gone astray, doth he not leave the ninety and nine, and goeth into the mountains, and seeketh that which is gone astray?"

The children all shouted, yes! The shepherd would go in search of the lost lamb.

"And if it so be that he find it, verily I say unto you, he rejoiceth more of that sheep, than of the ninety and nine which went not astray. Even so it is not the will of your Father which is in heaven, that one of these little ones should perish."

Jesus continued to teach, telling parables and posing questions. "Moreover if thy brother shall trespass against thee, go and tell him his fault between thee and him alone; if he shall hear thee, thou hast gained thy brother."

Peter held his face in his hands. I wondered if he had been struck by a sudden pain, but then I saw his eyes fix on John, and I thought of how Peter had struggled to find common ground between the two of them. They were such different men. Finally, Peter approached the Master. "Lord, how oft shall my brother sin against me, and I forgive him? till seven times?"

Jesus shook His head and looked at Peter with unbending love. "I say not unto thee, Until seven times: but, Until seventy times seven."

His teaching continued, but I kept watch on Peter. He slowly backed away and found his path from the courtyard. I took heart knowing that I was not the only man who struggled to live as Jesus would have us live.

In an effort to practice what He taught and to spread the gospel with an increased speed, Jesus sent seventy men to go out in pairs. Jesus then asked me to accompany Him to Jerusalem for the Feast of the Tabernacles. We shared fond memories of the season. Joseph used to take great pride in constructing the temporary booths out of boughs and lumber to remind us of the tents our Israelite forefathers dwelt in on their journey through the wilderness. Hundreds now dotted the roads and yards around the Holy City.

It was a time of rejoicing and remembering.

As always, Jesus lodged in Bethany in a booth made by Lazarus, the brother of Mary and Martha. I was grateful to have Deborah with us. She had grown closer than ever to Mary and Martha.

There was no time for rest. The rituals of the festival were soon underway, requiring the service of at least 446 priests and that many Levites. I scanned their faces, thinking how many of those holy men had followed Jesus, had heard Him preach, had either accepted Him or rejected Him.

Hundreds of Jews waved palm branches as one Levite walked to the Pool of Siloam to draw the special water. I had heard Jesus preach so many times of living water, and I sensed that was the sermon He would preach now.

The Levite who approached the pool was a small man with a large voice. With much drama, he drew two pints from the holy pool and pronounced the water "living." He then poured it into the golden ewer.

We all trod to the temple altar.

The chant began. The multitude recited the Psalm and the water was poured from the ewer into a silver basin close to the altar.

"Praise ye the Lord!"

The chant rose and fell and rose again, while palm branches rose and fell and rose again.

I waited and when Jesus gave the signal, I moved to clear the way for Him to open His mouth to preach. I wasn't the only one watching Jesus; almost every eye in the crowd watched Him, wondering what He would say and do. The Pharisees and all their allies were ready and eager to take Him at the least provocation.

Jesus opened His mouth and told the truth. "If any man thirst, let him come unto me, and drink. He that believeth on me, as the scripture hath said, out of his belly shall flow rivers of living water."

"Of a truth this is the Prophet!" cried one. I turned to see a man I recognized. Jesus had unstopped his ears so long ago it was hard to recall the details, but I remembered his face and his gratitude at the miracle.

A woman who often followed the Master, one whose sins had been cleansed, cried out, "This is the Christ!"

The Pharisees rumbled like a quake along the Great Rift Valley. But even those who served the Pharisees had to confess, "Never man spake like this man."

For a moment, I had hope. Would a mighty miracle occur? Would the Pharisees and all the holy judges of Jerusalem finally have their eyes and ears opened to the Master who stood before them offering true and lasting living water?

How I hoped!

Seventy-seven

My hope was dashed the very next morning. Jesus was seated at the temple, surrounded by His usual throng of both believers and nonbelievers. All the sights, smells, and filth of the city took me back one memory at a time. So many of my pivotal moments had occurred here.

Jerusalem seemed to mark Jesus' destiny even more profoundly.

"Master, teach us," the people cried.

Rabbi Zeev wasn't present, and I thought that he must be plotting a way to accuse Jesus. He was not the eldest Pharisee or the most respected, but I thought he was the most cunning.

I wasn't mistaken. He came shortly thereafter with fellow Pharisees and scribes. They brought with them a woman who was small, like Peter's wife, and who had the light-colored hair of Judas' wife. She had obviously been crying hard and still wept. Her eye was black and her lip swollen. She wore only one sandal.

Rabbi Zeev swept both hands toward her, making a show as though she were a sacrificial animal at market. "This woman was taken from a booth last night, caught in the very act of adultery."

People hissed at her like wild animals. She cowered at their cruelty.

I thought of the hundreds of branch booths set up for the Feast of Tabernacles. I remembered that when I lived in Jerusalem, the first days of the festival usually deteriorated into drunken acts of immorality and lasciviousness.

Jesus looked upon the woman with compassion. The glance that passed between us told me that He also remembered the day so long ago in Sepphoris. He'd been only a boy then, but the rabid Jews had sunk their fangs into an accused woman . . . stone by stone.

I'd tried to protect Him then and had failed. Nor could I protect Him now. For I understood with terrifying clarity that the woman wasn't the only one in peril; the holy men were there on an *un*holy errand—to accuse the Lord, to condemn Him and put Him to death. I knew that Rabbi Zeev and his cohorts would not be satisfied until the Lord's blood was shed.

The dark rabbi bowed before Jesus with mock reverence. "Master, Moses in the law commanded us that she should be stoned; but what sayest thou?"

Their trap caught Jesus between two laws. The Roman law despised stoning, but the law of Moses demanded it. Stoning was such a cruel and barbaric form of execution that most Jews, under the thumb of the empire, swore off stoning. Jesus and I knew better.

My head hung in fear. Whichever way Jesus chose, He would break a law.

"Master, which is it?" Rabbi Zeev asked, showing impatience. "The Roman law or the law of our Father?"

A woman came forward and spit in the bowed face of the accused. People cheered.

I felt sick. The bitter taste of blood filled my mouth, and I realized I had bitten the inside of my cheek. What if the crowd should turn their murderous hunger toward the Master?

The men who brought the accused woman shoved her and formed a circle around her.

I waited, not daring to move, but ready to spring should anyone dare to take hold of my Lord. My fingers wrapped around the handle of a small dagger that Peter had presented me as a gift. I remembered a moment when my hand had held another dagger—one posed to protect my father from three robbers. This time, I would spring fast and drive deep.

Jesus appeared unconcerned. He acted as though He did not even hear their questions.

The accused woman began to bleed from her nose, but she did not bother to wipe the blood. She just bowed her head and trembled.

Jesus stooped down. I thought I saw Him look at me, but I could not read the expression on His face. I recognized His action, though.

It was one I had performed every day of my life since meeting with Joseph.

Jesus knelt, smoothed out the sand, and then began to write in the sand with His finger.

Even I could not read the words.

"Give us the answer we seek, Jesus."

"Yea, tell us if it is lawful to stone this woman."

Their questions mounted first to shouts, then to demands.

One man drew from his pouch a handful of stones that he passed to outstretched hands.

"Lord, what sayest thou?"

Like a billowing sail, Jesus rose to His full height and majesty. He looked Rabbi Zeev in the eyes, then scanned the crowd and returned to stare at the anxious rabbi.

"He that is without sin among you, let him first cast a stone at her."

Jesus knelt again and returned to His writing.

The air went still. The stones went unhurled. One by one, the crowd backed out of the temple courtyard. Rabbi Zeev followed the eldest among them. They did not go far, but waited on the other side of the arch, curious to see what Jesus would do.

When only Jesus and the woman remained, I too, stepped away, convicted by my own sins . . . sins of my childhood . . . sins of my youth . . . sins of jealousy and fear.

I paused at the arch and saw Jesus rise again. "Woman, where are those thine accusers? hath no man condemned thee?"

I heard her sobbing answer, "No man, Lord."

Jesus spoke to her as He spoke to every penitent sinner. "Neither do I condemn thee: go, and sin no more."

What would those words spoken to *me* mean?

Jesus met the waiting assembly, and with arms outstretched, testified, "I am the light of the world: he that followeth me shall not walk in darkness, but shall have the light of life."

Rabbi Zeev's pride had been slashed. He alone challenged the Master. "Thou bearest record of thyself; thy record is not true."

At that the faces of the rest of the scribes and Pharisees burned red. They had wanted to stone the woman and had been restrained by the barbs of their own consciences. Now their rage rose again, boiling just beneath the surface.

Jesus showed no fear. "Though I bear record of myself, yet my record is true: for I know whence I came, and whither I go . . . "

He went on to testify and teach. His words went on to divide the truth-seekers from the truth-destroyers, but I did not hear them all, for someone touched my elbow. I turned to see the stricken face of Deborah. She had come with Lazarus from the house in Capernaum.

"It is Anna. She lies at the door of death."

My eyes asked if they had come to seek the Master for a miracle.

"No," said Lazarus, "we came that He might be with His grandmother at her bed of departure. That Jesus might be present to give His grieving mother comfort."

Deborah spoke softly. "Anna is old and ready to depart this world. It is Mary who concerns us."

We looked over the throng. Jesus stood before them all, proclaiming, "If ye continue in my word, then are ye my disciples indeed."

Lazarus put his hand on my shoulder. "It was error for us to come here. Jesus is about His Father's business. Mary is a woman of faith. Anna is prepared. Tell Jesus when the time is at hand, but do not disturb Him now, for the work He does here is greater than the work He would do there. Let Him come when He comes."

At Lazarus' words I recalled the words exchanged between a scribe I'd known at the temple and Jesus. The scribe had professed, "Master, I will follow thee whithersoever thou goest."

Jesus had appeared so saddened. "The foxes have holes, and the birds of the air have nests; but the Son of man hath not where to lay his head."

A friend of the scribe's had also professed his unbounded loyalty to Jesus and had said he would follow him whenever and wherever the Master went. But, he had said, "Lord, suffer me *first* to go and bury my father."

I will forever remember the look on Jesus' face as He said, "Follow me, and let the dead bury the dead."

I had thought His words harsh then, but now I understood that He had talked of dead hearts and dead works. Why did I not always remember that Jesus' words carried more than one interpretation? It was His way of teaching to many levels of understanding.

Now His voice rang off the stone walls and archways of the holy courtyard.

Deborah gasped. "Oh, Almon! Who is that pitiful woman?"

The crowed was parting to let the accused woman pass.

Deborah hurried to her to offer a cloth for wiping the woman's face, to put an arm around her stooped shoulder.

To my betrothed, it mattered not who the woman was . . . only that she was in need.

I loved her all the more for such an act of kindness, and I realized then that Jesus' words were most powerful not when they were spoken, but when they were *lived*.

Seventy-eight

The Pharisees did not cast their stones aside, but kept them in tightly curled fists, ready to sling at Jesus as He went about doing good.

Deborah and I were walking through the city when we came upon a man telling all who would listen that he had been born blind, but now could see because of a prophet named Jesus.

"Tell us your story," Deborah pleaded.

The man touched his eyes. "These were blind until Jesus spat upon the ground and anointed my eyes with clay from His spittle."

"I do not understand, sir. Be more specific," she asked.

"For years I sat begging right here. I lived in darkness until the day Jesus came by and stopped to give me sight."

"How so, sir?"

"He came with a multitude, and someone from within asked, 'Master, who did sin, this man, or his parents, that he was born blind?'"

I thought of Deborah, who stood beside me now, her face healed. I thought of my own mute tongue. Had we sinned? Had our parents sinned to bring upon us such flaws?

"Jesus rebuked both speculations," said the man.

The man then quoted the words of Jesus: "Neither hath this man sinned, nor his parents: but that the works of God should be made manifest in him. I must work the works of him that sent me, while it is day: the night cometh, when no man can work. As long as I am in the world, I am the light of the world."

"He commanded that I wash the clay from my eyes in the water of Siloam. I did, and I came away seeing! Glory be to God!" the man cried.

"Yes," said Deborah for us both, "glory be to God."

The blind man's eyes grew sad. "They seek to stone Him for my miracle. The Pharisees questioned me and found that while my miracle was real, it was performed on the Sabbath. They called Jesus a sinner!"

Just then the crowd came around the corner; in their midst was Jesus. Deborah and I stayed near the man as the Master approached him.

"Dost thou believe on the Son of God?" Jesus asked.

"Who is he, Lord, that I might believe on him?"

I realized then that the man had not seen Jesus before.

"Thou hast both seen him, and it is he that talketh with thee."

The man who now saw with his restored sight also saw with spiritual eyes. He fell at the feet of Jesus and, worshipping, said, "Lord, I believe."

Deborah wept behind her veil. She whispered, "The Master does only good, and yet look at that man there—the Pharisee."

I looked and saw one of the elder holy men, a friend of Ovadya, the Pharisee from Galilee.

"He plots to put Jesus to death, doesn't he?" Deborah asked.

I ached to tell her that her fear was unfounded, but the horrible truth surged through the sinews of my body, and I could not deny it.

The assaults did not cease. The more the Master gave, the more cunning men wanted to put Him to death. I longed to leave the Holy City and return to the shores of Galilee. At least there when the press grew too demanding, we could sail onto the water. Here, there was no corner we could turn without encountering a crowd.

We sat listening to Jesus teach, our eyes watching for anyone who might try to harm Him.

"They think he poses a threat to the empire," said Simon beneath his breath.

Peter said, "No, the empire does not fear Jesus. Antipas and the Jews fear Jesus. Pharisees never leave Him alone now, but seek to accuse Him continually."

A lawyer stood up to throw a question the Master's way. "Master, what shall I do to inherit eternal life?"

"What is written in the law?" asked Jesus. "How readest thou?"

The man looked smug. "Thou shalt love the Lord thy God with all thy heart, and with all thy soul, and with all thy strength, and with all thy mind; and thy neighbour as thyself."

Jesus smiled. "Thou hast answered right: this do, and thou shalt live."

But the man would not be seated. Instead he asked, "And who is my neighbour?"

Jesus looked over the faces in the crowd and when He saw John, He smiled. "A certain man went down from Jerusalem to Jericho, and fell among thieves, which stripped him of his raiment, and wounded him, and departed, leaving him half dead.

"And by chance there came down a certain priest that way: and when he saw him, he passed by on the other side.

"And likewise a Levite, when he was at the place, came and looked on him, and passed by on the other side.

"But a certain Samaritan, as he journeyed, came where he was: and when he saw him, he had compassion on him.

"And went to him, and bound up his wounds, pouring in oil and wine, and set him on his own beast, and brought him to an inn, and took care of him.

"And on the morrow when he departed, he took out two pence, and gave them to the host, and said unto him, Take care of him; and whatsoever thou spendest more, when I come again, I will repay thee."

Jesus paused. "Which now of these three, thinkest thou, was neighbour unto him that fell among the thieves?"

The lawyer was no longer arrogant. "He that shewed mercy on him."

"Go," said Jesus, "and do thou likewise."

Of all the many parables I'd heard Jesus speak, this one went straight to my heart.

It was doing as Deborah had done to the accused woman. It was doing as Judas had done when he opened the purse without judgment. It was doing as Joseph had done to me. That was living the gospel.

The sermon was such a success that we went back to Bethany for a season of rest. When Jesus entered the house, Mary sat at His feet and asked Him to tell the parable again—that, and any other word He was willing to impart. Mary could sit for hours listening and basking in the spirit of the Master's words.

I smiled when I saw Martha rushing around, tending to the many chores of meal preparation. She reminded me how Peter looked when

John sat at the feet of Jesus when there were nets to mend and chores left undone.

Flustered, Martha bid *me* wash the feet of the Master. How long had it been since I had taken a basin and a towel to wash the dust from Him?

She sighed again and again, louder and louder, as she rushed about stirring, dipping, serving.

And Mary sat and listened.

Finally, Martha lost her composure. "Lord, dost thou not care that my sister hath left me to serve alone? bid her therefore that she help me."

Jesus smiled as He answered. "Martha, Martha, thou art careful and troubled about many things: But one thing is needful: and Mary hath chosen that good part, which shall not be taken away from her."

I took the basin and towel, now black with dirt, and went out into the garden. I dumped the water, washed the basin, and wrung the towel. I then knelt beneath the fig tree and prayed, asking God to grant me a favor for which I never thought I'd ask.

Father, I implore Thee, if it be Thy will . . . give me voice that I might testify of all that I have learned washing the feet of my Master.

Seventy-nine

Winter had come and we were back in Jerusalem. The Feast of Dedication—Deborah's favorite feast—was here. It was a time to remember our heritage, to remember that the light had burned for eight days when there was not sufficient oil. It was a season to give gratitude and to recommit our lives to the life that Jesus lived every day.

The light was still burning, brighter than ever, but blind eyes could not see it.

God had not granted my prayer. My tongue was still mute, but my heart sang the praises of my Master and I felt His mission rising with a new power.

I followed Jesus to Solomon's porch on Temple Mount. A small but dogged group of Jews surrounded us. "How long dost thou make us to doubt? If thou be the Christ, tell us plainly."

Were they crazed? Jesus had taught and testified of His divinity throughout His entire ministry.

"I told you," said Jesus, "and ye believed not: the works that I do in my Father's name, they bear witness of me."

He sat down, and His next words raised images of His childhood in the hills above Nazareth.

"But ye believe not, because ye are not of my sheep, as I said unto you. My sheep hear my voice, and I know them, and they follow me: And I give unto them eternal life; and they shall never perish, neither shall any man pluck them out of my hand. My Father, which gave them me, is greater than all; and no man is able to pluck them out of my Father's hand. I and my Father are one."

Peter rushed at a man who raised his hand to throw a stone. I somehow found the courage to stand in front of Rabbi Zeev, my eyes challenging him to make a move. He muttered something under his breath, but he could no longer intimidate me.

Jesus stood and said, "Many good works have I shewed you from my Father; for which of those works do you stone me?"

A few nervous laughs sounded, even from the throat of Peter.

Rabbi Zeev stepped toward Jesus, and I stepped in front of him, blocking him, intimidating him—not of my own strength, but of the strength that ran through me . . . of power from on high.

He glared at me with bitter hatred.

"For a good work we stone thee not," said a priest, "but for blasphemy; and because that thou, being a man, makest thyself God."

Rabbi Zeev attempted to move past me, but I blocked his way again.

"Be gone," he said to me.

I did not budge.

The Lord spoke on while Rabbi Zeev whispered deadly threatenings against me. "I will have your tongue on the tip of my blade as surely as Antipas had John's head on a platter."

Fear not, but believe. The Lord's words returned to me when I needed them.

When the crowd grew too angry, Jesus beckoned us to follow Him. We left the Holy City to go to a place I thought we would never visit again—the shores of the Yored-Dan, where John had immersed Jesus and where the voice of the Father had declared His Sonship.

There we found a moment's peace by the river's edge, through our memories of John. I knew Jesus missed John's presence and his strength, but I also knew that Jesus knew John was in the kingdom with His Father.

All was well with John.

There on the banks of the holy river I woke to discover that Jesus had wandered off to seek solace and strength. I did not follow, but waited until He returned.

Father, give me the courage and the strength to do that which I should have done so long ago. Let me fear not.

When Jesus returned, I had stoked the fire so He could warm Himself. He thanked me, accepted the waterskin, and sat down on His mat.

I waited, my heart pounding, my dead tongue gone dry. Then I handed Him a scroll that I had carefully written. Years of my sins confessed. My greatest fears. My sorrows. My heart's desire.

Jesus took the scroll but did not read it.

I fell at his feet and poured out my soul in silence.

My Master heard.

Eighty

Judas came into camp in haste.

"They come for the Master!"

"Who?" asked Peter.

"The Jews! They that seek to kill Him. Jesus, you must leave now!"

Judas did not come alone. Pharisees and Nicodemus were with him. I wondered why Judas was in such company, but kept my thoughts private.

"Get thee out, and depart hence, or Herod will kill thee," said one of the Pharisees.

Jesus would not be moved. *Fear not* were not only words He spoke—they were words He lived by.

Instead of running, He taught us parables I had heard before. The parable of the lost sheep . . . the lost coin . . . the wedding guests and the great supper. But in the setting of John's wilderness, they took on new images and meanings.

I felt as though I dined at that great heavenly table.

James and the other brothers of Jesus joined us and I rejoiced at their reconciliation. Though some were more receptive than others to His message, Jesus cherished His family ties.

A donkey carrying Mathias trod to the rim of the crowd. "Come quickly," Mathias called. "The Master is needed!"

Jesus bid us all to be quiet that we might hear.

Mathias told us that he was on the errand of Mary and her sister, Martha. "Lord, behold, he whom thou lovest is sick."

We all knew the love Jesus had for this family; Lazarus was like a brother to Him. I feared that the Master could not afford to lose yet another friend. But He received the news with no show of grief, saying, "This sickness is not unto death, but for the glory of God, that the Son of God might be glorified thereby."

I did not know what to expect. Bethany was situated close to Jerusalem, the city where most sought to kill Jesus. It was unsafe and uncertain. Still, Jesus loved Lazarus. I wondered if He would send His word to heal His friend. He had done it before; I knew He could do it again.

Instead, Jesus waited. He let two days pass while He taught more parables and testified of His divinity.

At the rise of the sun the next day, He said, "Let us go into Judea again."

"Master, the Jews of late sought to stone thee; and goest thou thither again?" Peter asked.

"Are there not twelve hours in the day? If any man walk in the day, he stumbleth not, because he seeth the light of this world. But if a man walk in the night, he stumbleth, because there is no light in him.

"Our friend Lazarus sleepeth; but I go, that I may awake him out of sleep."

One stepped forward and said, "Lord, if he sleep, he shall do well."

Jesus groaned. He did not speak of rest, and needed to make Himself clear. "Lazarus is *dead*."

Now there was no misunderstanding.

If we went to Jerusalem, there would be stones waiting. Death for us. If we did not, there would be nothing waiting.

Thomas stood even before Peter could get to his feet. "Let us also go, that we may die with Him!"

His faith aroused ours, and we went.

On the fourth day after Lazarus died we finally arrived at the outskirts of Bethany. Reports told us that the house was surrounded by the cries of mourning. Jews were playing their music of death. Their songs were wails.

Martha came first, hearing that Jesus had arrived. Her head was covered in ashes, and her face was just as gray. "Lord, if thou hadst been here, my brother had not died. But I know, that even now, whatsoever thou wilt ask of God, God will give it thee."

Jesus looked on her with compassion that only He could measure. "Thy brother shall rise again."

Through her sobs, Martha said, "I know that he shall rise again in the resurrection at the last day."

"*I* am the resurrection, and the life: he that believeth in me, though he were dead, yet shall he live: And whosoever liveth and believeth in me shall never die."

His hands gave her shoulders strength.

"Believest thou this?"

"Yea, Lord: I believe that thou art the Christ, the Son of God, which should come into the world."

Martha then headed to the house to fetch Mary. When Mary approached, Jews followed her, and I knew that trouble awaited.

"Lord, if thou hadst been here, my brother had not died," she said, weeping. Her friends wept with her.

Pain shadowed the Master's face. "Where have ye laid him?"

"Lord, come and see."

Jesus wept.

The Jews, seeing Him weep, whispered, "Behold how he loved him!"

Again came cries like those Jesus' brothers had cried when Joseph had died. "Could not this man, which opened the eyes of the blind, have caused that even this man should not have died?"

Jesus went to the cave where Lazarus lay. "Take ye away the stone."

Martha tugged at His sleeve. "Lord, by this time he stinketh: for he hath been dead four days."

"Said I not unto thee, that, if thou wouldest believe, thou shouldest see the glory of God?" Jesus asked.

The stone was removed and the Lord lifted His eyes. As always, He gave thanks before He gave the miracle. "Father, I thank thee that thou hast heard me. And I knew that thou hearest me always: but because of the people which stand by I said it, that they may believe that thou hast sent me."

We all waited. Judas stood beside me, and I could see the anticipation on his face.

Even I did not know what Jesus could do with a corpse already rotten.

"Lazarus, come forth!" He called. His voice was like a whip cracking in the air.

And he that was dead came forth.

The weeping and the wailing ceased. Lazarus, a man we all knew and loved, walked out of the grave, still bound. The napkin still covered his face.

"Loose him, and let him go," said Jesus.

Hands rushed, my own included, to free Lazarus from the bindings of death. I turned to rejoice with my old friend Judas, but when I looked, I saw him leaving, headed down the road toward Jerusalem.

Eighty-one

The division was now clearer than ever. Those who believed were few yet fierce. Those who did not were many and murderous.

I could only guess how they knew so quickly of Lazarus. But why would *Judas* tell the priests and Pharisees? *Why?*

When Antipas murdered John without as much as a trial, Jews rose up only to be hewn down like so much dross. Now their fear of Jesus' power burned like a torch. They accused Him of so many untruths I could not keep an accurate record. Some said He was a Samaritan, possessed of a devil. Others said He was a fraud. Rabbi Zeev alleged that Jesus was seducing the people away from loyalty to Herod—and, ultimately, away from the empire.

Joseph Caiaphas had been appointed by Rome to be the Jewish high priest. Simon despised him and asked me to accompany him to a meeting addressing their concerns.

Caiaphas wore his full regalia—his glittering gold robes, his blue fringes. His hat sat crooked on his head, and his cloak needed more cloth to accommodate his well-fed belly. Judas could have sold his jewel-encrusted breastplate for enough to feed a multitude of multitudes.

Caiaphas' voice was thin and wobbly like that of a wailing woman. "Ye know nothing at all" he shouted, "nor consider that it is expedient for us that one man should die for the people, and that the whole nation perish not.

"This Jesus . . . He is a rebel. It is said that if we leave Him alone, all men will believe on Him, and the Romans shall come and take away both our place and our nation."

A violent cry rose from the bloodthirsty crowd.

"See that group?" Simon asked, pointing with his eyes. "Look at the man with the braided beard. Does he not look familiar?"

The man's fist waved in the air. He shouted lies about our Master.

"Look closely," Simon urged.

I looked and saw the face of a man who had come in the night, begging for mercy. He had crawled on all fours like a beast. His eyes had bulged, his mouth had foamed. He had claimed to be possessed, and had sworn he was a man of faith.

The Master had touched him and sent him away whole.

Now he stood upright and cried vengeance, spreading lies like disease. He was not alone. Many of the very people Jesus had helped were now intent on harming Him. The reality broke my heart.

We returned to Jesus, and Simon told the Master that it was unsafe for Him to travel along the shores He so loved. The towns and cities that had synagogues also had spies. To be safe, Jesus had to go into hiding.

It wasn't in His divine nature to hide. Jesus was a man who loved people and I knew He would wither—as John must have withered in the dungeon cell, locked away.

A day's walk from the Holy City was a region called Ephraim. It sat on an isolated hillside, reminding me in some ways of Nazareth. We stayed there for a short time, leaving those we loved behind at both Bethany and the house in Capernaum.

Deborah's mother, Naomi, had come with Malik and his family to Capernaum. Joel was sailing on the Great Sea, all the way to Alexandria, in search of the finest lumber. He talked of moving his business and his household closer to the Holy City.

Malik was very much changed—more serious and settled on business. He was kind to Deborah, and she seemed very happy when they rented a house and the family took up residence near the household of Lazarus.

Jesus continued to teach and to testify. More and more I found Him walking alone, seeking to commune with His Father. One night I woke to hear Him weeping, and my own heart broke for the suffering He knew: "For the Son of man is come to seek and to save that which was lost."

Jesus was driven by His desperation to teach every truth and to reach every person. As He addressed the crowds, He taught a new parable—one even I had not heard: "Two men went up into the temple to pray; the one a Pharisee, and the other a publican. The Pharisee stood and prayed thus with himself, God, I thank thee, that I am not as other men are, extortioners, unjust, adulterers, or even as this publican. I fast twice in the week, I give tithes of all that I possess. And the publican, standing afar off, would not lift up so much as his eyes unto heaven, but smote upon his breast, saying, God be merciful to me a sinner.

"I tell you, this man went down to his house justified rather than the other: for every one that exalteth himself shall be abased; and he that humbleth himself shall be exalted."

Mothers brought their babies, even those new to life, to be in our Master's presence. Nathaniel and Jude were weary, and the children came in droves, bringing with them noise and chaos. They asked Jesus to send the children away.

But Jesus had a great love for children. He called them to Him and taught, "Suffer little children to come unto me, and forbid them not: for of such is the kingdom of God. Verily I say unto you, Whosoever shall not receive the kingdom of God as a little child shall in no wise enter therein."

Jesus gave Himself to much fasting and prayer, and then He came to make an announcement I expected—still, it hit me like an anvil to the heart.

"Behold, we go up to Jerusalem; and the Son of man shall be betrayed unto the chief priests and unto the scribes, and they shall condemn him to death, and shall deliver him to the Gentiles to mock, and to scourge, and to crucify him: and the third day he shall rise again."

I heard all His words, but the ones that clung to my mind were these: "they shall condemn him to death." Everyone was there—the disciples, the Apostles, and their families. He left no doubt in our minds of what was to come.

Never had our faith been so tested.

Thomas said our feelings best. "It is not fair, but it is right, for God's compass directs this path."

Zebedee's wife, the mother of James and John, approached Jesus with unusual boldness.

"What wilt thou?" asked Jesus.

"Grant that these my two sons may sit, the one on thy right hand, and the other on the left, in thy kingdom."

Jesus sighed and addressed His two Apostles. "Ye know not what ye ask. Are ye able to drink of the cup that I shall drink of, and to be baptized with the baptism that I am baptized with?"

"We are able."

"Ye shall drink indeed of my cup, and be baptized with the baptism that I am baptized with: but to sit on my right hand, and on my left, is not mine to give, but it shall be given to them for whom it is prepared of my Father."

Peter and Andrew backed away. I knew they were angry; so were the other eight.

Jesus called them to Him. "Ye know that the princes of the Gentiles exercise dominion over them, and they that are great exercise authority upon them. But it shall not be so among you: but whosoever will be great among you, let him be your minister."

Now Jesus beckoned me to stand beside Him, His words making sense of every minute I had spent standing in my Master's shadow. "And whosoever will be chief among you, let him be your servant.

"Even as the Son of man came not to be ministered unto, but to minister, and to give his life a ransom for many."

Eighty-two

We turned one final time toward Jerusalem.

I had no words to describe the weight that our hearts carried as we looked to Jesus . . . knowing what was to come, because He had told us.

As we passed through Jericho, two blind men sat on the roadside calling out, "O Lord, thou Son of David."

The multitude with us meant to protect Jesus and rebuked the men, but they only cried the more. "Have mercy on us, O Lord, thou Son of David."

Jesus stopped. "What will ye that I shall do unto you?"

"Lord, that our eyes may be opened."

Jesus, weary beyond measure, weighed down with the crush of the multitude, stooped to touch their eyes. Immediately their eyes were opened, and they joined our growing throng.

Deborah walked beside me while her aunt, the mother of Jesus, rode a donkey that reminded me of old Boaz, the donkey from my youth.

Zacchaeus, a short man who was an acquaintance of Matthew, ran ahead of our crowd.

"What is he doing?" asked Judas. "He's the size of a child."

"He's a sinner," said Simon. "He collects tribute for the empire."

The comment was meant as a stab at Matthew, but Matthew was calloused to such arrows and paid no mind.

I watched Zacchaeus scurry up a sycamore tree for a better view.

Jesus saw him and said, "Zacchaeus, make haste, and come down; for to day I must abide at thy house."

Simon was indignant. The man was a sinner and a spectacle.

Zacchaeus stood and stretched himself as tall as he was able—which was half the height of Peter. "Lord, the half of my goods I give to the poor; and if I have taken any thing from any man by false accusation, I restore him fourfold."

Jesus smiled. "This day is salvation come to this house."

The next day our journey continued, with Jesus teaching and telling parables. Our sadness multiplied with every step that brought us closer to Jerusalem.

I had heard Jesus tell His Apostles that He was going, as Isaiah had prophesied, "as a lamb to the slaughter."

How long ago had I imagined Him a sacrificial offering? I had shoved the idea aside at the time—but now it walked behind me like a haunt, like a dreadful truth.

We passed great gray boulders, with caverns hewn out to bury the dead.

I could not imagine Jesus dead. Gone. What would my life without Him become?

Our final journey took us through the regions of both Galilee and Samaria. I could not set sandal on the land without recalling our first time here—at the well, when the woman believed and brought so many with her.

Now Jesus sought out a village of lepers and found ten men who kept their distance, but raised their voices, "Jesus, Master, have mercy on us."

"Go," said Jesus to them, "shew yourselves unto the priests." And they were all cleansed.

Only one returned to give thanks. He fell on his face at the Master's feet.

"Is he not a Samaritan?" Jude asked.

"He is," replied Simon.

Jesus asked, "Were there not ten cleansed? but where are the nine?"

And as the Master forgave the cleansed man's sins, I thought how the scene had been played out so many times before. One from ten thought to thank Him, to honor Him, to give His Father glory.

An olive tree rose thick and high and gnarled before us. We paused in its shade. Caught between Bethphage and Bethany, at the mount called Olives, Jesus motioned for my service. James, John, and Thomas were right beside me, as eager as I was to do whatever the Master bid.

"Go your way into the village over against you: and as soon as ye be entered into it, ye shall find a colt tied, whereon never man sat; loose him, and bring him. And if any man say unto you, Why do ye this? say ye that the Lord hath need of him; and straightway he will send him hither."

Such a request was not unreasonable. It was a time in Jerusalem when goodwill and hospitality was set to overrule the greediness and selfishness common in most other places.

Devout Jews hung curtains over their front doors as a sign that all passersby were welcome, that the household was willing to take in boarders.

Thomas, James, and John went with me, and we found the colt just as Jesus had described.

"How did He know?" Thomas asked.

I had no answer.

"Why loose ye the colt?" a man asked. We looked to see the owners of the animal.

"The Lord hath need of him," said Thomas.

"Take him freely," they said, "and be not concerned if your lord has not the means to return him."

We expressed gratitude and went quickly to Bethphage with the colt. There was a gathering of no small numbers already surrounding Jesus. Each of us was eager to spread our garments upon the colt, upon the ground, to make His final journey into Jerusalem worthy of the king He was.

One murmured that Jesus did this to fulfill the prophecy, "Behold, thy King cometh unto thee, meek, and sitting upon an ass, and a colt the foal of an ass."

We passed into the Kidron Valley, where Zacchaeus and Matthew and their friends were ready with branches they had cut from palms. These they spread upon the ground and waved in honor of Jesus the Christ, the true King of the Jews.

Mary, the mother of Jesus, walked slowly among the multitude, held by the sure arms of Deborah, Naomi, Mary Magdalene, and

Martha. I looked at the women and thought how different, how void our ministry would have been without their faith and service.

Soon the way would be open for my marriage to Deborah. My heart was divided knowing that the time was coming, but that Jesus would not be there among the honored guests.

Eighty-three

I had never felt such a mounting sense of anxiety. My hands would not quit shaking, my heart would not slow its pounding.

Simon feared that the Romans would stop Jesus—that they would take Him captive at the very gates. Thousands of people, both from the city and from the outlying villages, waved peace palms and shouted, "Blessed is he that cometh in the name of the Lord; Hosanna in the highest."

Soldiers were everywhere, with swords, clubs, and daggers ready.

The scribes and Pharisees shouted, "He is a rebel!" Jesus did not look the part of a rebel. He came on a colt, not a horse, and looked to be nothing more than a heralded teacher. A humble Jew.

Jesus, Lord of all, came in lowliness and humility.

"Hosanna to the Son of David!"

Had he been a crazed fanatic, a Druid or a Phoenician who practiced human sacrifices, had His followers breathed out threatenings against the empire, Jesus would have been pulled from the colt and put in chains.

The great number of His followers was cause for alarm. At Jesus' beckoning they could have started a rebellion that would have been difficult to put down. Jews in every corner would suffer bloodshed at such an uprising.

The disciples were on high alert. Many carried weapons; almost all carried stones.

"No soldier here will take his eyes from the Master," whispered Simon, glancing upward, where warriors lined the high walks of the walls.

"And I will not cease to watch *them*," Peter vowed. He hid a freshly sharpened blade and was eager to use it.

The poor and needy lined the streets, their hands stretched out in hope of alms.

I looked for Judas, but did not see him. More and more he seemed to vanish with no explanation. More and more I did not know my old friend at all. I feared for him. Once Jesus was not among us to fill the purse, what would Judas do?

The night before, when we had been talking among ourselves, Jude had asked the same question of all: "What drew you to Jesus?"

Each person had given his own answer, but Judas' reply had opened a window into his soul. "I saw in the Master unbounded prosperity." If he talked of money, I could not imagine how bitterly disappointed he must be. If he referred to eternal wealth, how great must be his joy.

Where could Judas be at this moment of triumph? What work could be more pressing?

Jesus moved to the Temple Mount and did not shy from speaking against the scribes, the Pharisees, the Sadducees, and the priests who sought so diligently and now openly to take His life. "O ye hypocrites!"

I did my best to stay close to Him, to be there as I swore to Joseph I would. I brought Him water and dates. He neither ate nor drank, but bowed in heartache that surely even heaven felt.

I had wept many tears in my life. I had also seen Jesus weep. But the depth of His agony as He groaned beneath the shadow of the great walls of that holy place was a suffering so deep I feared His life might end at that moment.

"O Jerusalem, Jerusalem, thou that killest the prophets, and stonest them which are sent unto thee, how often would I have gathered thy children together, even as a hen gathereth her chickens under her wings, and ye would not!

"Behold, your house is left unto you desolate.

"For I say unto you, Ye shall not see me henceforth, till ye shall say, Blessed is he that cometh in the name of the Lord."

His disciples came asking, *When?* When would the temple be destroyed? When would the kingdom come?

"Take heed that no man deceive you. For many shall come in my name, saying, I am Christ; and shall deceive many."

Jesus taught and blessed and prophesied. Two hundred thousand people—maybe more—packed the temple courtyard, pushing and shoving, hoping to get a glimpse or hear a word from the Lord who had raised the dead and challenged the highest holy men in all of Palestine. Once again, He looked out on the countless faces who looked to Him, and Jesus blessed the disciples, those who truly longed to follow Him.

Deborah was with the women in their court, but I thought of her and how she understood my life, my heart. As I did every day, I gave God thanks for her.

We returned to Bethany that night, where Jesus sought refuge in the home He knew, among the people He loved. It was a bittersweet night and I did not sleep, but sat awake outside in the garden. What more could I do? I felt as though I hadn't done anything that truly mattered. Did He know how much I loved Him? Did He know that I would trade my life to save His?

Jesus had gathered His twelve, and now those Twelve came out of the house, joining me for a time in reminiscing.

None of us dared to speculate on the future.

Toward morning, when the sky changed from black to pink, Jesus joined us.

"Fear not, but believe."

His peace dried our tears and gave us strength. The words He spoke to us were so holy my pen will never write them, but my heart will always treasure them.

The household stirred, and Jesus announced that it was time to return to the Holy City. Tears were shed and good-byes said. It was thought best that Mary stay at the house, safe and separated from whatever hardships were to be faced. Deborah agreed to stay with her, but the mother of Jesus insisted on coming. She would be with her Son to the end.

Mary dressed and packed her shoulder bag. "I am prepared."

Jesus embraced His mother and though their tears were dry, I knew that their hearts wept.

"Is there no other way?" Deborah asked, whispering in my ear. Her own cheeks were wet, her eyes swollen, and her voice raspy with emotion.

All I could do was shake my head. Jesus had answered that question over and over. There was no other way.

He was the only way, the only truth, the only life.

And so the women joined our assembly, and came with us as they always had. Only this was no ordinary journey, and we all sensed it.

After we were dusty from our journey, once the people came again by the hundreds, Peter took me aside. "Lazarus is not safe, either."

My eyebrows rose. *Lazarus?*

"He is a living witness to Jesus' power. The Sanhedrin wants to put him down, to silence him so he cannot testify for the Master's authority."

Lazarus himself did not seem occupied with anything but lifting the spirits of our assembly. "Be of good cheer, brethren!" he said, slapping me on the back. "Peter, wipe that frown off of your face."

Peter scowled. "Lazarus, how can you feel cheer at a time such as this?"

Lazarus lifted his palms to the sky and smiled. "How can I not? For I of all people here know that death is but a sleeping."

And he went off to share his joy and testimony with the next group.

I understood now why the Sanhedrin would want to silence Lazarus.

Jesus paused, and the crowd paused with Him. He pointed to one of the common fig trees planted along the way, providing fruit to any traveler who hungered. He asked the group if anyone hungered.

"I hunger," said Peter.

We could not hold back a shared laugh. Peter was always hungry.

Jesus went to the tree. Because it was spring, I knew its fruit would not be ripe, but perhaps there were figs that remained from last season.

Jesus lifted the large leaves, but found no fruit.

The tree looked healthy. It appeared productive, yet it bore no fruit. And in a lesson that never left my mind, the Master cursed the tree, and it began to wither before my eyes.

"How soon is the fig tree withered away!" said one of the disciples.

"It is a lesson," John said, lifting his voice. "Jesus teaches us that hypocrites appear to be fruitful, but they bear no living fruit."

"Now you speak for Jesus?" said Peter, always annoyed by John. He gave John no time to respond, but moved forward like a bull, looking at each member of the multitude, suspecting.

It wasn't the entrance Jesus had made the day before, but the crowds were still there, following Jesus to the Temple Mount. I certainly didn't expect Him to do what He did . . . The day before, He had made His way past the money changers, the merchants, and the filth. Today, He stopped, and with thousands of people trailing Him, Jesus cleansed the temple courtyard.

He had done it two years earlier, chasing animals and men, scattering coins and weights.

I said nothing.

Doves beats their wings, some freed, others still penned. Sheep bleated. The stench that filled the air was thick with dung, urine, and fear.

With a braided cord, Jesus sent the sellers and the buyers scattering. Many of the men recognized him and shouted out their threatenings. Still, they ran from His wrath. "It is written, My house is the house of prayer: but ye have made it a den of thieves."

Peter looked on with pride.

John looked on with wonder.

I rushed about, throwing myself in the face of anyone who dared to approach the Master. One of the priests I'd known years before warned me, "Caiaphas will know of this destruction and your Master will pay."

On all sides, we were surrounded by enemies.

Pharisees.

Priests.

Sadducees.

Scribes.

Herodians.

Romans.

Merchants and money changers.

Liars.

The deadliest were those who had been blessed by the power of Jesus and yet turned away from Him.

His own.

There were also those loyal to Jesus, willing to give as I longed to give.

It was impossible to divide the dark hearts from the light. Jesus did not seem to care; He only wanted to teach and to testify. His parables held thousands captive now that the lower yards had been cleansed and He was returned to the temple courts.

There was a sense of peace in His preaching.

I walked with Andrew, James, and Nathaniel around the walls, looking to head off trouble. Andrew, not revealing His brotherhood with the Savior, made inquiries among the Pharisees.

"They take counsel with the Herodians and others, trying to entangle Jesus in His own words."

We looked at each other, knowing that no human being could trap Jesus with His own words.

Jesus *was* The Word.

"What think ye of Christ? whose son is he?" Jesus asked those who held the traps in their hearts, ready to spring at and maim the Master.

He smiled, though I knew He did not feel like smiling.

"The son of David."

"How then doth David in spirit call him Lord, saying, The Lord said unto my Lord, Sit thou on my right hand, till I make thine enemies thy footstool? If David then call him Lord, how is he his son?"

No one would answer Him, and their deceitful and deadly traps went unsprung.

Eighty-four

Jesus was gone before sunrise. He needed time to pray and seek His Father's company. He left while it was still dark so the multitude would not follow Him.

I stayed at the house while the other disciples went into the Holy City to prepare for the day of the feast. There were always tasks to perform and people to address, seekers who came looking for Jesus.

This was the day that 260,000 Paschal Lambs were brought to the temple altar to be slaughtered, their blood drained, their bodies split and cleansed. It was a day I despised, though I had still never voiced my feelings to anyone. The sights, sounds, and smell that hung in the air made my stomach turn.

The children sat on the rooftop, the older ones counting the men who passed with the remains of their sacrificed lambs in their arms, headed to prepare the meat for the feast. Most of the disciples had gone into the city to sacrifice lambs for our own feast.

The women tended the younger children. Deborah was hardly ever without a baby in her arms.

Judas' wife came by the house inquiring of him, a child on her hip and a child by the hand. She seemed frantic to find him.

"He is in Jerusalem," Naomi told her, not mentioning that he had left in anger the day before.

"The priests of Caiaphas have this day stopped by our house asking after my husband."

We all stood frozen. What had Judas done to warrant such personal attention?

"Why would they seek Judas at your home?" Naomi asked. "Do you suppose he is in jeopardy?"

"I fear it is so," she said, turning not toward Jerusalem, but back toward her own house.

Deborah called after her, "Come, drink. Rest and wait with us. Surely your husband will return soon."

The woman shook her head and tugged her son's hand, but the boy had seen his father coming around the road's curve, and he ran to meet him.

Judas, upon seeing his family, called, "Why are you here?"

His wife did not wait for him to come to her, but called so we could all hear. "The priests of Caiaphas have sought you in our very courtyard."

Now Judas' feet rushed to meet his wife and children, moving so quickly that he kicked up the dust. "They come seeking me only to locate the Master," he said, lifting his voice so we would be sure to hear. "They know I hold the Lord's purse. They demand to know by whose authority Jesus teaches, and who will pay for the damage He caused cleansing the temple courtyard."

His words made no sense. But Judas did not stop when he reached the house. He continued on, taking his wife by the elbow. Judas paid rent on a one-room house on the edge of Bethany. It was a small privilege he said a treasurer deserved.

A sense of disbelief filled me. Judas hid a truth, but what was it?

That night Jesus called His Twelve to Him and counseled together around the fire. I kept watch to hold back the people desperate to approach Him.

Judas seemed quiet, but not surly. Whatever had troubled him that afternoon seemed to have passed. He even greeted me with kindness, though I heard him make no mention of Caiaphas' priests.

Though the branches were in bloom, the air was cold, and I went to fetch wood. I quickly backed away when I saw the men gathered around the fire, sensing the Master's time with the Apostles was sacred. Later, He ate with those He loved and spent His nighttime hours in solitude.

The next morning John came and bid me follow him into the city.

"The Master has asked that Peter and I go to prepare for the feast."

I smiled, thinking how Jesus often paired Peter and John, knowing that they struggled to remain friendly, even though they loved each other like brothers.

Peter waved me come. "Join us, Almon. The Master said, 'When ye are entered into the city, there shall a man meet you, bearing a pitcher of water; follow him into the house where he entereth in. And ye shall say unto the goodman of the house, The Master saith unto thee, Where is the guestchamber, where I shall eat the Passover with my disciples? And he shall shew you a large upper room furnished: there make ready.'"

I went with them. On the way, Peter spoke of another experience that reminded him of this errand. "When the Master bid me to fish for our tribute, I went because I believed him, but I thought, *How can this be?* Yet it was. The first fish I caught held the needed coin in its mouth."

A trio of men, armed but without official regalia, approached a group of men who walked ahead of us. "Ye are disciples of the Healer, aren't you?"

The men vehemently denied knowing Jesus.

"Keep your head down and walk on," Peter said.

We were not harassed, and I understood that Peter simply did not want to be caught up in anything that distracted us from the Lord's errand.

Smoke burned my eyes. Thousands of Paschal Lambs were being fired for the day's feast. Usually, the aroma of roasting meat made my stomach rumble, but not this day.

The streets swarmed with pilgrims. The scent of fresh blood still hung in the air from the previous day's slaughter. Soldiers mingled among the Jews, searching for any sign of insurrection.

The man was just as Jesus said he would be, and the house he led us to was not a poor man's abode. The carved wooden door reminded me of the elaborate door on Joel's house. We did not enter, but went around back and climbed the ladder to the rooftop. There was a large chamber there, a room ideal for the Master's purpose.

It was laid with all of the necessary items: pillows, rugs, and cushions. Peter set right to work moving the main table.

"It must accommodate Jesus and His Twelve."

A brief wave of jealousy swept through me, knowing that this was a feast I would not attend. But the jealousy lasted only an instant, and my heart was good again.

I helped the lord of the house while Peter and John set the spit. Then I was sent to meet Jesus and the others and lead them to the chamber.

When we arrived the lamb was roasting, the unleavened cakes were delivered, and John had found the bitter herbs. Mary Magdalene had sent a roasted shank with Jude.

Judas brought the wine. He did not complain of the price he'd paid, but offered it without his usual word of complaint.

Jesus thanked me for my service and I stood outside the door, dismissed, free to do whatever I wished.

For a long time I stayed right where I was, longing to remain close to the Master. I did not wish, however, to intrude, so I left and headed for Temple Mount. The sun was headed west, and the courtyards were not as crowded. Most people were feasting, just as Jesus and the Twelve.

I knew I could go back to Bethany and join with those who feasted there, but my feet were restless. They could not decide the direction they wanted to go.

I wandered the holy grounds. I wandered the city. The animal pens were mostly empty now, the ground thick with dung and urine. I hated the smell, which mingled with the scent of thousands of feasts being prepared.

Something felt wrong.

Without a purpose, I went back up to Temple Mount, and that is when I saw him.

Judas Iscariot.

My friend.

His sandals were hurrying across the great stone floor. Where could he be going? He was supposed to be with Jesus at this hour.

I rushed to inquire, but stopped like I was cast in stone.

Judas headed straight for the temple treasury. Before he reached the arch, two priests came out to greet him.

My eyes had to be failing me.

Judas in the temple treasury? With the very men who devised ways to murder Jesus? What was this about?

I did not know. Yet I knew. My friend was a friend to no one.

With one thought on my mind—to protect Jesus—I hurried back to the upper chamber. The last strains of a hymn penetrated the air.

They emerged one by one, the Savior coming out last.

I tried to get Peter's attention. He would know what to do about Judas.

But Jesus, who knew everything, had to already know.

"Almon, join us," said Andrew. "The Lord's most faithful are headed to Mount Olivet." I had never seen him wear such sorrow.

More than the Twelve—many more—joined with Jesus, and I fell in beside Andrew and Matthew. I looked to be certain that Judas was not present. It was growing darker, and I searched the faces by the light of a torch. Judas was not among us.

Quietly, feeling like I was a betrayer myself, I wrote on my tablet to tell them what I had witnessed.

Andrew showed no shock. "Jesus sent him forth. He told him to do quickly what he had to do."

"Yes," Matthew said, "Judas has gone to purchase a gift for the poor. You know we are commanded at Passover to give such an offering."

Andrew attempted a smile. "Do not fret so, Almon. Judas is probably meeting with the priests to extract a lesser price for whatever gift he has chosen."

I wanted to argue, but the men walked burdened with emotion. One day I would read from Matthew's account the events that transpired in that upper chamber. I would know for myself that Jesus had washed the feet of His Apostles. That He had broken bread in remembrance of His soon-to-be-broken body.

We crossed the Kidron Valley and then began the ascent up the slope of Mount Olivet. Jesus chose a different path than He had just days earlier; this time He turned toward an ancient olive orchard called Gethsemane.

The air was cold and the moon was rising.

The Master stopped and turned to look upon us. I had never seen Him so determined. Whatever He had to do, He was about to do it, but His heart was obviously heavy.

Heavier than I could know.

"All ye shall be offended because of me this night: for it is written, I will smite the shepherd, and the sheep of the flock shall be scattered abroad. But after I am risen again, I will go before you into Galilee."

I wanted to step forward and vow to Jesus that I would never find offense because of Him.

Peter spoke for my heart. "Though all men shall be offended because of thee, yet will I never be offended."

I thought I saw a glint in Jesus' eye. "Verily I say unto thee, That this night, before the cock crow, thou shalt deny me thrice."

"Though I should die with thee, yet will I not deny thee."

Every disciple echoed the same promise.

Jesus took only His chosen three, the same three that had gone to the rise of Mount Tabor with Him: Peter, James, and John.

Later, from the account of Matthew's pen, I would read that Jesus said unto them, "My soul is exceeding sorrowful, even unto death: tarry ye here, and watch with me."

He went a little further, and fell on His face, and prayed, saying, "O my Father, if it be possible, let this cup pass from me: nevertheless not as I will, but as thou wilt."

And He came unto the disciples, and, finding them asleep, said to Peter, "What, could ye not watch with me one hour?

"Watch and pray, that ye enter not into temptation: the spirit indeed is willing, but the flesh is weak."

Then He left them a second time and prayed, saying, "O my Father, if this cup may not pass away from me, except I drink it, thy will be done."

After this, He found them still sleeping. And He left them again, and prayed the same words again.

Finally He came to His disciples and said to them, "Sleep on now, and take your rest: behold, the hour is at hand, and the Son of man is betrayed into the hands of sinners.

"Rise, let us be going: behold, he is at hand that doth betray me."

I stood alone down the pathway, away from the gate. That is why I first heard the multitude coming. I thought they were more disciples, more needy begging for blessings.

I was wrong.

As their orange torches came closer, as I heard their vicious cries slither through the night, I realized that they were not disciples, but destroyers of the Master. They came with murder in their hearts and staves and swords in their hands.

They did not come alone, for out of the blackness appeared a familiar face. Leading the multitude was Judas.

Eighty-five

Though he had to pass so close by me on the pathway that our shoulders touched, Judas did not acknowledge me. If he had not been my friend these past three years, I would not have recognized him. His face was twisted and his eyes black, even in the illumination of the torchlight.

Those with him were not the elders or the chief priests, but blood-thirsty men, servants of those cowards who stayed behind to plot murder.

From Matthew's record and his very tongue, I later learned that Jesus did know that he would be betrayed. While the Twelve yet supped, He told them, "Verily I say unto you, that one of you shall betray me."

And the Apostles were exceeding sorrowful, each one asking, "Lord is it I?"

"He that dippeth his hand with me in the dish, the same shall betray me. The Son of man goeth as it is written of him: but woe unto that man by whom the Son of man is betrayed! it had been good for that man if he had not been born."

"Master, is it I?" asked Judas.

"Thou hast said."

Judas had gone out; some, like Andrew and Matthew, supposed he had gone to buy the required gift for the poor.

I was startled back to the present by the voice of Peter, which cracked the dark air like a whip. "Stand back!"

At that moment I realized it was not too late for Jesus to escape. *The road!* Jesus had to know that if He ran back through the orchard and up the slope, He would meet the main highway out of Jerusalem and could find His way to obscurity and safety. He could flee.

But Jesus came toward the raging mob, a force that wound its way to meet Him as surely as any black viper. "Whom seek ye?"

I felt the same evil and fear that I'd felt as a nine-year-old boy. Back then it had frozen me, but now it thrust me forward. My body sprang like a beast in front of Judas. If only I'd brought my dagger, but I had left it at the house in Bethany.

A point of steel caught me at the throat, but did not slit my vein. A boot met my stomach. Another met my back. It felt as through a rock split my head, and a great weight crushed my spine.

I was on the ground at the feet of Judas—feet I'd washed how many times?

I was not alone, for the whole multitude fell backward at the power of the Master. Even Judas landed beside me—taken not by the power, but by a sinister stronghold. And though the mob was armed and intent, none could take Jesus—not unless He *allowed* Himself to be taken.

The searing pain I felt eased, but only for an instant.

"Whom seek ye?" the Master asked again.

Judas and the others struggled to their feet. "Jesus of Nazareth," said a man, a servant of the high priest.

That is when I heard the voice of Judas whisper, "Whomsoever shall I kiss that same is he; hold him fast."

"I am he," said Jesus, making Judas' brutal plot unnecessary.

The armed mob moved forward.

Disciples who had sworn to protect the Master now backed away in terror. I managed to get to my hands and knees, only to be kicked again. Through a thick maze of legs and waiting swords, I saw and heard Judas approach Jesus.

"Hail, Master." Judas fell forward, embracing Jesus and loudly kissing Him—not once, not twice, but laying kiss after kiss on His face.

Jesus allowed Himself to be kissed and then drew away. "Friend, wherefore art thou come?"

Judas reeled back.

"Judas, betrayest thou the Son of man with a kiss?"

At that moment the whole world quaked. Swords and staves glinted in the moonlight, and the men surged forward at the Master as though He were a vile criminal caught in the act.

"I have told you that I am he: if therefore ye seek me, let these go their way." He lifted His chin to gesture at those He loved—at the

Apostles, at His disciples, at Judas, at me. When Jesus saw me there already half-broken, His lips turned up in gratitude and love. Though feeble, I was His devoted servant, and He knew it.

He continued. "That the saying might be fulfilled, which he spake, Of them which thou gavest me have I lost none."

I looked to Judas. I knew that if he were lost, it was his own doing.

"*This* is the mighty Jesus of Nazareth?" The servant of the high priest, the man who stood next to Judas, mocked and spit at the Master. "He is nothing but an ordinary man."

The roar of hell's laughter brought me to my feet. My vision was blurred, but I could see the Master, ready to be bound and brutalized.

His eyes locked with the eyes of Judas. Jesus did not blink, but wept at His friend's betrayal until Judas looked away.

The mob mocked, but Jesus did not struggle.

His very silence sang to me. This *was* the Son of God.

This was also Satan's blackest moment of glory.

"Lord, shall we smite with the sword?" Andrew cried.

Instinctively, I went for the throat of Judas. *What have you done? What have you done?*

Peter raised his sword and smote off the ear of the high priest's servant. The man screamed in pain and clutched at his bloody face.

The silver blade, as long as a man's arm, rose again, and Peter cried in defense of the Master.

"Put up again thy sword into its place," said Jesus, "for all they that take the sword shall perish with the sword."

My hand was on the throat of Judas, squeezing the very life from him. I had grabbed him so swiftly and unexpectedly that he had not made a sound except to gurgle. Now we stood so close his breath made cold clouds on my face. Horror reworked his features until again he appeared as a complete stranger.

Who was this man, Judas? What could his purse buy him now?

At the Master's command to Peter, I let go.

Gasping, Judas fell back against one of the men who had come with him. The man would not hold Judas, but let him fall to the ground.

Torches lifted high, and within the flicker I saw the Master's face. It was gentle and at peace. He moved toward the wounded servant.

"Malchus."

The Master's touch healed man and restored his ear. It was a miracle. All who were there saw it and could not doubt. But it was a miracle that mattered not to them.

"This arrest is illegal," shouted John. "You cannot take Jesus. What you do now is not lawful."

The men only laughed.

Jesus lifted His voice. His breath showed in the cold night air, and I thought to myself, *I must run and get the Master's cloak. My Master must be cold.*

Jesus spoke softly, yet with a power far greater than their weapons. "Thinkest thou that I cannot now pray to my Father, and he shall presently give me more than twelve legions of angels? But how then shall the scriptures be fulfilled, that thus it must be?"

And Jesus *allowed* himself to be taken.

Turning to the multitude, He asked, "Are ye come out as against a thief with swords and staves for to take me? I sat daily with you teaching in the temple, and ye laid no hold on me."

"We have hold of you now, Jesus, King of the Jews!"

A chill more biting than the air went through me. Part of me knew that if I stayed and pledged my loyalty to Jesus, the swords of evil would point at me. They would not spare my blood again. I would never marry Deborah. Never have a family.

Jesus, His hands bound, made His way past me, and I felt His presence.

I looked up and saw pain on His face—an expression no tongue could describe. He had been betrayed by those He had lived to save. His final hours were come.

A hand shoved my shoulder. "Are you with Him or not?"

My feet fell into line. I *was* with Jesus . . . now and forever. But where were all the others? The devoted disciples? Men were fleeing by the hundreds, hiding their identity and falling in with the thousands that came to see the famed Jesus of Nazareth arrested.

My head throbbed, my shoulder and back felt crushed, and my feet would not move at the pace I ordered. Peter moved ahead, faithful and determined to stay by the Lord.

"Almon."

I turned at the sound of a voice I knew too well.

It was Judas, on the ground, cowering and whimpering like the dog he was. All the others had gone ahead, thousands with their torches and their tales to tell of the night the Son of Man was betrayed.

I turned to leave.

"Almon." His hand reached out for me to lift him.

I laughed.

"Almon."

My mind had a thousand questions for him, but none of the answers mattered now. I reached out to grip his hand, and with my own wounded strength, I lifted him. The very touch of his traitor's flesh against mine made me shudder.

I walked away without looking back.

News of Jesus' arrest had spread throughout the city. I was sure it had even reached Bethany by now, and I wondered at the heartache in the house of Simon.

By the time I caught up with those who had taken Jesus, He had already been presented to the great Annas, former high priest and director of the Holy City's affairs. His unbounded wealth came from the coins that Jesus had scattered twice on Temple Mount. He both loathed and feared the Master. I could only imagine how unlawful and degrading was his interrogation of Jesus.

Now I pushed my way through the crowd to the palace of Caiaphas, the son-in-law of Annas and the man who had prophesied Jesus' death. No matter what laws he had to break, he had to find a way to make his own bloody foretelling come true.

I knew him from my days of temple training. Ambition drove him with the same force that greed drove Judas.

I knew that he would have the required twenty-three men assembled—the highest priests, scribes, and elders, members of the great Sanhedrin. They would be insatiable for vengeance against Jesus, the Galilean who had called them hypocrites and worse.

I feared my bruised legs would not carry me up the endless steps to the palace. My mind tried to grasp all that I knew of the laws. The tribunal had power to judge both civil and criminal charges. They were able to pass and impose judgment for violation of the law. Yet

Rome had never granted the Sanhedrin authority to execute death by crucifixion. And crucifixion was the death they sought.

Jesus would face them alone and would have to defend His innocence.

Nothing was fair. Nothing was lawful.

I did not fully understand what Jesus was being accused of . . . Insurrection? Blasphemy?

Those who voted against Jesus now could later reverse their judgment, but those, if there be any, who found him innocent, could not change their vote. I prayed that all twenty-three men would find Jesus guilty. That would mean a mandatory acquittal because under the law, He would have no defender.

If He was found guilty here of a capital offense, there would be a second trial, and members of the Sanhedrin would be implored to fast and pray.

Inwardly, I smiled at the thought of these bloodthirsty men fasting and praying so God would grant petition for them to murder His Only Begotten.

I made it to the top of the steps, out of breath. Men were everywhere, waiting and hoping to hear a guilty verdict.

"Almon."

This time the voice I turned to was friendly. Peter stood before me, blood still on his sword.

Eighty-six

There was a small fire burning, and Peter was among those warming themselves by the flame. They were not soldiers, but common men. I had no way of knowing if they were in favor of the Lord or against Him.

A soldier stepped between us.

"Are you with Him?"

I wasn't sure if he meant Peter or Jesus.

Peter stepped back toward the balcony at the same moment I stepped forward.

Yes, I was with Jesus.

"This man is the servant of the one they call the Master," Peter said.

A hand grabbed my injured shoulder, and I tried not to wince. That quickly, I was ushered up the walkway, taken past the guards, and allowed into the palace.

"Do not move from this place," the soldier said. He used his blade to point to a section by the first arch. I stayed where I was told and leaned against the cold stone wall to keep my balance. My whole body felt broken and ready to collapse.

The chamber was large and made of giant stone slabs. The air was even colder inside than out, and though there were lamps burning, it was dark. It took time for my eyes to adjust, and when they did, they focused in on a lone figure that stood in the center, surrounded by mocking judges.

It was Jesus and the holy men of Israel.

I drew in a breath and filled my lungs with the smoky air. I felt sick at the sight of my Lord. Someone had doused Him with water to wash the blood away. He stood there dripping and degraded.

I had a vision of Him just hours before, the spikenard poured onto His head by the tender hand of Mary Magdalene. Had Jesus been anointed for such a time as this?

Now he wore a napkin wound and tied about His head, a blindfold. Did they not know that Jesus saw all things—even into hearts—and they could not shadow His vision? The left side of His face bore a dark, straight mark, and I realized He'd been struck.

"Art thou a prophet?" called out a scribe who had once taught.

The others laughed. They sounded like dogs gone too long without meat. The horrid sound echoed off the walls and into my pounding head.

If they were accusing Jesus of being a false prophet, there was no law against that.

My Master stood with His head unbowed, His back straight.

I shut my eyes and tried to think clearly. They had allowed me into the chamber for one reason: so Jesus could not claim He had no defender. Others were there, too—men ready to bear witness against Jesus. I looked desperately, but saw no Apostle or even a faithful disciple.

Caiaphas, the reigning high priest and head of the pack of dogs, sat on his throne, a cushioned seat cut of the same stone as the rest of the palace. "Step forward if there are witnesses against this imposter."

No man moved until the high priest glared at one of the guards, who promptly prodded a man to approach the council.

"What is your witness against Jesus, the great prophet come from Galilee?"

At the mention of Galilee, the council scoffed.

The man looked uncertain, but lied with ease. "We heard Him say, I will destroy this temple that is made with hands, and within three days I will build another made without hands."

Caiaphas gloated. "He said He would destroy our holy temple?"

"Yea."

I wanted to lunge at the man. More than three years earlier, Jesus had made that statement. I knew that every elder in the circle knew that Jesus spoke of His own body, and had not made a threat to tear down the holy temple.

Another witness was encouraged forward. He too claimed that Jesus prophesied the destruction of the great temple.

The men cawed like famished ravens, nodding and recounting the times Jesus had taken a whip to drive the merchants and money-changers from the temple grounds. By what authority did He have the right to do so?

My mind recalled the first time Jesus had cleansed the temple courts. These very men had then sung His praises. Now they were set to stone Him.

The holy men grew enraged. By what right did Jesus speak such things?

The two witnesses countered each other. No agreement could be drawn, and I knew that under the law Jesus would have to be set free.

But nothing in that chamber was lawful or ordered. It was chaotic and driven.

Caiaphas hated Jesus and would find Him guilty no matter where He had to look for evidence.

The debacle continued. I surged forward when one of the priests spit at my Master's feet.

"Stay put or leave," warned a soldier. He held a small dagger to my face.

The council continued, mocking and spitting and scorning Jesus. There was nothing lawful or holy about the ordeal. My knees began to quiver.

Caiaphas crept closer and closer to the edge of his seat. He was angered and anxious to draw this feigned trial to a close. "Art thou the Christ, the Son of the Blessed?"

It was a trap. The very word *Blessed* referred to God.

"I am:" said Jesus, and His voice filled the chamber with thundering truth, "and ye shall see the Son of man sitting on the right hand of power, and coming in the clouds of heaven."

Fear gripped me. The word *power* also denoted God. Jesus was giving them grounds for a charge of blasphemy, and yet He spoke the sacred truth.

Caiaphas made a dramatic stand, feigning great offense on the part of Jehovah. His whole body shook. His arms waved high like a billowing sail. His council cried in a united wail.

Jesus did not flinch.

"Blasphemy!" was the decree that caused Caiaphas to rend his garments.

The other members of the council also tore the hems of their cloaks. The ripping sound combined with the wailing made my head ring.

"What need we any further witnesses?"

A torrid of insults were slung at Jesus.

"He makes Himself equal with God," one of the priests cried.

They moaned and groaned and suffered as if their feet were atop burning coals.

Now Caiaphas rent his inner garment as well, and the others mimicked him, tearing their own tunics in sympathy.

"Ye have heard the blasphemy: what think ye?"

"Death!"

"Death!"

"Death!"

"Prophesy unto us, thou Christ. Who is he that smote thee?"

At that moment the holy men rose as one, coming toward Jesus. When they were close to His face, they spit. It was a gesture to declare that His guilt would not be on their shoulders.

At that point I could not be restrained. When I ran toward my Master, four men came at me and cast me out of the chamber, back out into the cold night air. I did not leave so fast that I did not hear the council smite Jesus, slapping Him with their palms, spitting again and again, gloating in their guilty verdict.

I did not know what to do. Jesus had never needed me more, and yet how could I help Him?

There were people all about me, and I looked through the darkness for Peter. I found him by the fire just as a woman, one of the palace servants, approached him. "Thou also wast with Jesus of Galilee."

There was fear on his face as he looked at her. "I know not what thou sayest."

I could not believe what I had heard. *Peter denying Jesus?* It was impossible.

Though it was yet the third watch, the crowd was hardly thinned. How could anyone know who was for Jesus and who was against Him?

Peter went rapidly toward the porch and I followed him, wanting to beg his advice on what to do for Jesus.

Another woman pointed at him and called for all to hear, "This fellow was also with Jesus of Nazareth."

Heads turned toward him.

Peter swore an oath. "I do not know the man."

Again, I questioned my own ears. This was Peter, defender of the Master. No one was more devoted to Jesus. I wanted to tell him that we had only a short time to make a move for Jesus. Now that Caiaphas and his council had declared Jesus guilty of blasphemy, a sin punishable by stoning, there would be a required delay before the second trial.

Peter was not alone, but surrounded by questioning skeptics. "Surely thou also art one of them; for thy speech betrayeth thee."

He launched into a fit of cursing and said, "I know not the man."

Immediately, a sound rang through the air that I'd heard hundreds of times while I lived in Jerusalem: the call of a bugle atop the fortress. This one, the *cockcrow,* signaled the end of the third watch.

Peter looked upward at the bugler. The sky was just beginning to turn pink and the man's silhouette was evident against the sky. The fear was gone from Peter's face, replaced by sudden sadness.

Morning was coming, and with it a new trial. We had to do something to help Jesus. The law dictated that we had time, but the Sanhedrin had no interest in keeping the law. Caiaphas was after Jesus as surely as Herodias had been after John.

The realization sickened me.

I looked to Peter, but found him gone, vanished among the ever-present throng.

What choice had I but to wait?

I listened to the guards and the murmuring crowd to discover what was happening next to Jesus. The partial council of the Sanhedrin that had convened earlier now added numbers until it was a full quorum. It had been fewer than three hours since the first trial. I could only imagine the indignity and suffering Jesus was enduring.

Judas.

Where was the traitor? I had not seen him since Gethsemane.

I hoped he felt guilt for what he had done. I hoped he was suffering even as Jesus.

Where were the others that Jesus had chosen? Where were His followers now?

I was surrounded by thousands curious to see what would become of the famed Jesus of Nazareth, yet I had never felt so alone.

Apart from Jesus, I was no one. I was nothing.

When I approached the palace gate, I was sent back.

I waited.

Another trial. What more could they do to make Him suffer?

I huddled with strangers around the fire to keep warm. I thought of ways to free Jesus, but none seemed plausible.

I prayed, but wondered if heaven had closed its doors and windows to my pleas. Jesus, the very Son, was suffering like no man had ever suffered.

I heard the cheers before I heard the second and clenching verdict. "Guilty!"

No one had to tell me that such meant Jesus—my Jesus, the boy whose eyes I'd tried to shelter from seeing such a fate—would now endure death by stoning.

The law required His body to then be suspended from a tree.

No! God would not allow it. Surely, He would send a miracle to save His Son.

"Crucify Him!" a voice called.

"Yes! Crucify Him!" another joined in.

Soon, I was surrounded by a crazed mob, possessed of evil. Their cries caused the very earth to tremble. They longed to see the self-proclaimed Savior nailed to a cross.

My feet stumbled, and I leaned against the stone wall.

Only a reigning Roman had authority to crucify. Even the high priest Caiaphas could not call down such cruelty.

"Let it be not so." A woman fell against me, weeping. Her veil was torn from her face, and I saw the tears that drenched her cheeks. She was not familiar, yet I realized I was not the only one there mourning for the Master.

"You cry for Jesus?" a guard asked her.

"Yea. I weep for the Lord."

In the same instant, she was pulled away and gone.

Now I understood that the Apostles were hiding, and why they hid. It was not safe to vow loyalty to Jesus, but I did not understand Peter's denial. I would never understand Judas.

A Pharisee came out of the palace. I had to move closer to be sure it was him, but when I knew it was, I ran to him. It was Ovadya, the Pharisee from Sepphoris.

"Almon, you wear fear with the same ease a woman wears silk," he said. "Your Jesus is condemned. Now they take Him before Pilate."

Not *Pilate!*

Pontias Pilate, the Roman governor, was a hard man. He had taken up residence in the Fortress Antonia during Passover. It was his responsibility to keep the Jewish pilgrims under control during the feast season. Any hint of Jewish insurrection was met with a swift sword.

He was a lavish man, prone to excess. His palace by Caesarea was built after Roman opulence. It was said to hold a sports arena, a full theater for vile entertainment, a breakwater harbor, and a freshwater aqueduct that ran the full distance from Mount Carmel to the palace.

Now he was in Jerusalem, his only entertainment the ravenous pilgrims crying for the blood of one of their own.

Jesus was bound and His blindfold askew. He was still covered in blood, water, and spittle. His body had been beaten and His spirit bruised. I saw Him being led by Annas, Caiaphas, and other indignant members of the Sandhedrin, a prisoner moved to the Fortress Antonia, a heathen place close to the holy temple.

Those who shouted out accolades to the Master were immediately put down. I silently shouted my own praises, praying Jesus would hear them when no one else could.

The accusing party treated Jesus like He was filthy and His proximity would soil them. They approached the fortress with the same disdain. Neither Annas nor Caiaphas would step onto the unhallowed ground of the Gentile dwelling, not willing to defile their holy selves. Yet they felt no hesitation in pushing Jesus forward, into the hands of the Roman soldiers, into the judgment hall of a Gentile.

Eighty-seven

What was I to do?

Morning was coming, and with it the dawn of a day that had to be halted. In the book of Jasher the sun stood still in the midst of heaven, and hasted not to go down a whole day. Could not that miracle occur again on behalf of the true Son?

Rabbi Asa was the only one I could think of who might have an answer. He was in Jerusalem for the Passover feast; if I could locate him, I could beg him to plead for an audience with any member of the Sanhedrin—to talk with Ovadya or even the loathed Rabbi Zeev. Rabbi Asa would understand that everything that had been done to Jesus was unlawful. I knew the laws and the prophets so well I could cite them to support a case for Jesus.

I left the Fortress Antonia gate, pressed through the crowds, and went right to the temple, where I thought he might be. It was my only chance.

Hear, O Israel: The Lord our God is one Lord. Shema came out of my mouth as unheeded as breath.

I did not find Rabbi Asa, but I did find Judas there, just outside the temple treasury. He looked the age of Methuselah.

"Almon." He came toward me and grabbed hold of my arm. His breath was short and he shivered violently. "The Master, is He yet well?"

Well? I jerked away. Let Judas freeze in the cold air. What was that to me? This was the man who had betrayed Jesus. His kiss was venomous.

"I did not know. I did not know it would come to this."

I did not care. I only wanted to leave Judas, but he made such a pitiful figure, my heart would not allow me to turn away.

Something was different. It wasn't just that Judas looked ancient and defeated; something about him was different. I had to study for a time until I realized what it was. The purse! The purse he never let slip from his heart was gone.

He held out his hands to me, palms up. They trembled. "I have His blood on my hands."

I looked and realized that Judas told the truth. When Jesus had emerged from the depths of Gethsemane, He had been drenched in blood. Every pore cried red. Judas had touched Him—kissed and kissed Him again.

The Master's blood *was* on his hands.

"It stains my soul also," Judas said, collapsing as if he'd been beaten. His face touched the stone floor. He lifted his head and let it fall. Lifted it and let it fall again . . . and again. The sound was brutal, but no concern of mine. I was on an errand of greater importance.

I took my departure, but Judas screamed my name. "Almon!"

I stopped.

Through convulsive sobs he poured out his story. "It was a tithe," he said, "the money I took to betray Jesus was a simple tithe of the ointment Mary Magdalene poured on the Master's head."

Had the ointment been sold, it would have brought three hundred pence. *Judas sold Jesus for thirty pieces of silver?*

I might have killed him then if we had been alone, but there were other men there, temple priests and clerks. Servants still scrubbing the filth left from the days of feasting. This day the final sacrifices were to be made to complete the season. People stared at Judas, down on the ground, weeping without control. He was a spectacle.

No one bothered to help him. I certainly didn't.

He desperately wanted someone to listen to his sad, sad story.

"I knew Jesus had power from on high. I have seen His miracles. He healed my own son from the river fever. He *is* who He says He is."

Why then did you prove such a traitor, Judas?

My hand closed into a fist. I remembered what it felt like to have my fingers squeezed tight around Judas' throat. I feared I might attack him even though there were witnesses all around us. I wanted to see him dead for what he had done.

If Judas could only see what I had witnessed: The Savior drenched and shivering, standing innocent before His guilty accusers. If only Judas could see the blood, the pain, the spittle dripping from Jesus' face.

What did Judas matter?

"Almon, I beg you—stay. I beg you! Never did I mean for it to go so far. The Master has power . . . why did He not use it to save Himself?"

I had asked myself that very question.

Judas was struggling to stand and without thinking, I reached out to help him as I had before. Now the Savior's blood was on my hands as well.

"Almon! Wait! Is it true that the elders have condemned Jesus?"

I nodded and battled the desire to kick Judas as the guards had kicked me. Over and over. How I wanted him to suffer!

His cry turned inward, and I thought he might choke on his own sorrow. "I brought the thirty pieces of silver back to the priests and elders. I emptied the whole purse at their feet, saying: 'I have betrayed innocent blood.' They only laughed and said, 'What is that to us?'"

Jesus, too, had been laughed at during the night. He was no doubt being mocked even as Judas sought to rid himself his guilt. I had to leave him. I had to find Rabbi Asa and do what I could to prevent Pilate from sentencing Jesus to crucifixion. People were filing into the city, just now hearing of the trial. Those who had waited through the night were growing frenzied, anxious to hear the fate of the famed Christ.

"Go if you must, Almon. Leave me now, but *know* that I *know* I have sinned and I sorrow greatly."

A smirk turned up my lips. *What did Judas know of suffering?* And what right did he have to confess to me? The One whom he betrayed should hear his confession.

For years Judas had been my friend, but now he was my enemy. Though I had the thought to take him in my arms and embrace him as a brother, I followed my darker thoughts and turned. I hurried away, not once looking back.

As my sandals slapped the stones, a thought came to my mind. Judas claimed that he did not really anticipate that his betrayal would have such a grievous consequence. He said he believed Jesus would find a way to free Himself. My own father had sold me for profit, just as Judas as sold Jesus for profit. Always, Father anticipated that I would not suffer permanent bondage, but that he would find a way to set me free.

My suffering could not be compared to that of the Master, but still I saw the parallel: We had both been betrayed, sold for money by those we loved.

What did that matter now?

I hurried as quickly as I could, feeling more and more desperate—even hopeless.

There were rabbis and priests, elders and scribes. The Temple Mount was jammed with the holiest men in all of Israel. If they weren't part of it, they had come after hearing the rumors of what had happened to Jesus, the Healer, the Miracle Worker . . . now a blasphemer. Rabbi Asa was not among any of the faces I searched, but I did get word that Pontias Pilate had not yet granted the demands of Annas and Caiaphas.

My heart took courage, and I forced my aching feet to hurry back to the fortress.

Along the way I encountered John. He was alone and looked like a lost lamb amid a pack of wolves.

"Peter is grieving," he said. "His courage has failed him."

Knowing the friction that existed between the two Apostles, I was surprised to see John so tender toward his rival—a rival I knew he loved much.

"Peter told me that he denied the Master . . . thrice."

I thought how that fact was only partially true. He did not deny the Master . . . he denied *knowing* the Master. My own surety of Jesus had gone up and down as a wave upon the sea. But now . . . now a burning within me left no doubt. Judas was right—Jesus was who He said He was.

The crowds were crammed and crazy. In the morning light thousands waited to hear the final fate of Jesus. Among the loyal portion were Mary, Mary Magdalene, Salome, and Naomi. I was not surprised to see Lazarus, but I was surprised to see Malik; he was joined by the brothers of Jesus.

Deborah flung herself into my arms when she saw me. Though the air was still chilly, her body was warm from worry. "A guard has reported to us that Pilate has not arrived at a decision. That's a good sign, isn't it, Almon?"

I drew her to me and held her until I felt her own heart beat next to mine.

Deborah could not be stilled. She drew back and spoke her words in haste. "They tell us that Pilate came out and asked Caiaphas what accusation he brought against Jesus. The high priest said that if Jesus were not a malefactor, they would not have delivered Him."

At that moment Pilate appeared again on the landing and the people drew quiet except for a solitary voice. "What is your rendering, governor?"

Pilate raised his hand. I had a clear view of him and I thought he looked harrowed. "Take ye him, and judge him according to your law."

The crowd cried for blood.

"He is a traitor!"

"He steals from Rome!"

"He stirs the people!"

A handful of the other Apostles broke through the crowd and went to protect and comfort the family and loved ones of Jesus.

Annas and Caiaphas put their heads together in whispered frenzy. They were surrounded by members of the great Sanhedrin. I saw the tallith of the Pharisee Ovadya, but I did not see Rabbi Asa—not that it would matter now.

Caiaphas failed to tell Pilate that Jesus had already been tried twice, unlawfully. He called to the governor. "It is not lawful for us to put any man to death."

I realized in that clarion moment that the Jews, who had no authority to crucify, would not settle for a rock when it was a cross they craved.

Pilate waved the men to be still and went back through the massive doors into the judgment hall.

What indignities was my Savior now suffering? Could they be worse among the Gentiles than they had been among His own Jews? Were they smiting the Master, spitting on Him, mocking Him?

Pilate seemed a man who sought true justice, and for that I gave thanks.

Those of us who loved Jesus huddled together, suffering and comforting as one. When Peter joined us I did not let on what I had heard—and I did not judge him. I knew that no heart beat harder for Jesus than the one in his broad chest.

A guard came out of the doors and was immediately set upon with questions. John went forward to get any information he could.

We waited, and I saw the look on Mary's face. She wore fear like a mask.

John came back to tell us, "Pilate asked Jesus if He was King of the Jews."

"What did He say?" Peter asked impatiently.

"At first Jesus did not reply. Pilate asked Him if He could hear all the witnesses against Him. They say Jesus stayed silent for a time. 'Art thou the King of the Jews?' Pilate asked again."

We waited for John to continue, but his voice choked with emotion.

"Say on," Mary urged gently.

"Jesus said of Himself, 'Thou sayest that I am a king. To this end was I born, and for this cause came I into the world, that I should bear witness unto the truth. Every one that is of the truth heareth my voice.'"

That same burning returned to warm my belly, my chest, my whole being. I had hope that Jesus would find one more miracle . . . one for Himself.

"Pilate asked, 'What is truth?'"

"And?" asked Peter.

"And now we wait." John put his hands to his face and wept.

Eighty-eight

Sand fell through the hourglass as if it were wet. Time became torture while the crowd shrieked accusations, spurred on by Caiaphas himself. Mary Magdalene appeared drawn and colorless. I feared that she would faint. Deborah went to her, and Mary rested her head upon Deborah's steadfast shoulder.

Finally, the great doors swung open and Pilate reappeared.

The Jews seemed possessed; they were sure that Pilate would sentence the false prophet to death. I could hardly hear over the shouts and accusations.

I could see the profile of Caiaphas and read his anticipation.

It was too painful to look at either Mary. The women held each other while Pilate made his declaration, but it was not what we expected.

"I find in him no fault at all."

My heart danced, but the great throng was outraged. The Jews were furious. They shouted and screamed and would not be silenced.

Pilate appeared nervous and uncertain. He went back into the fortress, but returned quickly. The words he said to Caiaphas were drowned out by the bellowing crowd.

"What is it? What has become of my son?" Mary asked, turning to Peter.

Lazarus and James went toward the fortress looking for answers. They came back shortly, their faces ashen.

"Jesus has been sent to stand before Herod Antipas."

"No!" cried Mary Magdalene. "That murderer has sought Jesus ever since he beheaded John. He will surely kill my Lord."

"It makes no sense," said Peter. "Pilate and Antipas are not friends. For these many years they have stood at odds."

"Their friendship will be forged this day," said John.

"Hurry!" called Lazarus, "We must hurry to the Hasmonean palace. Herod is in the city for the festivities. There, he will judge Jesus."

"No!" both Marys cried.

Our band divided at that point. The women did not go to the palace of Antipas, but stayed at the Fortress Antonia.

"Jesus will be brought back here," said John. "The final verdict will be announced by Pilate."

"We will go to the palace of Herod," said Lazarus. "Peter will come with me."

But Peter was already gone.

No one instructed me where to go or what to do. The time had come for me to live my own life . . . free of servitude . . . but never free from my bond to Jesus.

For a while I waited with the women. But Mary was drawing strength from her sons and her sisters. Deborah seemed strong and occupied, giving comfort where comfort was needed. I chose to mingle with the crowd, to place myself by the palace guards so I could glean whatever information was being rumored about.

I learned that Herod Antipas was overjoyed to have Jesus stand before him. For so long he had sought an audience with the Master, believing Him to be John returned from the dead.

Outside the gates of the Hasmonean palace people were telling rumors into the ears of strangers. "Herod asks for a miracle, but the Nazarene stands silent."

The closer I got to the palace, the more I felt it. It was the same presence I had felt in the small desert village while I had waited for Jesus those forty long, long days.

It was the feel of evil, and it was so real it hung in the air and burned my lungs.

"The chief priests and scribes are vehement in their accusations against Jesus."

"He speaks not a word."

How many times had I heard Jesus quote from Isaiah? *He was oppressed, and he was afflicted, yet he opened not his mouth?*

The soldiers that seemed to be everywhere—Herod's soldiers—were dressed and poised for war.

I waited. The press and craze of the crowd was so intense that I could not see any familiar face, but I heard the rumors as they spilled out of the palace.

"Herod and the others mock the false Lord."

"They have Him arrayed in the white robe of royalty."

"Jesus refuses to speak in His own defense."

"He refuses to speak at all."

"Herod is outraged."

"Herod and Pilate are now allies."

"Antipas mocks the self-proclaimed king!"

I made my way back to the fortress, all the time thinking that Jesus was with the very man who dined at the table where John's severed head had rolled upon a platter.

I pictured the gore in my mind and could not chase the image away.

What more could they do to Jesus?

What more?

Fear drove me on. Everywhere I looked soldiers were armed and starved for the slightest provocation.

The women were as I had left them, huddled and tearful.

John, Peter, and Lazarus returned.

We waited, knowing that the burden of judgment now rested with Pilate.

We prayed. We prayed again. I prayed that Jesus was praying down the powers of heaven for Himself.

A servant from the palace came to us with sympathetic news. "You are His mother?" he asked Mary.

"I am."

"The governor does not desire your son's blood."

She bowed her head in gratitude.

"The governor's wife, Claudia Procula, has a belief in Jesus. When Pilate was set down she sent word to her husband imploring, 'Have thou nothing to do with that just man; for I have suffered many things this day in a dream because of him.'"

Peter pressed the man for more information, longing to find a shred of hope that would tip the scales in our Master's favor.

When word finally came from Pilate it created a perfect escape for Jesus. The Passover custom permitted the governor to release one convicted criminal. He'd already found Jesus guiltless. His attempt to transfer the responsibility to Herod had collapsed, and now the ravenous Jews demanded Jesus.

"Pilate knows our Master stands innocent," said John.

Peter scoffed. "He knows that Caiaphas and his priests stand guilty."

Thousands of people roared as Pilate made his proposal. He would release one. Would it be Barabbas, who had taken an innocent life during an insurrection? Or would it be Jesus, an innocent life who had taken nothing, but who had given only?

Jesus or Barabbas?

The waiting continued, choking us with fear.

"What transpires within?" was the question everyone posed.

The truth was that Pilate was doing his best to convince the Jews to release Jesus. Three times he declared Jesus innocent. The third time his words were hardly heard for the evil desires of the scribes and chief priests. "Why, what evil hath he done? I have found no cause of death in him; I will therefore chastise him, and let him go."

"No."

Pilate was beside himself. "What shall I do then with Jesus which is called Christ?"

The holy men and the multitude gone mad could only cry one word: *Crucify!*

In the end, it was Barabbas who was let go.

Pilate understood that crucifixion was a hideous form of death— so cruel and vicious that it was reserved for only the most heinous crimes. It was evident that Jesus had done nothing to warrant such a black fate.

"Why, what evil hath he done?" Pilate asked the Jews.

Thousands of mouths opened, screaming lies and demanding the blood of Jesus of Nazareth.

Pilate was a coward, fearful of the rising mob. If they wanted to crucify one of their own, what was that to him?

Yet he performed dual acts that demonstrated his conviction that Jesus was innocent. First, in private council with the leading Jews, including Annas and Caiaphas, he rose from his seat of judgment before his mouth announced the decree.

Second, before us, he washed his hands for all to see that unlike Judas, his hands did not bear the blood of Jesus.

The Jews had gone insane. "His blood be on us, and on our children."

Deborah came to me and leaned against me for support. In turn, I leaned on her. The whole world was coming apart, and there was no longer a way to stop it.

Eighty-nine

Like we were headed to our own executions, our little band moved to the place where Jesus was to be scourged. All around us, evil cried out victory!

Jesus was to die, and no plan or person could stop it.

Peter was vocal and brute. He pushed our band forward, faster and faster, shoving people out of the way so we could reach the place where Jesus was to be readied for the cross.

We arrived at the open entrance of the common hall.

"We are with Jesus," Peter announced. "His mother is included in our assembly."

All fear that ran rampant in the night's darkness was gone. If they were to kill us because we were with Jesus, so be it.

I remembered and felt Thomas' vow when we had first returned to Jerusalem, knowing that Jesus' blood was sought. "Let us go with Him that we might die also."

The soldiers were both Roman and Syrian. They allowed us to move forward to a place where we could glimpse the Master.

The women wailed at the sight.

Jesus had already been stripped naked. Now He was being strapped to a great wooden pillar.

Mary Magdalene lunged forward and fell on her face. "My Lord, my God."

Jesus lifted His chin, but said nothing.

Hundreds of soldiers, arrayed against one man, stood ready. Pilate was there in person. He wore the same look of shame and horror that I had seen on the face of Peter. Pilate, too, had denied knowing Jesus.

I had been witness to men's deaths before. But this was no ordinary man's death. The mass of people present only encouraged those who were employed to mock and brutalize the condemned.

Men circled Jesus, wolves moving in and out, howling and biting, spitting and cursing. Then came the man with the scourge in his hand. As brute as Peter, he raised the leather device so we could all see how it was weighted with shards of sheep bone and blades of lead.

Its first tear was deep and long. Jesus bled a river of red down His back. He cried out with the second tearing. The third caught at His shoulder and ripped through flesh deep into the muscle. The forth time the scourge sunk into His flesh, Mary, the mother of Jesus, collapsed into John's arms.

Deborah buried her face in her hands and sobbed behind her veil.

Again, the scourge landed. And again. And again. And again.

People all around us cheered with every blow, but my ears went deaf to everything except the sound of Jesus' body being torn and shredded.

At one point the initial scourge was traded for a different one, this one heavy with leaden balls. It hit the spine, and Jesus arched His back in agony. It hit again, and again, and again, bruising and breaking the skin that was already butchered.

I wondered why Jesus did not die from that beating. *Oh, Joseph, how I have failed to protect your son.*

Finally, Pilate called a halt to the stripes, and Jesus was unstrapped. I marveled that His shaking legs could hold Him upright as the Syrians brought forth the woolen robe of a Roman general. It was purple . . . Jesus' favorite color.

They clasped it tight over His shredded right shoulder and slapped it against the bleeding flesh of His back. Someone carried out a plaited crown made of long, sharp thorns. It was placed on Jesus' head and then forcefully shoved into His flesh so that the thorns sent tiny streams of red running down His face into His eyes.

The disciples and Apostles and women who worshipped Him suffered agonies of their own.

Caiaphas stood near Pilate. I saw their faces. Pilate looked ill. Caiaphas looked to be relieved.

A laughing soldier brought forth a great reed and put it in the Master's hand. All the soldiers bowed their knees in mockery crying, "King of the Jews!"

They came at Him again, slinging spit into His bleeding face.

A man took the reed from Jesus and struck Him on the head over and over.

Then Pilate turned away, signaling an end to the mockery and scourging.

It was on to the crucifixion.

We did not push ourselves forward, but allowed ourselves to be pushed with the crowd, back to the Fortress Antonia.

Scourged and already dying, Jesus was presented at the hand of Pilate.

Upon seeing Him suffering so, the crowd cried—some in agony, most in victory.

"If thou let this man go, thou art not Caesar's friend: whosoever maketh himself a king speaketh against Caesar."

That was the dagger, for Pilate could not afford Caesar to think him in any way disloyal.

He brought Jesus forth—a bruised and battered, but not broken, man.

"Behold the man!"

The dogs around us growled and barked; men turned to animals. "Away with Him, away with Him! Crucify Him!"

Pilate asked, "Shall I crucify your king?"

"We have no king but Caesar!"

The holy men chose their words carefully, knowing which words would sway Pilate.

"Away with Him! Away with Him! Crucify Him!" the Jews cried.

Pilate made one last pathetic utterance. "Take ye him, and crucify him: for I find no fault in him." Then he turned Jesus over to the waiting soldiers and disappeared behind the massive doors that could not hide his shame.

All of Jerusalem and most of the outlying villages had emptied themselves to come and see the sight. He who had raised the dead would fall dead Himself.

There was one solider, a Roman, who took pity on Mary. He made way with his horse for us to pass through the crowd, for us to follow at a viewing distance the trek from the judgment hall to the city gates. No Jew could defile the Holy City with a crucifixion within the walls.

Now I understood with clarity the hypocrisy that Jesus had so often preached against.

Two others, convicted thieves, also bore crosses that would bear their own dying bodies. They hardly were noticed. All eyes stayed on Jesus, King of the Jews.

The women were stronger than I imagined they could be. All three Marys walked together, the mother in the middle. They walked with straight backs and steady step. My own sorrow was like sand poured into my legs; each movement was a mighty effort. Deborah walked beside me, and I had never been more grateful for her presence.

We wound our way through the cobbled streets, up and down, and caught glimpses of Jesus only now and then.

The soldiers had removed the purple robe from Jesus and had dressed Him back in His own blood-drenched raiment. The crown still pierced His head. His body was bent now beneath the weight of the patibulum—two beams bound together, the second part of the cross on which He would be crucified.

I rushed to help Him carry it.

Hands pulled me back.

At the gate the soldiers compelled another man. "Your name?"

"Simon."

"Carry this man's cross."

The man looked mortified. "I have just come from the fields. I beg you, no."

I understood his hesitancy; a cross was a symbol of shame, but he did not know Jesus and did not understand that this man had no shame.

A sword was lifted, and Simon bore the burden I longed to bear.

Relieved of the weight, Jesus straightened Himself. I moved as close to Him as I could, positioning myself ahead by only a step or two. His eyes lifted, and through lids stained with dried blood, He saw me.

We had never needed spoken words to understand each other, nor did we now.

I was there, and my Master knew it.

The place outside the city was called Golgotha, the place of the skull. I knew when I saw it that Jesus would be lifted up on the center cross.

It was a site fit for death. Three beams were already set in the hard earth, awaiting their crossbars and victims.

Though it was spring and the grass should have been tall and green, it was dried and yellow. The rock escarpment that fell behind the hill was jagged and white, like the very color had been drained from the stone.

The sun beat down, and the sky that had been cloudless was beginning to gather in a storm.

"Our brother did not save our father, nor our cousin John. He will not save Himself." I turned to see James standing beside me. His eyes were red and swollen. His chin quivered. "I now understand why."

I wanted to ask James what he meant, because *I* did not fully understand. But James was back with his family, offering consolation and strength. They clung to each other as the Savior of the world was laid upon the ground, ready to be nailed.

A herald went forward and fastened a tablet to the cross. Pilate had written in Hebrew, Greek, and Latin: JESUS OF NAZARETH THE KING OF THE JEWS.

Pilate broke through the crowd on a high-stepping black horse, surrounded by his inner guard to protect him from the Jews devoted to Jesus. Caiaphas came with his own inner guard, members of the great Sanhedrin. They were revered by the Jews who hated Jesus, the vast majority.

When they saw the sign that Pilate had written, they implored him, "Write not *The King of the Jews;* but that he *said,* 'I am King of the Jews.'"

This time, Pilate was adamant. "What I have written, I have written."

Deborah came forth with a cup one of the women had brought. "It is gall, to ease his great suffering."

She took it to Jesus. He put it to His lips, but did not drink.

When she returned the cup was still full, its dark, pungent contents sloshing. "Jesus wants to be fully present for His suffering."

All His life, Jesus had been fully present. A vision of Him playing as a child, chasing butterflies, running with the lambs, brushing His hand over the top of the growing grain . . . picture after picture went through my mind. In the workshop. In the synagogue at Nazareth. In the tomb of Lazarus. Racing the children along the shores of Galilee.

And now.

Deborah wept at her own memories.

I could not bear her pain. This was the man who had touched her and, with a word, made her malformed face smooth. This was her kinsman. Her childhood friend. I ached to take Deborah in my arms and to never let her go.

We could do nothing but watch as they stretched the Lord's arms wide, and drove giant iron nails into His palms.

Those He came to save now cheered and danced at His torture.

Lazarus went to Jesus and whispered words of comfort. He and Jesus were as brothers and more. Lazarus lived because Jesus had called him forth from the tomb. Now Lazarus stood as only a man, unable to call forth anything but love.

The sun seemed to call for a blanket, and cloud after cloud moved with haste to cover her, to put out her light.

Jesus winced and then cried out as the second set of nails severed the nerves in His wrists. There is no sound on earth to match that sound.

My mind took me back years, to Joseph's workbench. Shafts of light shone through the wall planks, sawdust lay pungent on the floor. Jesus' pudgy little fingers wrapped around scraps of wood, chiseling, carving, and shaving them into wooden nails.

I closed my eyes and saw Him. I heard Joseph's pride and laugher.

And then my world went black. I did not faint. I did not fall. I remained conscious and standing, but everything around me went dark.

Time passed in that clouded state and the crowds began to thin. Only the most vehement against Him and the most loyal to Him remained.

The ground beneath my feet trembled.

"Have you seen Judas?" Thomas asked me.

I blinked, and reality came back into focus. Jesus hung before me on the cross. On either side of Him hung two convicted thieves. Already, the support props were nailed as a sort of seat and stool to help bear His weight. Nails had been thrust through the Savior's feet—feet I had washed and walked beside.

Round drops of dark red blood dripped steadily into the hard sand beneath him.

Judas?

The women gathered at the foot of the cross. They wept and mourned and stayed there for the Master's final agony.

His family stood close by.

His disciples.

His Apostles . . . minus one.

Judas.

Yes, I had seen Judas, but I did not see him now.

The sky was now completely covered, the clouds growing darker by the tick of the clock . . . a clock that was running out of time.

A group of angry Jews approached the Master. I thought they were merely curious, but because He hung so low to the ground, their hands were able to reach Him, to strike Him, to spit upon His bleeding wounds.

"*If* thou be the son of God, come down from the cross."

Jesus had heard those very words before . . . out in the wilderness, facing Satan himself: *If* thou be the Son.

Jesus looked down upon these men with a look I'd seen so many times. His eyes were filled with mercy.

He was innocent, and yet He was dying the most hideous death imaginable. When would their hatred be appeased? What more could they do to debase Him?

"He saved others; Himself he cannot save," they taunted.

In spite of the darkness and the churning elements, the soldiers also came and mocked Him. They slapped, they spit, they cursed. They fought among themselves as they divided the Master's inner garment. They did not know the great gift they had been given.

Jesus responded with seven words that seared my soul forever: "Father, forgive them; for they know not what they do."

Before me was the living lesson of forgiveness.

The Master did not forgive their sins and cleanse these men, but He did pardon their acts of the moment because He understood they were doing as they were compelled—by Jews. By Rome. By Satan.

They wore their holy garments, they raised their holy voices, but the words they spoke were unkind and unholy. "Let Him now come down from the cross, and we will believe Him. He trusted in God; let God deliver Him now."

One of the thieves dying beside Jesus derided him also. "*If* thou art the Christ, save thyself and us."

The more penitent thief struggled to cry, "Dost not thou fear God, seeing thou art in the same condemnation? And we indeed justly; for we receive the due reward of our deeds: but this man hath done nothing amiss."

The man bowed his head. I took him for a praying man and watched his head turn slowly toward Jesus. "Lord, remember me when thou comest into thy kingdom."

Jesus answered the man with mercy. "Verily I say unto thee, Today shalt thou be with me in paradise."

They were the first words spoken that brought comfort to Mary, the mother of Jesus, and the women with her. She raised herself and stood at the foot of the cross.

Even the most vile mockers were drawn back by her presence.

She whispered words to Him that none of us heard. She prayed so loudly we all heard. She mourned in a way that none of us could comprehend.

Mary looked to die herself.

"Woman," said Jesus, looking down at His mother, "behold thy son!"

Then His eyes locked on John's. "Behold thy mother."

John and those with him took Mary to His home in Jerusalem. James borrowed a donkey, and Mary was led away in hopes that she would be spared the agony of her eldest Son's final moments on earth.

Just then someone approached Jesus and struck Him hard across the face. His lip split open; His face bled afresh.

Rabbi Zeev!

I wanted to lunge at him, to beat him with a force that would break every bone in his body.

But Peter moved to him first. He leaned down and thrust his face into the face of the rabbi. I did not hear the words that were spoken, but I saw the color drain from the rabbi's fat cheeks. I saw him back away, retreating to his pack of fellow dogs.

Deborah came to me and offered drink. I could not swallow.

The penitent thief next to Jesus moaned. He was given gall, and he drank it gratefully.

We waited.

Thomas again asked me, "What of Judas?"

I only shrugged. *What did Judas matter?*

At the back of Golgotha's crown was the escarpment—the white, jagged rocks. I moved toward the ledge and looked down. I touched the drying grass around my feet.

I went back to the cross. Jesus had closed His eyes, and for a fearful moment I thought He might be dead.

Mary Magdalene remained at the foot of the cross. Deborah and the other women stood nearby.

The agony went on.

The sky darkened.

Then Jesus opened His eyes, raised His head, and said so all could hear, "*Eli, Eli, lama sabachthani!*"

My god . . . my god . . . why has thou forsaken me?

There were a few around me who took pleasure in believing that Jesus had been forsaken, but a spirit within me interpreted my Master's meaning. Father God, in all His perfectness, could not stay present at the moment when His Only Begotten Son bore the sins and sorrows of every sinner everywhere.

Such Godly goodness could not reside in the presence of such ungodly evil. Not even for a final moment of perfect Atonement.

Somewhere in the far distant corners of heaven I imagined the Father, His holy face turned away, His body bowed, weeping His own red tears of sorrow.

Yes, He had forsaken His Son, but son He would embrace Jesus, never to leave Him alone again.

The suffering of that moment was beyond human comprehension. I felt it. The trees felt it. The sky felt it. The ground beneath our feet heaved and sobbed.

The Jews did not feel it. They rose refreshed. Even Rabbi Zeev returned to chant and jeer. "This man calleth for Elias . . . let us see whether Elias will come to save Him." Their mockery brought back the memory of John.

In the distance thunder rumbled.

"I thirst," Jesus said. His voice was so low, yet I heard it and ran to bring Him a sponge and a reed for sipping.

Jesus tried to open His mouth, but He did not partake.

Everyone who loved Him gathered close to Him now. I knew their faces; more than that, I knew their hearts. I felt grateful that

Jesus was not alone or forsaken in His final moments on earth.

I looked around and noted Judas was gone, and I felt his absence. A pain went through me, a sense I did not expect. I knew that Jesus loved His errant Apostle, and I knew that Jesus also felt Judas' absence.

We waited.

When the end came, we all heard the Master's final words: "It is finished . . . Father, into thy hands I commend my spirit."

He gave up the ghost. They did not *take* it from Him. He *gave* it freely.

His believers wept.

His non-believers cheered.

Ninety

The world—*my* world—was as black as a tomb. The ground split and the rocks rent.

I had never known such darkness or such despair. The very earth itself was in mourning. The heavens wept great tears of sorrow. The ground beneath our feet quaked and I thought it might swallow all of us . . . those who wept for Jesus and those who heralded His final breath.

The Apostles banded together, Peter at the center.

The women smote their breasts and wailed.

Time no longer mattered—but eventually, the light began to return and the world went from black to a sodden blanket of gray.

Deborah looked at me with hollow eyes, dry and bitter. Though she was the age of a woman, her demeanor was that of a child. I wanted to hold her, but I felt as lost as she looked.

The Master was gone.

Without Him, who was I? Where did I belong?

A Roman centurion, the man who had shown kindness to Mary, cried aloud, "Truly this was the Son of God!"

Pilate's horse reared and nearly threw him to the ground.

The Jewish leaders, Caiaphas at the helm, rushed to the governor. "In order to keep the law fully, the bodies must be removed before the dawn on the encroaching Sabbath."

It was impossible to tell the hour by the sun, but I knew it had to be well into the afternoon.

Pilate simply waved a hand to dismiss the pesky holy men. His concern was for the darkening skies and the churning elements.

Pilate called to one of his officers. "Break the legs."

I looked at the dying men on either side of Jesus. Neither of them had much life left in them, but none of the bodies could be removed from the crosses until the men were pronounced dead. By breaking their legs, the shift of their weight would collapse their lungs, bidding death to hurry.

But Jesus had already died. When the soldier came to break His legs, Mary Magdalene stood up to the raised club. "He is gone."

The soldier was offended by a woman so bold. He took his spear to pierce the side of Jesus, to be certain what Mary said was true.

Blood and fluid came gushing out.

"Almon?"

The man who whispered my name looked familiar, but I could not place him at that moment.

"I am Joseph," he said, "Joseph of Arimathea. I know you as the servant of Jesus and I seek your help."

Joseph was a friend to Nicodemus; he was here somewhere—I'd seen him earlier. I knew them both to be kind to Jesus. I offered myself to help in any way I could.

He kept his voice low, and I had to listen carefully in the whipping wind to hear him. "Pilate has granted me leave to take the body of Jesus for burial. I have secured a sepulchre in a nearby garden. Help me lift and prepare His body, Almon."

I was relieved and grateful to have a task, one so final and so great.

"We must hurry," he said. "The elders grow angry at my request. Caiaphas argues that it is unlawful to give an honorable burial to a crucified criminal."

I knew that Jesus had been crucified for political reasons and not for blasphemy, so even under the law He was entitled to an honorable burial.

Mary had left to go to John's home, but was now returned with burial linens.

She wept with the other women as Lazarus, Joseph, and I lifted Jesus down from the cross. His lifeless body fell into my arms. Its weight was welcome. His brow was damp, His body broken and bloody.

I took one of His hands and turned it with my own. The nail had been removed and the wound was still wet and red. An identical scar was torn through the wrist. For that moment, I held His hand, thinking how many miracles its touch had wrought.

I could not bring myself to believe that Jesus was dead.

Nicodemus came carrying a great supply of myrrh and aloes with which to anoint the body.

One of the dying thieves whose legs had been broken made a final cry. A Roman soldier waited ready with his spear. I was not convinced the man was dead when the spear went through the flesh.

Curiosity kept a few of the most dogged Jews around, but the darkness and the trembling earth sent most back to the shelter of their homes.

If I left, where would I go?

Disciples helped to bear the weight of Jesus, who was now a corpse. I was given the honor of bearing His feet. I tried not to look at the nail prints and to fathom the pain He had felt every time He had shifted His weight on the cross.

Father, forgive me. How can I ever forgive them for what they have done?

Someone had given Mary a sheet of linen to wrap Jesus' body in for transport, but the linen quickly soaked through with blood. I grew unbalanced when I saw the Savior's back, so scourged the white steps of his spine were visible. His flesh was shredded, as if by a lion or a wolf.

How He must have suffered!

And how He must have suffered in Gethsemane, bleeding from every pore. What kind of pain could cause a man to bleed like that?

Judas! I thought of him again and wondered how he could have missed the crucifixion. How I hated him.

Father, forgive me. Forgive me now before this poison blots Thy light from my life.

And forgiveness came with haste.

My hatred and anger toward Judas thinned with the realization that my love for Jesus was so great it crowded out any feelings that were less.

The journey from Golgotha was short, but every step made Jesus' death more real.

The women's tears grew to full-throated mourning.

Lazarus held the Master's head. The man who had raised him from the dead was now being laid down in death.

"He will live again," Lazarus said. "I know it for myself."

Mary put a hand to her heart and uttered a prayer for only God to hear.

The tomb was set in a well-tended garden; flowers burst in the soft colors of spring. The death chamber was divided into dual rooms, and we first laid the Master's body on a polished stone slab in the outer room. There it was washed, anointed with oil, sprinkled with perfume, and wrapped in fresh traveling clothes, for Jesus was now on a journey to a place where His Father waited.

I knew it. I knew it. I told myself I knew it.

Never had I seen a body so mangled. It was torn and bruised on every surface—His hands, His legs, His arms, and His face, His back . . . oh, His back!

I was given the honor of washing my Master's feet one final time. The blood, the dirt, and the memories all swirled in the basin and stained the towel. As Mary Magdalene's tears had once washed His feet, my own weeping now fell like rain.

Nicodemus asked if there was more he could do. The Apostles merely looked at him, their eyes asking the same question.

Carefully and lovingly His body was cocooned. First the aloe and myrrh were made into a paste that was packed between the strips of *tachrichin* wrappings. His body was wound and His head was turbaned with a linen napkin. A long strip was twisted and tied to hold His jaw from falling open. His neck and face were left uncovered.

The inner chamber held a never-used niche, carved from the stone. In it was laid the body of Jesus, the Son of God.

The women's wailing had melted to whimpers.

The men stood looking for anything more they could do.

And then we backed out, lifting the leftover scraps of linen and placing them in a basket as we had lifted the scraps of bread and placed them in a basket.

I am the bread of life.

His words came back to me again and again.

Peter and Lazarus—others too—helped roll the disk-shaped stone in front of the entrance. It was meant to keep wild animals and intruders from harming His body, but to me it enclosed the Savior in utter darkness and solitude. Another memory rushed back to me:

how Jesus used to sleep up on the rooftop beneath the glow of the moon and the stars because He was afraid to sleep in the house where it grew so dark at night.

Oh, Master, fear not. How many times had He said those words to me?

We mourned the passing of more than a man, more than a mere mortal. The three Marys, Naomi, Salome, Deborah, and the other women . . . all of the rest of us, the men of the Master. All of us mourned. Thomas worried me. He looked so frail. John stayed near Mary and those of her sons who were still with her.

Lazarus was on his knees, weeping.

Peter bore on his face a determination that I had not seen for a long time. Just looking upon him gave me strength.

Again, I thought of Judas, and I missed him. What could have kept him so long?

Rabbi Zeev came past the tomb and offered his final words of mockery. "He said He could not die, and yet your Jesus *is* dead."

His laughter did not penetrate my soul, but echoed off into the mist that hung around us.

"We must leave now," said Nicodemus. "The Sabbath is coming."

Knees that were bent straightened. Bodies moved. The holy day was upon us, and it would not be lawful to be found here mourning the death of Jesus . . . though He was Master of the Sabbath.

Ninety-one

The others went away. Deborah and some of the women went back to Bethany. Mary and those with her went to the house of John, which was nearby. Nicodemus went to the temple. Joseph went to his fine house in the city. The Apostles went to a place of hiding, for there was mounting rumor that they would be next to die for their loyalty to Jesus.

I stayed in the garden until a moon shone down on me.

Judas.

Again, his absence haunted me, and I lifted my sore body up and went in search of the lost Apostle. I had not gone down the road far when I saw three men approaching. At first fear filled me, but then I heard a voice I knew.

"Almon."

It was Rabbi Asa and his sons. I rushed to greet him.

"Is it true? Jesus is crucified and now entombed?"

I nodded and pointed toward the garden.

Rabbi Asa's knees buckled and his sons had to grip him tightly to keep him from collapsing. I offered my waterskin and he sipped from it. Slowly, we moved to the side of the road and helped him sit on a boulder.

After a time he spoke with the voice of a true teacher. "Jesus yet lives, though I fear to tell you of Judas."

My spine went straight, though my heart fell.

"He repented of his betrayal, but hung himself in sorrow. His body was dashed in a field that will forever be cursed."

A new wave of sorrow ripped through me.

Judas, my friend. He had called out to me in his deepest sorrow, and I had turned away to look for Rabbi Asa. Now Rabbi Asa stood before me telling me that my turning away had left Judas alone.

Father, will my sins never cease?

"I spoke to Judas before he hung himself," the teacher said. "He knew what he had done and could find no way to make it right."

We sat there for a time. "It is not lawful for me to mourn on the *Shabbat*, and yet my heart sorrows at the loss of such a man as Jesus."

A man?

Did not the rabbi know that Jesus was more than mortal?

He lifted himself up and headed toward the tomb while I took my leave and went toward the city.

The guards were out and Jerusalem was nearly deserted.

"State your business," a soldier of Herod's demanded.

I held my hand to my throat to indicate that I was mute.

He did not search me for weapons, but let me pass.

Shabbat used to be my favorite day of the week. Candles were lit. Prayers were said. Families were joined. Worship went on and on.

This day I loathed.

Without a plan, my feet returned me to the places I had been the day before. To the palaces of Annas and Caiaphas. To the Fortress Antonia. To Temple Mount. I made the trek slowly, back and forth.

I was lost without Jesus.

Lost and so alone I wanted to die, too.

Fear not, Almon, but believe.

His words echoed as my sandals slapped the stones.

By the warming fires of the fortress I heard the rumbled rumors. Guards told me, "Caiaphas still fears the one they call Jesus of Nazareth. He and his own have sought another audience with Pilate. They remember the Nazarene's promise, 'After three days I will rise again.'"

"They have implored Pilate, 'Command therefore that the sepulchre be made sure until the third day, lest his disciples come by night, and steal him away, and say unto the people, He is risen from the dead; so the last error shall be worse than the first.'"

"Our lord granted the terrified Jews their request." He laughed and the others laughed with him. "First, mighty Caiaphas feared a new king, but when we laid eyes on Jesus and saw He was nothing more than an ordinary man, we smiled. Now . . . they have put Him to death on the cross and Caiaphas still trembles, fearful of His ghost."

The guards were still laughing as I moved out through the city back toward the garden tomb. The city had a feeling about it that I had never felt.

Before the gate I encountered a maimed man who had no legs, but bore his body forward with the strength of his arms. He slid toward me across the stone. "You! Do you see them?"

I did not answer, only looked at him.

"At the King's death graves were burst open and the dead walk again. Can you not see them?"

I shook my head and kept walking.

All the while I thought about Deborah. I was free now like I had never been free. I could return with her to Nazareth. We could marry. We could live in our home that was already almost complete. We could raise a family . . . it was everything I had ever wanted.

No. That was not true. I had wanted to be forgiven of my sins and I had wanted to be given a living tongue so I could teach and testify of all the things I knew.

People had often asked me why I did not seek the Master's touch for my own healing. For so long, I did not ask because I felt unworthy to ask. My sins were dark and hidden. I feared that Jesus would turn me out if He knew.

Yet He knew before I ever confessed.

What no one knew—save Jesus and me—was that on that final day in the Judean hills, just before we turned toward Jerusalem for the last time, when Jesus and I were alone by the shores of the green waters of the Yored-Dan, I had bowed before Him and poured my heart out with not one word.

I had begged forgiveness.

I had begged mercy.

I had received all that I'd requested and more.

In return, Jesus had made a request of me. He had bid me to tell no man until He was risen again from the dead. Now my tongue that could talk could still tell no one, not even my Deborah.

Oh, the temptation . . . to tell those who scourged and crucified my Lord. Oh, the temptation . . . to try to comfort Mary and those who mourned beside me.

Oh, the temptation . . . but more important, the need to believe and wait for the time when Jesus would rise from the tomb where we had laid Him.

When I arrived at the garden it was as the guards had said. Two soldiers stood at the entrance, now sealed so the stone could not be moved.

I waited and watched. What was I to do?

Then at the first rays of dawn came Mary Magdalene and Mary, the woman I thought of as my own mother. They were come with spices to refresh the body of Jesus.

I looked at Mary, the mother, and remembered a night so long ago when I had overheard her story of an angel appearing to her.

The women were determined, but the soldiers were prepared to kill anyone who attempted to enter the tomb unauthorized.

As we stood there another quake took hold of the earth.

A stab of light shot down from heaven and I fell backward.

When my eyes opened the stone was unsealed. The keepers of the grave lay as dead men. Mary and Mary Magdalene were embracing in joy. I stood still as stone, uncertain of the vision before me.

Mary was the first to see me and she ran telling, "The Lord is risen! An angel announced the glorious truth! Oh, Almon, the Lord is risen!"

The women there danced in joy. Then they ran. They *ran* to tell the good and glorious news that Jesus was no longer dead.

I moved toward the open tomb. I stooped to enter the chamber and I saw for myself the truth. There was no corpse—only grave clothes still wrapped to hold the Master's shape. There was no scent of death.

The tomb was empty.

Had Jesus really risen?

My heart told me that it was so.

I was still there in the garden when John and Peter came running. John hesitated at the doorway; he was fearful of desecrating the chamber.

But Peter came barreling like a bull unpenned. He pushed past John and went right in, not stooping low enough to keep his head from hitting the stone. It didn't stop him. His eyes had to see for himself that the Master had done what He had promised to do.

He had risen from the grave to live again!

When Peter emerged he saw me and came and stood before me. In a moment of doubt, he expressed fear that Jesus' body had been stolen by thieves, yet he wanted to believe the words the women had told him. He looked deep into my eyes. He groaned with longing and said, knowing that what he asked was impossible. "Almon, tell me that it is true. Tell me that our Master is risen."

"Yea, it is true," I said, speaking my first words. "The Master lives again."

I was not the first to see the risen Lord. Mary Magdalene was given that singular honor, she who sat at the empty tomb faithful *beyond* the end.

Later, she told me that the risen Lord had appeared to her in the garden.

"Woman, why weepest thou?" He had asked.

"Because they have taken away my Lord, and I know not where they have laid him."

"Woman, why weepest thou? Whom seekest thou?"

At that moment she had mistaken Him for the gardener.

"Mary," Jesus had said.

And she had known Him. "Rabboni." *Master.*

My eyes *did* behold the risen Lord, but that is a story I may never write, for it is holy and sacred to me.

I do not profess to know *how* He rose from the grips of the grave. I only know that He *did*.

After my marriage to Deborah, we made our home in Nazareth, just as we had planned. Joel grew old with haste. It gave Deborah comfort to be there to help him during his final years.

Her mother moved in to live with us while Malik and his family took over the ancestral home with the great wooden doors.

I earned my living between two trades. I worked with words as a scribe. I also worked with wood, for the husband of Salome was a carpenter who revived Joseph's old workshop.

My pen was never still. There was so much worthy of recording.

The night before I began to pen this tale to you, I was favored with a dream. It was so vivid, so real, that it moved me to write the things I knew of the Master—that I might raise my voice once again to testify that Jesus was who He said He was.

In my dream I saw an old friend . . . Judas.

I saw him standing along a sandy desert roadside. To his left there was a path, and to his right another path. He seemed at odds, lost and unsure which way to go.

He waited as if he expected a guide to appear and take him by the hand.

I moved closer and saw that that his face was scarred. His hands were maimed. His whole body looked as though it had been scourged over many, many years.

Oh, Judas . . . what agony had you suffered? What had the purse cost you?

Tears streamed down his cheeks. He fell on his face. I heard the thud—I *felt* it—as his flesh met the packed ground.

How sorry I was that I had not helped him when he had cried out my name. My anger had turned me away. Had I learned anything since that regretful moment? Oh, I hoped so.

In my dream, Judas prayed. He prayed words that I could not interpret, but I understood them nonetheless. He prayed the same prayer I had uttered at the feet of the Master.

Forgive me, Jesus. Forgive me.

Then I saw a shadow cross the sand. I turned, and in the amber light of sunset I saw the Master. The white of His robe was brighter than the white any angel ever wore.

I looked at His feet before I looked at His face.

He wore the tattered sandals Joseph had tooled for Him.

He carried nothing, but He moved with haste.

My heart raced. I thought He was moving toward me.

"Master!" cried a voice.

It was *Judas* that Jesus ran to.

He ran with such effort that small clouds of sand shot up around His heels.

And when He reached the betrayer, Jesus fell to His knees on the ground next to Judas. Jesus' arms embraced Judas, and He held His disciple fast.

I heard the sobs of both men. I felt their joy *and* their sorrow.

I woke from my dream in a sweat, the blood pounding in my head, my heart beating like an ancient drum. I did not wish to wake Deborah or our sleeping babies, so I moved outside, into our small courtyard.

The night air was cool and I pulled my cloak around me. My bare feet felt the damp coolness of the earth and I let it seep into my toes, my feet, my legs, and up until my flushed cheeks went chill.

I felt alive and so grateful for my every blessing.

I could not sit still, so I walked out the gate and up to our rows of grapes, fruit that hung heavy on the vine. I popped a purple grape into my mouth and savored its sweet nectar.

What was the meaning of my dream?

Did Judas finally find a way back to Jesus?

Did Jesus love him no matter how dark and bloody his sins?

All I had were questions.

Father, after all that I have seen and known, there is still so much I do not understand.

The one true thing that I had come to understand completely was that Jesus did not only die for all mankind, but He lived for all, and His life presented a pattern by which we should all live. He was the great and final sacrifice, the unblemished lamb, and His Atonement covered even the blackest, most vile of sins and sinners.

He and He alone could judge completely and righteously.

My responsibility was to try to live as He did, every act motivated by love.

I stayed outside, walking and wondering.

I continued to pray, and when morning came I offered *Shema: Hear, O Israel: The Lord our God is one Lord.*

At the first stirrings of morning, a man approached our gate and called out when he saw me. "Is this the home of Almon, servant to the one they called Jesus?"

I nodded, uncertain if he was friend or foe. Jesus still had both.

"I am come from the Holy City. My grandfather resided here in Nazareth. He is long dead. I am called Alim, as he was."

The old Arab who used to wave to Jesus! Yes, I remembered him.

The man stepped closer to me. Through the open window of my home I could hear Deborah singing to our babies, twins named Joseph and Joel, in honor of two fathers who would always be treasured.

"I am restoring my grandfather's old home," said the man, "and I have a commission to offer for your skills in both letters and carpentry."

I smiled. It seemed the Lord provided work whenever it was most needed. I had a sense that the young Arab and I could become fast friends.

"I am curious about something," he said. "I do not wish to give offense, but I have heard much of this man they called Jesus. What was He to you?"

I smiled as broad as the desert. The peace that came so often now descended like the morning dew as I spoke from my heart. "Jesus *was* . . . He *is* . . . and will *always be* . . . my *Master*."